D1123145

gone dark

ALSO BY AMANDA PANITCH

gone
dark

AMANDA PANITCH

MARGARET K. McELDERRY BOOKS

New York London Toronto Sydney New Delhi

MARGARET K. McELDERRY BOOKS
An imprint of Simon & Schuster Children's Publishing Division
1230 Avenue of the Americas, New York, New York 10020

Text © 2022 by Temple Hill Publishing LLC.
Jacket photography by robynmac/iStock
Jacket design by Greg Stadnyk © 2022 by Simon & Schuster, Inc.
For information about special discounts for bulk purchases, please contact Simon & Schuster Special Sales at 1-866-506-1949 or business@simonandschuster.com.
The Simon & Schuster Speakers Bureau can bring authors to your live event. For more information or to book an event, contact the Simon & Schuster Speakers Bureau at 1-866-248-3049 or visit our website at www.simonspeakers.com.
Interior design by Irene Metaxatos
The text for this book was set in Minion Pro.
Manufactured in the United States of America
First Edition
10 9 8 7 6 5 4 3 2 1
Library of Congress Cataloging-in-Publication Data
Names: Panitch, Amanda, author.
Title: Gone dark / Amanda Panitch.
Description: First edition. | New York : Margaret K. McElderry Books, [2022] | Summary: When a terrorist attack cuts electricity across North America, teenaged Zara and her would-be boyfriend Gabe set out to find Gabe's sister—her best friend Estella—relying on skills Zara learned from her survivalist father.
Identifiers: LCCN 2020046390 (print) | LCCN 2020046391 (ebook) | ISBN 9781534466319 (hardcover) | ISBN 9781534466333 (ebook)
Subjects: CYAC: Survival—Fiction. | Terrorism—Fiction. | Fathers and daughters—Fiction. | Survivalism—Fiction.
Classification: LCC PZ7.P18933 Gon 2022 (print) | LCC PZ7.P18933 (ebook) | DDC [Fic]—dc23
LC record available at https://lccn.loc.gov/2020046390
LC ebook record available at https://lccn.loc.gov/2020046391

This book is for Hudson,
who lights up every room he's in.

gone dark

1

Somebody is going to die tonight.

Preferably, it won't be me or Gabe. We've worked for weeks figuring out how to stay alive, gathering magical items, stocking arrows of all different status types, and cloaking ourselves in armor that will deflect sword points and turn us invisible if necessary. Now we're waiting to get our hands on the boss ruling over this set of abandoned towers in our unnamed postapocalyptic city.

"You ready?" Gabe asks me over my headset. I flex my fingers, prepping them to dance over my keyboard and punch buttons like they've never danced and punched before. My character waits patiently in front of me on the center monitor, her shoulders rising and falling in a way more understated manner than mine would be if I were the one about to put my actual life at risk.

That's not the only difference between us, of course. She's tall.

Strong. She moves as fast as a whip and says funny, clever things in her smoky voice whenever I give her the command to joke or flirt. Meanwhile, I'm all business. "Ready. Let's go."

Gabe is already moving toward the gaping black hole of a door. Gritty sand rises around his character's combat boots with every step, and the moon shines down on him from overhead, just as it does through my real-life window. "If we can pull this off . . . ," he says into my ear. It catches me off guard, and I jump a little from surprise, as if he were really standing beside me speaking huskily into my ear. Which he is not, and which he never has, no matter how many times he's driven me home from school. "It'll be a realm first. It'll be worth all those nights of skipping out on my friends to train."

I give him an unconvincing laugh. "Yeah. I've been skipping out on my friends too."

What friends? he's polite enough not to say back. It's hard to lie to someone when your best—and only—friend is their sister. Thank goodness for headphones, or Estella would be rolling her eyes on the other side of their shared bedroom wall right now.

But whatever. We've got a boss to kill. I make my character follow his silently, her feet moving so lightly over the dust left behind by a thousand battles that they don't stir any of it up. That's our party configuration: Gabe is the warrior who charges in and draws all the attention and the attacks, and I'm the rogue who slinks in behind him and destroys everybody from the dark. Most parties have at least a healer, as well, and we will too, as soon as we can convince Estella to join us.

I direct my character forward, and we disappear into the blackness of the room. I tell Gabe to hold back for a moment so that anything there can show itself before we stumble upon it. In the void I think I can hear my dad's voice in my ear for a moment. *Very smart, playing to your strengths.* Though I know it's in my head, I still jolt, jittery as I am. *You're small and should rely on your speed and your evasiveness, not up-front brute strength.*

Those skills were part of the reason I chose to be a rogue in the first place, though much of the reason I love gaming is that I can be anything on that screen. Anything at all.

Besides, who am I kidding? There's no chance my dad would approve of what I'm doing. I picture him back on the compound my mom and I left him at years ago, a self-sustaining home in the thick of the woods, unmarked on any map. He's shaking his head at me. *Frittering your time away on silly games when there's a doomsday coming? Can you shoot a bow like your character can? Can you scale the side of a building? Can you creep soundlessly behind your prey before you cut them down?* I don't need to answer him. *No. No, you cannot. You're soft. When doomsday comes, you will fall with all the rest of them.*

I realize I'm blinking very fast. "Zara?" Gabe says through my headset. "Are we good?"

"Sorry! Yes!" I send my character rushing forward, and for a while I manage to lose myself in the melee, in the spray of digital blood and the crunch of digital bone. Exhilaration floods hot through me. Gabe cheers in my ear.

"I'll distract the final guard while you climb up high and attack from above, okay?" he says.

"That's just what I was about to say." My character climbs like a spider, digging fingers and toes into almost invisible crevices, and then I settle her on a rafter, where she can peer down on the carnage below. She loads her crossbow. Sets it. Waits. Allows the doubt to creep back in.

Wait. That's me. *You should be exercising more than your fingers, Zara,* says my dad, his voice disapproving. *Like we used to. Drills with the rising sun. Hunting as that sun beats down on the back of your neck, burning it to a crisp. Falling to bed exhausted and hungry after failing to bag that deer you were hunting, because that is how you learn your lessons.*

He wanted what was best for me. I knew that then, and I know that now.

It's just that his idea of what was best for me was different from the rest of the world's.

I refocus on the game as the final guard between us and the boss's chamber lets out a loud roar and charges at Gabe. The guard is almost a boss himself, with impenetrable silver armor covered in swirls of browning blood from his many kills. This is where every party has been wiping so far, because they didn't notice what we have: the opening in the shoulder of his plate. His only weakness. Since he's so tall, Gabe and I knew we couldn't hit that spot from below. Someone would need to climb up high. Someone who has skill with a crossbow.

Gabe's sword meets the guard's with a clang and a grunt. I twitch my finger. *Thwip.*

The guard roars again, only this time it's in pain. His fingers scrabble at his shoulder, but it's too late. My arrow landed smack in the middle of his weak spot, and his armor is crumbling, falling off him as fine bits of ash. "Yessss," I hiss into the headset. "It worked." Now that his armor is gone, Gabe makes quick work of him, me contributing with arrows to stun and poison from above. When I leap down, a distance that would in real life potentially break an ankle but in the game just takes away a few hit points, he gives me a high five.

"It's finally time," I say. Electricity courses through me.

His character gives me a bow. "You do the honor."

I trot forward, door key—which was a whole other quest to obtain—in my hand. My heart thumps. My fingers tingle. The door flies open and the boss cries out. We lunge in, ready to do battle, and—

Everything goes black.

2

There are definitely worse times to lose power. Like, I could be splayed on a cold steel operating table, blades and fingers probing my heart, tiny electrical pulses the only thing keeping my blood going *glub-glub*.

But I'm not. I'm in my bedroom, seated in the cushioned black chair that spins so I can go back and forth between my three computer screens. All of which are currently black.

We were so close to finishing that battle. So close. As much as I try to tell myself things could be worse, that I could be bleeding out during surgery, I still release a string of curses loud enough to wake the dead. My fists ball at my sides, and I push my chair back so I don't put them through the center screen.

I hear my mom's feet hit the ground from the other side of the house, and all my muscles tense at once. Like magic, she appears in my doorway. She's nothing more than a shadow, at least until she speaks. Her voice is low and deadly. "Zara. Elizabeth. Ross."

I kind of wish I'd woken the dead instead.

"I'm sorry—" I start, but she bulldozes right over me.

"Do you realize that this is the first good night's sleep I've been able to get all week thanks to the budget crisis at city hall? Did I not tell you to keep quiet unless the house was on fire and you couldn't figure out a way to *quietly* put it out?"

I want to apologize again, but I know better than to interrupt her once she starts going. We're alike in that way: when we're onto something, we don't let it go till we run out of energy, which is great when it comes to studying for a test or defeating bosses, but less great when you're on the wrong end of a lecture.

My mom takes a deep breath. I brace myself, but something catches her eye outside my window, and she squints. I can just barely see the lines of her face and the wild tangle of her hair. "Did the power go out or just the streetlight?"

I seize upon any opportunity to spin a bit of her rage off me. "Yes! The power. Can you believe it?" I wave my arm at the window, which is a square of darkness, the moon a pearl in the top corner. "It's not even raining or anything." I glance at her sidelong to see if she's buying it. Her lips are set in a thin line, and her eyes are still slits. "Our power company is the worst."

I hold my breath for a moment, and then she sighs. I sigh with her. Lecture averted.

"They *are* the worst," she says. "But let's look at it as a positive: they got you off your computer."

I roll my eyes. "Very funny."

"I'm not joking," she says. "Don't you have to wake up in seven hours?"

"It's easier to wake up early if you don't go to sleep at all. It's just like one very long night."

"Zara!"

"Fine." I glance at my screens. They're still all too blank. "I'll go to bed, even though I won't be able to fall asleep. I'll lie there and stare so hard at the ceiling that I might light it on fire, but don't worry. I won't scream and wake you up. I'll just quietly burn to death."

"I take it back," my mom says, eyebrow raised. "The power company isn't the worst. You are."

"Good night, Mom." I step forward and let her kiss my forehead, then wrap her arms around my shoulders and squeeze tightly.

"Good night, Zara," she says, and she lingers a moment, like she wants to say something else. But she doesn't. She knocks a hand on the edge of the doorframe, then turns and leaves. Her footsteps pad back down the hall, her door creaks closed, and I'm alone again in the darkness.

My fingers itch. Everything itches. It's been only maybe ten minutes, but I miss my screens so fiercely that I don't know what to do with all the energy coursing through me. We were *so close.* How can anyone expect me to relax?

I grab for my phone; the itching calms a bit as its cool glass slides into my hand. It vibrates as soon as it hits skin; it's Estella. I picture her hunched over her phone, long black hair tied in a messy bun that wobbles on top of her head. I hear Gabe cursing through the wall, I assume you're cursing too?

I send her a frowny face and, just for good measure, the bursting-into-tears face. Then the crossbow. She gets it and responds immediately. Sounds like it's time to blow up the power company.

I hide a smile. Some of the tension drains away. I don't think that will help the situation. She sends only a shrug in response.

I let out a groan and flop facedown on my bed with my phone still gripped in my hand. It feels good to have the only working device held tight against my chest—almost like a security blanket. I curl up around it and bury my face in my old stuffed walrus, letting exhaustion carry me off to sleep.

3

I wake to the jaunty tune of my phone alarm, sweat matting my hair to the back of my neck. I grab for it and switch it off, then remember the whole power outage thing. I hop up, ignoring the dizzy tilt to the room that reminds me how stupid early it is, and settle back into my computer chair.

The screen blinks on. Relief washes over me as my computer runs through its system diagnostics. Power's back. Everything's okay again.

And school can wait a little while. I'll skip my shower this morning. I'll eat my Pop-Tart cold on the bus instead of taking the time to heat it up in the microwave.

After clicking into the game, I scroll through the logs from last night and swear. Several hours after we were kicked off, some other party achieved *our* achievement. We could log back on tonight and try again, but we'll no longer be the realm's first.

I have to kill something right now. I port my character into the nearest free-for-all arena, where I content myself by mercilessly slaughtering some other players, which gives me a surprise quest, so I might as well—

"Zara Elizabeth Ross."

I jump a little in my seat. It takes a moment to disconnect from the world of the game, to transport myself from the gritty, bomb-blasted arena to the bland eggshell-white walls of my suburban Los Angeles home. Another moment to translate the ominous in-game music to the stern voice of my mom. "What?" I say, irritated.

"Aren't you going to miss your bus?"

As if on cue, the roar of the bus echoes from down the street. I jump to my feet. "Crap." So much for a Pop-Tart at any temperature. I grab my backpack, wash some toothpaste around in my mouth, allow a precious second for my mom to kiss me on the forehead, and make it out front just in time to stumble up those gum-crusted steps.

Estella's already in our seat in the safe back-middle: not far enough up front to be smirked at, but not in the best places in the back (the best, at least, until senior year finally rolls around and we're allowed to drive to school).

"You look grungy today," she says in greeting. She is the opposite of grungy, as always: her eyelashes are dark and full against her light brown skin, and her thick black hair is tied back in two long, frizz-free braids. "Have you ever heard of a brush?"

I flop down in our seat. "Good morning to you too."

She graciously grants me use of the comb she keeps in her purse along with some of her mascara. By the time we rumble into the school parking lot, I feel like a vaguely presentable human being.

"This is a waste of time," I say as we push our way through the crowd. Cigarette smoke drifts inward from the edges somewhere. The main school building looms above us, a monstrosity in white stone and peach stucco. Estella stops occasionally to wave at someone she knows or greet somebody with a "Did you do the homework?" while I wait silently at her side.

"Being here is always a waste of time," Estella agrees.

"It's so stupid that they make us come in these last few weeks. We don't actually have anything to do." We pass through the front doors. The air-conditioning hits us in the face with a wave of cool air; it should smell sweet and sterile, like air-conditioning everywhere, but instead it always smells faintly of dirty socks and floor polish and whiteboard markers. "It's June. AP tests are over. All the teachers are phoning it in." We're both in as many AP classes as we could fit into our schedules, the exception being gym (not offered as an AP class, which is good, because I'd probably want to take it for the GPA boost, and I don't know if I could handle AP gym). "Can't wait to watch more movies from the nineties."

"We've been doing stuff in comp sci."

"Yeah, but that's hardly work." Estella and I are the only girls in AP Computer Science, and we're partners for basically every project we've needed a partner for.

Funnily enough, I feel brighter and more alert today than I ever have at school—guess that's what happens when you get more than five hours of sleep on a school night. Too bad it's wasted mostly on pretending to watch movies. AP Bio's film of choice is some documentary about cells, which plays at the front of the room as our teacher snores on his stool and kids whisper around me. I keep my eyes on my phone in my lap, fingers dashing over the screen. Estella is off in chemistry "watching" a movie about genetics or eugenics or something, but really she's sending me snapshots of her face through different filters. Estella as a dog. Estella with heart eyes. Estella with rainbows pouring out of her mouth.

And then a notification pops up from Gabe. He drives me home sometimes, so it's practical to have his number in my phone in case I have to let him know I'm running late or ask him how long he's staying after school. We don't text each other much, sticking generally to talking in the world of our game. Giving each other battle advice. Planning strategy for the fights ahead. It feels strange to say that my voice sticks in my throat around him when we're together in real life, given how easily it comes out over the headset.

We're both different in the game than we are in real life. Him? He plays sports, goes to parties, has a million friends. Sometimes I see him walking through the halls with his arm thrown around a pretty girl's shoulders, even though he doesn't have a girlfriend right now. He doesn't, right? I would know. Estella would tell me. Wouldn't she?

And me? Do I really even have to say it? Just look at me sitting here in AP Bio. Everybody around me is buzzing to one another, whirling with activity: showing each other things on their phones; whispering in friends' ears; making plans to do something later. They're like a school of fish, and I'm like a fish that's not part of their—no, I'm more like a rock. Or a sea cucumber. I'm here, alive, but I can't even communicate with all the other fish.

My phone buzzes again. Another message from Gabe. I bow my head to read it. How you doing today?

Bent double under the crushing weight of my disappointment, but

I'll probably survive, is what I want to say, but I'm already second-guessing myself. Does it make me sound too weird? Probably. So what I actually send is, I'll live. How about you?

Hobbling around under the crushing weight of my disappointment, he says. A smile tugs at the corners of my lips. But I think I'll probably live too. Carry on!

I send back a fist-pump emoji, then tuck my phone away and sigh. Gabe and I have been playing together since the night almost a year ago that I slept over Estella's house and heard him shouting at the screen through their shared bedroom wall. He padded out for breakfast in the morning, yawning and scratching, and maybe it was the fact that he was still half-asleep that gave me the courage to ask him what game he played. Apparently, he'd just begun the journey into *Dark Avengers*, and I offered to help him level up. Of course, I didn't tell him I had to pay real money to transfer to his server. The rest is history.

My hands fidget in my lap. I wish I could go to comp sci early and work on one of my passion projects, but that's during last period. I reach for my phone again, thinking maybe I'll send Estella some funky selfies of my own, when a ball of paper hits me on the side of the head.

The situation deserves an annoyed look and maybe a scowl in the direction of the thrower. I know that. It's just a ball of paper, and it didn't hurt me.

And yet I overcorrect, nearly falling off my chair, making its legs squeal nearly as loud as the sound that comes tearing out of my throat, because for a second my lizard brain thinks I might have to fight. My head falls into my hands, and I make myself take deep breaths, trying both to calm myself down and to avoid the stares of the suddenly silent room. "Hey," says Mitch Brown, who was almost certainly the thrower. "You okay? It was just a ball of paper. I was trying to throw it at Josh and missed, not—"

He stops short, as if someone's elbowed him in the side. And then someone hisses, "Stop talking, you'll make it worse."

I know that voice: it's Callie Everett, who has extremely shiny hair and even more extremely white teeth. I smile into my hands in appreciation for her words, and then she continues. Quietly, like she thinks I can't hear her. "Did you not go to our middle school? She's the one who used to have panic attacks all the time. The more you focus on her, the worse she gets. Just stop."

Murmurs rise again, and the blackness of the backs of my eyelids is soothing, and chairs start to screech, and soon it's like Mitch never threw anything at all.

My phone buzzes again, but I don't even reach for it this time. Callie's words are still spinning around in my head.

Panic attacks. Middle school. All the time.

A beat of silence. The thud of my stomach dropping. The feeling of my father's ghostly fingers digging into my shoulder and squeezing hard.

No. Think about your projects. The coding you're going to do later. Make up for all the time you missed with your fingers around tree branches instead of on keyboards. Staring at screens is as far away from your past as you can get, and that's what you need right now.

But his fingers are still on my shoulder, and with them comes his voice. . . .

For a while after we moved, I'd hear my dad whispering in my head—the only place I'd heard him since I left, as he has no phone out there in the middle of the woods. *You must prepare yourself,*

Zara, for the end of the world. It is coming. The world is not ready.
You *must be ready.*

It took a long time for a flick of a switch turning into light, or the ease of plucking food off supermarket shelves, to stop being new and exciting. The sheer variety of food out here in the real world was something amazing—the first time I had french fries was a transcendent experience. And other kids? Well. There weren't any other kids on the compound; I grew up rarely speaking to anyone besides my parents. I didn't know how to play the games they played, or the jokes they had, or the strange rituals of beauty the girls were just beginning to participate in. Between those and the stress of being thrown into a world I'd always been told was about to end, it's no wonder I had panic attacks in middle school all the time.

Electricity was the thing he always said would get me. It made people soft, and he didn't want me to be soft. And it was too easy to lose. Much easier than people always thought.

One day my dad and I were on the perimeter of the compound, building traps. My dad was in the process of digging a deep hole we'd cover with brush. I was whiny and hot and impatient and wouldn't stop asking him when we'd be done so I could go for a swim in our cool, clear lake.

If I'd been needling my mom, she would've snapped at me. But my dad only looked at me gravely. "Almost, Zara. We cannot get impatient. We must make sure everything is done properly, so that, come the end, we are not left flailing in the dark. Pay attention to what I'm doing."

I paid attention for about two seconds and then started whining again, my foot kicking at the edge of the hole. "I don't know why we even need traps." My dad had been very clear these weren't for hunting; they were for security. "We're in the middle of nowhere, Dad. Nobody ever comes here!"

"They will." He pointed at my feet. "You are standing on the edge of that hole, Zara. What happens if you fall in?"

I was not in the mood for a lesson. "I don't know, I break my neck?"

"Exactly. Humanity lives on a knife's edge, dependent on their creature comforts. Without those, they will fall."

He reached for me. Thinking he needed me to help him out of the hole—which meant we were done!—I grabbed his hand, but he didn't just grab back; he yanked hard. Already balancing on the edge, my feet went skidding over the side and into the emptiness.

He caught me, of course. One second I was falling and the next I was cradled in his arms, my cheek on his broad shoulder. He leaned in to whisper in my ear. "That's how easy it is, Zara. That's how everyone will fall. And the things I've taught you here? They will catch you."

Only they didn't catch me, did they? I was thrown here into this world I wasn't prepared for, and now I feel like I'm always falling.

4

I'm mostly feeling better by the time AP Computer Science rolls around at the end of the day; as much as I hate gym, being forced to jog around the track did release enough endorphins to chill me out a little. Still, I walk into comp sci and dramatically collapse into my chair anyway, because sometimes dramatically collapsing into chairs is fun.

"Rough day?" Estella says sympathetically.

I shrug. It hasn't really been that bad. I've definitely been through worse.

She takes her seat beside me. Unlike my other classes, AP Comp Sci doesn't have the standard school-issue desks attached to chairs with metal baskets for your stuff underneath; the room is set up with hexagon-shaped terminals topped by computers, the chairs regular and basketless. In front, the teacher has his own computer hooked up to the SMART Board so that we can see his coding demonstrated in real time. "My English class turned into an arm-wrestling tournament. I could barely breathe through all the testosterone and Axe."

I rest my head on her shoulder in support. "At least you didn't miss out on a realm first like me and Gabe."

Her shoulder bounces up and down as she shakes her head. "Could've been worse. My cousin out in Barstow had her power go out while she was in the elevator. She was stuck there for three hours. Had to pee in her water bottle in front of some random guy."

"Gross." I wince.

"And did you hear about the people who got stuck on the roller coaster at Six Flags?" she asks. "Some kid threw up on them. I'd say you got off lightly compared to that."

"Maybe," I say dubiously, but then another thought occurs to me. "Wait, was that all last night?"

"Yeah, the power went out in bits and pieces all over the area," Estella says airily. "Weird, right? You'd think either we'd all lose it or none of us would lose it."

"Yeah," I say. "Weird."

Mr. Miller starts talking about our final projects, his voice a drone like a fly in my ear. I half turn toward my station, pretending to be looking at something on my screen as I pull my phone out of my pocket.

It's probably nothing—no, almost *definitely* nothing. Estella was just mentioning some offhand information to make me feel better about what happened last night.

And yet as I google it, I realize I'm holding my breath.

She was right. I squint at the map as I scroll through article after article. The power outages last night made for a weird swiss cheese of electricity, with some neighborhoods and communities still with power and others beside them left without. It's probably nothing. Some quirk with the wires. And yet . . .

As I walked back to the compound with my dad after building traps that day, I was in a sour mood. Not just because I'd scraped my arm falling into the pit before my dad caught me, but because he said it was too late for us to go for a swim. Mom was waiting with dinner back at the house, and "you wouldn't want dinner to get cold, would you, Zara?"

"I'd rather eat cold food than hot food today," I grumbled, flicking the sweat out of my eyes before it could burn. I didn't particularly want my dad to teach me another "lesson"—falling into the pit and getting a scraped arm was pretty mild as far as his teaching methods went, and many of them ended with way more bruises of my own making—but I was annoyed, ready to hear about people who would have it way worse than me. Ready to hear why all these bruises and scrapes would be worth it. "How is everyone out there going to fall?"

My dad loped along easily, his eyes set straight ahead. Somehow he never stumbled over dead branches or hit his head on living ones, unlike me. "They will never see it coming. It will happen little by little—an attack here, an attack there. They will be tested, and they will fail because they will not be paying attention. You must always pay attention to your patterns, Zara."

"My patterns," I said obediently. "Right."

He waved his arm in the direction of the deep woods. Shadows mottled his front with splotches of gray. "If you stumbled upon a large pool of blood on the leaves, with a trail leading away, what would you think?"

It strikes me now how blasé I was talking about large pools of blood. "I'd think that something started bleeding there, maybe a deer, and then tried to crawl away?"

He nodded, and I preened. "Right. That's a natural pattern, one that doesn't draw suspicion."

Again: large pools of blood should probably draw suspicion. I'm aware of that now. But things were different then.

"But say that you stumbled upon several small pools of blood, with no trails anywhere. What do you think then?"

"Something's fishy," I say.

"Yes. Something happened there that is not usual. Not natural. You will want to stay alert. Pay attention."

"But what would cause that?"

"People," said my dad. "But it isn't important. It was only an example."

Just then I caught sight of our house through the trees, and all thoughts of patterns fled from my mind as I skipped forward. My mom was waiting on the front stoop. Her eyebrows were knotted anxiously together, but as soon as she saw me, her face relaxed into a smile. "Did you have a nice day, Zara?" Her hair was tied back in a loose knot, her apron speckled with something brown.

I nodded. "Dad was telling me about how everybody who's not on the compound is going to die when doomsday comes. And it's going to be bad when they all try to come here, so we have to protect ourselves."

A wince crossed her face for a split second, just quick enough that I wasn't sure whether I'd seen it at all. She glanced behind me—Dad had stopped out on the boundary to fiddle with one of our traps—then crouched down to look me in the eye. "There's not going to be a doomsday. Don't stress out about it too much."

I blinked. "Of course there's going to be a doomsday. That's the whole reason we're here."

My mom glanced over my shoulder again, then licked her lips. She reached out to pat my arm, and her sleeve fell down to reveal bruises around her wrist. It was weird how she ended up with bruises like me, even though she didn't run around in the woods and fall out of trees like I did. She asked about mine sometimes, asking over and over how I'd gotten them, but she never answered my own questions about hers. "We're here because we love your dad, and because being here makes him happy. Everybody out there is not going to die."

She's wrong was what immediately crossed my mind. Obviously she was wrong. Because Dad said there was going to be a doomsday, and Dad knew everything.

But I wouldn't tell her that she was wrong. Like Dad never straight-up told me when I was wrong. He'd say I had to figure it out for myself, because otherwise it wasn't a real lesson.

Just as I was thinking that, my mom stood up so fast her knees cracked. "Don't tell your father I said that," she said quietly, and then her lips broke out in a wide smile. "Welcome back!"

I stepped away so that my parents could embrace, my mind buzzing. Just like my mind is buzzing now. And not just my mind. My stomach squirms. My throat dries out. My toes clench up in my shoes.

And all the while my parents' words war in my mind.

Doomsday is coming.

There's not going to be a doomsday.

Doomsday is coming.

It wouldn't hurt to do a little more digging, would it? It's probably nothing. Almost definitely nothing.

"Zara?" Estella asks. She's leaning in, obscuring the lines of code already scrolling down her screen. "You okay? Are you having trouble with the problem?"

"No!" I say, feeling scandalized. Not about the "okay" thing, but about the idea that I might be having trouble with the computer problem. "I could solve this in my sleep!"

When I left the compound and touched down here in LA, I wasn't entirely sure what to make of screens and computers. At first, the light radiating off them hurt my eyes, gave me headaches. My mom enrolled me in classes, saying that I had to catch up . . . and I realized it was the only thing I did that didn't remind me of all I'd left. The sports she tried enrolling me in made me flash back to running through the woods, dodging branches or firing my crossbow. Artistic and cooking projects made me think about canning fruit or the colors of the trees in autumn. I had no previous associations with screens. They didn't give me panic attacks. I could disappear into them, and I did.

Estella holds up her hands in surrender. "Okay, just asking."

She returns to the problem, and I return to obsessing over something that's probably, almost definitely—could be?—not happening.

5

The end of the day finds me trailing after Estella as she chats her way through the crowds in the hallway as we head out. She's bubbly. I'm determined. To get home. To figure out what's going on. To make my dad's voice in my head shut up about doomsday. To convince myself that I'm seeing things that aren't there.

Estella does not understand my urgency. She's talking to some girl from her art class, laughing over something the teacher did today, as I chew on the inside of my mouth and jiggle my foot beside her. Finally the girl says goodbye and speeds off to band practice. I exhale with relief as Estella and I take a few more precious steps toward the front doors, only to have her stopped by some guy who claims he wants to ask her what the homework is in calc but clearly just wants to flip his hair and flash his dimples and hope she notices. I glare at him until he goes away.

He does me the honor of casting a confused glance, one so quick that I know he doesn't mean me to notice. I do, though, and I know what he's thinking: *Why does* she *hang out with* her? The subject being Estella, the object being me. It's a fair question.

A couple of weeks into high school, I was pretty sure I'd be equally as friendless as I was in middle school. Which was fine. (Or so I told myself.) I was used to sitting alone at the lunch table and being stranded in class when we all had to pair up.

And then I went to the bathroom. Which is not generally a momentous decision. But my mom had made me drink a lot of orange juice that morning because she thought I was coming down with a cold, even though excess vitamin C doesn't actually do anything to heal the sick. So I found myself in the second-floor bathroom reading Sharpied back-of-the-door scrawls about who'd done what with whom (very informative) when a voice boomed from the loudspeaker: "Initiate lockdown. Initiate lockdown. This is not a drill. This is NOT a drill."

I sighed. Cleaned myself up. Left the stall.

Was met by a glare from the area of the sinks. "What are you doing?" The girl's voice ended in a squeak. I'd seen her around, but I didn't know her name, just that she was always surrounded by a group of girls with equally shiny hair and smiles. "Someone might have heard that!"

Spoiler alert: it was Estella.

I went to sidestep her so I could wash my hands, but she got in my way again. "There might be a shooter out there. We can't make any noise!" Her arms were shaking, and her eyes were currently shinier than her hair or her teeth. At that point I wasn't so great at reading emotions in other people, but even I could tell she was terrified.

I softened. Sometimes I still forgot that everybody else hadn't gone through combat training the way I had. And she was right to be terrified of a school shooter. I'd seen way too many smiling faces of kids my age on the news to take that lightly. "Say there's a shooter," I said, then lowered my voice to a whisper as her eyes widened. I watched my face in the mirror over her shoulder as I spoke, trying to make sure I looked sympathetic. Trying to make my dark eyes kind, my lips curve into a smile. It was hard to tell if it was working. "That would be bad. But the chance that they've been tactically trained and really know what they're doing is very small." I wasn't going to have a panic attack for this, ironically enough. Even if I hadn't gone through years of therapy to help me with them, my panic attacks in middle school had been saved for things that felt almost random, like wind hitting me at a certain angle. Not things I'd been trained to deal with.

Estella gestured around her, arm still shaking. "B-but look at this! It's not like we could even run!"

That was true. The bathroom was a small one: three stalls (one out of order), two sinks, a tiny window high up on the wall that I wouldn't have been able to fit through even as a toddler. "We wouldn't need to run," I told her, trying to sound as soothing as I could. Even if my stomach was starting to dance a bit nervously. If someone did actually come in here with a gun, we'd be in a bad position. But I'd spent so many years waiting for doomsday to come to me that now I was calmer than she was, she who hadn't thought about it at all. And the most important thing was that I keep her calm so that she wouldn't yell out and notify anyone seeking to do us harm.

She looked at me like I'd told her I took a sip of the toilet water and it was delicious. "What are you going to do? Fight?"

"Well, yeah," I said. "I . . ." I trailed off. She was still giving me that toilet-water look, and I realized she thought I'd lost my mind. She'd think it even harder if I went on and told her all about my past and how it had prepared me for something like this. I had to pick an excuse. "I . . . did a lot of martial arts as a kid."

Her voice rose to a fever pitch. "So you're going to karate-chop the gunman? Do you really think that's—"

A popping noise from outside cut her off. Whatever she was about to say turned into a shrill shriek as she dove into my arms. I stumbled back into one of the bathroom doors. "Those were shots!" she cried into my shoulder. Her hair was sticking to the sweat on my cheek. "We're going to die, we're going to—"

They hadn't sounded like shots to me, but I didn't want to say that and get her hopes up, just in case. I pushed her back by her shoulders so that I could look her in the eye. "We are not going to die," I said, and I must have sounded commanding, because she stopped crying immediately. "Come on. Come with me." I grabbed her arm and pulled her against the wall next to the bathroom door. If anyone opened the door, we'd be hidden behind it for a moment. Enough time for me to surprise them.

She followed, but she was trembling. "Hey, if you keep hyperventilating like that, we're going to run out of air in here." She looked at me with those glassy eyes, not even a hint of a smile on her face. "I'm joking," I said hastily. "But you do need to calm down or you're going to have a panic attack."

She fixed me with a glare. Her hyperventilating was such that she must not have been able to speak with her voice, but her eyes spoke for her. They said, *The only way I'm going to be able to stop hyperventilating is if I literally drop dead right now.*

"Listen to me. Look me in the eye," I said. I stared right at her. She stared right back. This wasn't about respect or anything—it was about getting her to focus on one thing. To concentrate. No matter how much looking a stranger in the eye made my spine tingle with nerves. "Tell me what color my eyes are."

She had to take a few shaky breaths before she could force the words out. "Brown."

"They're not just solid brown," I said. "Look closer."

She looked closer. Without her even realizing it, her breathing was beginning to slow. "I see . . . a streak or two of green. Black. Lighter brown."

"Good. Good." Her breathing was slowing even more. I took a deep, slow breath of my own. When I had been in a situation like this on the compound, whether I was stuck in the root cellar with the grumbling of what had to be a bear overhead or whether I was up in a tree hiding from the bad things my dad said were coming, I would focus on one thing to help calm me down. The repetitive whoop of a whip-poor-will out in the dark trees. The knot on a potato rough under my thumb. Filling your mind up with that one thing crowded out the other things, the stressful things. One of the reasons I'd had so many panic attacks here was because there was always so much going on around me in this new world.

But Estella's breaths were already beginning to quicken again. She hadn't done this before. There was only so long she could keep the terror away once she'd solved the puzzle I'd given her. "Now we're going to breathe together," I directed. I took another deep breath, but not deep enough where it made me dizzy. I glared at her until she took one too. "Good. Now another. Match me and count them. Tap me on the shoulder at every fifth breath."

Tap. . . . Tap. . . . Tap.

She opened her mouth between breaths. "But what if—"

"Breathing, not talking."

She didn't listen. "What if he does come in here?"

"*Breathe,*" I said. She breathed, but she squinted at me at the same time. Again, her eyes spoke for her. *No amount of breathing is going to protect us against a gun.*

I dropped my voice, made it low and deadly. "If he comes in here, I will destroy him."

She nodded. Her eyes weren't quite calm, but they were a whole lot calmer than they'd been before. She trusted me. Somehow she trusted me.

We huddled together in that bathroom for a hundred breaths, two hundred breaths. We didn't hear any more pops. We found out later that they'd come from a car backfiring and that the lockdown was called because a kid had snuck out to smoke earlier, gotten locked out, broken back in through an emergency exit, and tried to run and hide from the security guards. All we knew then, though, was that when the voice came back over the loudspeaker to announce that all was clear and we could proceed with our day, we were safe. Estella attacked me with the fiercest hug I'd ever received.

"If it wasn't for you, I probably would have had a panic attack," she said, her voice muffled by my shoulder. "Maybe even died. Thank you."

I squirmed in her grip, exhaling in relief when she backed away. "Um, I don't think you can die from a panic attack. But, um, you're welcome."

She left the bathroom first. I followed behind. We both nearly bumped into a group of kids coming our way. The boy at the front of the group gave me an annoyed look. "Watch where you're going."

My cheeks warmed. *You're the one who almost walked into me,* was what I wanted to say, but when I opened my mouth, nothing came out.

A presence at my side. Estella. She'd harnessed the fierceness of that hug and was projecting it now at that kid. He seemed to shrink back. I expected to feel her hair crackle with lightning, hear thunder roar from her throat. "Back off," she said, and she slung an arm over my shoulder. "Unless you want to try and fight her. *I* wouldn't try it. She'd destroy you."

He didn't even reply, just scurried off with his tail between his legs. Estella stepped away and flashed me her brilliant smile. "Well," she said. "Shall we go to class?"

So that day—and every other day since—is why I don't begrudge her this dallying on the way out, no matter how much my mind is stewing with thoughts of the potential coming apocalypse. I don't know where I'd be without her. She says the same about me, but it's hard to believe her.

She finally finishes with the guy trying to flirt and turns to me. "Want to get a ride home from Gabe?" she asks. "He had to leave too early this morning for me to hitch a ride, but for once we're both not staying after at the same time. He can drop you off, or you can come over."

Getting a ride with Gabe would get me home probably ten minutes sooner than the bus. And there are . . . other benefits. That don't include rehashing our loss last night. "Sure!" Am I blushing? I'm pretty sure I'm already blushing. "I should get home. Thanks."

"Don't thank me, thank him."

The crowd in the hallway's thinned out a bit, leaving enough room for us to walk through it rather than shove. She flings the door at the end of the hall open, and bright sunshine pours in. Walking into it almost feels like walking into another world. Cars zip past, too fast for the parking lot; the high white sun glitters off shining paint and hurts my eyes.

Gabe's shiny silver car is parked all the way at the end of the last row, an island unto itself. He's leaning against the hood, eyes closed and head tilted back. Sunlight washes his brown skin, his black curls. His Adam's apple stands out in sharp relief, and his legs, muscled—but not too muscled—from playing soccer, are on display from the shorts he always wears, even during the winter. His eyes drift open as he hears our footsteps approaching. "It's about time," he says. "What, did you crawl here?"

Estella presses the back of her hand against her forehead. "You're lucky we made it here at all. We were almost flattened by the thousands of cars we had to dodge on this endless journey."

Gabe's hand darts out and lands on Estella's head. She squeals and jerks away, but it's too late—he ruffles her hair, making her braids go lopsided. "You jerk!" she says, but she doesn't sound especially angry about it.

She goes to toss her backpack in the trunk. I hang on to mine so I don't have to make Gabe open his trunk when he stops at my house. The trunk slams shut, and Gabe steps around to the side of the car. I expect him to get into the front seat, but instead he opens the back door and does a funny sort of bow. "It's not quite a spectral warplane, but I hope it'll do."

The spectral warplane was a potential item drop from the boss we didn't destroy last night. "I guess we won't be able to fly over the line to get out of the parking lot, then." I climb inside as he flashes me a brilliant smile, like he's pleased I played along.

My cheeks are ablaze.

"That's fine, your own flesh and blood will just open her own door!" Estella says from the other side of the car.

Gabe and Estella keep ribbing each other in the front as we start driving, until Estella finally concedes. "Maybe I'll finally join up as your healer."

She won't. We know she won't. But we nod anyway. "Should we try again tonight?" I ask Gabe. Because I'll definitely finish up my power outage research early. I'll realize nothing is wrong, and then I'll be ready for round two.

He clicks his tongue. "I wish. But I have a college thing tonight. Some kind of virtual orientation for club soccer."

I droop, hoping he can't see me in the rearview mirror. I keep forgetting that he'll be going off to college after the summer: UC Berkeley, five and a half hours north of here. Will he still have time for me when he's at college, surrounded by new and exciting people and things?

"No worries," I tell him. "Have fun."

"I will," he says breezily. I don't think I've ever been that breezy. About anything. "As long as the power doesn't go out in the middle."

"We just had a power outage," Estella says. "They must have fixed whatever went wrong. I don't think you have to worry."

"You don't know that." The words burst out of me. "Maybe next time the power won't come back on at all."

Silence hangs in the car. Gabe clears his throat. My cheeks flame again, this time from embarrassment. Estella slowly turns to look at me.

"Sorry," I say before she can say anything.

"Don't be sorry," she says. "But . . . I don't think you have to worry about something like that."

Estella doesn't have my dad's voice living in the back of her head. She didn't grow up for ten years waiting for the world to end.

I venture, "It's my dad. I've been thinking about him a lot today. He was kind of into all that . . . doomsday stuff."

I hold my breath as she stares at me. "You never told me that," she says. She sounds mildly interested, and the thought that she might spin it off into more questions makes my heart thump. I could tell her. I could tell her everything.

I wanted to tell her when we were younger. I planned on it for ages, at every sleepover we had after I "saved" her from that car backfire. I did trust her. But I kept stopping, afraid that she'd think I was weird or too different after all, and I'd lose the one real friend I had. So I didn't tell her, and then too much time had passed and it just felt weird to come out with something like, *Hey, I spent my entire childhood on a hidden compound in the woods, waiting for the world to end. Want to go get frozen yogurt?* All she knows is that my parents got divorced when I was young and my dad still lives out east.

"I know. It's kind of hard to talk about," I say quietly. Sympathy dawns over her face, but I'm unmoved.

I'll tell her next time.

"You know, if you ever want to talk about it, I'm here," she says just as quietly. Her smile is tiny. "I always thought your story about knowing martial arts was bull."

I nod. I don't know if I can speak around the sudden lump in my throat. So I pull out my phone and pretend that I'm texting my mom until she turns around.

I hug her before I get out of the car. Just a tiny squeeze, one arm from the back seat, and I'm gone before she can touch me back. I shut the door after me, and it's like I leave the incident behind.

6

At home I eat the Pop-Tart I didn't eat that morning. I wash my hands carefully in the sink, whooshing every crumb down the drain. I take a deep breath before settling into command central.

And then the entire world opens up to me. My fingers dance over the keyboard, and with every click there's something new: new information, a new map. You might think it's different from the compound, that I've learned more in my short years with access to school and the internet than I did in all my time there. But I was learning all those years too. Aside from the homeschooling I received from my parents, teaching me math and reading and writing, I was learning about insect migration, and preserving food, and the precise slant of light through the leaves at every hour of the day.

I was learning about paying attention to something that doesn't look right. Because out there, alone in the middle of the woods, something that's off can get you killed.

So I load up a map and search for all of last night's power outages, then layer them onto the map, one on top of another. I see the outage in my part of LA, the outage around Six Flags Magic Mountain, the outage that made Estella's cousin pee in her water bottle out in Barstow. And those aren't the only ones. There were outages in Needles, in Palo Verde, in Carlsbad. In Ridgecrest, in Shafter, in Lompoc. None of the towns between or around those areas were affected, and there were no storms or accidents or anything that would have caused them in such disparate places. At least, not that I can find.

And I look. I look hard. For a car accident that strategically hit the wires that connected power stations. For a freak rain squall that might not have been noted on weather apps. For . . . well, anything that would tell me I'm being ridiculous and wrong in thinking something's up. In thinking that, like my dad always said, somebody is testing out a larger attack.

I don't find it.

7

I push my chair away from command central and bury my face in my sweaty palms. This is some kind of test for doomsday. Or at least, that's what my dad would say. The signs are here. Could it really be true, though?

Could it really be some person or organization hacking into the power stations and causing selective outages to prove that they can? To prove that they have control over our electrical grids and can do it on a much bigger scale? I've seen articles like this about Russia or Iran or North Korea sticking their fingers in our grids, trying to gain access and sometimes even succeeding . . . though they haven't actually caused power outages with their access.

Until now. Now somebody has.

My whole body is numb. I feel my heart hammering as if it's coming from somewhere far away. It's like all my years of progress, of learning to live in regular society, have unraveled in an instant, and I'm right back there on the compound, and the words don't sound quite so wild coming out of my dad's mouth in that serious tone.

But this *is* totally wild. Right? None of this feels quite real. I imagine turning around to find a dinosaur lurking behind me, and he'd laugh, and I'd laugh, because we'd realize we were actually in a dream. I pinch myself and it hurts.

I wish this were a dream. I wish I could close my eyes and pretend I haven't seen any of this, the way another person would. Who else would look at this swiss cheese of power outages and see the end of the world except for me?

Maybe I never became so "normal" after all.

I have to tell someone. Maybe someone will inform me that there's a logical explanation for all of this, except that I know in my gut there *is* no logical explanation for this, that my dad was right all along, that we should never have left the compound, that soon we're going to fall into a giant pit and I have to let everyone know.

My mom. I have to call my mom. She works with the mayor. After we left the compound, she got a job in city hall as an administrative assistant, then moved quickly up through the ranks until she was running the mayor's desk. She knows lots of important people—especially important people in other cities who could check their local power companies and make sure there aren't any insidious viruses lurking in their code. She might think I'm insane, but I'll convince her. I'll *make* her understand. I know she can—she wouldn't have lasted so long with my dad, living isolated out on that compound, if she didn't believe at least a little bit that the world might end, no matter what she said.

Or maybe you want her to tell you that you're seeing things again, a little voice whispers in my head. *That doomsday isn't coming.*

No. That's not what I want. My heart wouldn't be racing like this if I didn't see something real.

Right?

I call her cell first. When she doesn't pick up, I call her work line. She answers on the first ring. "Mayor's office, this is Dina Appel," she says all in one breath. Despite everything I'm feeling right now, I can't help but be touched by a small spark of pride that my mom's come so far and achieved so much.

"Mom," I say, and my voice breaks.

There's a rustling on the other end. Her voice sharpens in that way moms' voices do when they're worried. "Zara? Is everything okay?"

"Mom," I say, then stop. I don't even know where to start.

"Zara," she says, her voice sharpening further. "Do I need to—"

"Dad was right," I say, and now that I've started, everything else comes spilling out. I'm panting by the time I finish, but a bunch of the stress has drained out of me. My mom is going to know exactly what to do, and then she's going to help me save the day.

I wait. And wait. And wait, until she sighs. "Zara," she says, and it's like I've just leaned over and slurped all the stress back up. "Your dad wasn't right about anything."

I shouldn't have mentioned my dad. If only I had stuck to what *I'd* found, what *I'd* noticed, then she would understand. She hears my dad's name and it's like a door slams shut in her mind. But I saw a pattern. I *saw* it. "But it's not about him," I say. Tears prickle at the corners of my eyes. "I'm the one who discovered what's going on. He has nothing to do with it. Listen to me—"

"I can't do this right now, Zara," she says. That edge on her voice has returned, and this time I'm afraid I'm going to get cut. "I've been running around like a chicken without a head all day, and I'm exhausted, and I can't think about your father right now."

"But—"

"We'll talk about this when I get home. It won't be long. Okay?" She waits for me to mutter a chastened "fine." "I love you, Zara. It's not the end of the world. Everything is going to be okay."

She doesn't know that. She *can't* know that.

But I don't know what else to do. Who else to go to. I mean, I could try calling the local news or the power company, but there's no chance any of them will believe me. Still, I pick my phone up, google the local news hotline, hover my thumb over the five key, . . .

. . . and hesitate. Because what if my mom is right? What if I'm totally imagining things, seeing things that aren't there because I got all fizzed up from being reminded about my dad?

I tilt my head back, trying to keep the tears pearling up in my eyes from sliding out and down my cheeks. "I'm not losing my mind," I say aloud. "I'm not, I'm not."

But I can't even convince myself.

8

After a while of sitting there and wondering if I'm actually losing my mind, I can't take it anymore. Like, my leg is jittering and my fingers are drumming, and it's as if I just took something that's making my insides bounce all around. So I visit my happy place: a postapocalyptic future hellscape.

My character greets me with her typical stony face. I kill a few radiation-mutated animals with my crossbow, and my shoulders begin to slump with the release of all the tension built up inside me. It's good I'm getting the practice in. Well, kind of. This is probably what the world's going to look like soon.

I shake my head at myself. As if responding, my character tilts her head to the side and sighs. It's like she's telling me that my mom's right. That I'm imagining things. That of course if you're thinking nonstop about doomsday, you're going to see it everywhere you look.

My headset dings, the indication that a friend has just logged on. I have only one in-game friend. As I'm trying to figure out what to message him, he messages me. Hey, what's up?

Usually this is where I'd hook us up via the headset, but I don't really want to talk. Not out loud. Somehow things are easier when they're typed out. Just killing things out of frustration. Hey, don't you have your college thing?

Not for another half hour, so I thought I'd hop on and grind out some rep while I wait. Gabe and I are both working on building our reputation with one of the factions controlling parts of the city, which our characters can do by killing enemies of that faction. If we're in good with them, we get access to some shiny new armor and vendors.

Not that any of it will matter in a few weeks. My fingers tense instinctively at the thought that doomsday may very well be coming and I'm sitting here playing a game.

If doomsday is *really* on its way, shouldn't I be doing more to stop it? Doesn't the very fact that I'm sitting here playing my game show me that even I don't believe myself?

I'll join, I message back, pushing those thoughts away. It's kind of reassuring just to *have* them. Because if I were losing my mind, I'd lose all these thoughts, too, right? Isn't that how it works?

Once I've ported to Gabe's side, we carve a path of carnage through our newfound enemies. My heart slows down, but the drumbeat in my head doesn't stop. *Doomsday. Doomsday. Doomsday.*

My headset dings, the sign that he's trying to connect, but I hesitate only a moment before hitting decline. I don't know how much my voice will betray how I'm actually feeling. Gabe doesn't pressure me or anything, but the message chime sounds over my headset. Everything OK?

I take a deep breath, but my fingers are already moving. *Do you ever feel like you're losing your mind? Like everybody else sees the sky as its usual blue, but you're looking up and seeing red?*

The intimidating dot-dot-dot pops up and disappears twice, making my heart start racing again each time. Finally he says, I think everybody's felt that way. What's going on?

My fingers twitch, wanting to betray me, but this time I manage to hold them back. You know how I said my dad was into all the survivalist stuff in the car? How he thought the end of the world was always coming? I say, then pause, uncertain how much I actually want to share. Not all of it, that's for sure. Something triggered me, and now I can't stop thinking about it. Thinking that I'm seeing the end of the world coming. And it's driving me kind of insane.

That's the most vulnerable I've ever been with Gabe, and it feels a little bit like I've reached an ice cream scooper into my stomach and carved out some of my guts, then plopped them in a bowl and handed them over. We don't typically *do* vulnerable. We don't typically do real life at all—all our discussions over the headset and in-game pretty much stick to what monster to kill and what goal to chase next.

This time the dot-dot-dot appears and disappears one, two, three, four times. I bury my face in my hands. I shouldn't have shared so much. Now he's going to think I've gone insane, just like my mom does. He's going to tell me not to worry, that of course the end of the world isn't coming, that I'm seeing things, that—

Chime.

I lift my head to see his message: If the end of the world really is coming, is there anything you can actually do about it?

The only thing I can really do in my current position as a broke, nonfamous teenager is try to raise the alarm and tell people. I've already done that with the person most equipped to believe me, and she didn't. I'm not sure now if even I believe myself . . . and if I don't believe myself, how can I make other people believe me?

Not really, I say.

Gabe's character claps his hands together. Then why stress out about it? What's the point? He doesn't wait for a response, which is probably wise. Let's just kill stuff.

He's right in a way—that there's no point stressing and worrying about something you have no control over. If only him saying that were enough to turn it off. Still, I return with him to our flurry of weapons, our characters scattering bits of pearlescent carapaces and chunks of armor around us, some of them with flesh still inside.

Something about sharing the news actually makes me feel a bit better, and the murder spree helps. Forty-five minutes flash by, and then I'm blinking at the clock, thinking that there's somewhere I'm supposed to be—no, that's Gabe. Hey, I message him, don't you have your virtual college thing?

His answer comes quickly. I can do another one. I wanted to make sure you were okay.

Hearing that makes a knot untwist deep in my gut, one I didn't realize was tied so tightly in the first place. I'm totally fine. You should go.

You sure?

Positive. Our characters wave goodbye to each other, and then he sinks to his knees and is enveloped in a virtual tent that then fades from view. I stare at the spot for a moment longer, then log off myself. Somehow doing this alone seems a lot less fun now.

I take off the headset, then take in a few deep, cleansing breaths. "You're not losing it," I tell myself, listening hard to see how truthful my voice sounds. "You're really not."

A tap on my door. It's gentle, but the noise makes my stomach fall to my feet. "Zara?" It's my mom, of course. I push my chair back slowly from command central and stand, stretching out my back. Maybe if I stay really quiet, she'll understand I don't want to talk to her, and she'll go away.

But that doesn't work on moms, or at least not on mine. She pushes the door open, silhouetting herself in the entrance. Her eyebrows meet over her nose in the most frowny way possible. "Who were you talking to?"

"Estella," I say, then hold my breath.

She nods and I exhale. She must have heard just my voice, not the actual words I was saying. "I'm glad to find you here," she says. "I was worried."

The unapologetic relief in her voice makes me scowl. "What did you think I'd be doing? Running naked through the streets wrapped in neon lights, screaming, 'Doomsday is coming, doomsday is coming'?"

The corners of my mom's lips twitch. "Technically speaking, you can't be both naked and wrapped in neon lights."

I scowl harder.

Her smile falls off and she steps forward. She's now within reaching-for-me distance, but she doesn't reach for me. "Zara. I'm worried about you."

I press my lips together. Somehow I don't think it would help if I told her that I'm worried about me too.

I saw what I saw.

Right?

She doesn't help dispel my fears. "Those allegations you made earlier—and just now—were and are pretty wild. And not true. You know that, right?" She looks sincere, the way she's searching my face for an answer, but that doesn't make it okay.

I just press my lips together harder. If I start bleeding, she'll go into panic mode about something else, which might be nice. I press my teeth into my bottom lip, but it turns out that drawing blood is a lot harder than books make it seem. And a lot more painful.

"Should we call Dr. Nguyen again? There's no shame in needing someone to talk to. God knows I went to Dr. Hall for two years after we got away from that place."

Finally. Something I can seize on that doesn't involve my mental health. "Got away? You make it sound like a prison." I roll my shoulders, trying to ignore how her face has slipped from sincere to sad. "You're the one who chose to marry Dad and leave your job and go live and raise your child in the middle of nowhere to make sure we were prepared for the end of the world."

The sadness is still there, sagging on her lips and her eyes, but something else joins it. Something that narrows her eyes and makes her chin pucker a bit. I don't think I've ever seen it before, and I don't know what it is, and that unnerves me. It's almost like she knows something I don't, and she's considering how much to tell me. "Zara," she says slowly and patiently, "you remember, right? You remember we left when—"

A scream fills the room. I freeze in place, my eyes darting around. Where is it coming from? Is someone else in the house?

My mom keeps talking as if she can't hear anything at all. My heart skips in panic. I know I need to do something to help who-ever's screaming, but it's like my hands have a mind of their own—they raise themselves and clamp over my ears.

My mom frowns at me. I blink, and then squint because I can't see her. All I can see is green. Green leaves rustling overhead and green light filtering through the trees, and just ahead, that's where the scream is coming from, hurtling at me over an earthy green carpet, and there's blood, a big puddle of it and lots of little puddles besides. . . .

"Zara!" Hands grab me by the shoulders, and the spell is broken. The room is a room again, enclosed by walls and a ceiling and a floor. I lower my arms. Silence rings in my ears.

I've heard that scream before. Long ago, all the way across the country. And here, right before I'd have those panic attacks at recess. Only it was only an echo then, like it was an echo just now.

"Are you okay?" my mom continues. Her dark curls, the same as mine, frizz wildly around her face like they're as anxious as she is. "What were you doing? Are you—"

"Nothing. It's not important," I interrupt loudly, letting my words fill up the small space until there's no room left for hers.

"It *is* important, Zara. I need to know that you're—"

"I'm doing fine." My voice comes out louder than I mean it to. "The only thing that isn't fine is that you think I'm losing it. And you're my mom, and you shouldn't think that." I turn my head so that she can't see the tears burning in my eyes. "You're the only one who's never supposed to think that."

Finally, finally, she reaches for me. Her hand on my shoulder is as light as a bird landing. "Zara, you know I don't think that," she says. "I would never think that, ever. None of this is your fault."

I'm about to ask her whose fault it is, then, when I realize that, duh, she means it's my dad's. He's supposedly warped my mind, made me what I am. Doesn't she realize it's been almost seven years since I left the compound? If she handed me a dead squirrel right now, I'd drop it and wash my hands, not skin it and roast it.

"They said a backslide at any time is normal. Normal," my mom repeats. "So we'll go back to Dr. Nguyen. You always liked Dr. Nguyen."

"I don't need to go to Dr. Nguyen."

But my mom's mind is made up. "I'll set up an appointment for next week. No, this week. You're free on Friday, right?"

"No."

"Okay, good." It's like she can't even hear me. "I'll pick you up after school. It's all going to be okay." She dusts her hands together, like she's just finished making something with them. "Dinner? I'm starving all of a sudden."

No, it's not like she can't hear me. It's that she *won't* hear me. "I'm not hungry," I say flatly. "I think I'm just going to bed."

"But it's not even eight o'clock—"

"Good night," I say, and turn away.

She sighs. She's so close, it shivers the little hairs on the back of my neck. "Good night, Zara. I love you."

The words are on the tip of my tongue—saying it back is a reflex—but I clamp my lips shut and pull away.

9

I lie awake that night and make some Wednesday resolutions—like those you'd make for the new year, only on a random weekday. One, I will not let myself think I'm losing my mind, because I know what I saw. Two, if I *am* losing it and didn't actually see what I know I saw, I will not let it show. I fall asleep before I can think too much about how much my two resolutions contradict each other.

I'm woken up by the pleasant sound of my mom hammering on my door. "I'm up," I groan, and I know she can hear me, but she gives a few more ear-shattering bangs for good measure.

My mom loves mornings.

I hop in a quick shower and brush my teeth and even have time left over to microwave my Pop-Tart for ten seconds, which is the ideal amount of time to microwave a Pop-Tart (warm, runny middle, crust not dry or falling apart). My mom stands by the oven, facing me. I look everywhere but at her eyes. She doesn't look anywhere *but* at mine. It's pretty uncomfortable. I can stand it for only nine seconds, one second before the microwave beeps. "If you have something to say, just say it," I snap.

I take my Pop-Tart out as she exhales deeply. "Have you given any more thought to what I said last night?"

I slam the microwave door with a bang. She jumps. "Nope."

I flee before she can say anything back. Estella waits for me on the bus. She scoots over as I walk down the aisle, making room for me. "Hey, Zara. You okay?"

I can't help but scan the rows in front of me with new eyes. Or maybe it's that I'm using my same old eyes, but I'm just no longer entirely sure I can trust them. "Hey, has Jodie always had hair that pink?"

Estella furrows her brow. "Um, no."

My heart stops.

Then Estella continues. "I think I'd call it more magenta."

I let out a breath of relief.

No matter what I told my mom, I can't help but roll her words over and over in my mind as Estella chatters on. Not the ones she wants me to think over (take that, Mom)—the ones she said when I told her the compound wasn't a prison. *Zara, you remember, right?* And that weird look on her face. I can't get over it. *Zara. You remember. Right?*

I remember the clean smell of the forest and how it changed with the seasons: crisp and piney in the winter; warm and grassy in the summer; the mineral smell of rain in the spring; the earthy scent of decay in the fall. I remember the fierce pride in my dad's eyes when I downed a deer or a pheasant in one shot, or successfully jerry-rigged a water filtration system using sunlight and clear plastic to collect evaporated water that was safe to drink after our main water filtration system broke. I remember the three of us swimming in our lake and racing out to the fallen tree, the three of us sitting around our table every night to eat the food we made with our own hands, my mom spending days every summer canning our abundance of tomatoes and my dad raving over her tomato sauce. I remember my mom bribing me with a rare piece of chocolate to clean out the chicken coop. (The joke was on her—the chickens and I were friends.) I remember drowsing to sleep beside a crackling campfire and listening to my mom laugh as she tried to teach my dad to sing.

I remember that we were happy. Tired and bruised and scraped, but happy. At least until the end.

I don't like to think about the end. *The blood and the scream and the . . .*

I'm still keyed up by the time computer science rolls around. We're still supposed to be working on our final projects, but I can't focus on the letters and symbols and numbers on the screen, so I just stare blankly into the light.

Until Estella nudges me. "Hey," she says. "This function keeps giving me an error. Can you take a look and see what I'm missing?"

I move closer and technically look at the function, but I don't read it. I scroll up and down, up and down, everything blurring before me. She asks me cautiously, "Are you okay? Do you want to—"

She stops as a kid walking by slams into her chair, sending her oofing into the table. He barely glances over his shoulder, a sneer flickering over his face. There are a few kids like him in this class: kids who resent that Estella and me—the girls—have the best grades of us all. I've seen the memes they pass around, pictures swiped from places like 4chan and overlaid with text that implies we're not valid, not equal, just because of our gender. My blood boils.

Estella gives him a disgusted look but stays in her seat. My blood boils more, and suddenly it's all whistling in my ears like a shrieking teapot: *Crazy doomsday girl stupid feminists power doesn't deserve—*

I leap to my feet. "Hey," I shout after him. "Say you're sorry."

The kid's already in his seat. He turns fully to face me. I think his name is something generic like Joe or Dave. "Didn't do anything," says Joe or Dave.

My fists ball at my sides. "Apologize to her," I say, my face heating up.

I can't read the look he's giving me. Did he go to middle school with me? Is he thinking the same thing as Callie Everett and Mitch Brown? *She's the one who had panic attacks all the time. Leave her alone.*

Estella tugs at my arm. "Just leave it, Zara," she says.

But you can't just leave things. Leaving things, pretending they don't exist and trying to stick your head in the sand? That's how they fester. Get worse. That's how the world ends.

This is about Estella, though. She needs to learn that you can't just let people walk all over you. That's how people die when the world ends. "*Apologize to her*, or . . ." I trail off, because just now I realize that all the eyes in the room are on me.

Joe or Dave snickers. "Or what?"

I take a breath and open my mouth. "Or—"

Everything goes dark.

The computer screens turn black with a startled hum. The lights flicker off. The air-conditioning clicks to a stop. I'm left blinking into Joe or Dave's face; in the dark his cheeks are hollowed out and filled with shadow, his eyes pits of black.

Mr. Miller claps his hands together at the front of the room, where he was taking questions from other classmates who needed the help. "All right, everyone! Let's sit tight until the power either comes back on or we get further instructions."

Estella tugs more insistently at my arm. "Come on, Zara. Please. Just leave it. It's not important."

I thud back into my seat. My whole body is numb as I shake my head.

It's more important than ever.

10

I sit silently next to Estella, a statue as she browses her phone, her face lit by the light of the screen. Cell towers are run by generators if the power goes out (a fact Estella checks on Google), so we still have a signal for now, if not Wi-Fi. I don't pull out my phone, though. I just sit there, my back rigid against the hard plastic of my chair, and I hope. I cross all the fingers I can that the glaring, fluorescent lights that make us all look pasty and sick come flickering back on. I wait for the computers to chime in a chorus and begin their rebooting process. Beads of sweat form across my forehead in the newly stuffy heat, and I pray silently to every god there is that the AC comes whooshing back.

It doesn't.

Usually if the power's out, they have to send us home early, but since we're already almost at the end of the day, they just let us wait it out, with only after-school activities being canceled. Estella nudges me with an elbow. "It's so weird," she murmurs. Somehow it seems only appropriate to whisper in a dark room. "There are people online saying that the power's out in all of New York City and Chicago and LA." My heart sinks into my stomach. I feel vaguely nauseous. "Isn't that weird?"

Though we didn't ask him, the kid at the hexagon in front of us turns around. "My cousin texted me from Texas that the power's out there. And my sister in college in Seattle—they're blacked out too."

The class erupts into whispers about what this might mean. I don't participate. I just sit there as solid as a block of stone, not even hoping and praying anymore.

I wasn't seeing things after all.

Though now I'm kind of wishing I had. Because this is it. The entire country's power is out—that's three separate grids. No accident or storm or random series of coincidences could have caused it. This is the attack I was waiting for.

Right? Maybe it's not. Maybe it's another test, and the power will come blinking on in another day or two. Maybe, maybe, maybe . . . but if there's anything I learned growing up, it's that I can't wait around for a maybe.

The march out to the student parking lot or the courtyard, usually a seething mass of humanity I always escape grateful to have all my limbs, is kind of zombielike today. Everybody's speaking in whispers, and I understand why. The power's out all over the country. Nobody's sure what this means. It's never happened before, and the new is scary, and people's phones are beginning to die, and generators keeping cell towers and hospitals going last only as long as they have gas to run them.

Whispers rush over me as Estella and I move through the crowd. Eyes that usually skip over us meet ours, as if they're seeking answers anywhere they can. "They still have power in most of Europe and Asia, but Toronto and Montreal and Mexico City are blacked out. . . ." "Was it a bomb?" "A sunspot?" "When is it going to come back?"

Nobody asks *if* it's going to come back.

A girl I know vaguely from gym—she always came in first in the mile—is talking confidently to a group of other astoundingly tall people. "We've had widespread blackouts before. Worst-case scenario is we're screwed for a few weeks."

"I think my family has a little generator," another girl chimes in. "You guys can come over and charge your phones and take a shower."

High fives all around. I shake my head. I'm tempted to stop and tell them that phones and showers are the least of our concerns right now, but who knows if they'll believe me?

Our trip home in Gabe's car moves at a crawl; everybody must have left work or school at the same time. And of course traffic lights aren't working. Traffic cops in orange stand in the middle of every intersection blowing whistles and waving their arms.

"Zara." Estella, in the front, twists around.

I blink. "Yeah?"

She grips the side of her seat. Her knuckles blanch. "Did you see this coming?"

My dad used to say we were the ones who'd see it coming. I was going through his wallet once and found a card with a symbol on it: two circles, with an eye inside the smaller one. When I asked him what it meant, he told me, "It means we see everything. What's already there, what has happened, and what is still to come."

Even so, I'm not sure what exactly Estella's getting at here. "What?"

"It's just . . . yesterday you were talking a lot about that dooms-day stuff, like with your dad. . . ."

I rest my forehead against the window. It's cold. The vibration of the car rattles my teeth. "No, I didn't know this was coming." But that's not quite true, is it?

Maybe she hears how down I sound, because she doesn't ask anything else, not even when we get to my house. She only gives me a quick, tight hug as I hop out. "I'll call you later," she promises. I smile back in response and don't say, *Your phone might be dead later.*

My own phone is almost dead, but my external battery pack powers it up—I should probably get in touch with my mom. As if she read my mind, she calls me. Her picture pops up on my phone, one I took of her first thing in the morning before she'd even had her coffee or brushed her teeth. She's squinting into the camera like she doesn't know what it is, her upper lip curled as if she might try to bite it, her hair standing up and down and all around.

She's begged me to delete it more than once, but it's basically art. You don't delete art.

"Hi, Zara," she begins, but I bulldoze right over her. I want to dig an apology out of her, an acknowledgment that I was right and she was wrong, but that can come later.

"Please tell me you're taking this seriously."

Her hesitation *kills* me. "Zara," she says finally. "Of course I'm taking it seriously. Most of the country seems to be blacked out. We might be without power for a while. That's a big—"

"Not a while," I interrupt. I want to scream so loud and sharp, it breaks all the glass in the house. "We need to prepare. The way we used to." I can practically hear her wince over the phone, but I don't care. "Do you remember step three? I remember that step one is making sure I'm safe for the moment, and step two is water, but I don't remember what—"

It's her turn to interrupt me. "Zara," she says for the third time. "We're readying our emergency supplies in case we need them, but I really, *really* don't want you to panic." I hear the sound of her sighing on the other end of the line, or maybe it's just static. Or maybe it's the generator failing and the cell tower going down.

She keeps on talking. "I would say you should come meet me here, but the roads are a mess right now. I'm sure Uber's prices are sky high. But don't worry, Zara. Everybody's on it, and we're working hard to fix it."

She's speaking to me like I'm one of her constituents, which makes me screech in frustration. I know better than to believe in the power of the government too much. And not just because of my dad: even my mom's admitted under pressure that no part of the government, federal or state, has an actual plan for a full-scale, countrywide disaster like this. Assuming it's all really down for good. *Please, please, please let me be wrong.*

But I don't think I am. I feel it in my bones.

"Why don't you give Estella a call? She's good at . . . at making the best of these kinds of things."

I know what she was going to say: *She's good at calming you down, Zara.* "Fine," I say abruptly. With that, she lets me hang up. She may or may not know I have no plans to call Estella right now, but she's not going to press. Which is good. Because if she's not going to prepare for herself, I need to prep for both of us. I'm safe inside, which means the next step is water: I fill up as many containers as I can, plus the bathtub. I google the process for keeping water in a city after a power outage. Gravity will keep water flowing into our pipes from the water tower for a while, and a generator will be able to pump water up into that tower, but if the generator runs out of gas, that's it. I'm not that thirsty, but I force an entire glass down. When I move, I feel it sloshing in my belly. Over it my dad whispers, *A person can live only three days without water.* That's not something I have to look up.

Water. Okay, I have water. And I'm safe. So. Next steps.

I head up into the attic, breathing in cool, musty air, each footstep making a hole in the layer of dust. I haven't been up here in years, but this is where my mom and I stashed a bunch of the gear I brought with me or bought in those frantic first few months in the real world, when I was convinced the world would end at any moment. Now the supplies lie jumbled up on shelves, making spooky shadows on the far wall. I pause, taking a deep breath and pondering our supplies' importance, then sneeze, which makes dust fly up all around me.

Pepper spray is a good thing to have on hand; I grab one for myself and one for my mom. Fortunately, they haven't expired. Iodine tablets for water purification and a thermos with a built-in filter for clean water—also good things to have. What else?

I have a few solar-powered headlamps; it can't hurt to have a ready source of bright light. A Swiss Army Knife with about a million attachments—it's not the exact same one I had on the compound, but picking it up feels like grabbing an old friend's hand. The bottles of sunscreen and boxes of crumbling protein bars are long expired, so I give them a pass.

With all these necessities gathered and stuffed into my backpack, I trudge down the ladder. As long as I'm safe and have clean water and canned or packaged food, I'll be fine for now. My neighbors should be fine too. It's really when the water stops that chaos begins.

When I get downstairs, I find a missed call from Estella. She picks up immediately when I return it. "Zara! No school tomorrow, says the robocall." My mom must have gotten it on her cell phone. "Not until they get the power back on."

Until. She sounds so certain. "Oh," I say after a moment, because it's clear she expects me to respond.

"So guess what?"

"What?"

Estella's voice fills with glee. "We're having a party tomorrow night. On a school night. End-of-the-world party, Gabe deemed it. Bonfire, canned food, the works. You in?"

"Are you insane?" The words burst out of me before I can help myself.

"No," she says. "Are you?"

Well. I'm not sure how to answer that. So I say instead, "Stell, I'm really worried."

"I know. You're always worried," she says. *Thanks a lot.* "I know this is serious. Especially if you grew up with this kind of thing discussed all the time. But it's going to be okay. They're going to get in there and fix it. In the meantime, it'll be like camping for a little while. It'll be fun." Her voice is confident. I don't know if she's convinced herself since our car ride or if her family convinced her.

The only thing I can do in response to that is make a mental note to bring enough emergency supplies for Estella and her whole family.

"So you're coming tomorrow, right?"

Do I really want to? No. I feel like I should be doing something more than what I'm doing now. But I've got enough food and water and safety for a while, and I can't make any long-term plans without more information. And, of course, without my mom. So I might as well go. "I guess," I say. "Should I bring anything?"

"Just your sweet ass," she says. That I can do. We hang up, leaving me unsettled.

I pass the night alternately scrolling headlines on my phone—there's still no consensus on what's going on, just wild speculation—and powering it off, because my heart flutters with panic every time my battery drops a percentage. I think about going for a walk, but I don't really feel like going outside—it looks pretty normal, with maybe a few less people jogging or walking their dogs, but wandering around out there feels like exposing myself. I'll get enough of that when I walk to Estella's tomorrow. I fall asleep before my mom gets home, all curled up with Elroy, my stuffed walrus, in my arms. Cuddling with him always made me feel better as a kid, but it does nothing for me now.

The next day dawns warm and bright and still powerless. My mom's already at work, a note tacked to the fridge telling me to be safe and that she loves me. I don't want to waste water washing myself, but I do slather on more deodorant and change into clean clothes. The bell skirt of a flowered dress—picked out by Estella, naturally—swishes above my knees. It's been a couple of days since I've shaved, but nobody'll notice the pricklies unless they squat and stare directly at my calves.

My stomach gives an unpleasant lurch. It takes me a moment to realize why: if this is really happening, I won't be shaving in the shower anytime soon. There won't be showers anymore.

It's the little things that get you. Which is why my dad used to say it's better not to have any of those little things in the first place. Then you can't miss them when they're gone.

11

I might be wearing what Estella called "the cutest dress I've ever seen, oh God, it's burning my eyes out with its sheer adorableness," but I don't pair it with the strappy silver sandals she deemed its perfect sole mates (get it?). You can't run in strappy silver sandals. Instead I put on my metallic silver Converses, which are comfy and good for running away from thirsty hordes. Though I don't see any thirsty hordes on the way to Estella's. I don't see much out of the ordinary, in fact. Normal cars sitting in normal driveways, normal people jogging in the street, normal mail being retrieved from mailboxes.

Sure enough, she raises her eyebrows skeptically when I present her with her very own survival pack. I've gone around the side of her house, a neat little ranch like mine, into her backyard. There she's waiting on her deck, with Gabe and a few of his friends chatting near the side of the pool. My own lawn is brown and crunches when you step on it, but Estella's is lush and green, her pool bright blue and crystal clear. My mom says it's because Estella's dad is retired and has nothing better to do than lawn care, which sounds like jealousy to me. "That's okay," Estella says. "I don't think I'm gonna need it."

I don't withdraw it. "Take it for my sake," I say.

She reaches out to unzip it but doesn't take it off my hands. Instead she gingerly pokes inside, like she's performing an operation. "What's this? A water bottle? I have, like, eight hundred water bottles."

"Not one with a built-in—"

"And what's this? A headlamp?"

"Estella!" Gabe calls behind her. He gives me a wave. I wave back. "What?" she calls. When he only motions for her to come over, she rolls her eyes. "Be right back. You're sweet, Zara, but seriously. I don't need it. Take it home for your mom."

She turns and pads over to Gabe. *You're being stupid,* I beam at the back of her head. I imagine that I can see a few strands of her thick black waves sizzle.

Still, if she doesn't want my survival pack, I can't exactly shove it down her throat. So I step over to the sliding glass door and toss it inside.

"Zara!" It's Estella's turn to call over from where she stands in the knot of Gabe and his friends. There are a few of them, two of whom I recognize vaguely from the school hallways. And . . . Callie Everett of the shiny hair, who gives me a small smile. I didn't know she was friends with Gabe or that she lived nearby. I nod a greeting as Estella leans into me, her voice hissing in my ear. "Are you going to smoke? Irina brought some weed."

"Is it good?" I ask. I have no idea why I even bother, because I'm not going to smoke or vape any of it, nor do I have any idea what makes a particular bundle of weed good or bad. Not tonight. If I were going to smoke, I might as well have thrown all caution to the wind and worn my strappy silver sandals.

Estella shrugs. "How about a drink? We've got vodka we can mix with soda or orange—"

"I'm not going to *drink* right now." My voice comes out as a scold. How can she even think about impairing her mental state at this time? I need to be alert. Ready. Not giggling and swaying if something bad happens. Well, if something even worse happens.

She sighs at me, but before she can say anything, the sliding glass door whooshes open. Estella's mom leans out and shouts, "The president's giving an address!"

Estella takes a long sip of her soda and doesn't move. I shift from foot to foot. When Gabe and his friends don't move either, I say—a bit too impatiently—"Well, should we go in and watch it?"

Gabe cocks his head and studies me. "Zara, how are you doing?"

That's just another way of asking if I'm okay. I'm really sick of being asked if I'm okay. But I don't say that. I just say, quietly, "I'm fine."

I've spent so much time with Gabe online, and yet somehow here in person, it's hard to say anything at all.

"We should all know what's going on," I say finally, and is it my imagination, or does it come out really loud?

"I'll go with you," Estella says quickly, thwapping Gabe on the shoulder. He clasps his hands to it like he's been mortally wounded and makes an exaggerated crying face, which causes everybody to laugh again. "Come on, Zara. Let's go watch it on my dad's phone."

Estella's dad's phone is practically as big as a tablet. She and I and her parents cluster around it in their kitchen, bowing our heads to get the best view. It makes me feel like we're people in the old days, bunching around a radio to hear FDR's snappy voice. Though, instead of listening to him soothe a Depression-weary populace, we're looking at a live feed of an empty chair behind a desk. Static spits every so often, and the low rumble of voices fills the background.

Then she's there, the president, sitting in her chair with a creak. She's staring straight into my eyes, though I'm sure everybody watching feels the same way. "Citizens of the United States," she says, her voice low and measured, and I feel like she's not just looking into my eyes, she's looking past them, into my brain. "As I'm sure you've noticed, our electrical grids have gone down, causing extended blackouts throughout the entire country. Canada's and Mexico's are down as well. We do not yet know the cause." Her face stays impassive, and that, I know, will be the topic of conversation among the people once she's done: how composed she was, how confident she sounded, how reassuring her eyes were. *It couldn't have been an attack,* they'll say to one another, *or else she'd be panicking. It's all some weird natural coincidence.*

Most of those people won't notice the working of her throat, the slight twitching of the muscles along the rings of her trachea. Like she can't stop swallowing, or like she's trying as hard as she can not to scream.

"We have authorized FEMA and local governments to distribute emergency supplies if the blackout persists throughout the week." A key word there: "if." She's planting doubt in everybody's minds without any of them realizing she's doing it. *If.* There's no *if* about any of this.

"Please do not be alarmed," the president continues. Her gray-blond bob is shiny, framing her face like a helmet. Maybe it's meant to protect her like one too, from whatever's about to come. "We ask you to remain calm and shelter in place while we work to fix the problem. Do not panic, and please stay off the roads unless you are an emergency vehicle." She gives me—the audience—a tight smile, and then the video flickers before her speech begins all over again. "Citizens of the United States . . ."

Estella's dad swipes her away, stopping her midword. I look over just as he yawns so wide, his jaw actually creaks. "Waste of time," he says.

Estella's mom snorts. "A whole lot of nothing. Well, at least she doesn't sound all that alarmed." I want to shake them and scream, *What were you watching?!* Instead I just stare over their shoulders, taking deep breaths. They've got a map pinned up on their bulletin board. I trace the freeways with my eyes, plotting a course to take us back to sanity. . . .

Estella grabs me by the hand and tugs me back outside, where a few more of Gabe's friends have gathered. They've set up chairs around the pool, which still glitters blue despite the lack of buzzing filter. Some clumps of sand have gathered on the bottom. A few more days with no filter or vacuum, and it'll be murky and brown, swimming with dirt and leaves.

How quickly everything falls apart.

A few more people show up over the next hour, mostly Gabe's friends. All people who live close by, since none of us are supposed to drive right now. Estella's parents stay in the house, though her mom comes out every so often to check on us—mostly, I think, to make sure we're not getting wasted on her watch. The world might be ending, but she's not going to abandon her sacred parental duties. So much for that. She must have a really stuffy nose not to notice the skunky smell drifting from the far corner of the backyard.

My red plastic cup is cold in my hand and wet with condensation, but it's filled only with soda—decaf, at that, because caffeine just makes me jittery. Gabe and his friends are already giggling in their circle, swaying as if to a beat, though there's no music.

Like they're reading my mind, Gabe turns around. "Stell," he says. "Want to sing for us?"

Estella's cheeks are red. When she speaks, her words are loose, like they're falling out of her—she disappeared into the weed corner for a moment earlier. "Just play some music," she says, leaning on me. She's wearing a bare-shoulder top, one with ruffles all around the front, and I can feel her sweat rubbing off on my own skin. I don't pull away, though.

Callie steps forward. "Nobody wants to use their phone battery to stream anything, since we don't know when we'll be able to charge them again," she says, voice hushed.

Everybody sobers. They're quiet. It's enough for me to feel hope for a second, that maybe I'm not the only one who is thinking that this is all a big deal.

Another girl waves a hand in the air. "We lived without electricity for thousands of years, we can do it again," she says. Her eyes sparkle. "Besides, it might be kind of exciting, don't you think?"

Do none of these people realize how much of our lives depends on electricity? I step away from Estella, making her stumble. Nobody here will think it's "exciting" or thrilling when they're eating wormy cornmeal for a week straight because we no longer have refrigeration and they don't know how to hunt and we can't pump gas for the millions of trucks carting food around the country. Or when they're eating nothing at all. I tip my head back to look at the sky so nobody will see the consternation on my face. It's almost entirely dark now, the last golden shimmers of the sunset melting into a starry sky.

"I'd sing if there were music," Estella says.

Somebody claps. Somebody else joins in, and I'm confused for a moment, thinking I missed something, when somebody else starts slapping their thighs, and somebody else starts beatboxing. I look down and can't stop the snort that escapes me at the sight of Gabe and three other guys smacking their hands and tongues all over the place.

Estella shrugs. "Okay, then." She opens her mouth and unleashes the soulful rasp of her voice, something wordless and tuneless that somehow flows into the spaces left by the boys' drumming and clapping. It's wild, primal, perfect. The stars spin above me, and her voice spins around me, and for a moment I lose myself in all the stars of the sky.

At some point we migrate forward into the circle, the grass damp and ticklish on our bare ankles. The air smells like chlorine and salt and something artificially sweet, maybe drifting up from the others' cups. I close my eyes. The dark allows me to swing my hips from side to side, toss my head back and forth. The movement makes me feel free. Like I might fly away.

I wonder if Gabe is watching me. I crack an eyelid to find that he's turned away, laughing with Irina of the good weed. Something like jealousy sparks in my stomach.

One of the other girls grabs my arm and pulls me into the middle of the circle; everybody around us whistles and claps as she spins me around. I tip my head back and look up at the sky, and my hair takes to the air behind me. Everything feels light. This must be what normal feels like.

It feels good. And then I remember that it's all going to end soon, and it's like someone's thrown me in the pool. The realization washes over me, weighing me down and popping my eyes open. The others are still singing. Someone else is dancing in the middle, though it's so dark, I can't even tell who it is. A wave of loneliness sweeps over me. It's like the old cliché: alone in the middle of a crowd.

A hand alights on my shoulder. I blink and glance over it—Callie's just tapped me, Callie of the shiny hair and *Isn't she the one who used to have panic attacks all over our good Christian suburb?*

"Zara," she begins, and I stiffen. But all she goes on to say is, "Are you okay?"

I move back a couple of steps, melting into the shadows, away from the circle. The hole I left closes behind me like I was never even there. "Fine," I say. I take a deep breath.

She breathes out through her nose. "So you did hear me. In bio," she says. Her lips press together. "I thought you might have. I'm really sorry."

I turn away from her. Somehow her hair is still incredibly shiny even out here in the dark. How can that be possible?

"Sorry," she says again. She crosses her arms like she's cold, though it's not so much as cool out here. "Are you sure you're okay? You don't look . . . um . . ." She trails off.

I assume she was about to say something along the lines of *You don't look good.* I open my mouth, ready to insist that I'm the finest I've ever been, but something stops me. Maybe it's my frustration with Estella and Gabe and the others for not taking this seriously, or the paralyzing helplessness I feel about the state of things right now. "Actually, Callie, no, I'm not okay. Do you want to know something horrifying?" She's kind of looking at me right now like *I'm* horrifying, but I can't stop myself. "In a large-scale catastrophe where the entirety of the United States loses power for a year, ninety percent of the population will die. Ninety. Percent. That's about two hundred ninety million people." That's another thing I don't have to look up; it's branded on my brain even after seven years. My dad repeated it often enough that I don't think I could forget it if I tried.

And I have tried.

This is exactly the kind of attack he was talking about. The pattern I saw—and now I *definitely* know I wasn't losing my mind—was insidious. Sinister. If someone was able to pull that off, then this attack is the real thing.

I can no longer try to forget.

"What do you think about that?" I continue, like I'm daring her to do something, though I don't know what. I don't think it matters. *She* doesn't seem to think it matters; she's still staring at me like my head's been tipping off my neck, farther and farther, slowly revealing more blood and viscera.

She blinks at me. I'm not sure whether I'm expecting her to cry or to scream, but she does neither.

Instead she bursts into laughter.

I look at her warily as she nearly doubles over with it, wiping tears carefully from her eyes so as not to smudge her eyeliner beyond repair. Brace myself for her to straighten up and tell me I'm insane.

But she defies expectations once again. "Okay. Say you're right. What are you going to do about it?"

"Me?" I've gathered my water and food and supplies. But that's about it. "I don't know."

"Exactly." She swishes her hair. She must practice it at home in the mirror, admire how perfectly it falls in a gleaming sheet behind her. "So if we're all going to die, we might as well enjoy tonight." She glances behind her at the others. "They're all full of bullshit, you know that, right? They're way more scared than they're acting. It's like they're having a competition to see who can pretend they're worrying the least."

I have no idea what to say to that. Fortunately, I don't have to respond: a whoop goes up behind us, and then there's a flare of light. We turn and shade our eyes from the brightness. The smell of burning wood fills the air. When the hoots fade, the sound of crackling is like static all around. It's a bonfire. The others have gathered together a pile of wood, and they've struck a match and lit a fire.

My immediate reaction is to tell them how stupid it is to light a fire in an area that hasn't been properly prepared, because it only takes a split second for wildfires to start—seriously, that isn't even from the compound, that's just general knowledge from living in a state that burns half the year—but I go limp before any of it can come out of my mouth. Callie's clapping, her question forgotten, and the others are cheering, and shadows flit over everybody's faces too quick to catch.

Light. We have light tonight, and that has to be enough. For one night.

Before everything goes to hell.

12

I wake up way too late the next day, sticky in sheets that smell of unfamiliar soap, my body so warm it's practically cooking itself. I groan and kick at the lump of blankets at my feet—only the lump of blankets kicks back. *That* wakes me up in a hurry. I blink hard, eyes so dry they burn, and find myself in Estella's bed. Estella herself sprawls beside me, her legs slung over mine. Atop our pile of legs is curled Twinkle, the family cat, a fat orange creature with the eyes of a fawn and the snore of a lawn mower.

I manage to ease myself out of bed without waking Estella or Twinkle; there's a moment where Estella snorts, and I freeze, but she only rolls over. My phone sits on the nightstand beside a glass of water. I go to drink it, then hesitate. Estella hasn't stockpiled water the way I have. That glass of water could literally save her from dying.

Probably not, but I leave it where it is anyway.

I texted my mom last night to tell her I'd be staying over, but she didn't text back. This morning I see why: there's no signal.

That's annoying.

I turn the phone off, then hold my breath as I turn it back on, my heart thumping quick and light like a rabbit's. Still no signal. Not even one flickering bar.

No. No, it can't be. Not already.

I grab Estella's phone, because obviously I know her PIN, and try to call myself. It doesn't ring or beep or anything, just gives me dead air. We have two different service providers, so it can't just be one acting up.

The generator powering the cell tower must have blown. A sour feeling fills the pit of my stomach, creeping up the back of my throat. My fingers itch. I'm suddenly swamped by the urge to stream some music or text classmates I've never texted before or look up the definition of "palimpsest," which is part of a poster on Estella's wall I've never bothered to decipher before. It's urgent that I know what "palimpsest" means right now.

I shove my phone into my bag and swallow hard over the lump in my throat, trying not to cry.

So phones are gone now. What next? No internet or data, obviously. No laptops or computers. Nothing that needs to be charged or that needs to grab a signal from the sky. Anything that uses a battery should work, at least for a while—I'm thinking about flashlights and smoke alarms. Everything else . . .

Everything else will be useless. The loss hits me hard, like an actual kick to the stomach. What about my character in *Dark Avengers*? She's just floating in cyberspace, alone.

If I can't reach my mom by phone, I'm going to have to meet her at home. Estella might sleep till the evening—if competitive sleeping were an Olympic sport, she'd have a pretty good shot at the gold medal—so I creep out the door, shutting it gently behind me, and tiptoe down the hallway.

I pause in front of Gabe's door, which is half-open. Through it I can just see his foot sticking out from the bottom of his covers. Should I say goodbye? I take a step closer, holding my breath.

Then back off. *No.* I'm not going to wake him up. I'll talk to him later.

I forgot that moms tend to have supersonic hearing. Just as I'm easing the front door open, a creak sounds behind me. I jump. "Zara," Estella's mom whispers. "Everything okay?"

I paste a smile on my face before I turn around. She smiles too when she sees it, but her brow stays creased. Maybe she's more worried about the blackout than I thought. "Great," I whisper back. "Just heading home. The phone's not working, and my mom might be worried."

She nods once, jerkily. My words aren't a surprise. She must have already turned on her phone to find it nothing but a shiny paperweight. "Don't forget your bag."

"My bag?" Oh. "It's for you guys," I say. "It's got some water tablets, a filter, a headlamp. Some stuff just in case . . ." I trail off, not wanting another well-meaning lecture. If I have to hear one more person tell me brightly and confidently how everything's going to be fine, I'm going to vomit all over their shoes.

She shakes her head. "You should keep it," she says. I wait for the *You're being paranoid, it's just a blackout, we have blackouts all the time, everything is going to be fine, fine, fine,* but she only says, "We have a lot of that stuff from when Gabe was in Boy Scouts. We even have survival blankets and a tarp. Hold on to your stuff. Your mom might need it."

The only reason she would know they have survival blankets and a tarp is if she's checked. Maybe her "she doesn't sound all that alarmed" statement about the president was more wishful thinking than observation.

Before she can move, I dart forward and squeeze her tight. She makes a surprised little choking noise, but she hugs me back. She's warm and soft, and she's going to keep Estella safe. "Let me know if you do need anything," I say, stepping back.

She smiles at me for real this time, all the lines in her forehead smoothing out. For a moment she could be Estella's older sister. "The same to you, Zara. You know we're always here for you."

I wait a moment before grabbing the bag and leaving. It feels nice just to stand there with someone else who's scared too.

But only for a moment. Because if this is really the end, then I have to shut myself off from other people, the way my dad did so many years ago. Because all the strategies he taught me were for *me*. Not other people. He said other people only brought you down, made you soft. So he'd approve of me not having really any other friends. He'd say that I was made for this new world.

There are more people outside today than there were yesterday. Maybe the loss of the cell tower has made them crave human connection in other ways. The Garcias and the Markowitzes huddle together in the latter's yard, heads bowed together in conversation. I wave at them, and they wave back, but there's a hesitation. Or maybe I'm only imagining it. I'm certainly not imagining the look of suspicion a woman walking her dog gives me. I give her a tentative smile as she passes me on the sidewalk, but she only strides quickly by, tugging her dog after her. I don't recognize her. Maybe that's why she eyed me, because she's wondering if I'm casing the neighborhood now that alarm systems are all dead. The joke's on her—if I were going to case a neighborhood, it would be a much nicer one than ours.

The road is mostly empty, cars parked safely in their garage homes or in their driveways, but one does cruise slowly by. Two little kids have their faces pressed up against the back windows, noses smushed against the glass, eyes goggling at me. The rear window is nearly blocked with suitcases. I wonder where they're going. Do they think anywhere else in the country is doing better? Maybe they're making a run for the woods, planning to camp out near a lake and hunt until this is all over. It's not a terrible idea, as long as too many people don't have the same one and hunt the area to nothing.

One neighbor is standing outside my house on the sidewalk, frowning down at his phone. He doesn't move as I approach. I have to step on the grass to get around him. It crunches beneath my feet. "Cell tower's down, I think," I say, because all the suspicious glances are getting to me, and I want to show I'm helpful and good, damn it. "Nobody's phones are working."

The neighbor looks up. Actually, I have no idea if he's one of my neighbors, because I've never seen him before. He's older than me but younger than my mom, with hair somewhere between brown and blond, medium height and weight. Usually, I'd shrug and assume that he's such an excruciatingly average person that I may very well have met him—may very well know his name—and just not remember, but the ends of tattooed vines crawl up from the collar of his T-shirt, ending at the bottom of his neck. That's something I would remember.

"Thank you, young lady," he says, which makes me grumble inside—I've never liked being called pet names. I nod an acknowledgment and go to step around him, but he goes on. "You doing okay out here?"

"Yup," I murmur. I've stopped on the grass to his side and glance at him from the corner of my eye. He's not looking at me or at his phone. He's staring up at the sky. Hasn't anyone ever told him he'll go blind if he stares at the sun?

"Nobody seems worried enough. Shouldn't they be more worried?" He shakes his head. "They should be gathering food and making plans for what they're going to do when this all goes to hell." He makes a scoffing noise deep in his throat, one that sounds like he's about to spit. "It's going to be soon."

Those vines creeping up from his chest are beginning to resemble tentacles. "Maybe," I say, shrugging my backpack higher. I don't like how much this guy's thoughts are mirroring my own. "Whatever makes them happy, I guess."

He centers his gaze on me. "What do you think?"

There's a heaviness in the pit of my stomach. I can't pinpoint exactly what it is about this guy, but I don't want to stand here and chat with him. Something is creeping me out, and it's scary that I don't know what it is. If I have a chance, even a chance, of surviving the end of the world, I need to be able to identify wrong and right. Certainly not bond with other people.

And I have to stop worrying about being polite. Ignoring my mom's scandalized *Zara, don't be rude!* in my head, I forge forward. "I have to go," I say over my shoulder.

He nods as if I responded to his question. Off to my right, a bird tweets from the bushes in front of my house: a short whistle, then a long one, then another short one. Another bird answers from my left, behind—or maybe beneath?—someone's car parked at the curb.

That something-is-wrong feeling bubbles up again. When I first arrived here after years of living in the forest, where I would fall asleep to the sounds of croaking frogs and hooting owls and rustles in the brush outside my window, I couldn't relax to the sounds of cars and air conditioner creaks. To make myself feel better, I did what my dad had made me do all throughout my childhood: catalogue every single thing I heard, from the cars to the birds. I know the coo of the mourning dove. The distinctive caw of the American crow. The rumble of the next-door neighbor's car with the broken muffler.

I've lived here for seven years and have never, ever heard that birdcall before. I stop in my tracks, a memory bubbling up from the depths of my mind.

Me and my dad, deep in the woods, tracking a group of three deer. (Yes, most deer hunters work from blinds, climbing high up and waiting for the deer to cross down below, but that was too easy for my dad. He said it wasn't fair to the deer.) Hoofprint to hoofprint, indentations in the soft ground and smashed clumps of damp leaves. It took a few hours of our careful movements, knowing that even a single crunched branch could send them racing off, but we finally caught up to them. My chest puffed out in pride. It was the first time I'd managed to get to this point in tandem with my dad.

But he raised his eyebrows at me, a reminder not to get cocky too soon. I nodded. No point in feeling triumph before I had the deer's warm blood slick on my hands. "We'll split up," he whispered, his words no more than a rush of wind. I never could match his volume; if I tried to respond, I'd spook them. So I only nodded. "Once we're in place, I'll make some noise in the right spot so that they run right at you. You won't be able to miss."

I widened my eyes, a question. He understood, because he always understood. "You'll know I'm in place when I do my birdcall," he whispered. "Take your time and make sure you're moving quietly. When you get into place, behind that grove of trees, do the same whistle back, and I'll send them your way."

I pull myself out of the memory, gasping, suddenly unable to catch my breath. The specific whistle was different from my dad's, but . . . I can't help spinning to look the man in the face. "What's going on?" I say, and even though my mind is spinning, my heart is somehow beating slow and solid and so loud, it sounds like it's echoing between my ears.

Thud-thud. Thud-thud. Thud-thud.

The man quirks an eyebrow. One corner of his mouth lifts in a smirk. "What's wrong, Zara?"

Thud-thud. Thud-thud. Thud . . .

"I never told you my name," I say, and my voice is deafening in the sudden silence.

I'm the deer.

13

The first birdcall came from my right near the hedges. Another from my left near the car.

So there's at least three of them. I take a giant step back, out of the closest one's reach. I don't know who they are or what they want, but it can't be good.

That smirk on his face. My mind won't stop racing in circles— *Should I run where should I run should I try to talk my way out should I find out what they want what do they want?*—but that smirk is the one thing that makes it still.

He thinks he's got me.

"You knew the blackout was coming before it came," he says, and though I know I should already be running, I can't help but want to hear what he has to say.

Though, how would he know that? I told only my mom. Unless

maybe she told somebody at her office? Or maybe her phone line could have been bugged? Or listened in on? She does work for the government. But why would they be listening in on her line? She's just the mayor's assistant.

Are they police? FBI? But these guys can't be police or FBI, or this one would already have announced himself and flashed his badge. Right?

Wrongness twists in my gut. And I'm not going to ignore my gut.

"You're going to have to come with me. I can't take the . . . ," he begins, but I'm already spinning on my heel, loosing a clod of grass, and sprinting as hard as I can down the empty street. I pray to the beat of my feet, the bounce of my backpack on my back: *Please let there be only three of them, please please please.*

It occurs to me too late that I could have spun and gone back the way I came, running for Estella's house and barricading myself inside with her family for protection.

"Stop!" the guy shouts behind me, like I'm going to listen to him. If I weren't running so fast, I'd scoff. Survival depends on the individual—being forced to depend on or trust others is how you get killed. Like, if I trusted him, trusted that he knew what was best for me, I don't even want to know what would be happening to me right now.

My feet pound the pavement, sending jolts up my ankles. The road ahead is clear and empty, no potholes to leap or cars to dodge, so I dare to glance behind me.

I almost wish I hadn't. It's best to have all the information, but it's hard to keep all the liquids in your body when you see three big, burly dudes careening straight toward you, their legs flying them over a hell of a lot more ground than yours, their faces set in grim determination. The one in the middle—the one I spoke with—isn't smirking now.

The world blurs around me, less from moving so fast and more from the tears pressing on my eyes. I'm coming up on the end of my street; I'm going to hit the big road soon, but I can't depend on sheer speed to save me. I'm panting, my lungs burning and my legs screaming in protest at all this activity. I glance over my shoulder again and suppress a groan. They've gained on me already and can't be more than a house length or so behind. If I don't do something, they're going to catch me.

The middle guy's lips are spreading in that awful smirk again, and it's that more than anything that makes the blur around me clarify. I feel almost like I'm a wolf. I can hear everything and see everything, the flies buzzing in the air and the worms writhing in the dirt and the rumble of a car up ahead.

A car. There's a car up ahead, coming down the main road. My ears perk. My legs pump.

"Give it up, Zara," the middle guy shouts. He sounds like he's right behind me. I grit my teeth and push my legs *faster, faster, faster*, but it's no use.

Nails rake over my back. I cry out more from surprise than pain, the adrenaline pushing me forward so hard, I might actually break something if I tripped and slammed onto the ground. All three of them cry out in something like triumph. They think they've got me. The noise leaves their lips and crawls up the back of my neck.

I can still hear the rumble of the car. This might just be the stupidest thing I've ever done. *Just a little farther come on Zara you can do it you can do it you can . . .*

I leap onto the main road. The car is coming. I stand there for a split second and watch it hurtle toward me, frozen, feeling for a moment the way I imagine a deer in literal headlights feels. The driver's eyes widen; his lips part in a shout, and there's the screech of slamming brakes, but there's nowhere for him to go except into a guardrail and—

I throw myself to the side, squeezing my eyes shut as I feel the heat from the car scorch my arm. The guys shout and the brakes squeal and there's a horrible thud, but I don't look back. I don't know if it's that I can't spare the time or I can't handle the thought of what I might have done. I'm in the right, I know that. It's self-defense. And I don't regret it.

But I also really, really don't want to look.

Across the big road is another neighborhood like mine: smallish houses that might as well have come from the same cookie cutter; browning lawns; the occasional towering tree. I race down the street like I did before, cursing myself the whole way, struggling in vain to unearth another helpful memory from my past. But it's no use. My feet pump along as if of their own will, while my brain is no help at all.

I've gone only a few houses, my whole body blazing white-hot with panic, when I hear the footsteps pounding again behind me. I risk a look back. Only two of them are left, the guy with the vine tattoos one of them. That horrible thump replays itself in my mind. This time I feel triumph. It's tempting to yell something taunting back at them, but I don't want to do anything that might give them a shot of adrenaline.

Okay. What next? Nothing around me sticks out as especially helpful. A loose dog loping down the sidewalk. The sound of a lawn mower buzzing from a yard ahead, because while the world is ending, why not mow your lawn? A middle-aged woman pushing open her screen door to come outside, maybe to track down the loose dog.

Wait. That last one. She leaves her front door open. All that separates me from her house is that flimsy screen door.

I veer hard to the right.

My feet pound over her lawn, passing her, and leap all three of the front steps at once. She shrieks something incomprehensible behind me, but I don't slow down even a tiny bit. I'm inside, and I slam the front door behind me, hoping it locks automatically and it'll put a pause on the two guys still following me.

It doesn't. I've barely gotten inside, skidding over the laminate of a small living room with a couch and a pair of armchairs, when the door goes flying open behind me, hitting the wall with a crack. *Damn it.*

"Stop," one of the men pants, and it's gratifying that he sounds more tired than me.

I shove one of the armchairs in his direction. Miraculously, it slides, knocking right into both of them. They shout in surprise. I respond by knocking over the woman's enormous flat-screen TV, which lands squarely on someone's leg. Sorry, lady—it's useless now anyway. The sickening crack of what must be the leg bone.

The injury gives me enough time to dart through the open sliding glass door and slam it behind me. I hear its lock snap shut, buying me an extra precious second.

The backyard looses a cloud of dust with every footstep. I'm dying for a moment just to stop and clear my head, but I have to keep running. I veer to the left, darting between two small ranch houses, then race across the street and through someone's front lawn, then back to the right. It probably won't take them long to come after me, but it's enough to get out of sight. I need to figure out somewhere else to go in this neighborhood. It's not like I can dart from tree to tree, hiding in their—

Wait. The trees. The *trees.* My feet tense, like they're ready to bound into branches. I spare a moment to glance up. It's not like I'm running through the middle of a forest, but formidable trees dot this neighborhood like they dot mine, giant trunks with fans of leaves and branches like ladders. When I first moved here, I'd sometimes climb a tree outside our house and perch as high as I could go without it swaying too dangerously. It was peaceful up there with the chirping birds and whispering leaves, everything else far below.

One of those trees stands before me. A thrill zips down my spine. Maybe I can actually pull this off.

I skid to a stop beneath the tree, and before I have a chance to think about it too hard, I bend my knees and leap as high as I can. I just barely grab the bottom branch with my fingertips, which is enough to swing myself forward and connect the bottom of my feet to the trunk with a thud. I run them upward until I'm nearly horizontal. My stomach is hanging queasy and heavy like my backpack, which is threatening to conspire with gravity to pull me back to the ground, but it's suspended for only a moment, and then I'm launching myself up legs-first. My knees hinge over the branch, and my stomach crunches to pull myself into a sitting position.

I have only a moment to take a breath and shake out my limbs before I have to propel myself up, up, up. I hop from branch to branch as lightly as I can, trying not to rustle any leaves in case the men are in sight—it's tough with the bag swinging from my back. My skirt keeps catching on branches. The rough bark scrapes my skin. Back on the compound I had calluses like armor on my fingers and palms; coding and gaming haven't had the same effect. But I grit my teeth through the burn and shrug the pack higher on my shoulders and keep on going until I'm close to the top and the trunk isn't much thicker than I am. I look down and finally let myself sigh with relief. Leaves knot themselves so thickly around me that it's like I'm in a cage.

When I hear the footsteps below, every part of me clenches. It might not even be them. It sounds like only one person, actually. Maybe it's some random person who lives in the area, out for a pleasant afternoon walk.

And then I hear him mutter, and there's nothing pleasant about it. "Zara Ross." I can hear the hiss all the way up the tree, the rasp of the words in his mouth like he's about to spit. "Where did you go?"

I wish I had my crossbow. Not to attack, but to defend myself if he tries to climb up after me or waits until I get tired and come down. It would be nice to have anything, really. Even a knife.

I remember standing outside with my dad, practicing shooting at targets. I lowered my crossbow and asked, "What about other weapons?"

"What about them?" he asked. "I've shown you how to shoot a gun, though we agree a crossbow is preferable because of diminishing ammunition."

I kicked at the ground. "I don't know, like, a knife or something," I said. "My crossbow won't be any good up close if someone comes after me."

He laughed. "On the contrary, nobody would expect you to use your crossbow close up," he said. "Someone like you should not be using a knife."

"Someone like me?"

"Small and comparatively weak," he replied. I bristled, but I knew what he meant. I was strong for someone my age and size, but not compared with a grown man like him. "I've shown you self-defense moves in case someone tries to put you in a headlock, but you shouldn't be focusing on using a knife in close combat unless absolutely necessary; you should be focusing on running far enough away for you to use your crossbow."

Which made sense. So I focused on the crossbow, and on running. He would be proud of me right now. Or half-proud, I guess. For the running.

I cling to my branch, trembling like a leaf. I've downed both the man's companions while getting away. If he wasn't happy with me before, he must really despise me now. He mutters again, "Murderous bitch," and his footsteps tromp away. Did his friend die when he got hit by the car?

Well. I might not be happy about it, but I wouldn't change it either.

14

The guy might be gone, but that doesn't mean I'm safe. He could still circle back. Maybe he even knows I'm up here and he's hiding around a corner, waiting to pounce on me once I feel safe for maximum sadistic pleasure.

So I move not a muscle.

For.

Five.

Hours.

Five hours feels like a really, really, *really* long time when you're balanced on an uncomfortable tree branch high off the ground, your shoulders ready to break from the strain of your pack, and you really, really, *really* have to pee. Especially when you can't think anything but *Oh my God oh my God oh my God.* I try to occupy myself by tracking the movement of the sun in the sky and seeing how much I remember, but it's not all that much, and it's not all that distracting. Five hours is an estimate. Maybe it's longer. I rest my head against the trunk and close my eyes. Somehow five hours didn't seem so long when I was immersed in the postapocalyptic hellscape of *Dark Avengers*. Those nights already feel like a thousand years ago.

I can't go home. Those guys know where I live, and the chance that somebody's watching my house right now is too high. I wonder again why the hell they were chasing me. Why they were so set on me. City hall gets crank calls all the time, not just about the world ending, but about actual, genuine threats to people's lives. And it wasn't like I had any specific details, just wild thoughts. And my mom shut me down right away. So why me? Why this? Could there be some other reason I can't think of? I'm baffled and horrified at the same time. Borrified. Horaffled.

I may be losing my mind a little.

My arm stings, scratched raw from my encounter with the car and the road. Normally, I wouldn't even think about it. I've had much worse. But with no medicines and no hospitals . . . if it gets infected, it could rot me from the inside out.

Trying to hear my own thoughts right now is like trying to hear a song through heavy static. It's enough to stress me out, but not enough to decide on anything substantial.

I need time to reflect. I might not be able to think right now, but I need to get there. Which means silence. Sleep. Safety.

By the time I get down from that tree, my legs are shaky from all that balancing and my body is stiff. This dress has definitely looked better. I take a precious few moments to do some stretches and jumping jacks so that I don't feel like I'm about to break in half, but that's all I have time for. I have to keep moving.

It's beyond weird, walking around the neighborhood at night when there aren't any lights on at all. It feels like I'm on a different planet, or like I've slipped through a portal to centuries past. There are supposed to be streetlights shining overhead and TVs flashing in windows and lights glowing to deter burglars.

There aren't many people out; the utter blackness seems to have frightened them into staying in their safe suburban homes. A few bonfires dot the distance, or maybe they're actual house fires, but I steer clear.

Suspicious things keep rustling in the dark, too. Probably just the neighbors' cats, but I can't help picturing men lurking with blood-spattered machetes or slavering beasts with stinking fur and teeth as long as my middle fingers. There is the occasional light inside that illuminates the skittering silhouettes of cats and squirrels, probably thanks to a generator still stocked with gas. But for the most part, I have to step a lot more slowly than I'd like.

I do spare a moment's thought for the woman whose house the men and I raced through. I hope she's okay, even if looking after myself came before worrying for her welfare. I hope they didn't do anything to her house. I hope they didn't do anything to *her*.

But there's nothing I can do for her, so I soldier on.

My neighborhood is full of small houses, mostly middle class, but a mile or two down the road is a hill of big, fancy rich-people houses. My legs protest at the thought of hiking that hill right now, but it's probably my best bet. They'll have sheds and pool houses that'll allow me to curl up in relative safety and comfort, and their alarm systems will be as dead as my computer.

By the time I find a shed set far enough back from the owners' house that they can't possibly hear me, I'm ready to drop and crawl on my hands and knees the rest of the way. I make it inside, jam a rake through the door handles so that no one can pop in and surprise me, collapse onto a foam pool raft, and drop off to sleep.

Even though real life feels like a dream right now, I dream anyway. About my past. This flight isn't the first time I've run from a mysterious threat.

I was eight, maybe nine. It wasn't that long before we left the compound for good. My dad had just made me my very own miniature crossbow with a green stripe on it. I was so proud of it that I kept it with me all the time, except when I was sleeping.

Which turned out to be a mistake, considering that was when the attack came.

I woke to the sound of splintering wood and shattering glass from the hallway. I sprang out of bed in shock, but my door was already opening. By the time my feet hit the floor, a tall, bulky figure was looming in the doorway, cloaked in shadow.

I stared at him for a moment with no idea what to do. My dad had always been the one who told me what to do. Why wasn't he yelling for me to attack or to flee or to—

What if my dad was already dead?

The figure took a big, menacing step forward, revealing an empty void of a face. No. A black mask stretching over his face. Nobody good wore a black mask over their entire face like that.

That settled it. *No close combat. Run or use your crossbow.* In one fluid motion I leaped back onto the bed. Using my mattress like a trampoline, I bounced as high as I could and vaulted out my open window.

I hit the ground running even as I winced at the sharp pains in my ankles; it was good the entire compound stood on one story. A roar behind me: I spared a precious moment to glance over my shoulder. The man in the mask stood at my window now, still in shadow. But wait . . . was he climbing over the ledge? Was that his leg swinging over the—yes, yes he was. He was following.

I had to keep going.

It didn't occur to me till later that somebody probably wouldn't come alone to murder my family and take me hostage, or whatever. I had no idea what the man in the mask might have planned, or if he had companions along for the ride. All I knew was that he was from the outside world, and the outside world was bad. And all I could hear right then was my dad's voice. He'd recently instructed me on what to do if an outsider ever came to the compound.

Do not talk to them, Zara. No matter what threats they may make or what they may say about me and your mother. Use your strengths. You know this place better than any outsider. If you cannot escape them, use your knowledge of the compound to outwit them.

I wished I could dart off into the woods, but my room overlooked the warren of storage rooms and sheds my dad had built to house all the equipment we needed to run what was basically a functioning mini society. They were made of wood, but that was the only commonality. The ground around them had been shaved clean for ease of movement, and if I tried to climb one of them, my footsteps would be heard loud on the tin roof.

No time to waste. I plunged into the shadows. The spaces between the buildings were narrow, the turns sharp and sudden. I could use this. It was dark here, even more so than in the woods, where the moonlight glinted off the trees, but my eyes were used to this. My feet raced nimbly over the bare dirt, finding mercifully few sticks. My heart raced along with them.

I didn't have to stop and look to know the man was following me. I could hear his heavy footsteps thumping behind.

My breaths came in squeaky little gasps. He was keeping up with me even as I whipped around corners and darted between doorways. How was he doing that?

Okay, then. If I wasn't going to be able to escape him for the deep woods, I had to fight. I knew without thinking that the nearest shed was full of farm equipment—no crossbows, but I could work with that. I burst through the doorway, making plenty of noise this time so he'd know where I went.

The space inside was packed full of shadows that loomed above me, their shapes odd and spiky in the few shafts of moonlight that snuck through the window. For a second I reeled—I'd never come here in the dark before and was left with the odd feeling that I'd interrupted a meeting of old gods and monsters.

But only for a second. By the time the clock hit the end of that Mississippi, I was hopping up the rungs of the ladder that led to the loft, where my dad kept the various farming implements that didn't need as much height. I tipped the ladder over. It clattered on the floor, but somehow it didn't sound as loud as that man stepping foot inside.

I crouched on the loft, placing my hands gently on something heavy and round. I could probably guess what it was in the light, but in the dark I had no idea. It felt almost like a cannonball. If the masked man came any closer, I'd push it over the edge of the loft and crush his head in.

He came closer. Closer. He was within reach of my cannonball now, and yet I hesitated. *If he comes a little closer . . .* , I thought, my stomach swimming at the idea of causing this man—no matter how frightening he was—pain or death. *I need to be absolutely sure this would be self-defense. I am not a killer.*

"What are you doing?" the man in the mask said. His voice was muffled by the cloth. "Why have you not acted yet?"

What?

My heart sped up. "Come any closer and I will," I threatened. My hands shook, and not just because the cannonball's surface was ice cold. "I'll smash your skull in. Just you watch."

The man in the mask chuckled. "I bet you would." His voice was still muffled, but it sounded almost like he was . . . *proud* of me? "You'd be safe up there while you hurled everything in your arsenal against me. My bones wouldn't stand a chance."

My eyes nearly bugged out of my head. *"Dad?"*

He stepped back, then reached up and tugged off the mask. Sure enough, there were my dad's glittering eyes, black in the dark. "I'm proud of you, Zara. Very proud."

I blinked hard. Then harder, like I might be dreaming. "What did you . . . ?"

"What better way to test your understanding of my lessons?" he said. I wasn't sure what to say back to that. "You did an excellent job trying to lose me in the warren and then hiding up here with ammo when you realized you couldn't. My only critique is that you should not have waited to attack. You should have hurled whatever you had at me as soon as I came within range. I would have dodged it, but a normal person would not have."

"What would you have done if I had my crossbow with me?" I asked. I was shaking again now. I could have killed my own father. Even he couldn't have dodged my bolts.

His laugh was deep and gentle. "You would not have shot me."

He sounded so sure of himself. I wondered how he knew. Later my mom mentioned that he'd gone in to check where my cross-bow was right after I'd gone to bed. It didn't change anything in my mind. My dad knew everything. And if I spent the next several days waking up screaming in the middle of the night until my mom rushed in to rock me in her arms and soothe me back to sleep, well, that didn't matter. My dad had done the right thing, like he always did. He always knew what was best for me.

It's still dark in the shed when I wake, but light filters in through the cracks between the walls and the roof. I perk my ears, straining to hear outside. It doesn't sound like anyone's out there, but I can't be sure. Better stay inside until it's time to go.

My head is clear again, which is such a relief, it almost swamps me. I decide immediately that I need to find my mom. No matter what's going to happen, and what we're going to do, it needs to be together.

Last time I heard from her, she was at work. In LA, at the mayor's office. Which means that, since I can't go home whether she's wait-ing for me there or not, I need to go to the mayor's office. If she's not there herself, I can leave word there for her.

Now for the hard part: I actually have to get there. Normally, this would be easy, the phone mounted on the dashboard of my mom's car chirping directions at me in my GPS's soothing Austra-lian accent for the half hour it takes me to get to city hall, maybe an hour with traffic. Or I'd take an Uber.

No car. No GPS. No phone. I don't even have a map.

Without knowing the exact route, walking it is probably going to take me more than a whole day, three if I want to play it extra safe and avoid well-trafficked areas where the men—or anyone else— might find me (and obviously I do). I don't just need a map, I need food too. All I have in my pack is pepper spray, a water filter, the water purification tablets I brought to Estella's, the headlamp, and the Swiss Army Knife. I could probably survive off them for the time it takes me to get to city hall, but I'd be weak and hungry, and totally off my game. Which could get me killed if the men show back up. And it's not like I can just pop into a convenience store on the way, assuming they're even still open. Owners and cashiers could have been told to watch out for me. At a time like this, I might turn in some random stranger for something that would increase my odds of survival. No, I need someone I trust completely.

"Estella." My lips form around her name before my mind catches up. What did her mom say? *You know we're always here for you.* Time to test that. Estella probably doesn't have maps or anything, but her parents are old people, and old people hang on to their old things. Right—I remember seeing that area map in their kitchen. And I bet Gabe will be furious when he hears what I've been through. Maybe he'll even be gallant and swear he's going to kill them or something. Or at least drive me where I need to go.

There's always the chance that the men are watching Estella's house too, but I doubt it. If they'd known where I was, they would've waited for me outside Estella's house rather than my own house. To think that they'd be watching every place I could possibly be is madness.

Right?

15

Somehow the journey to this neighborhood—Estella's house to mine, then mine to here—felt a whole lot longer when I was running for my life. You'd think all the adrenaline would have made it go faster. Every time I spot someone through a window or see someone striding purposefully in my direction, I duck away just in case it's *them*. A few more cars drive by than I saw yesterday, suitcases visible in the windows.

If the drivers think that's going to be enough to save them, they're wrong. I told Callie that 90 percent of people would die, and she laughed, because it's impossible for us to really process death of that magnitude.

That's nine out of every ten people. More in places like LA, where people are piled up next to one another, depending entirely upon trucks and electrical wires to ferry in everything they need for survival. There'll be mass starvation. Poisoning from ingesting something you're not supposed to, food or water tainted with human waste. In parts of the country where the temperature rises or dips below balmy, people will scorch or freeze to death. Here, with the ongoing drought, people are most likely to perish of thirst. Foreign countries might mobilize and send ships of aid, but it won't be immediate, and it won't be enough. Think of ten people—me, my mom, Estella, Gabe, Callie, Mitch, my snoozing bio teacher, Mr. Miller, Irina of the good weed, the guy beatboxing at the party— and odds are that soon nine of us will be dead.

I really need that map.

Estella's street is quiet, quieter than any of the neighborhoods I've passed through so far. Somewhere, in the distance, there's the sound of breaking glass. A dog trots down the middle of the road, something little and fluffy, its tongue flopping out the side of its mouth. It barely looks at me, but it does look behind itself every few steps like it's waiting for someone to follow. Or like it's afraid someone will.

The hair stands up on the back of my neck.

I don't know what I'm expecting, but I keep my eyes trained on the red peaks of Estella's roof. As I near it, my stomach drops to my feet with a sickening splat.

Her door is yawning wide open.

Without turning at all, I reach around and pull the pepper spray from my pack.

I hold my breath as I creep up her front steps, like that's going to keep someone from hearing me. My ears strain at the entrance. I can't hear anything but the door creaking as it sways back and forth in the breeze.

Should I yell inside for her and Gabe? Anyone inside is going to hear me coming anyway. I open my mouth, then shut it and step inside as quietly as I can. Nerves tingle all through me like static.

Somebody's been here. More than one somebody. People who have upended the couch and sliced its cushions, so that white stuffing puffs out, and smashed Estella's mom's carefully curated collection of carnival glass on the floor, where light glints on its oily sheen. Ripped the legs off chairs and shattered plates all over.

I want to back out and run down the street behind that dog. Instead I take a step forward. "Estella? Gabe?" My voice comes out high and thin. "It's Zara. Are you here?"

Nobody answers. Not even Twinkle the cat. Holding my pepper spray carefully, I check every room. Nobody's there, just torn-up bedding and splinters of glass glittering on the carpet.

I lurch toward the back door, which leads into the yard from the kitchen. They're not here, but there's no blood or bodies, either, so maybe they ran. Just before my hand hits the knob, my eyes land upon the map tacked to the bulletin board. Just the map I need. Still, I hesitate before grabbing it. What if the Ramirezes come back and need it?

But they're not here, and I am.

I grit my teeth and tear the map from the board. It rips at the top around the thumbtack, but I take it anyway. Without looking behind me, I throw myself out the back door and, once again, run. Tears sprinkle the grass beneath me, but I don't stop.

It's not until I'm a safe distance away, several houses, that I let myself think that maybe I was wrong and the men did know where I'd come from.

That whatever happened to the Ramirezes was because of me.

Please let them be okay.

The guilt is a rock in my stomach, weighing me down, but I keep moving. The sobs jump out of me, and I want nothing more than to stop for a bit and wail until I'm empty, but I keep moving.

The world is ending, but I keep moving.

16

After eight hours of walking, my legs start to feel like they're going to fall off. But then I look up at the sky and realize that the sun hasn't moved nearly enough across for it to have been eight hours, that it's really been only about three hours that *felt* like eight, and I'm not sure whether I'd rather scream or cry or shake my fist cartoonishly at the heavens.

I'm sticking to small side streets and tromping through backyards, consulting my map often and avoiding any roads where the men might try to find me. The sun beats down on the back of my neck, roasting it to a shiny red crisp. My footsteps crunch on the dry grass. The occasional helicopter buzzes overhead. And I keep reaching for my phone, to check my GPS to make sure I'm still going the right way or to send Estella a shot of me glaring into the camera, something we do when we're not happy.

Did. Something we *did.*

I would give up a finger to be able to listen to some music or a podcast or an audiobook right now. If I could put my headphones in and hear anything other than dead silence, the world wouldn't feel so . . . scary. So empty. I could have given my mom a call already, asked her where she was and assured her that I was okay. A shiver runs through me; I could be dead and she wouldn't even know. *She* could be dead right now and I'd have no idea.

How did people ever live like this?

Speaking of people, I don't pass many—I've isolated myself from areas with a lot of them, and though we're not far from LA, there's still plenty of empty space—and the few I pass just give me wary looks. Or maybe they're looks of pity. More than one catches me singing softly to myself, first anything I can remember from the radio, then, once I've exhausted that supply, TV show theme songs, commercial jingles, nursery rhymes.

The one song I avoid is the lullaby my mom used to sing me when I was a kid. I can't let myself think too much about my mom. How, failing to find me, the men might have gone in search of her. Waited at home for her. How our house might be as smashed up as Estella's right now, but with streaks of her blood across the wall. Whenever those thoughts drift through my mind, I have to lean back against something hard and take deep breaths to avoid hyperventilating. I tell myself that they aren't that thorough, that my mom works late every night, that they didn't find her. That she'll be there in LA, whole and hale and ready to protect me.

I don't think of Estella or Gabe. I can't. Not if I want to keep going.

I pass a restless night in another shed and dream of tentacles scrabbling after me in the green, then wake with my legs stiff and sore and my neck throbbing with sunburn. I want nothing more than to stay here and rest in this cozy shack that smells like chlorine, but I force myself to stand, wincing all the way, and get going. My muscles will feel better when I've loosened them up, even if my aching feet won't. That's one thing I remember from days-long hunts or scouting missions back on the compound.

Day two goes much the same: a blur of aches and pains and haunting music, a night tucked away beneath an underpass, where I jolt awake at every noise.

LA itself is almost the opposite, seething with people. There's nowhere to go to avoid them. People sit on stoops and stare at me suspiciously when I pass them on the sidewalk. Children play in the street. Cars still drive by, but they move slowly, with the lack of traffic rules in play. I wonder how far each car will make it before it runs out of gas. Where the drivers think they're going.

A whistle cuts through the air. I tense up right away, picturing the man with the vines signaling his friends, but I look over to see a group of men on the sidewalk. I scowl at them, wanting to give them the finger or something, but what if they are the type of men who'd get violent with me? Better not to encourage them, even if there are people around. I speed up, glancing over my shoulder again and again until I'm absolutely sure they're not following me.

It's a new sense of danger, something more raw and real than when I was whistled at or catcalled before. I always rested assured that I could go somewhere for help if I really needed it: call 911, or run to a public place with a lot of people, or whatever.

But what now?

I feel a surge of victory as I approach the mayor's office, but this trickles away as I notice the locked door, the curtains drawn tight over windows. Walking up slowly, I notice a page nailed to the front door. FOR ASSISTANCE AND CRISIS MANAGEMENT, PLEASE FIND US AT THE ROSE BOWL.

I grimace. More walking. But my mom's going to be at the end of it. I can do this.

I focus on putting one foot in front of the other as I skirt the edges of LA, passing parked cars and long, low warehouse buildings, tall brick apartment complexes and bike racks, and wonder who did this to us. It has to be a foreign government—I remember reading reports about how Russia was digging into our electrical grid. It could be them, or North Korea, or somewhere else seeking to cripple us. I can't see a smaller group, no matter how brilliant, doing something on this scale.

As I get closer to the Rose Bowl, around three hours later, I join a trickle of people walking on the sidewalk, which turns into a stream walking in the middle of the street. The air is dry and dusty, and the sun is bright and hot on my cheeks. Everything smells faintly of gasoline.

I hear the Rose Bowl before I see it. It's like something is roaring just ahead.

Deep breath. My mom needs to be here. She needs to be.

Otherwise, I don't know what I'm going to do.

17

The crowd around the Rose Bowl is a monster, ferociously loud and thrashing every which way. I shrink as I move through it, trying not to touch anyone. People press on me from all sides, and the smell is something else: BO and unwashed hair and sweaty socks and human waste. The porta-potties scattered along the edges make me gag when I drift too close. I'm not sure how they're going to clean them out or move them. Maybe they don't plan to.

I clear my throat as I start moving closer to the stadium. I have no idea how I'm going to find my mom in all this mess.

If she's even here.

No, I tell myself firmly, and then, to drown those dark thoughts out, start to shout. "Dina Appel! Looking for Dina Appel!" I shove my way through the crowd. If she's here with the government distributing supplies, she'll probably be close to the stadium. "Mom! Dina Appel!"

The stadium finally rises above me. It's a relief when I step into its shade, even if the air still smells like it's cycled through a bunch of other people before it hits my nose. Workers wearing fluorescent orange vests are shouting through megaphones: "THE LINE BEGINS AT GATE A. HAVE ALL OF YOUR FAMILY MEMBERS PRESENT AS YOU PASS THROUGH THE LINE. YOU WILL RECEIVE WATER AND RATIONS. IF YOU ARE HAVING A MEDICAL EMERGENCY, REPORT TO GATE B OR FIND YOUR NEAREST REPRESENTATIVE IN AN ORANGE VEST."

Gate A. If my mom's not there, someone will be able to point me in the right direction.

What stretches before the large opening of Gate A is less a "line" and more an amorphous blob, but people still shriek when I cut them. "Hey!" one guy shouts, stepping in front of me. He's a massive boulder of a person. Each of his shoulders is about a Zara wide.

"I'm not trying to cut you," I yell as loud as I can. I'm still not sure if he can hear me. "I'm just trying to find my mom."

"Get to the back of the line!" he bellows.

"I don't want to cut you," I try again to explain, "I'm just trying to find my—"

His eyebrows form a terrible *V* over his eyes. "My kids and I have been here for nine hours," he says. "If you think you're getting *my* water and *my* rations, you've got another think coming."

The man in front of him turns around. "Let the kid through," he says loudly. "Don't make trouble picking on a little girl." His hand goes to his side, where I can see a handle of a gun poking out of his jeans.

The first man turns to him, his eyes roiling. "What? You going to shoot me?" His own hands go to his sides. "Go ahead and try. You'll have a bullet through your—"

"Whoa, hey." I insert myself between them, my heart beating quick and shallow like a rabbit's. "Everyone calm down. No weapons." A crowd like this in the heat, where supplies are limited and wait times are long, is a tinderbox, and a gun is a match.

"Then you'd better find your place." The first man glares down at me, and I can practically feel his eye-beams scorching the hair on the top of my head. Other people around him are beginning to grumble too.

As much as I want to find my mom, I want to avoid a shooting even more. "Fine," I say, turning, but then I catch a glimpse of orange from the corner of my eye.

It's not my mom, but it *is* the woman who works at the cubicle next to her. Denise. I've exclaimed over photos of her grandchildren enough times where I'll be insulted if she doesn't remember me. Sure enough, her eyes widen and she claps her hands over her heart. "If it isn't Zara Ross," she says. At a time like this, she's still wearing lipstick, though it's smeared at the corners of her lips and over her front teeth.

"It is," I say, and let her hug me. She smells like baby powder.

When she pulls away, she shakes her head. "You know your poor mother thinks you're dead." If my mom is thinking, that means she's alive and okay. The relief is so great, it nearly makes my knees buckle. "She went home to get you and found your house torn apart, with you nowhere to be seen." Denise leans in again. "She's been a total mess. Just came back to work yesterday after the mayor personally begged her and promised to send the remainder of the police force after you."

A pang in my chest. Those men must have searched my house after they lost me. Or at least the head one, with the tattoos. I feel another pang at the thought of Elroy, the stuffed walrus I've slept with since childhood. They probably slashed him open and pulled out his stuffing just for funsies.

"Let me take you to your mom," Denise says, and I trail along behind her, keeping a careful eye out around me, eyes roving over every sweaty forehead and slumped set of shoulders.

They're still out there looking for me.

18

Denise leads me around the group of people and through a side door into the stadium. It's immediately cooler and darker; the smell of old popcorn and hot dogs hangs in the air, probably burned into the dusty concrete walls. She takes me past shuttered cotton candy and funnel cake stands, their striped roofs painfully bright and cheerful, to an orange barricade. People are queued up behind it, and there, facing them, her arms full of water pouches . . .

I can't hold myself back. "Mom!" I shout. It echoes epically against the high ceiling: *Mom-mom-mom-mom-mom-mom*.

She spins, and her jaw falls open. The water packets make a horrible squelching sound as they land on the floor, but I hardly have time to process it before she's leaped the barricade like a champion hurdler and wrapped me in her arms. She rocks me back and forth, sniffling into my hair. She's probably getting snot on me, and her arms are so tight I think they might actually be cutting off my circulation. I don't mind at all. I let her hang on, and I stare down at the floor, at her infinitely practical black sneakers. As much as I usually make fun of her for them, I bet those thick old-lady soles are helping her feet ache much less than mine in my now-tattered silver Converses.

When she finally pulls back, her eyes are red. She keeps her arms on my shoulders like she's afraid I'm going to run off. "I'm so happy you're okay," she says. The "kay" turns into a sob.

"I'm okay," I say. I've already decided I'm not going to tell her about what happened to Estella and Gabe and their house; I don't want to panic her any more than I need to.

Plus, I don't want to think too much about it myself. I'll face it once I'm no longer in immediate danger.

Speaking of immediate danger . . . how much should I tell her about the men chasing me? As little as I can, I decide. Partially because I don't want to freak her out, and partially because I don't know enough about them to speculate myself.

"Some men showed up outside our house. They came after me. I don't know if it was random or not. I escaped, but they must have gone back and ransacked the house."

My mom shudders. "Thank God. I came home and . . . and . . ." A muffled sob. "I didn't know what to do. I drove around searching for you, talked to as many neighbors as I could, put up flyers. I talked to the police, but there wasn't much they could do for me, with everything else going on. I finally came back to work to keep myself busy. I figured you would come here if . . . if you could."

I nod. "It was a long trip. But I made it." I force a smile.

She's so happy to see me, she doesn't even notice how fake my smile is. My mom tells me about what they're doing here at the stadium: the state and city disaster relief agencies came together after people started running out of supplies to distribute clean water, iodine tablets, packaged and canned food, medicines, and things like emergency blankets, even though people don't really need emergency blankets in this heat. They carted all their supplies to the stadium and catalogued them, then spread the word that anyone in need should come here. If this all keeps going—which it will—they'll transform the stadium into a shelter. Once they sort out the bathroom situation, because with no working plumbing it'll become a nightmare right away.

There turned out to be way more demand than they'd expected. "I couldn't believe how many people didn't have more than a four- or five-day supply of clean water or food," my mom says, quietly enough that none of the people crowded behind the barricade can hear. "It's almost . . . like . . ." She shakes her head, and I know she's thinking about my dad. Maybe about how she should have prepared more too. "Never mind. But I'm worried—we can last maybe three days at our current level, less if more people keep showing up." Her voice wavers. "I don't know what we're going to do."

I wish I had a second survival pack. Or even just one full survival pack. It's going to be tough stretching everything in there for the two of us, but we'll manage. "We'll figure it out," I say. "It's going to be okay."

She sniffles. "You're right. We'll be okay as long as we have each other."

That's definitely not true, because we could very easily die together, and having someone else depending on you opens up more avenues for you to fail, but at least she doesn't look like she's about to dissolve into tears anymore. "Sure," I say.

She backs away a tiny bit, but she doesn't take her hand off my arm. It's like she thinks I'll disappear if she's not touching me. "You relax, Zara. Find a seat and chill for a bit. You look like you need it."

As tempting as it sounds to put my feet up, I'm vibrating with nervous energy. I don't want to sit and relax. If my body is idle, it will leave space for things I don't want to think about to squirm their way into my mind. "No, I want to help. What can I do?"

"You can help by resting. Zara, please—"

"I need to help," I say firmly, and her eyes soften.

"If you insist," she says. "Why don't you go back to the field and see if you can help with sorting supplies?"

Sorting supplies. That sounds good. Lots of data to occupy my mind. I nod, heading deeper into the stadium.

19

I wind my way through the concrete underpass of the stadium, walking toward the bright white light. When I cross into it, I emerge onto the football field. Rows of seats unfold around and above me like they're cradling me in a massive hand. I can practically hear the echoes of crowds past cheering us on, though the stands are largely empty today. Only scattered spots in the first few rows are filled, mostly by people in orange vests taking a rest.

It's the field that's full. Spread from goalpost to goalpost are boxes and supplies placed right on the grass. From here I can spot pouches and bottles of water, prepackaged meals, the bright shiny foil of emergency blankets. It's like a relay race: people are unloading boxes at the far end and spreading their products out to be gathered by other volunteers and placed together in boxes for families or groups.

I approach the volunteers on the distribution end, but their hands are literally and figuratively full. They point me toward the unpacking end, whose volunteers shake their heads and point me toward the empty seats in the stadium.

I can't just sit here and do nothing. "Isn't there anything I can do?" I appeal to the closest volunteer, who's wearing a white coat under her orange vest. She must be a doctor or a nurse.

She barely gives me a glance. "If you want to be helpful, you can take a vest and head outside," she says briskly. "Point anyone who looks sick or hurt to Gate B. People are getting overheated, and it's a lot easier to deal with it when it's heat exhaustion and not heat-stroke."

A few minutes later I'm fully decked out in neon, and the crowd outside the stadium is parting before me like I'm Moses raising my staff at the Red Sea. I scan the crowd for anyone swaying on their feet or staring dully before them. It's a lot harder than it sounds, considering how many people are sagging from the heat and all the walking they probably had to do to get here. I send a pregnant woman sitting with her head between her knees to Gate B, then a man splashing water on his face, before approaching a group of kids who don't appear to be with an adult.

"Hey," I say. "Are you guys—"

We all jump as somebody shouts behind us. "We're okay," one of the kids says, slinging a protective arm around the other two. "But it sounds like they're not."

I head toward the commotion with a sense of trepidation, unable to get the vision of that guy flashing his gun at me out of my head. But nobody has a weapon out—yet. A group of guys stand looking at another guy, this one turned away from me so that all I can see is his head of black hair, his fists balled at his sides, and his shoulders bunched around his ears.

One of the guys facing me, who looks a little like a bull, says, "Dude, I'm sorry about your sister and your parents, but I think you've got the wrong person."

"I saw you get out of that bus!" the black-haired guy shouts. "It's just like the bus that took them!"

"It's a school bus," the bull says sympathetically. "It brought a bunch of us here from the city. There are lots of school buses. You got the wrong guys, man."

The black-haired guy's fists ball tighter, and I realize what's going to happen a split second before he throws himself, fists flying, at the bull. "Hey!" shouts the bull, dodging just as the black-haired guy swings around again, finally showing his face.

I don't know what would've happened if he hadn't seen me. "Zara?" he says in disbelief, his jaw hanging open, his fingers uncurling from his palms.

It takes me a second to recognize him. His face is mottled purple and black and green, bruises layered on top of bruises. His right eye is nearly swollen shut, and blood crusts his upper lip. There's blood on his forehead, too, though I can't see where it's from.

My mouth drops open, mirroring his. "*Gabe?* What *happened* to you?" A beat where his mouth closes and opens. The guys from the bus exchange glances and melt away into the crowd, seeming glad to be forgotten. "And . . . Estella, where's Estella?"

It's like hearing her name jump-starts him. "She's gone. They took her," he says, and the words keep coming, tumbling out over one another in a rush to get out. His eyes widen, wild with panic. "My parents, Estella. My abuela asked us to come stay with her up north for a bit, help her out with everything going on, and we got stuck in traffic. Gas ran out. I hiked to the nearest gas station to get more, but there wasn't any with the electricity out, so we decided to walk. We hitched a ride on a bus, but . . ."

He trails off, flattening his lips. So they weren't attacked by the guys chasing me; the Ramirezes must have already left before the guys paid their home a visit. Still, a pit's forming in my stomach, hollow and empty.

"The guys driving the bus made some nasty comments about Estella and what they were going to do to her, but the bus was going too fast to stop. I tried to fight them and get control of the bus, but there were too many of them." His voice breaks. "They pushed me out onto the side of the road. I'm lucky I'm not dead. I hitched a ride here to find the police. People said everybody was congregating here, including the police. I need to find help, Zara. I'm no fan of the police, but these guys on the bus have my family, and they're not going anywhere good."

He's shaking now, his whole body. His eyes dart from side to side, like I'm hiding the police from him. Air shudders with every breath, squeaking on its way out.

I'm reminded of Estella in that school bathroom the day we first met.

I place my hands on his shoulders, clamping down, trying to anchor him to the ground. "Breathe," I tell him. "Deep breaths. Focus on my voice. *Breathe. Breathe.*"

He breathes. When the squeaking stops, I have him start counting. His eyes change from wild and panicked to mildly surprised, like he didn't realize that I could calm him down like this. By the time he stops shaking, I've got tears in my eyes, because

I'm picturing being in that bathroom stall with Estella.

"Listen," I tell him. He nods. The blood on his face is dry, so he's not bleeding, which hopefully means he's not in immediate physical danger. "The police aren't going to be any help right now." I fill him in on what my mom told me, stopping a few times to remind him to breathe, because if he passes out right now, he won't be any help to anyone. "Let's go back to my mom. She can help us figure out what to do."

Anger flashes in his eyes. "If there's no police, I already know what I have to do. Find a gun and go after those bastards."

Now that I've seen him, I can't let him go. He's my point of familiarity in this incredibly unfamiliar world. "Let's just go to my mom, and—"

As if on cue, a shot rings out.

20

People scream and scatter. Someone knocks into me hard, their elbow jamming into my solar plexus. Stars burst all around me. Someone grabs my arm, drags me to the side. *Gabe.* My pack tilts my center of balance, and I waver on my feet, but he keeps pulling, and I stumble after him.

"We've got to move!" he shouts. All I can see is the back of his head, though I can picture his jaw working, his eyes filled with panic—but a focused panic this time. He doesn't need me to tell him: *You'll never save Estella if you die here.*

Another shot slices through the air, leaving nothing but cold fear behind. More screams tear from the center of the crowd.

The sound of stomping feet is like something I'd hear in a documentary on the African savanna. The rumble right before a herd of wildebeests comes over the hill, trampling everything in its path.

My heart leaps into my throat, and I need a moment to figure out what to do, but then the crowd is there over my shoulder, rising behind me like a wave, and I don't *have* a moment. We need to move.

Flash to my front: just empty ground, ripe for the stampede.

Flash to my left: the parking lot. We might be able to make it there before they're upon us, but we might not.

Flash to my right: a raised platform set a few feet above the ground, likely the former site of a concert or giveaway. A few stairs lead up to it, but not all around. It's our best bet.

Only a split second has passed, but it feels like minutes. The ground is shaking. I grab Gabe's arm, and my own limbs shake with it. We take off running. "Come on!" I already have to shout to be heard over the thundering footsteps.

Sweat soaks me as we run, diagonally so as to stay ahead of the crowd, because if we just go straight to our right, they'll grind us under their sneakered feet. Everything comes in bursts of sensation and sound. The sun beating down overhead. The yelps of fear. The smells of metal and hot earth.

They're close. They're so close. Too close. I can feel their rumbling and the stink of their fear and—

My shin collides with wood, sending a spark of pain jolting from my calf to my knee. The stage. We're here. Gabe hops up with his longer legs, then leans down to pull me after him. My feet hit the stage, my legs wobble, and then the crowd comes thundering past in a cloud of dust and shrill screams. A third shot sounds; people scream more.

I fall against Gabe and hide my face in his shoulder, breathing in the smell of boy sweat. I can feel his heart beating as fast as mine.

He hisses above me. "Someone went down." It's too loud to hear anything specific, but my stomach lurches as I imagine the crunch of cracking bone.

Not all of the crowd is running our way, I realize. The shots must have come from the middle of the pack: some people are running our way, but the other half—the front half, those earlier on in line—must be running the other way, into the stadium.

I push away from Gabe, eyes flying wide open. "My mom," I say. "My mom is in there." I swear my heart stops for a second. What if she . . . she . . . ?

She's going to be fine, I tell myself. Of course she is. She's strong and smart and was stationed near a barricade, which means she was right by the exit. She's probably saving people right now.

She has to be. *She has to be.* Though I tell myself this over and over, I can't stop my body from shaking the way the ground did. Gabe and I huddle together again, waiting for this all to be over.

It feels like we wait for an hour, but it's probably only, like, five minutes. With hundreds of people running as fast as they can, even with the glut and the panic, it's not that long before they've cleared the area, racing off into the distant parking lots and disappearing between stranded cars.

They leave bodies behind.

Not a ton of them, but I can see them even from far away, people collapsed on the ground. Some twitch. Others don't. My stomach twists.

Whoever fired the gun doesn't seem to be there anymore, at least. Nobody's left standing in the area—I can see a few people huddled in the shadows of trees or pressed against the stadium's side, but it seems like it should be safe to head back into the stadium to find my mom. She'll know what to do with the bodies and the wounded.

"I have to get to my mom," I say numbly.

"Ready?" Gabe asks. I take a deep breath before nodding.

Some of the people on the ground moan, and we see if there's anything we can do to help, but it's not like I can splint a crushed arm or fashion somebody a crutch right there. One of the people who were huddled by a tree approaches, followed by others, saying that he's a doctor, and another is an EMT, so we leave the wounded in their capable hands.

The people who don't move or moan—those I try not to look at too closely.

There are more people strewn over the ground as we approach Gate A—the gate's narrow compared with the open space outside, which means less room for the same amount of people to squeeze through. A little girl is crying out for her mother, though she miraculously appears unhurt. Gabe approaches, telling her not to worry, but she shrieks at the sight of his damaged face and scurries away.

I poke my head through the gate. It smells awful there inside the stadium—like urine and blood and something deeper, darker, like there are other fluids in the human body we're not supposed to smell. There are even more people lying here. I step over them and pretend I'm not, that they're sandbags, logs, piles of gold, anything but people. Because if I focus too hard on any of them, on the way they lie there unnaturally, their chests not rising and falling, it threatens to send me tumbling back into the woods, my crossbow hot in my hand, a different body beneath me. . . .

A man stands against the wall, rocking back and forth, his face in his hands. His words are coming in little gasps. "I didn't mean it. I fired in the air. I was just trying to make him back off. I didn't mean it. I didn't think he'd fire too."

Anger tries to climb up my throat at his sheer arrogance and stupidity, but I push it down. I'll let my mom deal with him.

Noise comes from the field: the screams seem to have died down, but the sound of a thousand people whispering is still an ocean.

I freeze when I see it. The shoe on the floor, the infinitely practical black sneaker with the thick old-lady sole.

Everything comes in fragments. The blurred scuff mark on the concrete floor. The splay of prepackaged meals fallen from a box and stepped on, something brown and viscous leaking from them. The metallic smell of blood hanging in the air.

The sign of a hot dog stand, broken in half, dangling from a creaking bit of tin.

The orange barricade, still standing strong.

The figure slumped against one section, like it's trying to use its orange vest as camouflage. Its arms raised against its head, now bent at awkward angles. The wild mass of dark hair hiding its face.

I don't need to see its face.

Her face.

21

I don't feel the pain I'd expect: a ripping-down-the-middle, jagged-edges-and-torn-seams, impossible-to-sew-back-together-again feeling. Everything is numb. Somebody could punch me in the face right now, and I wouldn't feel anything but a heavy pressure. I'm at her side, the slim hope she was only unconscious dashed. She's not only unconscious.

All around me is a roaring like we're sealed away in our own little wind tunnel.

I keep waiting to wake up. This can't be real. None of it can be real. Dreams can feel like they last forever, but eventually I'll open my eyes and the cool air of the AC in the window will brush my face. I'll flip on my bedroom light and turn on my computer and pretend not to hear my mom calling from the other room to see if I'm awake, because if I'm awake, I can bring up the recycling bins from the street. But she'll come knocking for me anyway, poke her head into my room, and smile at me like I'm the best thing in the world.

She's the only person who will ever love me that way, and now she's gone.

Hands on my shoulders. "Zara," Gabe is saying, and just like that, the spell breaks.

The roaring falls away and in its place rises weeping, muttering, and the moans of the wounded all echoing against the high, hard ceiling. My numbness dissipates, and instead there's a swell of panic and an ice-cold splinter of grief. They hit each other, and my body fills with steam, and there's nowhere for it to go, so it pushes hard on the backs of my eyes and my chest.

To try to let some of it out, I say, "This isn't happening," but it doesn't work, and Gabe's hands fix themselves in my armpits and pull me to my feet. I can't stand—somehow my legs don't work. They're as bendy and wobbly as cooked noodles, so I slump against him, and he holds me up.

"Don't look," Gabe is saying, and it makes me want to cry, because I've already looked, and it's not like you can unlook at something.

I take a breath, then another breath, and the numbness floods back through me. Finally I stand up straight, pushing away from him. It occurs to me that sometimes it might be possible to mistake numbness for strength. You're strong as long as you can't be hurt.

"I'm so sorry," Gabe says. He looks at me like he's looking through a ghost. "So, so sorry."

I almost want to laugh. "I'm so sorry to you, too," I say. But am I as sorry as he is? Because Estella and his parents are still alive.

There's still hope for them. "Actually, never mind. You can just be sorry for me."

"Zara . . ." He doesn't seem to know what to say to that.

People are beginning to filter back out from the field. Many carry water and food pouches, the sight of which sparks some fury deep inside me. "Hey," I say to the nearest person, whose arms are piled so high, I can't even see their face. "Hey!"

They don't respond, just keep moving slowly so that the tower in their arms doesn't topple. The spark flares, and I fling myself forward, fists flailing. Pouches go flying, and other people grab for them and dart away.

"Hey!" the person—a man—shouts. I don't back down. My chin juts out, and I glower at him beneath heavy brows. *Bring it on,* I think. Maybe he'll shoot me. I don't even care.

"Zara." Gabe's voice pours water on the fury. Just like that, I'm cold inside again. Empty. I fall back, and the man continues on his way, hurrying out with way more than his fair share of our limited supplies.

Fear. Cruelty. Selfishness. This is how the world ends.

"Zara, we can't stay here," Gabe says. He sounds serious. And much better than he sounded earlier, before I calmed him down. There's some irony: I calmed him so that he could calm *me.* "There are too many people, and some of them have guns, and all of them are going to want the supplies that are left. We don't want to get caught in another stampede."

"I don't really think I'd mind."

He sighs through his nose. "Let's go outside, at least. Where we can stay out of people's way."

I don't move. "I won't leave her here," I say. It feels wrong to be talking about her like this when she's right there.

"She would want you to be safe," Gabe says, and he's gentle, which makes me hate him. I wish he'd be impatient, or annoyed, anything that would allow me to yell at him without hating myself.

I still don't move. "I won't leave her here," I repeat. What if another stampede *does* come through and people's feet grind her into the ground? What if everybody flees and leaves her to rot and animals come to tear at her? What if she comes back to life and I'm not here to see it? What if, what if, what if? Tears sting my eyes. "We need to bury her before she . . . before she . . . we need to bury her."

I start to move now, but only in the form of a violent shake, my teeth clattering against one another so hard, I think they might actually break. There is no going back. Life is going to be different now. Forever. My mom is gone. Forever. Even if the power somehow blinks back on tonight, my mom will still be gone, and she's never coming back. I'm looking at her right now, at her familiar face and familiar hair and familiar hands, and I'm about to put her in the ground, and I will *never* see her again. *Never.*

My eyes blur with tears, but I can't stop looking.

"All right," Gabe says, and he stares at her for a moment, cheek working, and then in one fluid movement he crouches and scoops her up into his arms. It takes him some effort to stand, but he does, even as he looks as hard as he can into the distance, at me, at the wall, at anything besides what he holds in his arms. "We'll bury her, and then we need to get out of here."

He might have the luxury of looking away, but I don't. I can't. She's my mom. So I dutifully watch her legs swing as we move, and I pull her shirt down when it rides up and exposes the bruised skin of her belly.

She would do the same for me.

We settle back outside not far from where Gabe and I rode out the stampede. If I squint into the distance, into the cars gleaming in the parking lot and the people now ambling back toward the stadium, I can almost imagine it's a normal day, that I'm here for a football game. I take a deep breath and close my eyes, willing to pretend for a little while.

Gabe drags me back down to earth. "I can't stay here long if no one's here to help me," he says. "I have to go after my family. The bus was going toward Vegas, they said. Anything goes in Vegas." His laugh is harsh and humorless.

Words stick in my throat. I can't stand the thought of losing him. He's the only person I have left.

Well.

I still have my dad.

My dad might not even have noticed anything is wrong. He doesn't use electricity on the compound, and he's far enough from any populated areas that people likely haven't stumbled his way. He's probably just out there surviving as usual, hunting and farming and tracing the constellations in the sky. The things he gave me? Those are the things I need right now. I don't want them. But my tech is useless. I need to rediscover what he gave me.

I know what I have to do. But it feels like sacrilege to say it while my mom is right there. "I can't leave her here," I say. I feel something twist in my gut.

I don't go on. I root for Gabe to lose patience with me. I want to yell. I want to scream. I want to stomp on his feet and swing my fists at his chest. Maybe then I'll feel something.

But all that happens is that his voice goes even more gentle. "We'll bury her, like you said," he says.

I blink. My vision goes blurry for a second. I rub my eyes, and my fingers come away wet. "My grandparents are buried, like, an hour away."

"We can't bury her there," he says, and his voice is still kind, but now it's firm, too. It's like being in charge has reawakened that side of him that's used to being the captain of the soccer team, the vice president of the Future Business Leaders of America. "We'll bury her here." He waves his arm; the parking lot and sidewalks approaching the stadium are broken up by spaces of dirt and grass. "She would understand."

I'm powerless to do anything but nod. She *would* understand.

Gabe offers to venture back to the stadium and root out a shovel, but I choose to go instead. I don't think I can handle sitting there alone with my mom and not being able to ask her for help or advice. And I owe it to her to bury her myself. I owe her everything.

I avoid Gate A, where most of the people still knot, and slip in through the medical emergencies gate. It's dim and cool inside, entirely empty, all the medical professionals having fled to the people who need them. My heart is a stone as I grab some bandages, penicillin, ibuprofen, and antiseptic from the shelves—not all of it, just enough—and shove it into my pack. The dull pain of its weight has grown comforting. It feels almost like another part of my body.

It doesn't take long before I find a groundskeeper's closet with a shovel inside. It's half as tall as I am, but I carry it before me like an offering, refusing to let it drag on the ground. We pick a shady spot between two trees, and ignoring the glances of others in the area, I begin to dig.

"Let me help," Gabe says every few minutes, but each time I shake my head. I wipe trickles of sweat from my forehead and tears from my eyes every time they start to sting. I dig until my arms are trembling and everything is sore, and yet I'm only a couple of feet deep.

I want to collapse into my tiny hole and cry.

But Gabe reaches over and takes the shovel from my hands. My palms are sticky with the fluid of popped blisters, and they hurt when I rub them on my hips, but it's a good kind of hurt. If the inside of me isn't hurting the way it should be, then I can make the outside weep to make up for it.

He takes over; I stand at the edge and stare at him to make sure he's doing it right. He is. He's much better at hole digging than I am. "Maybe this can be your new career now," I say. "Grave digging." I laugh. He doesn't. Neither of us finds it funny. "We're going to need a whole lot of graves, I think."

He doesn't answer, only keeps digging.

The sky goes pink, then a blazing red. Most of the people leave the parking lot and the area outside the stadium—maybe they're going to pass the night inside or on the field?—but there are enough people around that I don't feel too unsafe.

But that's something that's going to have to change, I realize. I'm used to feeling unworried when there are several other people around to hear me if I scream. What would these people do if I screamed, though? They can't grab their phone and call for help. They can't use their bare hands to fight off someone who has a weapon.

Maybe I'm safer when there isn't anyone around at all.

It's still warm out, but I shiver. Gabe rests the shovel blade on the dirt with a clank. "I think it's ready," he says.

It doesn't look deep enough, but we can't stay out here all night.

I shiver again, then fall forward onto my knees. I brush my mom's hair out of her face. Up here it's hard to tell anything's wrong. She could just be lying on the couch, spacing out with earbuds in.

A tear drops onto her cheek. I brush it away. There's no point saying anything right now. She's not here anymore.

But still. "I love you," I say, and I want to say more, like how much I'll miss her, that I don't know what I'll do without her, but there's so much there that I choke on it. All I can do is sniff. No— all I can do is reach out and pass my hand over her cold forehead, closing her eyes.

Gabe manages to dig out a few steps and lay her gently in the hole, stretching her out so that it looks like she's sleeping. There's a jingle, and I go to ask him what it was, when he leans over and picks up her car keys. He hands them to me. I pocket them. It's like a sign: that she's giving me her blessing to go.

I stare down for a moment at her empty face. I can't help wishing that she were wearing a ring or something, maybe a necklace that I could carry with me. Keep one small part of her by my side and touch it when I felt like I needed her.

But she's never been the type for jewelry. I think she has some at home, but it's not like I can go back and get it.

"She would want me to say the Kaddish," I say hoarsely, stepping back. My mom is Jewish, my dad a die-hard atheist, and I'm kind of nothing. Most of the years I would've gone to Hebrew school were spent on the compound, and the next two years I would've spent preparing for a bat mitzvah were spent mostly in therapy. My mom tried to teach me how to read Hebrew a few times, but I don't remember a lot of it, much less the prayer for mourners said over the dead.

"She would understand," Gabe repeats. And the worst part is, I *know* she would. I'm not doing this for her. I'm doing this for me.

And that makes me feel even worse.

When I think too hard about my mom and how I'll never see her again, my chest fills with a kind of gaspy panic. But when I simply *don't* think about it, when I put her into that place in my mind I keep her when I'm hanging out with Estella or coding something new, where she's there but not *there*, I'm okay. Well, as okay as I can be.

As much as I want to make it to my dad, I can't abandon Estella and the Ramirezes. Fortunately, Vegas is on the way east. I convince Gabe that starting out in the night is a bad idea, because we don't even know where we're going, so we sleep for a few hours in my mom's car: him in the front, reclining in the passenger seat, and me stretched across the back seat. We roll up the windows except for a crack to let in air, and we lock the doors. It's stuffy and hot, but it feels safe. If anyone comes up and tries to menace us, we can just punch the ignition button and run them over.

I don't expect to get more than a few hours of restless sleep, but somehow I drop right off and am out. When I wake, the sky is light, and my mouth tastes sour. My mom is still dead, and remembering that sucks the air from my lungs all over again and makes me want to vomit at the same time. And to top it all off? Gabe is gone.

22

I can't bring myself to be upset at Gabe, because I can't blame him for leaving me behind. He was strong enough to fight off his attackers, while I barely managed to outrun mine. Maybe he found another ride out east. I'd be a burden on him, and he knows he has to save Estella right away. That's fine. Survival is about the individual, fewer people to share my supplies with and all that. Maybe I'll catch up with him on the way. It's fine.

Totally fine.

I roll my neck and stretch my back, trying to ignore the succession of cracks that pop out of me, and down a few sips of water to get rid of the sourness in my mouth. I squirt some toothpaste on my finger and brush my teeth dry, then grimace and swallow it down so I won't have to open the window to spit. After the toothpaste I'm too vaguely nauseous to think of eating anything real, so I get out my map. But not before glancing out the window to see if Gabe is coming. He's not, of course.

I figure I can drive my mom's car until I run out of gas—she has a full tank, so I should make it through most of the desert, which is good because I don't want to be on foot out there. No water. I should have no problem making it to Vegas, maybe even through Vegas to Cedar City if I'm lucky and find Estella quickly. If I'm even luckier, I'll find someone with gas to sell on the way. Gas stations won't be working, since the pumps run on electricity, but people might have supplies of their own.

A tap on the window. I nearly jump out of my skin, and I hit my head on the ceiling. I tense up, ready to mow right over someone, when I realize it's Gabe's knuckle against the glass.

I don't want to turn the car on and waste gas just to roll the window down, so I open the door. "I thought you left," I say. A flicker of warmth lights in my chest.

"Took a walk. Wanted to see what was going on." He glances back toward the stadium. "We have to go. People are fighting over supplies. I saw a guy literally knock another guy's teeth out. Blood everywhere."

I wince, both at the thought of flying teeth and at all those supplies lost to us. *At least I got medical supplies,* I think, when he reaches around and hands me a few prepackaged meals and water pouches.

"I nabbed a few before they saw me," he says. "Should tide us over for a bit."

Us.

Even though it might be easier for him to do this on his own, he wants us to do it together. I take a deep breath. We're going to save

Estella, but I want to make sure he knows we have somewhere to go after that, too. So I spill about my dad's compound. I don't share that I grew up there, which still feels too personal, but he's nodding by the time I'm through.

My face cracks into a smile. It feels different than it used to before. Maybe I'll never smile quite the same way again. "Okay," I say, and pat the seat beside me. "Hop in."

After a few false starts—I have only a permit, and it feels weird to be driving without my . . . *no, don't think about that right now*—I manage to get us moving in the right direction. My eyes are on the road, so I can't look behind me. All I can see is the pink of the sunrise welcoming us in.

23

The car is quiet, the air thick and tense, the way I imagine the air is inside one of those family tombs where generation after generation has been stuffed into stone drawers to rot for eternity. It's broken only by the occasional instruction of the GPS built into the car's dashboard, which is missing the Australian accent of the GPS on my phone: we might not have electricity, but the satellites are still up there in the sky, and it'll keep running as long as the car does. As long as we have gas.

I don't want to think about what happens when we run out of gas. The pumps need electricity to get gas out of the ground and into the car, so they'll all be useless. Hopefully, we'll be able to find gas in plastic jugs, but gas outside the ground degrades in less than a year, and it'll have been the first thing other people snapped up anyway.

Could this blackout really last more than a year?

Stop it, I tell myself firmly. I'm falling into the same traps that so many of my former classmates did. The trap of optimism, which assumes everything will get better, because it has to, right? The trap of hope, because hope was always a good thing in the past. It's easy to fall into one of those pits and never be able to climb back out. And can I really hope that things will get better when my mom is still dead? Things will never get better. I'm in this hole forever.

My fingertips drum the wheel. I glance at Gabe. He's staring out the window, his face surprisingly calm. Maybe there's an unspoken rule among pairs of desperate people that only one can freak out at once. "Do you know anything more about the people who took Estella and your parents, or where in Vegas they're going?" I ask. The thought of Vegas during this blackout makes me flinch. Even less water than LA, lots of stranded vacationers stuffed into a small, hot space. There are probably already riots there.

He flinches, and a small, dark part of me is glad. Because my mom is dead, and he doesn't feel the pain like I do, the pain that threatens to swallow me whole, and it's just not *fair.*

He clears his throat before responding. "They just said Vegas, one of the hotels," he says, and his voice is so hopeless, so dead, that even that small, dark part of me turns its face away with guilt. "That's all I know."

I force myself to look at him, but only for a second. I need to pay attention to the road. We crawled out of Pasadena—lots of stopping and starting in the line of cars—but now that we're on I-15, we're flying over a largely open road, cruising at a relatively fast eighty miles per hour. Cars whip past us going ninety and probably a hundred, and every so often we pass a tangled wreck. They're the ones who will hit roadblocks without enough time to slow down. They're the ones who block parts of the road, forcing us to slow down and go around them at a crawl. "That's not enough to find her," I say bluntly, and watch Gabe wince again. I don't look away this time. "Vegas is big, and it has a million hotels. We need more."

"I don't *have* more." He blinks hard and fast, like he's trying to force tears away.

Dirt stubbled with grass flashes by me, buildings with mountains towering over them in the distance. "You have something," I say, and focusing on this one thing makes the pain recede a little. It's still a mountain so high, it's impossible to climb, but now it's shrouded in fog. "You already told me. A school bus. Lots of men. How many men? What did the bus look like?" *Did any of them have tattoos of vines that looked like tentacles crawling onto his neck?*

Gabe gusts out a sigh. "It all happened so fast," he says, and then he's telling me from the beginning. How his parents were packing up a small bag to take to his abuela's cabin up north. How they left a note just in case, which must have blown away when their house was ransacked—I wonder if it was really the men who'd been following me or some random opportunist who saw them drive away. Then everything else he told me, the car breaking down and them hitching a ride on the school bus and the unsavory men planning a detour for their heedless passengers.

"How many?" I ask. It doesn't matter how thick the pain is in his voice. That's what my dad would say, anyway. He hated it when I cried, even when I was little. "Crying is useless. You're just wasting water," he'd tell me. "Don't cry over it. Fix it."

Gabe shrugs. He slumps against the door now, as if holding up his head costs too much energy. "I think there were six. Or five. Or seven. It was hard to tell. They all looked the same."

"What do you mean, they all looked the same?"

"They were all big, and muscled, and white," Gabe says. "And most of them were wearing these black leather jackets."

"Was anything on the jackets?"

Gabe shakes his head. "Not that I remember. But like I said, it happened so fast."

"Do you remember anything they said? Any hints they might have given about where they could be going?"

He doesn't reply, just keeps staring out the window, watching the landscape flash by. Gradually the grass grows less and less green, the dirt more and more red, until we're cruising through Nevada. Huge rock formations loom alongside the road, like a miniature version of the Grand Canyon. The gas gauge is hovering around halfway. "We're not too far, I don't think," I say.

He barely nods. I wonder if he's thinking about how hopeless our mission is. Before, we could've posted an appeal on Reddit or something, asking everyone in the area if they'd seen the people or cars we were looking for, and the internet would've sprung to our aid. I've seen the internet find missing children, uncover adoptive parents, even hunt down killers based on a drop of spit. Without the internet we're just driving into the vast unknown, somewhere east where these people may or may not be.

I want to tell him everything will be okay. That we'll have Estella back soon, safe and sound.

But all I can do is keep my hands on the wheel and my eyes on the road.

24

We slow at a gas station outside Vegas so that I can pee and Gabe can stretch his legs. I don't even bother with the gas station bathroom, which would've been disgusting on the best of days. This is definitely not the best of days. I squat in the shadow behind the convenience store, Gabe a safe enough distance away that he can't hear the trickle hit the sand but could hear me if I screamed.

When I return, I notice that the gas pumps themselves are all roped off with yellow caution tape, their screens, which usually flash digital numbers, blank and dead. A few cars are parked in the tiny lot before the convenience store, but nobody seems to be around. "We might as well check out the store," I tell Gabe.

The bell above the door tinkles as we open it. It's almost unbearably hot inside even with the shades drawn over the glass windows.

The shelves aren't as bare as I pictured them: sure, the freezers and fridges usually filled with ice cream and turkey sandwiches are empty, but the shelves are still littered with shining potato chip bags and tubes of Slim Jims. I run my fingers over the bags of chips, making a crackling noise. "I wonder if they have—"

"Honey butter?" Gabe says.

I blink with surprise. "How do you know that?" My mom always "forgot" to pick up my favorite chip flavor at the store—she said it tasted like barf. A fresh current of pain shoots through me, so strong that it actually feels like an electric shock. Another shock of pain as I remember how Estella always had them for me at her house.

Gabe doesn't quite smile at me—I don't think either of us is up for smiling right now—but the corner of his lip twitches in a slightly less grim way. "You mentioned it once while we were playing. How you wished you had honey butter chips at home, but that it was probably for the best that you didn't, because then your keyboard would be full of crumbs."

"I can't believe you remember that." We rarely talked about personal things in the game, but now I feel suddenly guilty for not having any idea what Gabe's favorite chip flavor is.

"Also, Estella used to complain that they were abominations and that smelling them while you ate them grossed her out. But she'd always tell me to get some for you at the store." He shrugs. "I don't see any here."

"It's fine," I say. "I don't think I'll be able to taste anything for a while." It's funny what grief does to you. I know I'll have to eat to stay alive, and that I need to stay alive to make it to Estella, but food is fuel now. Same with water.

I cast an eye around for bottled water but don't see anything except a few cans of soda.

Maybe there's still stock, because there's still a guy behind the counter. It's easy to loot an empty store, but harder to steal under the owner's wounded eyes. I jump a little when I notice him, a baseball cap pulled low over his forehead as he gazes suspiciously at me. "Hello," I say, because it feels weird to be looking at each other and not speaking.

He nods in response. If it were only me here, I'd probably just beat it, because this human-sized oven is uncomfortable enough without awkward silence. But Gabe strikes up a conversation with the attendant—whose name, we learn, is Avi—and soon enough they're laughing like they've known each other their whole lives. It's almost surreal. You could forget that we're alone in the world, careening across the country on a wild-goose chase.

"Everybody who stops in says, 'Avi, Avi, you should get out of here while you can,'" Avi says as I wind my way through the aisles, searching for a bottle of water someone might have left on a shelf and forgotten. No such luck. Only salty snacks, which will just make the lack of water worse. "But where am I going to go? I have nowhere else. I have only this store. So I will wait here until the power comes back."

"I get you," Gabe says easily. He's back to the old Gabe, the one who was the center of cheering crowds at school. You'd have no idea what he's going through right now if you didn't already know. Was this persona of his always a mask? How many other people are just putting on a show?

Life would be so much easier if I knew how to put on a show.

"Hey, we're actually looking for someone." Gabe straightens up, his face going serious. "A group of guys in black leather jackets driving a school bus." He pauses as Avi scratches his chin thoughtfully. "Have you seen them?"

Avi lowers his hand, then raises it again in front of him, his palm out, like he's trying to stop Gabe coming at him. "I don't want any trouble."

Gabe's eyes narrow. For some reason I don't want to see him break his mask. I step forward. "We're not the trouble," I say. "We're looking for the trouble."

Avi shakes his head. "I know they're the trouble. But if *they* know I sent someone after them . . ."

"So you've seen them, then?" I say. Wearing a mask like Gabe's must be exhausting. You always have to worry about breaking it with the wrong look or the wrong tone.

Avi hesitates a moment, then nods. "But like I said, I don't want any trouble."

"We already know they're going to Vegas," I say.

"They stopped here on their way through," Avi says. I snap to attention. Through? "Vegas is on lockdown, you could say. You know how many police and army are in Vegas? They are keeping order, they say, and these men, these criminals, they do not like order."

What do these men have planned for Estella and her parents? I can't say exactly. It sounds like the Ramirezes might have gotten caught up in something bigger than themselves, or maybe the men just want to take advantage of the country's current deterioration to fulfill some baser impulses somewhere else. But there are so many empty spaces in the US. Something like half the land west of the Mississippi is just . . . empty.

Which doesn't make it easy to track them down.

25

"You have to know something," I tell Avi again. His eyes are weary. Probably because I've said the same thing five times in a row.

Eventually he'll get so sick of me, he'll give in.

Right?

"I don't want any trouble," says Avi.

Not right. This isn't going to work. I slam my hands on the counter, leaning forward. He leans back just a tiny bit. "There are two of us and one of you." My heart is thumping so hard, it might come up my throat, but *this* has to work. He says he doesn't want trouble, so if I threaten some . . . "Tell us where they went and there won't *be* any trouble."

Avi stands silent for a moment. I see the rings of his throat working as he swallows over and over. Finally he says, "I don't know the specifics. I didn't hear any particular place. I just know they planned to go east, past Vegas. Maybe Utah, Colorado. Where there is water."

I study him for a moment. This man who claims to want no part of what those evil people have planned, yet who clearly chatted with them while they were here. This man who says he wants no trouble, but who stood here in his store and ignored that people were in trouble right there in his parking lot.

I hope I don't turn into someone like that.

Gabe glares at him. He seems to be thinking the same thing I did. That Avi saw Estella and his parents in distress and did nothing to help them. Maybe he couldn't have fought off a bunch of big, strong guys, but couldn't he have snuck up and opened the back door of the bus? Or refused to sell the men water? I mean, I can't expect him to risk his life to help people he doesn't know—would I even be brave enough to do that?—but I can expect him not to actively aid in oppression.

Suddenly, violently, Gabe tears a bag of chips off the nearest hanging rack. "I'm taking this," he says, making it sound like a dare.

"We'll pay for it," I say, reaching into my pocket and tossing some cash on the counter, because of course our cards won't work anymore. "And I'll take this case of soda, too." I feel a pinch of regret as the paper flutters onto the surface. Money might not be worth anything in the coming days, but on the other hand, these pieces of paper might still be worth something to people waiting for it to be over, and it's probably wiser to hoard it. Besides, he couldn't do anything to us. Look at him.

Look at you, Zara. I recoil in horror. It's my dad's voice, but not his words. Any one of us can be weak. I never want to be someone who takes advantage of it.

Never.

I grab Gabe, who in turn is grabbing a bag of ketchup chips. Are those his favorites? Or just what was closest?

"Thanks for your help," I tell Avi. He doesn't answer until Gabe and I are nearly out the door.

He says, "I hope you find her."

26

I stow the soda in the back seat, then take a quick survey of our remaining supplies. We have a full six-pack of water, along with plenty of food. Water's the important thing, though. We'll drive toward Cedar City and see if we can get any intel about the men there before canvassing some of the towns up that way. Hopefully we'll find more bottled water somewhere, but if not, I have my water purification tablets and water bottle filter. There's no water here in the desert, obviously, but we should be fine once we pass Cedar City and the country starts sprouting greener patches. I think. And if those men are looking for water, maybe we'll be following their same route.

Gabe is glowering as we pull out of the gas station. It's not until we're already back on the road that I realize we didn't get actual gas, but there's no way we're going back there. "At least we don't have to go to Vegas," I say in what I hope is an encouraging tone.

He does not look encouraged. "We have no idea where they're going."

"At least we've got *something* to go on."

He doesn't agree with me, but he doesn't disagree with me either, so I count it as a yes. "Music?" I ask. He shrugs, which I again count as a yes.

I spin the dial, but only static comes blasting from the speakers. I fiddle with it and finally find a station not affected by the blackout—maybe still running on a generator—but of course it's country music. I go to change it to something less obnoxiously patriotic, but Gabe starts bopping his head along, which makes me smile. I think this is my first real smile since . . .

The smile slides right off my face.

Gabe asks me a half hour in if I want him to take a turn at the wheel, but I shake my head. The driving's doing a good job distracting me from everything I don't want to think about, so I want to stay here as long as I'm awake.

But Gabe really needs a distraction too. He's drumming his fingers against his jeans, hard enough where I'm worried he's giving himself a bruise. "Hey," I say. "What were you going to major in?"

I wince as soon as the words are all out. Maybe the best distraction doesn't involve reminding him of what he lost—because even if the power does blink back on tomorrow, his sister and his parents have been kidnapped, he's been assaulted, and his life will never be the same.

I steal a glance at Gabe, hoping that none of my thoughts have winged their way through the air into his ear. All I see is that the drumming's stopped. Which is good. I think.

"Probably psychology," he says, which is a surprise to me.

"Why?"

He gives me an amused look. "You sound horrified."

"I'm not horrified," I say. *Okay, only horrified a little.* "It's just that the jobs in growing fields are mostly in STEM, aren't they?" Science, tech, engineering, math. Like computer science. Like me. "So why not major in a STEM field?"

"Because I don't want to major in a STEM field." He gives me a half smile, which is better than no smile. "We can't have a world full of only scientists and engineers and mathematicians."

That sounds like a perfectly nice world to me. "But why psychology? Isn't that the field where . . ." I trail off because I don't want to tell him his idea is terrible. The internet liked to joke about psych majors and English majors, saying that they'd never find jobs.

"I like psychology. I like knowing how people's heads work," Gabe says. "What's going on in there." He knocks on the side of his head. "And yeah, I know people say that psych majors don't get jobs, but don't more companies need to know how to communicate and use people's inner workings to make the companies better?"

I give Gabe a shrug. "Well, it's not like computer science is useful right now," I say, a concession.

"Psychology's more useful at the moment," he says. "People are getting reduced to their most primal instincts. Say we're face-to-face with a group of angry people, all yelling at you and wanting different things. Who are you going to want on your side, the computer science major or the psych major?"

I jam my foot on the gas. The car jumps forward. "Didn't help very much at the stadium."

"Nobody could have helped at the stadium," Gabe says. "That was a mob scene. Zara . . ."

I shake my head. It doesn't matter. What's done is done. I can't let myself get into the what-ifs. "What's really useful right now is what my dad taught me," I say. "I wish I weren't so rusty."

I can only imagine what my dad would say about a psych degree. I already know how he feels about college in general. "A waste," he'd say dismissively whenever my mom talked to him about how I should go to school. "Why should she get bused off to learn about dead old men and their pointless deeds when she should be here, learning the important things from me?" When I think back now, I'm almost surprised by how much my dad knew. He spent as much time as he could teaching me about the outdoors, about survival, but he also taught me math, science, how to read the classics like Steinbeck and Hemingway (he was really picky when it came to books and left most of the others to my mom). When I enrolled in school in LA, the only area where I was behind was in social studies. I was actually so far ahead in math, I tested into high school algebra.

"You probably know more about survival than me," Gabe says, then falls silent for a moment, maybe thinking about how that's not true. Because I've been pretty useless so far, aside from bringing along the car, and that he could've just stolen from the parking lot. There were a ton of empty cars there at the Rose Bowl. "Though I probably should've stuck with what I wanted to be as a kid. *That* would've been useful right now."

The land outside almost looks like the land in our game. Empty space. Sand and stone. Only there it was bombed that way, and here it's natural. Though is there really much of a difference?

"Let me guess," I say. "You wanted to be a farmer?"

He lets out a surprised "huh." "No. Is that really the first thing that comes to mind?"

"Obviously." I zoom around a car abandoned sideways across the right lane, whipping clouds of dust in my wake. "Food is extremely important, and so are people to grow it. People who aren't dependent on machines or grocery stores." He's still looking skeptical. "What?"

He rubs at his forehead. "Think more exciting."

What's more exciting than a farmer that would help in a post-apocalyptic world? "Engineer?"

He turns fully to face me. I'd like to look him back in the eye, but I'm driving, so bad idea. "I think you might actually have picked the one job *less* exciting than farming."

"One, you're wrong. Engineering is all math and science, which is the *most* exciting."

He actually laughs at this. Not a big laugh, and not an especially humorous one, but a laugh nonetheless. A tiny spark lights in my cold, dark soul at the sound.

"Two, you're still wrong. We don't want the end of the world to be exciting. If it's exciting, things are going wrong. You want it to be boring and full of rebuilding."

"I get your point," he says. "Still, I was thinking more of the *Dark Avengers* version of excitement."

Scoff. "A warrior?"

"Close enough," he says. "I wanted to be in the FBI. Hunting down bad guys and everything. That was back when I had a really idealized view of the police."

"Agent Gabriel Ramirez," I say. "Has a nice ring to it. I still think we'd be better off with a farmer or an engineer, though. Just on a practical level."

"You won't be thinking that when it comes time to storm the skyscraper."

I'm about to crack that I have no plans to storm skyscrapers IRL when I remember that we're on a rescue mission and may very well end up storming *somewhere*. A sigh streams long and low between my lips.

It's like he reads my mind. "Hey," he says. "It's okay. It's going to be okay."

"Says the guy whose mom isn't dead," I say flatly.

He flinches. Good. He should be flinching. But as soon as the thought flashes through my mind, it's gone. I don't want to make him hurt. I just want to make him laugh again.

But I can't lie and say everything's going to be okay when it's not. So I take the conversation down a level. "I don't think you'd be one of the guys storming the skyscraper anyway. I think you'd be one of the guys back in mission control, using your psych degree to profile the enemy or hunt them down or whatever."

"Maybe," he says, sounding relieved. "Today that's probably where I'd end up. But when I was a kid, I specifically wanted to be part of the Eyes."

"The Eyes?" I hit the brake, giving myself plenty of time to slow down before we have to navigate around a wreck still smoking slightly on the yellow line. I keep my gaze carefully trained on the road itself, not wanting to puncture a tire on stray debris. Fortunately, there don't seem to be any people still in the wreck—definitely glad because nobody is hurt, and *not* because if someone were there, Gabe would surely make us slow down and help them.

"The Eyes," Gabe echoes. He lowers the sun visor so that he doesn't have to squint. "I watched a movie about them with my dad when I was a kid and proceeded to hang my entire professional ambitions upon them until middle school."

"Kids are weird," I say. I can relate. When I was a really little kid, I wanted to grow up to be a mermaid who lived in our lake. My mom had told me that meant I'd be stuck there, never able to leave. "So?" I'd responded. I didn't care. I didn't know what else was out in the world, but I did know that I was happy there by the lake with my family.

It occurs to me now how her face had pinched up, how her eyes had reddened like she was going to cry.

"So what did the Eyes do?" I ask quickly, before I can think too much about my mom and start to cry myself.

He half smiles again. Though his sun visor is down now, he's still squinting. "In the movie they saved the president's daughter after she got kidnapped. They were called the Eyes because they had eyes pretty much everywhere. Like, they could see through everybody's computer cameras and phone cameras and could listen in to basically any microphone at will."

"Their tech sounds good," I say. The road ahead is clear, and the red desert is a blur outside. We're practically flying. For a second I imagine our wheels might actually lift off the ground. Leave all of this behind.

"The best," Gabe says. "Of course, it wasn't just tech. They were the only people with the stealth and know-how to infiltrate the terrorists' headquarters and rescue the First Daughter without getting any allies killed." He pauses for a moment. "Except for the squad leader, of course, who heroically sacrificed himself at the pivotal moment."

"Naturally."

He shakes his head. "I wanted to find the movie a few years ago, but it wasn't streaming anywhere."

"Too bad." Suddenly something under the hood rattles, shaking us from our teeth to our bones, and I yank my foot off the gas. The car slows. The rattling stops, but the shaken feeling doesn't.

"What just happened?"

I glance uneasily over the dashboard. No lights have blinked on. "No idea."

We're quiet for a few minutes, waiting to see if the rattling will come back, but I keep our speed steady and less than ridiculously high, and everything seems to be smooth. "Anyway," he says finally. "I wish I had their training. Or the training of our *Dark Avengers* characters. Because right now I feel pretty damn useless."

I would like to tell him he's not useless, but I'm not one for lying. "We're both pretty useless."

He shifts in his seat. "Maybe I should take a turn driving."

"If you really want to." I know it's about proving how not-useless he is or whatever, but I could use a break from the nonstop focus on the road.

I pull off to the shoulder and let Gabe switch into my seat. We take a moment to stretch our legs outside, wincing in the bright glare of the sun. I crack my neck. There's really nothing around— just road and red rocks, scrubby patches of green low to the ground, mountains in the distance.

When Gabe takes the wheel and eases back onto the road, sailing a good ten miles per hour faster than I was, he also takes the wheel of the conversation. "I assume you would've majored in computer science."

"Probably."

He cracks a slight smile. "Estella always talked about how the two of you were going to start a tech company one day. One of the few founded by women. She would be the face, and you'd be the brains."

"She'd be the brains too," I say.

"Yeah, I know." He's quiet for a bit. I kind of hope he'll jump in and say I'll be the face along with the brains as well, but he doesn't. "It'll still happen. It'll just take time."

"Maybe."

He turns the radio up till it blares. No way I could hear him talk right now, which might be the point. We pass a half hour or so whipping through the desert, the windows down and gritty air working its way into our hair and our eyes.

The radio's so loud, we don't hear the rattling start again until the car's shaking hard.

27

Gabe steers the car toward the shoulder. Just as he comes to a stop, smoke plumes out from beneath the hood.

He turns the car off. Shocked silence vibrates around us. "Get out!" He hurls himself out of the car, and I follow, and we race around behind the trunk. He throws an arm out to shield me the way my mom used to do when I was sitting in the front seat and she had to stop short at a red light, as if that protective arm emitted a force field that would save me from flying forward into the windshield or from the fallout of an explosion.

There's no explosion, though the smoke keeps billowing out from under the hood, changing from light gray to dark gray. It smells like burning rubber and oil.

"This is bad," Gabe says, the understatement of the year. But his pessimism doesn't live long. "We'll just flag someone down to help us. I don't know anything about cars. . . ."

We share a moment of silence, and I'm sure we're both thinking about the same thing: the days when you could just pull up a You-Tube tutorial of anything you didn't know how to do.

"But I'm sure someone driving by will," Gabe finishes.

I snort. "That's sweet that you still believe in the goodness of humanity." He should have realized by now that people suck. Just look at Avi. We can only really depend on ourselves.

No. Not ourselves, because am I really sure that I can depend on Gabe? *I* can only really depend on *my*self.

He gazes at me steadily. "'In spite of everything I still believe that people are really good at heart.' Anne Frank."

"Nice quote," I say. "You know she and almost her whole family were murdered after she wrote that, right?"

"Of course I know that." His eyes are wounded now, a kicked dog's. "But the sentiment is important. For the most part, people aren't going to hurt you or refuse to help you for no good reason. People are good."

"They won't be doing it for no good reason. They'll be doing it for self-interest. That's what motivates people above all." If people were asked to decide between saving the lives of their immediate family members and saving the lives of a hundred strangers, most would choose their family members, even though a lot more people would die senseless deaths. That's theoretical, but now it's in the real world too. If somebody had to weigh stopping at the side of the road and using their expertise to help us against the odds that we were pretending to need help so that we could steal their car or supplies, they'd choose themselves. I hate to remind him of this, but it proves my point, so, "Your family was just literally kidnapped by bad people on the road. And Avi didn't help them."

Gabe shakes his head. "The exceptions that prove the rule. Most people want to help."

He's so totally wrong. But I let him stand at the side of the road and wave frantically anyway. If we let the car cool down a bit, maybe we'll be able to see what's wrong, and we don't particularly want to be walking in the midday heat anyway.

His waves grow less and less spirited as more and more cars speed by us. We're both coated in a thin film of red grit now. "So much for the goodness of people," I say, just as a car slows and pulls to the side of the road ahead of us.

Gabe gives me a smug look over his shoulder as he trots to the person's car. It's a couple, a man and a woman, tan and weather beaten, probably in their forties. Two kids peer out at us from the back seat. "Hey there, thanks for stopping," he says, leaning in to talk to the man in the passenger seat. "Our car broke down, and we have no idea how to fix it."

The man and woman both climb out of the car. "You stay," the man directs the kids, who duck back down. One has what looks like an old-school Game Boy, which runs on batteries, in his hands. My eyes linger on it for a moment, wondering if I'd be able to hack it into something more useful, but I'm not going to steal a Game Boy from a kid. Or anyone. So I just follow the man and woman over to our car, which is still emitting puffs of smoke from the front.

Gabe pops the hood and stands over it with the man, staring down. The woman stands to the side, near our front window, her arms behind her back. I keep an eye on the woman, who's keeping an eye on me, too.

"So where you two headed?" the man asks, staring into the engine. A trickle of sweat runs from under his red baseball cap down his cheek. It looks almost like a tear.

"Cedar City," Gabe says. "Hey, you by chance see a bunch of men in black leather jackets driving a school bus?"

"Sorry, no," the man says. He points at something in the engine. "Here's your problem. You busted a gasket. I can fix it for you easy if you got a screwdriver."

"I'll check," I say. I pop the door unlocked and stick my head in to scout through the glove compartment. Gabe and the man's conversation drifts by overhead; they've struck up an easy rhythm about the road, the weather, the possibility of rain, all these things that normal people are somehow always able to talk about.

I bring the screwdriver around front, and the man thanks me. "Don't thank me, we should be thanking you," I say. I swing my arms, trying to air out my pits. I hate the feeling of underarm sweat, especially knowing I'll be sitting in close proximity to Gabe again very soon. Not that it'll do much. I'm still in my dress from the party, and it's dirty and smelly and tattered. Hopefully, in Cedar City I'll be able to bathe and change. "Seriously, thanks for stopping. I was starting to think nobody would."

The man shakes his head. "That's the problem with people around here. You from LA?" He doesn't wait for an answer. "That place, I swear to God. We've been living there for almost five years now, and I can't get over how fake people are."

Gabe's staring intently into the engine, watching what the man is doing. I should be doing that too, but the man's words strike a chord in me. "Right?" I say. "I moved here a while ago, and all people seem to care about is . . ." I go on, my arms gesturing animatedly around me as the man works. He's really getting in there, the screwdriver rattling the whole car. "Anyway, I'm never getting plastic surgery," I finish.

"Wise decision," the man says. He thumps the car, glancing over his shoulder. "Well, I think I'm done here." He steps back, dropping the screwdriver on the ground. "Oh, sorry."

"Don't worry about it." Gabe bends down to grab the screwdriver. The man backs away very quickly.

Too quickly.

My head jerks to the side. Our rear door is open. I didn't leave it open. "Hey," I say, taking a step toward the man, but he's stumbling over his feet, and now he's turning and running back to his car. The woman is running after him, her arms full of water bottles and soda and—

"Hey!" I shout, running after them. The woman turns and points a gun at me, shifting the items all over into one arm. I skid to a stop.

"I'm sorry," she says, pushing our items into her car with that one arm. The arm with the gun doesn't tremble. She climbs in, moving quickly so that the gun points away from me for only a split second before poking out the window. "Don't take another step."

It kills me to stand still, but what am I against a gun? What is Gabe?

Dead.

The man jumps into the car, and they're already moving, the tires drawing circles in the dust. "Hey! Stop! We need that!"

"I'm so sorry!" the woman shouts out her window. I can barely hear her; the wind of her going tries to tear the words away. "Our kids need it too!"

I run a few more steps, but there's no use. They're already back on the road, and then they're nothing more than a bright, shiny point in the distance.

All I can hear is my heart pounding in my ears. I turn slowly to Gabe, who's staring after them, his expression crestfallen. His forehead is getting very red, his cheeks, too. Sunburn or anger.

Or both.

28

I don't bother with some snarky comment like, *How's that for good at heart?* Well, I do, but only in my head, so it doesn't count. Instead I get right to inventorying what the couple took. "All the soda we got at the gas station, and almost all of our water," I report grimly. "They left us two bottles. Well, one and a half."

Gabe is silent for all of this. I continue, "Maybe he saw it as payment for fixing the car. It's fine. We only have about an hour and a half left to Cedar City, and we can restock there."

He nods wordlessly and gets into the passenger seat. I climb into the driver's seat and press the ignition.

Nothing happens.

Unease flutters in my stomach, or maybe that's the beginning of a deadly thirst. "Right, this happens sometimes," I say weakly, and press it again.

Nothing.

I jam it again and again, holding it short and long and over and over again.

The car doesn't so much as sputter.

I drop my arm and lean over, resting my forehead on the steering wheel. I close my eyes. We're in a broken-down car in the desert with one and a half bottles of water, and everyone driving by us is terrible.

Everything is terrible.

My head jerks up, eyes flying open, as Gabe pounds his fist on the dashboard. "Damn it!" he roars. "Damn it all to hell!"

He blinks at me with haunted eyes, clearly expecting me to tell him off. To tell him that I was right, and he should have listened to me, and that now we're more screwed than we were just a little while ago and it's all his fault.

I don't even feel the urge to be petty. There's just the beginning of a dull ache in my head.

We don't have time to waste on fighting. "We'd better get walking," I say.

29

Without the car's GPS, we're stuck following signs that we're going the right way. And not woo-woo signs from the universe, like a lucky charm or a license plate with my initials on it. Literal signs that say CEDAR CITY along with the number of miles away.

We're a lot of miles away.

Leaving my mom's car behind is a twist in my heart. I take everything with me that I can: the braided lanyard hanging from the mirror I made at camp long ago; the little plastic figurine of a dog she kept in the front cup holder for good luck. I even try to peel off the faded bumper sticker about saving the trees, but give up after I realize it's melded to the car.

We discover very quickly that we can't walk on the shoulder of the road. We lurch, our eyes stinging from dust kicked up by cars off the side of the road, where our feet crunch over the red sand and stone. At first we hold out hope that we might find an abandoned car we can hot-wire, or that one of the wrecks might not be too badly destroyed for us to use, or that somebody might stop for us, but no such luck.

Though it might be luck that no one's stopped for us, judging by the experiences we've had so far.

The sun beats down on us without mercy. I drape a scarf over my head and around my neck, but it can only do so much against the blinding heat. "Maybe we should rest during the day and walk at night," I suggest, but there's nowhere to rest. No shade. No mercy.

My throat is dry and as scratchy as sandpaper, but I limit my consumption of water to the occasional sip. I guard the last one with ferocity, knowing there's no more where it came from, but eventually I have to drink it. I squeeze every last little drop onto my parched tongue.

"We won't make it to Cedar City," I rasp. It's amazing how quickly your vision can blur and your legs can shake. Aren't we made of water? Isn't there still a whole lot of water left in me?

"There are places along the way. We'll stop there." Gabe's voice is a dry whisper too.

So when we see an exit pointing the way to a small town—Red Lake—we take it as a sign. A woo-woo sign. Because that's how quickly my sense of logic has dried up.

The universe doesn't give you signs. That's my dad talking to my mom, his voice full of scorn. A butterfly had fluttered past her face while she was telling me a story about her own mom, who'd died a few years ago, and she'd declared it a sign from her. *The universe doesn't care about you. The universe rewards the fittest. All we can do is make sure we're among the fittest.*

Am I fit now, Dad? My throat's clogged. I want to cry, but the tears won't come.

Good, Zara. Crying is a waste of water. And you need all the water you can get.

I'm not sure if that's me or my dad.

Night starts to fall, the temperature with it. At first I delight in the chill on my sunburned skin, but it's not long before I start to shiver. And it's not just a cold shiver either. My forehead is still scorching hot to the touch. "We should stop for the night." I can barely hear myself speak. I clear my throat and try again, but this effort's not much better. "We have to stop."

"We can't just stop in the middle of the desert." Gabe's definitely slowed down over the course of the day, but his footsteps are still plodding resolutely one after the other. He drained his own supply of water hours ago. "The sign said Red Lake was only three miles away. We have to have walked two already, right? We have to be almost there."

We're moving basically as slowly as it's possible to move on two feet. I don't think we've walked two miles, but I don't have the energy to protest. So we trudge on. And on. And on.

30

When I see the buildings rise before us from the desert, at first I think they're a mirage. They're blurry in the way I imagine a mirage would be, and the universe doesn't give us signs, and we're not fit enough to deserve a rescue, so . . .

But we grow closer, and the buildings don't disappear. And then . . . a pool of water before them, stretching out as far as the eye can see. It's dark against the red of the sand around it, but we lurch toward it, not speaking, afraid that opening our mouths will loose particles of H_2O into the air.

We don't even bother with the buildings, just keep going for the water, our eyes trained on one spot and one spot only. I wait to hear the lapping of the water on the shore, or smell the murk of water that's sat too long under the sun, and we near it, and—

We halt in our tracks. This was once a lake, that's clear. But the water is gone, and it's been gone a long time. The empty lake bed stretches out as far as the eye can see, cracks spidery in the dried-out ground, nothing but dust in the air.

The houses. There still might be water in the houses. There might be people in the houses too, but we can worry about that if we have to. We spin together, as if our minds are one, and drag our feet toward the closest building.

Again we stop. We missed it when we were rushing to the water, but the house is boarded up. So is the next one. And the next. They're all slumping to one side, the wood of their walls rotting. Spiky desert shrubs grow through decks; any unboarded windows are broken. Something rustles inside the closest one.

Anger swells within me suddenly. Red Lake. Once there was a lake here, and a vacation community around the lake, but the lake disappeared, and all the people with it. It lured us here under false pretenses. I want to scream and kick the ground and rage into the night.

But I don't have the energy. All I do is wilt.

"We need to rest," I rasp. "Let's stop in one of these houses."

We might be weak and weary, but the boards on the closest house are nearly rotted through, easy for Gabe to snap with a good kick. Something flies out the window as we go inside, but I pay it no mind. I'm busy raking my eyes over the room, hoping that maybe somehow there will be a case of water lying here forgotten, but no. It's only us.

31

When I wake, my head is pounding with a dull ache, and my throat is stabbed by every swallow. I sit up, wincing, which only makes it worse. The sun streaming through the cracks in the boarded-up window is turning the rest of the world fuzzy around the edges.

I poke Gabe awake with a foot to the ribs. From the way he winces, he's in as bad shape as I am. "We can't stay here," I say. Or try to say. I'm not sure anything actually scratches its way out of my throat. "Maybe we can get back to the highway. Maybe someone will help us."

But the sun glares into our eyes as we step fully into it, and immediately I'm off balance, everything tilting around me. Gabe catches me before I fall, but the effort nearly makes him fall too. His breath wheezes in my ears.

I'm going to give you a test, Zara. Show me how much you've learned.

Who was that? I glance around for the person who spoke but see nothing except—yes—a literal tumbleweed blow across the dirt.

Gabe gasps. "There!" He points into the distance. "Do you see it?"

I shake my head. I don't see anything.

"Water. It's water," he says, and lets me go to move toward it. I follow. He must be going toward the road. Anything else would be death—except then I see it too! A fresh pool of water, right in the sand! It must be runoff from the lake somehow, or—

I'm going to drop you into an unknown place, and it's your job to get back home.

"That's what I'm doing," I tell the voice as I drag my feet after Gabe.

Gabe turns and looks at me over his shoulder. His whole body shimmers through a haze of heat. "What?"

You have your compass, right? You should always have your compass on you.

"I don't have my compass," I whisper at the voice, nothing coming out from my dry lips, but somehow I know the speaker can hear me anyway. Because it's my dad, and he's not actually here, only in my head.

I can practically hear him shaking his head. *That was not smart of you, Zara.*

I blink fuzzily. "I know," I say. "But I don't see how a compass would help. What I really need is a . . . a . . ." I can't think of the word for one of those forked sticks that are supposed to lead you to water. I never needed one on the compound. It was located in an area with water everywhere: lakes, little streams, even possibly pumped up from underground if you needed it.

A dowsing rod, my dad says. *And they're just more woo-woo. You're smarter than that.*

"But I'm not. If I were smart, I wouldn't be in this situation."

True. I never knew my dad to lie. Not even to make me feel better.

He told me all these things years ago. I was probably eight or nine, and he decided it was time for me to learn how to navigate our world. He blindfolded me and walked me far into the woods, sometimes carrying me so that I wouldn't stumble over errant branches or trip over rocks. After what felt like ages, he deposited me onto the soft, leaf-strewn ground and tugged the blindfold off my head. "Go," he said, and while I was still blinking in the newly bright sunlight, he disappeared.

I can barely hear Gabe ahead of me. From behind, he moves almost like a zombie in a bad movie. "It's there. I see it."

I see it too, with every step. And with every step, it stays the same distance away. Either it's moving or I'm not. "What if it's a mirage?" I try to say. Sand stings my eyes. My body is a hollow husk, drifting over the ground like that tumbleweed. I can't really feel my feet, but they're probably still there, because I haven't fallen over yet.

In the woods that day I did all the right things. I had my compass. I had my instincts. I was able to forage up some water and had my crossbow in case I needed to shoot a squirrel or something.

And yet by the time night fell, I hadn't made it back home. It was a cold part of the year, nearly winter, and with the dark came the cold. I huddled under a tree, shivering hard. At one point I looked at my fingernails and, in the last strains of the dying light, realized they were turning blue.

I woke up in my dad's arms. He was carrying me back. "I won't always be here to save you, Zara," he said gravely. "You need to be able to take care of yourself."

"I know," I tell him now. "I know I do."

With the next step, my legs buckle under me. The sand is baking hot under my cheek. "I know." I try to get the words out, but the effort doesn't so much as stir the dust around me.

32

Don't cry, Zara. Crying is a waste of water.

I know, I try to tell my dad, but my lips don't seem to be working. It doesn't matter. There's no water left. I couldn't cry even if I wanted to.

33

My head is pounding.

Not pounding like someone knocking to get me to open the door. Pounding like a battering ram going to war with the front of a castle.

And it takes me a few seconds to wrench my eyes open. When I reach up to rub them afterward, my fingers roll a thin layer of *something* between my fingers. I marvel at it the way I'd marvel at dried Elmer's glue as a middle schooler, peeling its papery film off my hands.

Everything around me is white. I sit up, trying to take it all in, but the motion of sitting makes my head feel like someone's just kicked it, so I drop back down onto what feels like a pillow. My whole body trembles with the effort, making me pant.

I'm alone in a room, it looks like. A small room, painted a pure, shining, pristine white that nearly hurts my eyes. The blanket that covers my lower half is white too, and so was the quick glimpse of pillow I got. Everything is white except for the two photographs that hang side by side on the wall near me, both close-ups of some kind of purple desert flower. Pretty, in a spiky sort of way.

My clothes are white too. A loose white T-shirt, white jogging pants, and white socks. I'm not wearing any shoes, but my Converses are tucked into the corner of the room. I have no idea where my dress is.

I've been putting it off, but I know I have to do it. Inventory my body. My dad's voice echoes through my head again. *It's exceedingly important to know your own body. If you have an injury or a weakness, you must be aware of it or you will be at a severe disadvantage.*

His voice makes my head hurt worse.

Still. I roll my ankles, flex my calves and my thighs, poke experimentally at my stomach to see if it roils. It complains, but only because it's empty. I test out all my arm muscles, do the pinch on the back of my hand to check for dehydration. The skin there returns to flatness after a couple of seconds, so I am dehydrated, but only a little.

Aside from my head, everything seems normal enough. Considering the last thing I remember is collapsing in the Nevada desert, my mouth full of grit and Gabe desperately trying to move my dead weight.

Gabe.

I sit bolt upright again. My brain slams against the inside of my skull, but this time I don't care. "Gabe?" I call, or try to call. Only a papery rasp actually comes out. I clear my throat and try again. "Gabe? Gabe?"

I don't even want Gabe. I want my mom. I want her so bad, it claws at my insides. But Gabe is what I have. Well, had.

Could he have left me behind? I like to think I wouldn't leave him if our positions were reversed, but it's hard to say. If he really tried to rouse me and drag me along, and I wouldn't move . . . I couldn't blame him for going on and trying to survive. Survival is about the individual, after all. I wouldn't want to weigh him down.

A click. The door is opening. I grab for my pack, for pepper spray, anything, but my pack isn't here, and the door's already open, and it doesn't look like I need the pepper spray based on what I see, so I relax.

But not too much. Because you never know.

"It's good to see you awake!" the opener of the door says. She's dressed all in white too, a girl maybe a few years older than me. Her teeth are as white as this room, and her blond hair is scraped back into an extremely tight ponytail. "How are you feeling?"

"Where's Gabe?" I rasp. Talking is a struggle; every word scrapes painfully at my throat.

The girl moves closer to me, a glass in her hand. "Here, drink this. It might help you."

I look warily at the glass, which is full of what *appears* to be clear water, but I so recently almost died of dehydration that I don't stop to worry if it's been drugged or anything. I chug it all down to the last drop, then lick the rim.

"Easy there," she says, a laugh in her voice. "There's plenty more where that came from."

Maybe I did actually die of dehydration, and this is heaven.

Heaven isn't real, Zara, my dad says disapprovingly. *Religion is the opiate of the masses.*

My mom didn't feel that way. I swallow hard over a tender lump in my throat. She cared deeply about her Judaism, not necessarily believing in all the rituals and tenets, but appreciating her connection to her ancestors and her history and her culture. But Judaism as she learned it doesn't believe in a heaven.

I always thought myself perfectly rational, scorning the idea of an afterlife, but I can't help but wish very hard there's a heaven now. That she's there waiting for me, and that I'll see her again.

"Where's Gabe?"

"Your companion's in the next room. He actually woke up a couple days ago and has been in to visit you a few times," the girl says. "I'm glad you've woken up. We weren't sure if you would."

I appreciate the frank way she's speaking to me. "I'm guessing you saved us?"

The girl laughs. Like, throws her head back and all. "Not me personally!" she says. "But yes, you're very fortunate that relatives of one of our community members were driving here from Las Vegas, took a side road, and spotted you two collapsed in the desert. Vultures were already circling overhead."

"Thank you," I say, suddenly faint with how close we came to death. And that somebody saved us without even knowing who we were.

Maybe I was wrong. Maybe some people *are* good after all.

And then it clicks, what she said. "Wait. You said we've been here for a few days?"

"A week, actually," she says cheerfully. "I'm Brynlee, by the way."

My stomach is now churning along with my mind. A week is a *long time*. Like, too long. The people who have Estella must be way ahead of us by now. Who knows what she's been going through this past week?

And that's long enough for my dad to have realized something's happened by now. Which means he's probably expecting me soon. The churning turns to curdling with shame. I can practically see him standing outside the house, checking his watch, tapping his foot. If I take too long, he might consider me weak. Unfit. Not worthy of his protection.

"I'm Zara," I tell Brynlee. "How long until we can leave?" And then, something that should probably have occurred to me earlier, "And where exactly are we?"

"I'm afraid I can't tell you exactly where we're located, but we're in Nevada," Brynlee says. "You've been saved by the Church of Jesus Christ of Latter-Day Saints."

What's—oh. "You're Mormons?"

Brynlee's lips thin slightly. "We prefer the Church of Jesus Christ of Latter-Day Saints."

"Sorry," I say. "I didn't know. I'll use that from now on."

"No worries," she replies. But her telling me who she is stirs a memory. A conversation with my dad.

I'm starting to get sick of hearing his voice in my head. But I don't have a choice. *Religion is the opiate of the masses, but I do admire the Mormons,* he said. *They're smart. They know they live in an inhospitable world, and it's rumored that they have prepared more than we have. They have bunkers full of supplies, all hidden away in their compounds. At the end of the world, it'll be the Mormons who repopulate the States.*

Right. I remember now. The LDS Church has always taken the possibility of civilization collapsing seriously, whether from a nuclear attack or climate change, and a whole lot of their members have spent time preparing. And not just individually stocking up on bottles of water and dried food. No, they've formed full-on compounds where members of the church can live more or less normally while the world crumbles around them.

We must be on one of them now.

"Can I see Gabe?" I ask. She nods. I have to get Gabe, and then we have to go. We've already lost a week. We can't afford to lose any more time.

And yet as I go to stand, I nearly collapse back into bed. "Careful," Brynlee warns. "We've been massaging and working your muscles while you were out, but you're still going to be weak. Don't forget you almost died."

I could never forget that. My dad's voice will never let me.

34

I totter slowly out of the room and into a hallway just as blindingly white as my room. Brynlee nods at a boy around my age passing by us in the opposite direction. "Ronan," she says in greeting.

The boy—Ronan—nods back, then focuses in on me. "You're awake," he says. His voice is low and husky, a surprise coming from such an angelic face: blond hair, bright blue eyes, rosy cheeks like a porcelain doll's.

"I'm awake," I agree.

He stares at me a moment longer. I shift on my feet, trying to stand without leaning against the wall. "Where are you going?"

"To see Gabe," I say. When Ronan just looks confused, I go on. "My friend who was brought here with me. We're going down the hall to go see him."

He blinks. Long lashes, surprisingly dark compared to his light hair, cast shadows on his pale cheeks. "What? No, I mean, where were you going before you almost died?"

They really like bringing up this almost-dying thing. *That's unfair,* part of me whispers, but it's easier to blame them than myself. "East," I say. "We have to . . ." I trail off. I'm not sure how much I want to share. It might be better to keep things close to my chest before consulting with Gabe. What if they decide they don't want to help us anymore, since they might assume we're heading straight to our actual deaths? "Go east," I finish lamely.

"Come on," Brynlee says. "Unless there's something you need, Ronan?"

He shakes his head, almost too quickly. "Nope. Not me."

Still, I can feel his eyes lingering on us as we continue down the hall.

Brynlee stops at a door at the other end and knocks, three short raps. "Come in," Gabe's voice says from the other side, and my heart nearly stops with relief. It's like I wasn't able to believe he was alive and okay until I actually witnessed it.

Opening the door and seeing him in the flesh feels even better. He looks thinner than he did a week ago, skin clinging more tightly to his bones, the muscles in his chest and shoulders a little bit shrunken. His eyes widen as he sees me. I hope it's all relief, though after seeing him, I can only assume I've shrunken a bit myself.

"Zara," he exhales, and then his arms are around me, pulling me into him. I close my eyes and take a deep breath. Underneath the sterile smell of the room, there's still a trace of the Gabe I know. The Gabe who chose to collapse beside me, trying to pull me along, rather than lurch on alone.

When he backs away, his eyes are clouded. "It's been a week."

"I know." *You could have left without me,* I don't say. Because even though I know he'd be ahead of me if he had—assuming he survived—I'm glad he didn't. I'm glad we're together.

What would my dad have to say about that?

We both turn to Brynlee at once. She must know what we're about to say, because her response comes before we even say it. "You can't leave yet. You're both weak, and you don't know what it's like out there."

Right. I didn't even think about that. It's been two full weeks of no power. People will have run out of any stockpiles of bottled water they had. Maybe out in the east they'll be fine, as long as they're able to boil whatever plentiful water they find in lakes and streams and from rain, but out here we're in the desert. In temperatures and conditions like this, you get one or two days without water, especially if you're on the move. As Gabe and I so masterfully demonstrated. Here if you're not already near a river or another water source, you're screwed.

There must be so many dead. And so many more dying.

". . . can't even walk," Brynlee is saying. My attention snaps back to our conversation.

"I can so walk. I'm walking right now."

She raises an eyebrow. "Tell you what," she says. "I'll take you on a tour of our ward. Would you like that?"

She sounds like she's talking to a misbehaving ten-year-old. It makes my skin bristle, even though she's been nothing but perfectly nice to us. Saved us.

And yet it would be good to know where we are. Right now I know nothing but these two small white rooms and the long white hallway, with no idea what lies beyond either end. It's always best to be familiar with your environment, just in case—which here mostly means having to sneak out in the night if they won't let us leave on our own.

I take a deep breath. Straighten my shoulders. Try very much to appear like I'm hale and healthy and in control. "Okay. Sure."

"Great!" Brynlee gives us a gleaming smile and moves toward the door.

"Come on, Gabe." I link my arm through his as we follow, to hold the both of us up.

35

The door at the end of the hallway leads us into blinding sunlight. I blink hard, everything around me spotted with white.

When my vision finally clears, I'm confronted with a picture of startling normalcy. To our right are arranged a number of long, low brown buildings like the one we've just emerged from; they're probably work buildings, storehouses and granaries and the like. To the left: small, squat brown buildings with front porches. Clearly houses. In the distance rises a white steeple. "That's the church," Brynlee says. "The center of the ward."

She walks briskly to the right, looking over her shoulder frequently, her eyebrows raised just the slightest bit. She's doing this on purpose to see if we can keep up with her. My legs already feel wobbly, but I grit my teeth. No way am I letting her get the best of me.

We push on through people milling about. Not quite a crowd, but they're not sparse, either. Most are blond, all are white. Without exception, they nod or smile at us. "Welcome," some say. It's like they all already know who we are. I wonder which ones saved us, if we've passed them without knowing. Don't they want even a thank-you? Can anyone really be so decent not to want *anything* at all?

I glance sidelong at Gabe. I'm about as white as can be, even if I'm dark-haired and dark-eyed, so I could blend in. But he's brown, even browner after all the sun we got. There's no blending in for him. I link my arm even tighter with his, half to show support and half because I don't want to fall over.

Brynlee's still talking, the words flowing out of her in a continuous stream. ". . . views of the desert sky from the edge are just incredible. I'm from Salt Lake City, and I've gone hiking there, but the views here—"

"What are all these buildings?" I blurt. I don't care about desert views. I've seen enough of the desert to last me a lifetime.

She confirms that they're what I thought. "The ward has spent years and years preparing," she says, confirming what my dad said too. "We have enough food to last our whole population three years, and water, too, with a state-of-the-art water filtration and recycling system."

"I hope you have a good security system," Gabe says grimly.

Brynlee blinks at him, something clouding her eyes. I'm sure she doesn't like to think about it. That she and her loved ones will be safe here, fed and watered, while the outside world claws desperately at their gates. "We do," she says cautiously. She glances toward the wall.

It comes to me that all the noise I hear isn't coming from inside the wall, as I thought. I tune my ears as if I'm tuning a radio signal and realize, to my surprise: "There are people out there."

That cloudy look stays on Brynlee's face. "Yes. There are several people who have . . . camped out there." Maybe I was wrong. Maybe that cloudy look wasn't about not wanting to think about it.

Maybe it's from thinking about it too much.

"It was really good of you to save us," I say abruptly, like it's just occurred to me. It was totally random, and by all rights we should be dead out there, dried bones in the desert. Or camped out with the desperate souls pleading for entrance. I want to ask why they chose us and not them, but I can't bring myself to say anything, just in case she smacks her head and goes, *You're right, we'd better dump you out there.* "Thank you. Again."

Her face relaxes. "Brigham Young said, 'Go and bring in those people now on the plains.' The Bible says that to save one life is to save an entire world. We can't save the entire world." The clouds return. "But we could save you, two poor souls brought through the gate by my friend." I wonder if they would've saved us if that friend hadn't scooped us up. Probably not—we would've been just two more desperate souls on the other side of the wall.

I push that thought away and take careful mental notes as she shows us where the food stores are, a water tank, a warehouse for things like extra clothing and batteries. She notes that I can change into different clothes whenever I want to. "Oh, and this is the weapons room," she says, waving her hand at a building just as long as the others. "A distasteful business, but necessary."

No matter how distasteful, I perk up. "Can I see?"

Brynlee looks at me warily. She might have saved my life, but she doesn't trust me. She confirms it when she says, "We can look in from the outside."

Does she seriously think I'm going to grab a weapon and turn it on her? I'm almost insulted. Still, I don't argue with her, because arguing with her will allow me no weapons at all.

And these are *nice* weapons. My eyes rove hungrily over them, my fingers twitching with the desire to have one—or more—in my hands. Guns, freshly oiled and gleaming. Boxes and boxes of bullets. I don't love guns—my dad thought of them as easy mode compared with the more visceral use of a knife or crossbow, and he didn't like being dependent on diminishing ammunition—but they're better than nothing, and maybe you need some easy mode when the world's so hard. Elsewhere in the room there are knives, small and large and in between. Machetes. Rifles and shotguns. What look like hand grenades. And, saving the best for last . . .

Crossbows. A whole row of crossbows, shiny and poised and ready for action. My fingers curl, remembering how my own crossbow felt in my hands. It would be really nice to have it when we venture back out into the world. Especially considering we're both running from dangerous men and in pursuit of dangerous men. "Can I have one?" I ask.

"No." Brynlee gives me an odd look. "I can't give you a weapon. But we do have a manned range a bit farther down, if you'd like to practice shooting?"

Yes. That's exactly what I want to do. My curled fingers twitch.

"It's almost closed for the day, but I can take you tomorrow morning," Brynlee continues. "In the meantime, why don't you come to the cafeteria and have something to eat?"

I nudge Gabe as we walk to the cafeteria. "First thing tomorrow morning we're going to the range."

He glances at me sidelong. "Okay."

He doesn't sound that excited, and then I realize. . . . "Gabe," I say. "Have you ever shot before?"

He eyes me another moment, as if deciding how to respond, before shaking his head.

My dad would probably mutter something disgusted about having to carry another person. And I'd be lying if I said I didn't feel a flash of annoyance . . . but that flash quickly fizzles into something like relief. That I *am* bringing something to the table. That I'm *not* totally useless. "It's okay," I tell him. "I'll teach you."

Before he can reply, we reach the cafeteria. It's an odd hour, too late for lunch and too early for dinner, so there aren't many people spread out at the long tables. "I'll go get you some food," Brynlee says, motioning for us to sit down, but I resist. Even though my legs feel like overcooked noodles, there's no way I'm letting her know. So Gabe and I wait in line to have some beef stroganoff and creamy potatoes ladled onto our trays. I walk carefully back to our table to keep the brimming glass of cool water from overflowing. Just the force of placing the tray gently on the surface makes drops spill over the rim. I lower my face down to the tray to slurp them up, lapping like a dog.

When I lift my head, there's a familiar face sitting before me. It's Ronan, the kid from earlier in the hallway. He's got a salad before him, slicked with oil, and a wobbling bowl of Jell-O. I eye the salad curiously. There's no way they're farming out here in the desert, not with the amount of water it would require, and greens wouldn't last long enough even in refrigeration to still be edible. They must have a hydroponics farm in one of these buildings, where they're growing various vegetables and herbs and maybe even medicinal plants with only water, nutrients, and electrical grow lights. I wonder how much gasoline they have stored for the number of generators they must need.

"Did you want some salad?" Ronan asks. "I see you staring. It's not bad."

I shake my head. Salad is the last thing I need right now—I need fat, and calories, and carbs. I need to give my weakened body all the things it needs to rebuild itself. Quickly. As if illustrating the point, I shove a forkful of beef stroganoff into my mouth and chew. It's a little salty, but good.

Gabe sits beside me and chows down. Brynlee sits across from us, then waves at someone across the room. "You don't mind if I step away for a bit, do you?" I smile at her, my mouth full, and she pops up to go talk to an older woman eating cereal.

Ronan leans over the table toward us. "So, where you folks from?"

"LA," I say. Maybe not LA proper, but close enough. Gabe nods as he continues to shovel in the food. He has some biscuits on his tray too. I can't believe I didn't see them.

Ronan's face brightens. He sets his forkful of salad down. "LA, huh? What was that like?"

Gabe and I exchange a glance. In unison, we shrug. "I don't know," I say, because his mouth is still full. It's really impressive how quickly he can shovel it down. "It was home."

"But there's so much going on there, right? So many different types of people?" His eyebrows are raised. It's like he wants us to tell him something in particular, but I have no idea what it is.

"Sure," I say, hedging my bets. I shove a bite of potatoes into my mouth and nearly swoon at the amount of cream and butter clearly in there. "Lots of different types of people."

"And you must have friends of all types, right?"

I glance over at Gabe again, but Gabe has his head down close to his food. He's abandoned me to this bizarre conversation. *Thanks, pal.* "I . . . guess?" I mean, Estella may have been my only real friend, but I *did* know people of "all types" from school. Whatever that means.

Ronan nods enthusiastically. "Cool. Cool."

He's been asking me and Gabe questions this whole time. It's a rule of polite conversation that I should be asking questions back, right? "Um . . . so you're . . . from here?"

"Not here exactly," Ronan says. His enthusiasm fades; even his hair seems to droop. "But a small town not too far over the Utah border. Not more than a few hundred people. Three hundred and twelve, it said on the welcome sign, but a few of the old folks died since that sign was made."

"Wow, three hundred people," I say. "That's, like, the size of my neighborhood." He looks starstruck, so I go on. "That's, like, half the size of my class at school." His eyes widen even farther.

"How we doing over here?" Brynlee appears at the head of the table, beaming over all of us.

Ronan leaps up, leaving his salad nearly untouched. "I'm fixing to go to work."

"You'd better be off, then," Brynlee says. Ronan scurries away. She looks at his tray and sighs. "Shame on that boy, wasting food like that."

Gabe holds out his hands. "I'll eat it."

Brynlee and I both watch with amusement as he scrapes the bowl clean.

36

I'm still sure that I'm ready to get out of here, but my body disagrees. When I rise from the cafeteria table, it's all I can do to stand without falling over.

"You went through a real ordeal," Brynlee says sympathetically. "You can't expect to be up and at 'em right away."

But I can. Irrationally, I'm angry at my body. If I had only been in better shape before this whole thing happened, maybe I'd already have found Estella. Maybe I'd have been able to push through the heatstroke and dehydration until we found water.

It's easier to be mad at a collection of muscles and bones and blood than be mad at myself. I should've listened to my dad earlier. Stopped pushing his voice away.

But I can't go back in time, and now will have to be good enough. So I wake Gabe up early the next morning to make him go for a jog with me around the edges of the ward, which is surrounded by a wall, manned at every gate, with barbed wire on top.

As we round back to our home base, I'm struggling, each leg screaming in agony as I gasp for breath. Gabe moves a little easier, but he's still breathing hard. When Brynlee shows up, her forehead creased in concern, it's all we can do to stagger behind her to the cafeteria for eggs and bacon and grits. I wolf them all down, though I'm feeling vaguely nauseous.

Ronan stops by our table just as I'm chewing on the last of my bacon. "Morning!" he says, giving us a funny little head bob. "What are you up to today?"

"The weapons range," I say immediately.

I expect to get a look from him like the one I got from Brynlee, but he lights up instead. "What a coincidence, that's where I'm headed too," he says. "Brynlee, I can take them if you want."

It takes Brynlee a second to hear him; she's deep in conversation with an older woman at the end of the table. But when he gives her a poke, she looks over with a distracted smile. "Sure, go on ahead."

The range is everything I hoped and dreamed it would be. It's mostly empty, a long stretch of empty dirt with distances marked on the sand and all sorts of targets propped up against the wall. Maybe most of the people here are pacifists, or maybe they all already know how to use weapons and don't need the practice. In any case, Gabe, Ronan, and I are the only ones here besides the two guys checking the weapons in and out, making sure they don't disappear. Ronan exchanges some jokes with them, selects a shotgun, walks a comfortable distance away from the targets. He cocks his gun. Shoots. Nails the target three times in the center. Nods confidently. "Not bad."

"Not bad?" My mouth falls open. "You're an excellent shot."

He doesn't thank me, just smiles self-consciously and sets the gun aside. "Only get so many bullets for practice. I have to work on my bow skills, too."

As he starts shooting again, this time with a bow, I turn to Gabe. "Okay, let's pick our weapons."

I go for a crossbow, of course. A wooden one, shiny with the number of fingers that have rubbed over it, slightly too big for my hands. Still, I hold it lovingly against my chest.

It feels a little like coming home.

Gabe surveys the weapons on offer, his forehead creased. "I don't know."

"Why don't you start with a crossbow like me? I like crossbows because you can keep going with a fixed amount of ammo, as long as you can recover your bolts from where you shot. Can't do that with a gun. And I doubt they'll let us have enough bullets to practice for real. They probably want to save them, like Ronan said."

He blinks, considering. I would think him totally calm, except that his thumbnail is scraping the palm of his opposite hand. "Okay. Sure."

"Just pretend we're storming the skyscraper," I say.

I can't ignore the total lack of enthusiasm in his voice. "It's different in real life."

"You're just shooting at a target."

"But that's not why we're practicing," he says flatly. "We're practicing to put a bolt in an actual human being."

A shiver runs down my spine, leaving nausea in its wake. Because he's right. Shooting a real, actual human being is a thousand—no, a million—times different from shooting a fake person in a video game. Gabe had seemed all about it in his fury back at the stadium, but now the reality's set in. For one, a real person's blood doesn't turn into purple sparkles in the air—it pools around them in a sticky red-brown sludge, and when there's a lot of it, it makes the air taste like copper. And a real person's body doesn't fade away after their last breath. It crumples to the ground with a sickening thud, and it bends in ways no body should bend, and it—

"Zara? Are you okay?"

As Gabe touches my shoulder, I realize I'm heaving. All around me is green, and the birds are silent, and—

"Zara!"

There are no birds here, I remind myself. Not here in the middle of the desert. Other than the vultures who wanted to eat us. And bizarrely enough, that's the one little detail that recenters me back on this weapons range.

I force a smile. "Watch how I do it."

I pretend I'm moving slowly on purpose, though really it's because it's been so long since I've done any of this. Lowering the crossbow to the ground, stepping on it to cock it. Bringing it back up to load the bolt into it. Lifting it even higher to aim it, looking carefully at the center of the target. And, finally, hitting the trigger. *Thwip.*

The bolt punches into the side of the target. I roll my shoulders, clearing my throat so that I don't loose a few curses. Just a few years ago, I could've hit the center with my eyes closed.

"That was awesome." Gabe's voice actually sounds as if it's full of awe. Which makes my shoulders uncurl, my chin lift a little higher.

"It's really nothing," I say. The truth. "Here, let me show you."

Cocking it is the most complex part of it: it's several motions you have to do just right, the crossbow on the ground with your foot in the stirrup, or else you can damage the bow or misalign the ropes, which means your shot will go far and wide. So I stand right behind him, my cheek up against his back. Even through the scent of the industrial detergent on the clothes they gave us, I can smell the Gabe smell I used to breathe in in his car, that distinct blend of spice and soap and a little bit of sweat. It smells familiar. Like safety.

Like home.

I take in another deep breath, then reach my arms around him to adjust his. He's tense up against me, careful in how he moves so that he doesn't accidentally elbow me or step on my foot. "You have to make sure the strings are exactly even on either side of the barrel."

He makes some adjustments, pulls tight. "Like this?"

"Almost." I gesture to the right one. "That one's a bit off."

Gabe leans over. I can't see his face, but I imagine he's squinting. He nods, then tightens the right string. "I didn't even notice."

There's that sound of awe in his voice again. It makes me feel . . . I don't even know. It's something like uncomfortable, but it's not bad. It's something I'm not used to hearing directed at me.

"Good," I say, to distract myself from all of it. "Now bring it up, pull it until you hear the clicks. No, make sure you're pulling both ropes at the same . . ." I reach out to help, and my hand brushes his. My arm tenses at the feeling, but he doesn't yank his away. They touch all the way up. We've touched before on this journey, of course, but only at times that were necessary.

This doesn't feel necessary. It feels . . .

I clear my throat again to distract myself, though this time it's from the warming in my cheeks. "Good," I say again. "Now you'll want to load it. No! The odd-colored fletching should face down. Like this. Right."

He's clumsy, but he gets it in. "This is way easier online," he says. "Where all you have to do is click a few buttons."

"A lot of things are easier online." Like talking to people. Like dying. If you die in *Dark Avengers*, you respawn minus a few experience points and armor durability. "Now, once you turn off the safety, you should make sure your finger isn't on the trigger until you actually want to fire. And make sure the bow is always pointing down again until you fire."

"Like this?"

"Yeah." I move back so that he has room to bring the crossbow up, and now that we're not touching, another spark of irritation flashes through me at the thought that I could be refining my own form right now, scrubbing off all the rust until my skills shine. That's what my dad would say, anyway. Maybe that irritation I feel is my dad's.

Because my brain cocks its figurative head at it, creases its figurative brows. It's like it's saying, *You might not be alive without Gabe. So* what *if you take a little time teaching him how to shoot?*

I don't know which half is right, so I just focus on helping him aim. "I like to close one eye, especially when you're using one of these older ones without a scope," I direct. "Aim well, and shoot when you're ready."

Thwip. His finger twitches on the trigger, and the crossbow bolt flies straight and true. If only his aim had been just as straight and true—it sails right over the top of the target, thudding against the wall behind it.

I can't help it. I snort a laugh. Gabe steps back, lowering the crossbow and shaking his head, but he's smiling too. "It was my first time!"

"Thanks for making me feel better about how rusty I've gotten," I say.

"Anytime." He trots over to the wall to retrieve the bolt. "Okay, let's try again."

We take turns loading and aiming and shooting. After an hour or so, my arms are tired and aching, but I'm hitting the bull's-eye half the time, and Gabe is . . . well, Gabe's hitting the target half the time. It's progress. "You're not doing too bad," I say.

"Says the crossbow star!" Gabe says. "I'm extremely impressed."

You'd think that would make me happy to hear, but I'm left with that kind of jumpy, uncomfortable-like feeling again. Maybe because he's not really complimenting *me*—he's complimenting the things I got from my dad.

But why wouldn't that make me happy? I need those things now. I need them if I'm going to keep the two of us alive.

I turn away from Gabe and face the wall. "I told you my dad has this survivalist compound out east, and that I spent a lot of time there as a kid," I say. "But . . . there was more than that."

I imagine his eyes on my face, which makes my cheeks heat even more. "There were a lot of lessons I had to learn," I say. "I shot my crossbow until my hands bled. I tracked game through the woods, or sat up in the blind waiting for them to come by, until I was dehydrated and ready to pass out. That's why I'm so good at shooting."

"That . . . doesn't sound healthy," Gabe says cautiously, and the way he says it kind of makes me want to collapse in relief. Again, I don't know exactly why. Because it's good I know these things. It's good I have these skills. "Do you want to talk more about it?"

"I . . ." The words stick in my throat. I'm not sure what to say. I do kind of want to talk more about it. To unload all these feelings weighing me down.

But I'm not sure I want to revisit what's hiding under them.

Either fortunately or not so fortunately, I'm saved from having to respond by the sound of an explosion. I instinctively duck for cover, grabbing Gabe's hand and pulling him down with me, but once we aren't hit over the head by falling debris, I straighten back up. "What was that?"

Ronan responds from the other end of the range. I almost forgot he was there. "It sounded like it was coming from outside the wall."

My stomach clenches. The people camped out there. They'd be getting thirsty now. Desperate. "What do you think it was?"

Ronan shrugs. "I don't know. But I'd better go check in at the gate." He moves past us in a hurry.

It's not until he's already gone that I notice he's brought the shotgun with him.

Over the next few weeks we keep practicing with the crossbows. I hit the target every time. Gabe gets closer. We jog in circles inside the wall, trying to ignore the increasingly loud noises on the other side, the weapons now carried by the guards. Every day I ask Gabe when we can leave. Every day he tells me we need to be stronger if we're going to make it out there. And I don't argue, because as much as I want to get going, I know he's right.

"You should stay," Brynlee tells us at dinner one evening. We've just finished a jog, and our clothes are soaked through with sweat. We sit down at the table and immediately chug a bottle of water each. I still can't stop marveling at the slippery feel of it at the back of my throat, the way it slides into my stomach and quenches that desperate thirst. "This thing doesn't look like it's going to blow over anytime soon." By "this thing," I'm not sure she means the people clamoring outside or the fall of civilization. "We can get you jobs. Two strong young people is worth going through supplies a little faster. And if you stay, we can move you out of your rooms. The dormitories for single men and women are really much nicer than where you are now."

I don't answer. How can I repay her charity by telling her we need to venture back out into the inhospitable desert where we nearly died as soon as we're strong enough?

And we're nearly strong enough.

"Thank you so much for your kindness," Gabe says. "We really appreciate it."

Damn, he's good at peopling. From the way Brynlee smiles, it's obvious he flattered her, maybe even made her think that we would indeed stay. But he didn't actually answer. I take notes for the future.

At least, until Ronan sidles up to our table, tray of food in hand. Brynlee's busy chatting with a few other girls, so when he leans in, we're the only ones within earshot. "I might be overstepping here, but y'all didn't seem all that committed to staying."

I wait for Gabe to expertly people our way out of this, but he doesn't say anything. Glancing over, I realize he's in the circle with Brynlee and the other girls. I stare at them maybe a moment too long, not sure how I feel about them all laughing together.

"Zara?" Ronan prompts.

Turning back to him, I shrug. "Everybody here has been so kind to us," I say, echoing Gabe from before.

Ronan studies me. "But . . . ?"

"But nothing," I say brusquely. "I don't know." And I shove a mouthful of chicken casserole into my face so he won't ask me any more questions.

But he doesn't stop studying me, like he knows exactly what I wanted to say.

37

With all the exertion and the good, heavy food, I've been sleeping like a log at night. Well, a log with lots of little animals in it that stir it every so often, because after the compound I can never truly sleep like a log. Still, it's unusual when I jerk awake one night, my heart pounding a hundred miles an hour, sweat pearling all over my forehead.

I sit up straight, taking deep breaths, trying to calm myself down. There's the echo of a sound in my ears, but all I hear now is the whoosh of blood in my head. *You must have had a nightmare,* I tell myself. *That's it. Go back to sleep.*

But there's no way I can fall back to sleep like this. I get up for a drink of water, and that's when I hear it again. An explosion. A small one, not like the entire wall of the compound is coming down . . . but like *something* is going down.

Instinctively, I grab for my pack and my crossbow. I find my pack; of course I don't find my crossbow. My pack will have to do.

Gabe is already in the hallway, his pack slung over his own shoulder. I raise an eyebrow, impressed. "You're learning."

"From the best."

I hold his gaze for a moment, surprised. He looks back at me steadily. That's what he's been this whole time: steady. Steady by my side.

I don't know what I'd have done without him, I'm even more surprised to realize.

Another boom from the direction of the gate. Gabe says, "That doesn't sound good."

"We should be ready to run," I reply, my stomach filling with ice. Because what could those explosions be, other than people trying to get in? Trying to bust down the wall and come inside to take water and food and everything else our rescuers have?

The worst part is that I can't even fault them. I can't fault anyone on either side of the wall. The people on the inside want to protect what they have; if they give too much of it away, they won't have enough for themselves, and they'll die. The people on the outside are desperate: it's either break down this gate and get inside, or die.

Like all of them, I'll do whatever it takes not to die.

Even if that means stealing. *It's not* really *stealing,* I tell myself, and then say it out loud to Gabe, as if looking for affirmation. "It's only to protect ourselves in case the wall goes down," I say, because we'll definitely want weapons if that happens. And from the way the ground shook after that last explosion . . . well. I think we're going to want weapons.

Though it's the middle of the night, lights are blazing and people are rushing around as we exit the building. And yes, people are armed. We follow the general flow of people to the weapons shed, whose doors are flung wide open now. I'm pretty sure I have stars in my eyes as I take everything in. Not just with my eyes, but with my hands. I run them over the smooth butts of rifles, the wicked blades of knives, the flight groove of the nearest crossbow.

I know before my fingers even touch it that it's mine.

It's smaller than the other ones, perfect for my smaller hands, and it's not wooden, like some of the crossbows by its side. No. This one is shiny silver and black, and even though I know it won't blend into the forests and deserts and plains we'll need to cross as well as some of its wooden cousins, it reminds me a little bit of the legendary enchanted flaming crossbow my character has in *Dark Avengers*. Except not flaming, obviously. In real life that would probably be bad.

"That's the last crossbow," Gabe says.

Somebody shoulders me out of the way as they reach for a gun. I give the back of their head the stink eye. "That's probably for the best. Your skills still need work."

His eyes widen as he looks around. "I have no idea what to do." But he steps toward the guns.

"You're probably best off with something else," I say. "Something you don't have to worry about loading and aiming, or finding more ammo for. You're big and strong. Pick something big you'll feel comfortable holding."

His fingers linger on a knife before grabbing the handle of a machete.

"All right," he says.

Just in time. Because at that moment a great shout echoes over the space outside, followed by an even greater crack. We rush out the door to see an enormous plume of dust rising over a collapsed section of wall. People from our side rush to the opening as people from the outside rush through the new hole.

I raise my crossbow, instinctively ready to defend what's ours, but hesitate. Because the people pouring through aren't evil, black-masked intruders who want to murder us, the way my dad always said they'd be.

They're just dirty, gaunt, desperate people. Men, women, and children. The elderly. Some people hobbling, some hoisting big sticks in the air.

I lower my crossbow, mouth open with dismay. I can't shoot them.

I don't know what I'd have done if somebody else hadn't stepped through the wall after them. A man, the only one of them clutching a real weapon, a big black gun. He swivels in place, looking around—I'm not sure for what, but his eyes land on me.

I freeze. He stares at me. I stare at him, and at the vine tattoos crawling from the collar of his shirt.

38

If I really think about it, it's not an insane coincidence. Gabe and I left a trail of people who saw us—everybody at the Rose Bowl; Avi from the gas station; the couple who robbed us in the car; everybody who drove past us as we were walking on the side of the road.

But *why* has he tracked me all the way here from where he left me sitting up in that tree, holding my breath?

The man's lips curl into a smile. He takes a step toward me.

My hands are shaking too hard to aim my crossbow. "We have to run." I pull hard on Gabe's arm as I step back. *Damn.* The man is blocking the hole in the wall, and now he's raising his gun, and—

I pull Gabe behind a building before he can shoot. I don't know if the man wants me alive or dead, but I can't take any chances. "That's the guy who came after me," I hiss through my teeth as we run. Where are we running? I don't know. The whole compound is encircled by a wall, and he's blocking the only hole. Maybe we can run around in a circle to get behind him and then slip out the hole?

No. Our rescuers are probably blocking it off even now. Panic claws at my insides. We're mice trapped in a cage with a cat. There's only so long we can put this off.

"There's got to be another way out," Gabe says. We're still running, but the exertion is already tightening my chest. I'm not at a hundred percent. I can't run very long. I tug Gabe behind a building and flatten myself against the wall, gasping for breath. We just have to figure out what to do. There's got to be something to—

"Did I hear y'all talking about getting out?"

I turn to see Ronan standing there, his pale hair silvery in the moonlight. He looks at us with a blank expression, or maybe it's caution, not allowing us to see what he's thinking. I open my mouth to explain what I meant, then hesitate. Because not only will what I have to say take too long to get into, but it doesn't exactly paint me in the best light. I've brought trouble upon them with my very presence.

But as it turns out, it doesn't matter. "I can help you escape," Ronan says breathlessly. "I was actually coming to find you. It's the perfect time, with all the commotion."

Well, that's unexpected. I exchange a glance with Gabe. He looks as mystified as I feel. "Why would you do that?"

Ronan shuffles his feet, and I realize he's got a pack on his back, one as stuffed as and likely heavier than ours. The spout of a water bottle pokes out from the top. "And I won't just get you through the gate. You almost died in the desert before, didn't you? You'll die for real if you run out there with no plan. I have maps, and I know the area. I know exactly where we are, and you don't. There's a tributary of the Colorado River a half day's walk from here. If we stay along that, it'll take us to the Colorado River itself, and there are hiking trails along there too."

"Heading east?" Gabe murmurs.

Ronan nods eagerly. That's enough to unsettle a cloud of suspicion around him. Around me. I ask, "What's in it for you?"

Because no matter how often people claim to be doing something out of generosity or altruistic purposes, there's always a catch. There's always something in it for them, whether that's billionaires donating to charity to get their name on a building or my mom volunteering at the local women's shelter because it made her feel good to help people in need. The more people protest, the more it's usually true.

Except maybe for the people who saved us and brought us here. They never even introduced themselves to us. I hope they didn't include the guy to whom I gave the stink eye back in the weapons shed.

Though Ronan doesn't even try to pretend he's doing this only for us. "I have to come with you," he says. "There's a hidden gate in the side for emergencies. You need me to find it. Also, if you don't take me, I'll sound the alarm."

My fingers tighten on the crossbow. "You don't want to do that."

"You're right, I don't," he says. "I want to go with you on your trip. I know where to go, and I have a lot in my pack that I bet you don't. Like, do you have electrolyte tablets?" He must see the *no* in our faces. "They'll help you hold on to water. Important when water's scarce."

"You know it's going to be dangerous, right?" Gabe asks. "Do you even know where we're—"

"You can come," I say. Gabe shoots me a surprised look, but I only shrug in response. We don't have time to parse his motive or try to warn him away. We have to get out of here. If Ronan decides he's not up for it after we get through the gate, then he can always turn back.

Still, I hold the crossbow firm before me. "If you're doing this to trick us for some reason, to deliver us to that guy, I swear to God I'll shoot you first," I say. He doesn't have to know I don't believe in God. "In the throat. You'll die slowly, choking on your own blood. We might go down, but you'll go down with us."

Ronan shudders. I hope it's not because he's planning to betray us. Probably not. Probably anyone being warned they could die choking on their own blood would shudder at the thought. "I swear, this isn't a trick," he says. "I have to get out of here, and I can't go on my own. I don't even care where we go. You're the only outsiders— well, friendly outsiders—I'm likely to meet in the next few years."

I don't know if I'd call myself "friendly," and I think he's pretty wild for calling me that, considering I did just threaten to kill him slowly and painfully, but whatever. "Okay. Let's go."

I brace myself to find the man waiting for me, skeletal grin on his face, as we round the other corner, but there's just the same sense of general commotion as before. There isn't the sound of gunshots, at least. Maybe everyone will be able to talk this through.

Ronan leads us on a zigzag through the warren of storehouses, hesitating each time before bolting out into the open. My esteem for him rises the longer he takes us without getting spotted.

Though it's also probably because we're going in the opposite direction the man would expect from us. Not toward the hole in the wall, not the main gate, not the main area of the compound, where we might be able to hide. We're racing for the very back.

Still, isn't it kind of odd he didn't follow us?

No matter. I slow as Ronan pauses beside a section of the wall that doesn't look any different from the sections around it, aside from a thin black line in a rough door shape. Of course, the effect of innocuousness is kind of ruined by the armed guy standing guard in front of it.

I heft my crossbow. "How are we getting past? Should I shoot him?"

Gabe and Ronan both jump, staring at me with horror like I suggested killing him. Which . . . okay, I see how they could've gotten that impression. "Just through the leg or something!" I clarify. "Something that won't kill him, just stop him from following us or sounding the alarm."

Ronan is still looking at me like he just realized I'm a ghost. Or a serial killer.

Maybe he's finally realizing just what he got himself into.

"*No,*" he says, his voice loud enough that the guy at the gate turns around. "*Don't hurt him.* I can talk us through. Just wait here."

We obediently wait up against the side of the nearest storehouse, my crossbow raised, because I *will* hurt him if I have to. Gabe looks a lot less certain with his hand on his machete. Maybe I should have let him take a gun after all. Somehow it feels a lot easier to shoot someone from a safe distance than to slice into them up close with a heavy blade.

Ronan hurries over to the guy, who doesn't look that much older than us. They bow their heads together, speaking quietly; no matter how hard I try, I can't hear anything they're saying.

I shift restlessly on my feet. This is taking too long. The guy Ronan's talking to shakes his head, then reaches up to his eye and swipes. Is he . . . crying? Just as I'm starting to worry, he leans in and gives Ronan a huge hug. When he pulls back and wipes his eye again, he speaks a little less quietly. "Good luck," he says. "I hope I see you again."

"You will," Ronan says. "Stay safe."

His chest rises and falls with a deep breath, then he turns toward us and motions us over. I cringe as I step into the open, but nobody shoots at us or tackles us to the ground. We just hurry over to the gate. Ronan steps through, me after him, but Gabe pauses for a moment to look back at the guard. "Thank you," he says.

The guard nods. The second we're on outside ground, relief rushes through me. We're safe. Well, not quite safe. There are still lots of ways we could die in the very near future. But as long as we—

"Hey!"

The shout comes from behind us. I spin, my stomach falling, to see him, lurking outside the wall. Waiting for us, those vine tattoos clawing to get at me.

39

He knew. He knew where we were going.

Of course he knew, Zara, says my dad's disapproving whisper. *He's probably been out here for days casing the entire joint. As soon as he saw you running in that direction, he knew where you'd go.*

This is bad.

I spin back around. "RUN!" I shout at Gabe and Ronan, but I don't wait to see if they're coming before bolting myself. It's a random direction. In the distance there are rock formations, large and twisted enough that maybe we can hide in them somewhere. I don't know, now that we've been spotted, but it's the only hope I have.

Gabe lopes easily ahead—but not too far ahead, not far enough where I'm afraid he might leave me behind. Ronan takes the rear. And behind him? I don't look to see who is following behind.

I miss the trees of my youth—I feel way too exposed here, with nothing but dust shielding me from the spotlight of the moon. I streak across the ground, my feet skipping lightly over the packed red sand, but that won't help me hide.

I can already hear the footsteps pounding behind me.

I know it might make me lose a precious half second, but I still glance over my shoulder. The man with the vine tattoos is following us, his head down, his gait easy. He's gaining on us with every step, but it's just him, no one else.

A burst of energy jolts me forward. Maybe we can survive this after all.

Relief follows the energy as we dive into the warren of rock structures. The curving, twisting columns of red rock and granite climb up toward the sky, smaller pieces of them littering the ground beneath. Maybe we can get deep enough into them and hide. I mean, I'm already wilting. Adrenaline is driving me forward, but it's only going to last so long. I need to stop soon.

But he'll never stop chasing us. He will comb every little bit of this warren as we sit here and slowly wither away from thirst. And we can't spend so much time here that we deplete our water supply. We need to make it to the tributary of the Colorado River, and if I've learned anything so far, dehydration in the desert can down you pretty quickly.

No, I need to fight. What would my dad say? What would he do?

The memory's one I relived recently, so maybe that's why it bubbles up now. It's the one I thought about when I slept in the shed, where my dad pretended to be an intruder and sent me on a run for my life.

And then I know exactly what I need to do.

I scan the rock formations around me for one that looks sturdy. That one would tip with my weight on it, that one has a menacing crack in the middle, that one—ah! Yes, that one should work.

I skid to a stop and begin to climb. It's not incredibly tall, getting me maybe ten feet or fifteen feet off the ground, but that's all I need.

Gabe stops beneath me, goggling up. "What are you doing? Should I climb one too?"

I gesture to his feet. "Hand me that rock, then take Ronan and hide somewhere nearby."

I love him for not questioning me. He hands me the rock—nice and heavy, perfect, the size of a human head—and disappears.

It's not long before the sound of thumping footsteps follows. "Where are you, Zara Ross?" the man mutters under his breath. He comes into view, dressed in camo. He has his rifle at his side. My head whirls at the sight of it, nearly tipping me off the rock formation.

I'm not a killer. This *is* self-defense. I don't know what he thinks I've done, but I don't have time to stop and ask him—he can't be in his right mind anyway if he thinks I've done something bad enough for him to chase me to a different state. Still, I hesitate as he comes within range. *Zara, Gabe and Ronan are nearby!* I scream at myself, but my hands don't move. *If you can't do it for yourself, do it for them!*

My fingers don't start to loosen until I hear my dad, an echo of those words he said to me so long ago. *My only critique is that you should not have waited to attack. You should have hurled whatever you had at me as soon as I came within range. I would have dodged it, but a normal person would not have.*

I hurl the rock, reaching immediately for my crossbow in case I miss.

I don't miss.

The rock hits his head with a dull thud, and he drops like a stone. He hasn't been knocked out, though; I hear him groan. I clamber down from the rock formation and hit the ground just as Gabe and Ronan peer from around the corner, their eyes widening at the sight of the man at my feet.

The man moans something indistinguishable, wincing. There's some blood on his head, but I haven't dented his skull or smashed it in or done something totally irreversible. My aim must have been slightly off, hitting the side of his head rather than his head full on.

I find myself relieved.

"Okay, let's go," I say, just as the man starts to pull himself up.

"He's going to follow us," Gabe says.

"There's only one real place to go around here if you want water," Ronan says. He means that the man will know exactly where to go when he follows us.

My dad would say, *Kill him, Zara. You cannot live with a threat constantly hanging over your shoulder.*

I raise my crossbow. No hesitation.

I fire.

The man cries out as the bolt goes straight through the meat of his calf. Nausea roils my stomach at the sound.

You never forget the sound of something punching through skin and muscle, shattering bone. Or the screech a person makes when you pull your crossbow bolt back out and the blood starts to flow.

Ronan makes a choked noise. Gabe looks away, his jaw set. I lower the crossbow with a grim nod. "He won't be following us now," I say. I look down at the man, am briefly tempted to question him, but that would involve waiting until he sobers up. We need to get out of here ASAP. "You should be able to drag yourself back to the ward. Maybe they'll take care of you once they clear things up." I look back at the others, but still speak to the man. "This was your warning shot. If I ever see you again, it'll be through the heart."

The man mutters something that sounds a little more like words, but I don't stop to listen. I stride off into the night, Gabe and Ronan close behind and the man left bleeding into the sand, making those red rocks a little redder.

40

I start to breathe a bit easier as we leave the rock warren behind. "So we're going to a tributary of the river?" I say to Ronan.

He doesn't need a compass or a map. He's moving faster now, as if he can't wait to leave the man behind. "Yep."

Putting my trust in someone I barely know is disconcerting. I ration the water Ronan gives me as we spend the remaining cool hours of the night and a few warmer hours of the morning following him, keeping mental track of every landmark we pass just in case we have to turn back. As we walk, Gabe and I tell Ronan all about what happened to Estella and her parents, where we're going, how we need to find them. Ronan nods along.

Some green starts to sprout up as we continue our trek over the red sand, hiking downhill over steep rocks. At first it's not a ton of green—no trees or bushes—just some tall grass and small, spiky desert shrubs we have to pick our way over. Later there are a few trees, thicker and greener. And then there's the river itself. I sigh at the sight of water, immediately reaching for the closest bottle and drinking all I have, then stumbling down the rest of the steep slope to fill it up. I'll drop a tablet inside to make sure it's safe to drink.

"So we'll travel along here for a while, until we hit Lake Mead," Ronan says. "Then from there, along the Colorado River east. We can talk to people and see if we can get any intel on your family. We should be careful with our food. If we're lucky, we might find some big sheep or antelope, but we probably won't get lucky."

"You never know," Gabe says, but I'm nodding along. Partially to disguise the way my legs are shaking with exhaustion. I still haven't completely recovered from almost dying and then spending a week in bed and then fighting for my life, and I'm starting to feel it.

"I like that there are trees near the water," Ronan says. "Shelter and shade."

I look around. I'm surprised by the emptiness—in a desert area like this, I'd expect to see a lot more people near the water. "Where *is* everybody?"

Ronan looks at my grimly. "You were in the ward for almost a month. That's a lot of time out here. Do you . . . really want to know?"

I nod quickly again, even as Gabe looks queasy. In my mind, it's a lot better to know things than not know things. No matter what they are.

Ronan sighs. "Okay, then. We should keep walking. We can rest when it gets really hot."

He's right. We start walking along the river, Ronan double-checking with his compass that we're heading in the right direction. And then, against a backdrop of dramatic red rocks and majestic mountains, Ronan tells us what he knows about the world outside.

"There are bodies," he says. "Bodies everywhere."

The people in the ward have stayed put for the most part, avoiding the danger, but they do have a satellite linkup working with a generator for a few hours a day. What they've heard on it defies all belief. It's like I said earlier—when the water goes, people start to go too.

Especially out here in the drought-stricken West and Southwest. People out east might have more borrowed time, but here we don't have enough water to support the population. No rain. Few water sources, even fewer clean ones. People got sick from drinking unclean water, or died in fights over the water sources, or suffered severe dehydration after either being unable to find or being turned away from pools or reservoirs or lakes. Assuming there's water left in them. A lake might seem huge, but with thousands of people on its shores, it runs out pretty quickly, even assuming no feces works its way into the water and makes everybody sick.

Hence what Ronan said. "Bodies everywhere."

And of course, with bodies everywhere come lots of other things everywhere. Sickening rot. Scavenging animals. More diseases.

Still, I'm surprised we don't see more people as we trudge along the river. We do see some—other hikers picking their way east or west, looking suspiciously at us before nodding in greeting or giving us a muted "hey"; and there's the occasional growl of a car up above the rim. I guess this river is kind of out of the way for people, distant from a lot of population centers. If you had a car, you wouldn't stop here—you'd keep driving. And if you didn't have a car . . . well, you'd probably be dead before you made it here.

I make it about an hour and a half before I collapse.

One second I'm focusing carefully on putting one foot in front of the other, and the next my legs are buckling under me and I can't stop it. The most I can do is control the direction of my fall, so that I drop to my knees and hands like I've suddenly decided to crawl all the way east. Except there's no way I can crawl. Even my arms are shaking now. Shaking and burning.

I don't cry out, so it takes Gabe and Ronan a moment to notice my footsteps are no longer thumping along with theirs. I lower my head, not wanting to see the expressions on their faces as they look at me buckled on the ground. Scorn, surely. They'll be shaking their heads, reevaluating why they wanted to bring me along, considering leaving me here to rot on the shores of the river. Hopefully not too close to the river itself; my rotting body would pollute the water for everybody else.

Strong arms circle me; now that my bones and muscles don't have to perform all the work of keeping me up anymore, I melt into those arms. Gabe's arms. For some reason I'm certain that they'll hold me up, and then I glance at him and see him looking down at me with worry. Fear. Not scorn. Not leaving me behind. Why did I think he would?

"Get her some water," Gabe says over his shoulder to Ronan. Ronan nods and reaches into his pack for his water bottle, then thrusts it in my direction without a thought. His own water bottle. Even though I have water in my pack, he's giving me his own supply.

My dad would hate him, would think he's an idiot for potentially putting himself in danger to save another person. . . .

But maybe my dad would be wrong.

I blink. That's a thought that hasn't entered my head before, and it makes me squirmy. Too squirmy to really think about, because I don't have the energy to squirm. So I push it away, let Gabe bring Ronan's water bottle to my lips. I sip a few mouthfuls, then turn away. "It's not the water."

"You might be dehydrated." Gabe's eyes are so tender, so caring, that they burn my face. I can't look right at him. Though I know he's wrong, I take another sip just to push down the lump in my throat.

Ronan reaches out and pinches the skin on the back of my hand. "It's not dehydration. See, the skin here would stick together if it was."

I wipe my mouth with the back of my hand. I know exactly what's going on, but I don't want to admit to it. Because what if I'm wrong about them leaving me behind, and they do?

Tears prick my eyes. No. Oh, no. *Crying is a waste of water, Zara.* I turn my head so the others can't see me, but I can't stop the tears from beginning to roll down my cheeks.

"Oh, you're crying," Ronan says. He sounds uncomfortable. "Losing water. I'm . . . going to refill our water bottles. Be back in a bit." And he beats it.

But Gabe doesn't. He settles onto the ground beside me and rests my head against his shoulder. "You're not totally recovered yet, are you? Your body's still weak."

I turn my head so that my cheek is right up against his compound-issued white shirt. I hope they're okay back there. That they came to some kind of understanding, that they're not all going to die in the desert.

"It's okay," Gabe says. His voice is gentle. "You could've just said something, so that we didn't push on so fast."

When I speak, my own voice is froggy. "We have to push on fast. We have to get to your family. And away from the guy chasing me."

"It's no good moving fast if we're going to die doing it," Gabe says.

I let his words wash over me. They feel . . . strange. Like stepping into a shower you expect to feel nice and lukewarm only to find the water scalding hot. My dad would say he's wrong, obviously. That I can't show any weakness, because weakness gets you killed. Which makes sense if you're looking at it from an analytical perspective. It would make sense for Gabe and Ronan to leave me behind, because my current weakness is slowing them down.

But . . . maybe the world doesn't operate entirely according to my dad's perspective? I have to think about this more, but not now. Now I raise my face to Gabe's, allow him to see the tears dripping down my cheeks, and somehow the mere act of showing them to him, of not trying to hide them, makes me feel a little bit better. Especially when he reaches out his thumb and wipes one of those tears away.

When the tears stop and Ronan returns with the water bottles, I tell them it's okay to keep moving. And so we do. We limp along, with me leaning on Gabe and sometimes Ronan, but we keep moving.

41

We walk on through Nevada, leaving it behind. The tributaries take us up through Utah, through more hot desert, through jaw-dropping rock formations and steep slopes that make us grit our teeth with effort. Through forests that shade us from the heat and bring us some edible plants Ronan finds. It takes us way longer than it would have if I were in tip-top shape, weeks, but I heal and grow stronger as we move. We stop in the occasional small town or population center to ask people what they've seen.

We can't avoid the bodies. We find them in cars, the stink wafting over from hundreds of feet away, and curled up on the ground. Flies buzz everywhere, bugs crawl, and I hold my breath. I know the mere smell of a dead body won't make me sick, but tell that to my lizard brain. And to my stomach, which wants to vomit basically all the time. I reach into my pack and clutch the plastic dog from my mom's car when things get really bad, or wrap her lanyard around my wrist, and it feels a little bit like she's here trying to comfort me.

We distract ourselves with stories. Ronan's are the most interesting, since I've spent the last few years picking up information about Gabe, so I already know all the clubs he was in at school, that he's half Mexican from his dad's side and a quarter Honduran and a quarter Italian from his mom's, that he's had one real girlfriend and their relationship lasted eight months of junior year (her name was Nina, and she was gorgeous, and it's hard to feel any jealousy toward her whatsoever when she'll probably be dead soon, if she isn't already).

Ronan tells us that he grew up the fifth of seven children in his tiny hometown in the desert, that he was homeschooled by his mother, the way most of the kids in his area were homeschooled by their mothers, and that the person he was closest to in the world was his older brother Ammon, who was actually the guy he said goodbye to at the gate. "It seriously stinks that now I'm finally getting to explore the world, only to have it going up in flames," he says.

"Is that why you left? To explore the world?" I ask. It's not just personal curiosity (okay, that's a lot of it). It's also intragroup trust. If I'm supposed to be able to depend on him in life-and-death situations, then we need to be able to trust each other.

But he just turns his head away.

One night we're setting up our campsite: far enough from the river that we hopefully won't be disturbed by any animals or people coming to drink, but close enough that we can't possibly get turned around and lose our way. It's a dark, moonless night, which makes me and Gabe stick close together. I'm used to touching him now—his hand pulling me up from too deep a squat; me casually brushing a fly off the back of his neck—and sleeping beside him is no big deal.

Even if I've started staring at the back of his head before I fall asleep. Thinking about the way he's stuck by my side, and listened to me when I've talked like I'm someone important, and swiped a tear from my cheek so that I didn't feel too embarrassed.

There's no way *he's* thinking about me the way I'm thinking about him. I just don't feel all that desirable. I know there're beauty standards constructed by society, and that my body wouldn't grow hair all over if I weren't supposed to have hair all over, but the fact remains that the girls who waited till high school to shave their legs (a.k.a. me) got snickered at in the locker room. And now I'm not just a little fuzzy; my legs and armpits are full-on tangles of dark hair. My eyebrows are overgrown, and it's not like I used to wear facefuls of makeup, but brushing my hair and putting on a little mascara used to make me feel pretty.

Now I feel like a machine. A survival machine. Strong, but not pretty.

Nevertheless, here's me and Gabe lying side by side in our sleeping bags, close enough to wake each other with a touch or a kick if we sense a threat. We used to sleep in shifts, one of us staying awake to keep watch, but both Ronan and I are light sleepers, waking at the slightest crack or hoot nearby, so we've just succumbed to exhaustion. If somebody appears and tries to steal our supplies, we'll wake up. And if a mountain lion or bear feels confident and hungry enough to attack people, well, being awake wouldn't help us much anyway.

Ronan's set up several feet away, close enough that I could see if there were any light, but far enough that I would have to throw a rock at his head to wake him up. "Seriously, I would feel a lot better if you'd move closer," I tell him. "What if we get attacked in the night? You'd be alone. Vulnerable."

I hear a swishing noise: him turning over in his sleeping bag. I'd bet anything he's turning away. That seems to be his signature reaction to hearing things he doesn't want to respond to.

"And you're the one with the guns," I say. He packed away his favorite rifle and enough ammunition to last us quite a while, along with a spare handgun. "So we'd be in trouble over here."

He snorts. "You, in trouble? You'd have any attackers on their knees before I could even aim."

Asking around about Estella, we hit gold in the fifth town. I ask my usual questions of the townsfolk and get ready to hear the usual responses: "No, sorry." "Doesn't sound familiar." "Haven't seen them."

Instead a bald man with glasses stops and blinks at us. "Black leather jackets? A school bus full of people?"

I nod, holding my breath. Then exhale it hard as the man's face does something I can only describe as collapsing. Gabe tenses next to me. The bald man says, "Yes, it was horrible. Rolled through here a while back, and everyone on board was sick."

"Sick?" Gabe says. He's starting to look a little sick himself.

The man shakes his head. "Yeah, they all must've drank bad water. The bus driver stopped nearby and dumped them all on the side of the road to die."

Dumped. Side of the road. To die. It's like the words are swimming around my head. I can see them, feel them, but I can't take them in.

"They're all dead?" Gabe says, his voice breaking.

The man shakes his head again. "Not all of them. Most, I'd say.

Some of the younger folk made it through. Buried the others and hitched a ride on."

I can't process, but I turn to Gabe. He's just as good as been told that his parents are dead, and that Estella might be too. The color is slowly draining from his skin, leaving him a sickly ashy shade.

Ronan picks up the slack. "We're looking specifically for a girl named Estella Ramirez, and her parents," he says. "She's about this tall, with light brown skin and long black hair. Seventeen years old. Do you remember if . . ." He trails off as the man starts shaking his head yet again.

"Sorry," the man says. "Could be, but I don't remember specifics. We didn't want to get too close in case it was something other than bad water. I can tell you where the survivors went, though. There was a caravan came through about that time." He smiles slightly. "Probably better they hitched up with the caravan rather than riding on to whatever the guys in black leather jackets had planned for them."

"Where?"

"There's a community in Colorado where they're supposed to have electricity. They say they're opening the doors to everyone who makes it there," the man says. "Across the mountains. It was either hitch a ride with the caravan or stay here, and, well . . ." What looks like sadness flickers over his features. "We barely have enough for our own."

As if apologizing for not helping the survivors, the bald man spends the next several minutes with us, showing us where to go on our maps and giving us tips for heading in that direction. "You won't have to cross the Rockies on foot, which is good for you," he tells us. "You'll want to avoid Moab, before you cross the Utah-Colorado border. There's sickness there."

He's quiet for a bit, and I think he's done, looking for an excuse to say goodbye, before he clears his throat and speaks again. "If you'd like to pay your respects to the dead, we buried them over yonder." He points away from the river. "Marked with some wood crosses. Can't miss it."

We wait for the man to wish us luck and walk away before we speak. "I think we know what we have to do now," Gabe says, and he goes on with, "Go to Colorado," as I say, "Dig up the grave."

Both Gabe and Ronan recoil. "What's wrong with you?" Ronan blurts, then immediately looks apologetic, a kicked puppy. "I mean, why . . . ?"

"To know who's in there," I say. "Because if . . ." I swallow down something bitter. "If all three of them are in there, then . . . then we don't have anyone to chase anymore."

"They're not all in there," Gabe says confidently. "You heard the man; there were survivors. The Ramirezes are strong. You know that."

Still, we stop by the grave and bow our heads for a bit before moving on. None of us want to sleep here tonight.

I can't seem to sleep at all, actually. First there's a rock jabbing me through my mat, and then my neck won't stop itching, and then there's an annoying crunching noise coming from the side. I open my eyes, and they don't want to close again. Especially after I realize Gabe's sleeping bag is empty.

I slide out of mine, shivering in the cool night air. "Gabe?"

He sighs in response. He's not far, sitting several feet away with his back up against a tree, his head tilted toward the sky.

"Can't sleep?"

If this were a few weeks ago, I probably would've ignored him and tried to go back to sleep. But things have changed, after he didn't leave me behind, after I taught him how to shoot, after he told me it was okay to not be okay. I march on over to him and take a seat beside him. "Talk to me."

"About what?"

"About what," I mock, then realize that probably didn't sound very nice. "Sorry. I just thought it would be obvious. Like, your feelings and stuff."

The corner of his mouth twists. "I don't want to talk about it."

I nudge him with my shoulder. "Don't you remember what you told me?" No response. "It'll make you feel better to get it out."

He sighs deeply, his eyes still on the sky. I look up too. There are so many stars up there, cold and blue, all glittering against the black velvet sky. "What if they're dead?"

"They're not dead."

"But what if they *are*?" Now he looks at me, his eyes searching. Though I don't think I'm going to have the answer he's searching for.

"Then at least we have each other." That's seriously terrible, I think, and it's going to make him feel worse. But it doesn't seem to do so, actually. A faint smile crosses his face, and he throws an arm around my shoulders, and that's how we fall asleep, my cheek against his shirt.

I wake up with a cricked neck, but it's okay.

42

We venture away from the Colorado River as we move into the state itself. The land is greener, the desert behind us, and the map says there's a reservoir not far away. We pass through national parkland, and now one of us has to stay awake at all times while the other two sleep, armed and alert with bear spray. At least we have enough to eat. My foraging skills I learned back east don't help much in this western park, but Ronan is familiar with the plants out here. I never thought fresh, crunchy greens could taste so good.

Whenever we hear a car or a group coming, we hide. There aren't many of them, but people have clearly taken up residence here in the wild, where there's game and water and land. It won't be long before the land is picked clean of everything edible, I realize with dread. With only the three of us, though, it's not hard to avoid detection. There's just so much space out here.

More and more cars and groups come by as we near the community. I'm not sure exactly what it's called—there's no named dot on the map—so in my head I've started calling it Partytown. Because they still have electricity there, apparently, and what else does that mean in this world other than a big party?

It sure looks like a party is the first thing I think when we finally see it. We've been trudging over a gentle downward slope for a while, descending a mountain we climbed earlier. Partytown lives in a wide plain below. Farmland, except surrounded by a fence.

Or maybe not a party—a fair. One of those county fairs my mom used to drag me to right after we left the compound, with carnival games where you could dunk a clown in water or pop balloons with a dart, with all sorts of fried food for sale (or, because it was LA, everything avocado and salad), with people milling about and exclaiming how beautiful the weather was. Again, this was Southern California. The weather was always beautiful. And just like at one of those fairs, what we hear now is a tangle of voices and the rumble of cars and the squawk of animals.

Small white houses and trailers stretch through the valley; I can just see a cross on a high tower, probably a church, and what looks like a barn. This must once have been one of those off-the-grid communes, I decide, with a hippie ideology that translates perfectly into opening up their doors to everyone who needs them. Interspersed among the buildings and trailers are plastic tarps serving as tents. There's food for barter everywhere, random things, TVs and other electronics that will actually work here if they have electricity as promised. Backup phone chargers—I have to admit those pique my interest. Farm tools. Many of these booths are clustered outside the fence, but I can see more inside the commune proper.

"So who are these people?" Ronan murmurs from our vantage point. We're hidden behind some trees, not that any of them would likely look up and see us anyway. Though fortunately, I'm no longer in the white of the ward; Ronan brought us some changes of clothes. My head-to-toe brown won't win me any fashion shows, but it does help me blend in. I tell him my hippie commune theory, and he nods like it makes total sense. "So we should just be able to go down there and join in, right?"

"I guess," I say. Gabe is already picking his way down the hill, going faster and faster as he moves, a snowball gathering speed. Ronan and I have to hurry to keep up with him. "Gabe, we should have a—"

"Howdy, folks!" A man steps right in front of us, and we barely skid to a stop before hitting him. His wide white smile doesn't waver. "Welcome home!"

Well, that's a little presumptuous, I think as I take him in. He's probably in his forties or early fifties, with skin so smooth I can only describe it as stretched. His blond hair, unnaturally pale, crests into a wave over his head.

"I'm Philip," he says. "And I'd call myself a greeter for this here little town, where everyone is welcome." He gives me that huge, gleaming smile again. I'm pretty sure he expects me to smile back, but instead I just shift uncomfortably from foot to foot. "You're welcome to stay here as long as you want and take advantage of our public electricity setup. There are lines for outlets, and of course all indoor spaces with heating, air-conditioning, and lights have a waiting list hundreds long, but you're free to pitch a tent anywhere you wish!"

"Thanks," I say faintly. He leads us closer to the group; the smells of roasting meat and fried foods slap me in the face, just like at the county fair.

"There's only one thing you need to know." He spins around to face us, arms crossed over his chest. He's wearing khakis and a polo shirt, both of which have clearly been ironed in the recent past. "Everybody works to better the community."

I clear my throat. My eyes can't help but catch on the guns, which nearly everybody seems to have. Big black assault rifles hanging across backs. Shotguns held tight to sides. Handguns tucked into belt holsters. Which makes sense, considering what's going on out here, but . . . still, it's a lot of guns.

"We're happy to work," Gabe says. "But we're also looking for some people. The Ramirez family? My parents, Lydia and Ernesto? My sister, Estella? Around—" He stops short as Philip shakes his head.

"They might be here, I wouldn't know. Too many people for me to keep track of personally."

I take a deep breath as we move through the gate of the fence into the community proper. People throng around us, their odors rank. There seem to be a few outdoor showers, but either there are too few or people aren't taking advantage of them. The Ramirezes will be, I know. They're very clean people.

And they're going to be here. Definitely. Any minute now we're going to round the corner and they're going to be there, right in front of us. Hawking some of Mr. Ramirez's excellent chili. Setting up a campsite. Sewing tears in people's clothes.

Yup. Any minute now.

43

Gabe gets put on guard duty, and Ronan volunteers to hunt. I volunteer to hunt too, but Philip looks at me with a patronizing smile. "A strong young lady like you would be very welcome in the kitchen or the laundry. Unless you'd prefer to aid with sanitation? We always need more latrines."

Fine. Whatever. Kitchen or laundry it is. I grit my teeth and nod, whipping my hair around my face. We won't be here that long anyway. Just as long as it takes to find the Ramirezes.

Our patch of dirt and grass is located on the outskirts of the community. In the distance somewhere I hear the rumble of trucks. "You have gasoline?" I ask.

"A small gas pump," he says.

I nearly lean forward with eagerness. "How about computers? You know, I'm a skilled coder."

I don't really think there are things to do here involving computers. Unless they jerry-rigged some kind of satellite internet hookup to access overseas servers and things, the country's internet is down without electricity anywhere. It's really just a yearning to feel my fingers tapping over keys again.

What I expect is for Philip to shake his head, maybe give me a bemused smile. What I get is an attack. He grabs me by the shoulders, snarls right into my face. I arch my back, but I can't get away. "What do you know?"

"Nothing!" I gasp. "I have no idea what you mean! I just like computers!" For a moment vines flash before me, growing to wrap their way around my neck, and then they're trees, and there's a flash of brown in the distance, and—

"Let her go!" Gabe grabs me and pulls me free. It's with some surprise I realize I'm shaking. "Zara, are you okay?"

Just like that, the shaking stops. I focus on the scents and sounds around me: the roasting meat; the earthy smell of fertilizer; the rumbles of trucks and voices and something else, a motor running deep below. What is that? "Yes," I say. "I'm okay."

Philip backs off, a stern look still in his eyes. "You won't be needing any computer skills here," he says. "I'm thinking you'll do well in the kitchen. It's right over that ways." He points us where we need to go, and then it's like he can't get away fast enough.

Gabe lets loose a string of curses. Ronan does too, only his version of cursing involves "darn" and "stinking." "Something's not right with that guy," Gabe says. "Are you sure you're okay, Zara?"

It doesn't matter what I think. What matters is finding Estella. "I'm fine, like I said."

Ronan glances anxiously over his shoulder. "I hate splitting up."

"Don't worry," I reply. "We'll meet back here at the end of the day, okay?"

He chews on his lower lip. "Something's not right here."

We meet his words with silence. I'm the one who breaks it. "At least you get to carry a gun."

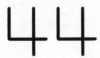

As I walk through Partytown, I can't stop being dazzled by the sight of solar panels. They gleam on the roofs of all the buildings, funneling electricity down into their own network. Definitely their own network, because if the solar panels had been connected to the main grid—like most of the people with solar panels on their houses—they would've lost power with the rest of us. It must have been expensive and taken a lot of work and know-how, but I admire their foresight now. So would my dad.

The kitchen is in a large, brown barnlike building. It's makeshift, set up to serve as many people as possible, which doesn't seem to jibe with how many people are making their own food outside. But then I realize this must just be one kitchen out of many, with the number of people here. Maybe this is the central one, intended to feed the actual residents of Partytown and not the numerous new-comers outside.

Inside, the ceiling is high and windows are few. But there's a big iron stove and ovens, and metal tables everywhere, and appliances hooked up to tangles of electrical cords. It smells like meat and beans and baking bread, what you'd expect a glorified campsite for manly men to smell like.

And it's crawling with people, most of whom appear to be women. I stand awkwardly in the entry of the room as people bustle about, clattering cans and mixing pots and doing other cooking-related tasks, and examine each of their faces for Estella's.

It's a gut punch when I realize she's not here.

I shake my head, trying to send that feeling flying. This is just one kitchen, one place in this town with probably a thousand people. There are so many places she could be. And really, a central kitchen is probably a good location from which to scout. Everybody has to eat.

Should I just jump in and start stirring something? I don't have much experience with stirring. Or cooking in general. Not unless you count microwaving Pop-Tarts.

I wonder if they have any Pop-Tarts here.

My wistful remembrance pops as someone approaches me. She's probably the same age as me, with deep brown skin—she looks like she might be Indian American—and long black hair. A scar stripes the skin beneath one of her huge dark eyes. "Hey, are you new here?"

I nod. She reaches out and grabs one of my hands, squeezes. I usually don't like people touching me without permission, but right now, for some reason, I appreciate it. It's like she's giving me a little bit of her strength. "Are you alone? I am. A lot of us in here are.

The people here with groups or families are mostly doing their own thing." She doesn't wait for an answer, just squeezes my hand again. "I'm Jasmine. It's going to be okay."

It's funny how she says these things like they go together. *I am Jasmine, that is who I am, and because of that everything is going to be okay.* "I'm Zara. Do you know an Estella?"

Jasmine blinks at me. "I don't think so?" Disappointing, but not catastrophic. Again, this place is big. "Why, who is she?"

I hesitate, but I plunge on. I don't want to share any more information than necessary, but in order to find her, it would be helpful to have the word spread around that I'm looking for her. "She's my best friend, and I heard she's here. So if you hear any word . . ."

"Will do!" Jasmine swings her arms. "Are you from the area? I hear people have been coming from far away."

A touch of unease. That much I don't have to share. "No, are you?"

Pain flashes over her face, and then she swallows hard and it's gone, replaced by a look of determination. She's strong. "No, I'm from New Jersey. I was here in Colorado for this Outward Bound hiking summer trip thing with my school when the power went out and we couldn't fly home. We were kind of floundering around blindly and got pointed here. Some of my group tried to drive back. I wasn't feeling well, and I didn't want to spend the whole trip throwing up, so I thought it would be safer to wait it out here and drive back soon." She bites her lip. "I didn't think it would go on this long. Or that there wouldn't be enough gas to spare for the trip."

"Jasmine! Get back to work!" The woman's voice is exasperated, like this is an order she's made many times before. And then she turns, waving a wooden spoon, and I see that she's not really a woman at all. She's a girl, like us. Well, maybe she's eighteen or nineteen, which technically makes her a woman, but I certainly don't feel like one at seventeen.

There are lots of women bustling around, but I somehow know that this girl's the one in charge, and not just because she's the one giving orders. She just looks like the chef. She's short and white, chubby and freckled, with reddish hair, a stubborn chin, and burn scars shiny all over her forearms. "That's Ina," Jasmine says, and then confirms, "She's the chef."

"Ina, like the—"

"Yeah, like the Barefoot Contessa on Food Network." Jasmine ducks her head in and whispers. "Don't ever let her hear you say that. She'll hit you with a wooden spoon. Not that I know from experience or anything."

I can't help but give a little laugh. I like her.

"I'm camping with a few other girls from my school out near the barn if you want to join," she says brightly. "It doesn't smell great, but it's ours!"

"I'm actually here with two guys." I tell her a little bit about Gabe and Ronan. She wrinkles her forehead.

"I thought you were here alone."

"I guess not quite."

Jasmine jerks her chin at me, and we fall into the line. I just do whatever she tells me: roughly chopping vegetables, stirring pots, washing dishes. I find a comforting sort of rhythm in all these repetitive motions and the noise surrounding me, and before I know it, we're filing out for the day.

"See, it's not so bad," she's saying as we walk through the community. The buildings and trailers seem to be laid out in a grid, with the more permanent structures—like this barn—in the center, and the trailers on the outside, with tents set up in a circle around all of that. "And we're always well fed. Look, you can charge your phone here if you want to!"

My heart leaps at the thought of accessing all my pictures and music again, that picture of my mom grimacing at the camera, then falls as I realize how long a line there is for the few chargers. "I'll come back later," I say, and am surprised at the sense of relief that rushes through me. A guilty sort of relief.

It's kind of easier not having those pictures on me.

Jasmine chatters nonstop as we keep walking; I wonder if she needs to fill the air with things that aren't horrible. I'm only half listening, combing the crowds around me as I search for Estella. "These are all storehouses, I think. And this building always has a humming noise coming from it; maybe it's for the beekeepers. This is the infirmary. Oh, and this is the laundry. . . ."

My feet skid to a stop, brushing up plumes of dirt. They match the puffs of steam emerging from the newly open door to the laundry. The figure who stands silhouetted there looks as if she's emerging from a fire. It's like I've been caught in smoke too, the way my throat closes up.

She sights me before I can shout her name. She steps forward, and her eyes swallow up her face. "Z-Zara?"

We run toward each other at the same time and collide so hard it hurts. She's sticky and smells like dirty clothes, but I cling to Estella tight, like I'll never let go.

45

Estella and I can't stop crying and babbling, hands rubbing all over each other like our skin might suddenly slip off and reveal a stranger underneath. Finally I step back, still clasping her by the shoulders, letting my tears flow freely down my cheeks.

She looks rough; she's much thinner than she was the last time I saw her, and she was already thin then. Dark hollows cave in the area beneath her eyes, and her cheekbones are so pointy they might cut me if I touched them. Her hair is tied in a high bun on the top of her head. It wobbles with every moment, threatening to bring her tipping over with it.

"Gabe is here too," I say, and that's enough to make her burst into tears again. I hold her as she cries with what I hope is happiness.

It's just then I remember that Jasmine's here. She's still standing awkwardly to the side, though her hands are clasped beneath her chin and her eyes are sparkling with joy.

I return my focus back to Estella and tell her about our journey to find her, about how we almost died in the desert and were saved by Ronan's people, how we tracked her east and heard the news about the sickness, how we finally found her here. I don't tell her about my mom, but she must know. Estella knows I wouldn't leave my mom behind if I had any other . . .

I swallow the tears down.

I don't want to ask her about her parents because that would bring up mine, but she tells me anyway. "They're dead," she says, and that brings a fresh wave of tears from her. "I can't . . . I don't know . . . I almost died too. It was either die there or come here. . . ."

"We have to stay alive," I tell her. "That's the most important thing."

She hugs herself as she follows me to our campsite, a half step behind me the whole walk no matter how many times I slow down so we can walk side by side. "I thought I was going to die," she says in a monotone. "The whole time, I thought I was going to die. The . . . the things they said to me . . ."

I stop slowing down. Maybe it's easier for her to say these things if she's looking at the back of my head.

Though I want to look at her. I want to hug her and let her cry into my shoulder. But it's not about what I want. It's about what she needs.

"At first we thought they were helping us. Taking us where we needed to go. But once Gabe realized something was up and they kicked him off . . ." She's quiet for a moment. "They filled the bus up. Packed people in the aisles. What were they going to do with us? I don't know exactly. I don't think they planned anything in advance. But we heard whispers. Whispers that didn't mean anything good. Whispers that almost tipped me toward pushing myself through a window while we were moving."

She draws a shaky breath. "I guess we were lucky. Lucky that the bad water got to us first."

I reach back for her hand. She grabs it. I squeeze.

Luck. Luck means something different now, I guess.

46

We walk quietly the rest of the way. "Gabe is going to be so happy to see you," I say, then sober as I realize he's not going to be so happy to learn about his parents.

But Gabe isn't waiting for us at the campsite. Ronan is, dressed in camo clothes he must have borrowed from another hunter and streaked all over with dirt. A few leaves stick out of his blond hair. His face breaks into a wide smile as he sees me hand in hand with Estella. "I knew you'd find her," he tells me. "I knew it."

Gabe sneaks up on us. Estella's been asking Ronan what seems like anything she can think of, as if hearing his favorite food or least favorite sport will fill her brain up so much that there won't be room for anything else, and then all of a sudden Gabe's pushing past me and scooping her into his arms, rocking her back and forth and squeezing her so tight she chokes a little.

I touch Ronan on the shoulder. "Let's give them some privacy," I say. "Guys, we're going to take a short walk."

Neither brother nor sister responds, which I take as permission to scamper away as quickly as possible. Because it's not just about giving them privacy, of course.

If I stay to hear them cry about their parents, then I will be forced to think about my mom.

"Where are we going?" Ronan asks. I can't exactly tell him I'm heading anywhere as long as it's not within earshot of the other two, so I wave my hand vaguely in the direction of the perimeter. We pass that humming building, a few closed storehouses, and fall into a row of small, houselike trailers. Lights shine out the front windows now that it's getting dark, and curtains flutter behind glass. I'm seized by such a strong hit of nostalgia that it almost makes me bend over.

"What you looking at?" The voice comes from our right. I turn. A big, burly guy sits on the front stoop of one of the trailers, his legs spread wide. If this were only a few months ago and he were sitting on public transit, he'd end up getting made fun of on one of those viral manspreading blogs. Smoke curls from a cigarette in the corner of his mouth; the cigarette moves up and down as he speaks. "You don't live here."

"We're just taking a walk," Ronan says brightly. "It's a nice night."

The man glares at us and spits his cigarette onto the ground, where he grinds it out with his boot. "You don't go that way."

Internally I shrug. None of this is worth starting a fight over. We'll just walk somewhere else. I go to turn around, and as I do, my eyes catch on the window above the guy's head.

Pink gingham curtains frame the window, showing off a pretty pink vase. The vase was once full of fresh flowers, which are now brown and wilted, hanging toward the floor. Through the opening I can see a photograph of two elderly people, a man and a woman, both smiling very hard into the camera. Below it, curly pink letters spell out WELCOME TO THE ALBERTSON'S!

One: whoever made that sign had terrible grammar. It should say "Albertsons." Two: as the man from the steps stands up and goes inside, slamming the door behind him, it doesn't look like the Albertsons live there anymore.

47

By the time Ronan and I finish our circuit and make it back to Estella and Gabe, he's nearly succeeded in convincing me I'm being ridiculous. It's amazing how quickly he's gone from, "Something isn't right here" to convincing himself everything is okay. I kind of wish I had an optimistic nature like that. I bet life would be a lot smoother that way. "That was probably their son or grandson or something," Ronan says. "Or maybe they left, and he moved in."

"Maybe," I say, but my heart isn't in it.

Estella and Gabe are sitting together on the ground as we approach, their faces red and raw and swollen, but dry. Their eyes open a little bit too wide as they look up at us. Shock? Maybe.

I sit beside them. "You have to eat," I say. Right: Ronan and I also traded some of the supplies he brought from the ward for some food with actual salt and spices on it, because Estella looks too thin and Gabe won't be hungry after hearing about his parents. "We brought you some fried potatoes with cheese."

Estella nibbles halfheartedly on a crispy brown edge. Gabe doesn't touch any of the appetizingly steamy taters. I push them again in his direction. He stares down at them. "Seriously, eat," I say. "You're going to need the fuel when we leave."

Estella wrinkles her brow. "When we . . . leave?"

Right. I haven't told her the plan. Gabe must not have either. Which isn't surprising. They had so much else to talk about. So I tell her now—that we're heading east to my dad's compound. "It should be safe there, and we can weather all of this with him," I say.

My heart drops as Estella doesn't immediately nod and say that sounds like a great idea. Instead she frowns. "But we're already safe here, where there's electricity and food and all this other stuff," she says. "Why can't we just stay?"

I turn to Gabe, ready for him to back me up, but he seems to have sunk into himself. Estella must have gotten to him. Convinced him we were ridiculous for being so worried about a "feeling" that things were off. Because why wouldn't he be convinced? She's been here for a while. And she's safe. Okay. At least physically.

Maybe I am being ridiculous.

"You know," Ronan says slowly. "She's right. The whole reason we were going to your dad's is because we didn't know where else would be safe. But here it seems like we have everything we need. I know I said I felt off here before, but a feeling might not be enough to plunge ourselves back into known danger."

He and Estella nod resolutely at each other, already a team against me. I bristle up my spine. "We said we were going to go east."

"I understand why you'd want to go to your dad, but it's a really dangerous trip," Estella says. "You and Gabe almost died multiple times already. Do you really want to risk it when we *know* we're okay here?"

"But we're not okay here," I say. Don't they get it? That weird, creepy vibe I got off Philip, the way he erupted at me when I asked a simple question, that grammatically incorrect sign made by sweet old people hanging in the house of a scary man? Something's not right.

And it's not that I just don't want to be here. It's not that at all. I tell myself that very firmly.

Estella places a hand on each of my shoulders. "I love you, Zara," she says softly. "But you need to think of us for a little while, okay? Unless you want to go alone."

Think of her? All I've done these past weeks is think of her. *Fine, then, I'll go alone,* I think very hard in her direction, trying to beam it into her head with my eyeballs. It's better that way. Survival is about the individual, and obviously the only person I can really depend on is myself.

And yet I don't actually say it out loud. Because there's that little nagging thought from earlier that tells me I might not be exactly correct.

I don't speak to her again that night. Not while we're eating the remnants of the fried potatoes, now cold and soggy and sticky. Not while I hear her quietly crying herself to sleep beside Gabe. Not while I rise after a few hours, the night around me loud with insects and people mumbling in their sleep, and prepare to move.

That guy said we couldn't go that way. Maybe there's something there. Something we're not supposed to see. Something that will convince Estella and them that we have to leave after all. So I steal off into the night.

So much of my dad's training had to do with being quick and sneaky. "You must work with what you have," he told me. "You're small and fast and light. You cannot stand up to a man in hand-to-hand combat, but you can sneak circles around him." Combat was an essential part of the survival skills he taught me—once dooms-day came, naturally everybody would be seeking a way onto our compound. And they wouldn't all be nice and friendly and polite. "Once you can sneak up on me, I will consider you accomplished."

So I practiced. All the time. I climbed trees above where I knew he'd be farming to patiently wait for him to appear down below. I tried to follow him through the woods while he was hunting. He always caught me.

The root cellar was key, I decided. It was dark down there. If I went down and hid among the bags of potatoes and apples and the shelves of cans and jars, he'd never see me coming. So I went down early one morning, before he'd be down there bringing more crops. I congratulated myself silently as I pushed myself all the way to the back, in the darkest corner, where I never went, where I never—

My fingers brushed up against metal. I blinked in surprise. The root cellar had been dug out of earth; its floor was dirt, and same for its walls and ceilings. What was metal doing on the wall? My fingers explored. It felt almost like a door, which was bizarre. That didn't make any sense.

A shout from above. My dad. I exhaled, waiting for him to exclaim that he knew I was hiding down there, that of course I couldn't escape him . . . but he wasn't yelling at me. "What were you thinking, Dina?" his voice was booming. My mom. He was talking to my mom. "Why would you wear that? Who did you think was going to see you?"

I scrunched my brows in confusion. I'd seen my mom that morning and told her how pretty she looked. Usually on the compound we wore practical clothes, like leggings and soft, comfortable T-shirts, but this morning she'd decided to wear a dress and flats with ribbons on them. She'd smiled when I complimented her.

"I wanted to look nice for you." My mom's voice was shaky. "I knew I didn't have any messy chores to do today, so I thought it might be nice to—"

There was a cracking noise. My dad must have smacked the wall. Sometimes he did that when he got mad. Though I didn't understand why he'd be mad about my mom looking nice.

Then nothing but silence. I stayed right where I was. Eventually my dad came downstairs. He took a step, then another step, then—

"Ahhh!" I jumped out right in front of him.

He startled, stumbling back a few feet. "Zara," he said. "Of course, there you are. I knew you were there."

But I didn't totally believe him.

Either way, all my training means I glide through the night like a shiver of wind, not stirring any tents, slipping past anyone who happens to be up moving about. Most of the lights in the buildings are out, but there are lights on around the perimeter and above doors, making sure I don't stumble over any sleeping forms.

It's not long before I reach the trailers from earlier that day. Normally I'd be tired, but energy runs through me as if I'm hooked up to Partytown's grid. The trailers are almost all dark, but the occasional porch light shines me a path through the night. I know exactly where I'm going. To the end of the row of trailers, where the man tried to stop me from going. Well, succeeded in stopping me from going. But not now. Now I'll see what they're hiding.

I'm at the end of the row. My heart pounds with anticipation as I tiptoe forward into the vast expanse of night. No light here, which means I'll have to give my eyes a few minutes to adjust to seeing only with the moonlight overhead. I use the time to wonder what I'll find. Philip and the other leaders of this place arranged in a circle with their heads bowed, loudly plotting how to harvest the organs of everybody here? A pile of stolen goods, elegant silverware and designer shoes and gold coins all tossed together like a dragon's hoard? Or—

A fancy flower garden?

I boggle at the sight before me. Rows and rows of roses and other flowers I don't know the names of, their blooms colorful and strong, pruned carefully. Signs are stuck in the grass every other row. DON'T STEP ON THE FLOWERS! BE CAREFUL! KEEP OUT!

I take a step back. The man just wanted to keep me from trampling their garden.

Maybe there's something beyond the garden? I venture out into the night beyond, but there's nothing there. Nothing but woods.

Discouraged, I retreat. *There's still got to be something out here,* I tell myself. *You just didn't find it tonight. Tomorrow, you'll find it. You'll find what's wrong.*

Because there has to be something wrong, right? It's not just that I want to keep going east. There has to be *something*.

I'm a little less careful on my way back, because so what if they catch me now? I still dart from house to house, keeping myself hidden, but I stop waiting before moving on to make sure there's nothing ahead of me.

So that's how I walk right into Ina. Or really, how I bounce right off Ina. She's solid and rooted to the ground, a tree trunk made human. Maybe that's how I mark her immediately and don't panic and scream, thinking I've run into some bad guy.

It's strange to see her outside the kitchen. She belongs there, in her chef's whites, the chef's knife in her hand.

Only she's still got a knife in her hand right now. I scramble back when I notice it so that I won't find myself on a spit, but she just rolls her eyes. "The knife's not for *you*," she says. "Zara, right?"

That makes me breathe a little easier. "Then who is it for?"

She shrugs. "Anyone who tries to stop me."

"From doing what?"

She pulls me to the side of one of the trailer houses, then takes something out of her pocket. I can't see much of it but a few gray blobs, but it's about the size of a driver's license. "I don't know if you can see, but this belonged to Maisie O'Halloran," Ina says. "She ran the communal kitchen before I came here. You know I was one of the first people to come here? Back when it was just a small commune. They welcomed me in with open arms. They welcomed *everyone* in with open arms." Her voice grows darker. "And then they all started leaving. Or at least that's what the new guys in charge said. Maisie left too. Only I found her wallet hidden in the back of a cabinet. Why would she go somewhere without saying goodbye to her kitchen workers *and* leave her wallet with all of her IDs and everything behind?"

My eyes are adjusting now. I can almost see the photo on the license, an older woman with a wide, weather-beaten face and a smile in her eyes. "Maybe she didn't need her wallet where she was going. Like, money is pretty useless right now."

"You really think so?" The scorn in her voice is enough where I feel a flash of worry she might stab me with that knife.

I hesitate. "No."

This is exactly what I wanted to hear. That something is wrong here in Partytown.

So why do I feel like I'm going to throw up?

48

The next several days pass in a blur of activity. Gabe spends most of his time not talking and not eating, and I worry more than once about him having a job where he carries a gun. Estella works her hands raw and red in the laundry and chatters nonstop about how lucky she feels to be here. Ronan becomes the golden boy of the hunters, bringing down so much meat that none of us have to worry at all about our food rations.

Philip shows up at our campsite a few days in to see how we're doing. He's wearing another sharply pressed shirt and khakis with a line down the center of each leg, his nearly white hair still swept into a wave above his overly tanned forehead. "How're we settling in here, folks?" he asks us. We're just rolling out of bed—well, crawling out of our sleeping bags—with our hair mussed and teeth unbrushed. "All good? Are you happy with your work assignments?"

His eyes linger on me. It's definitely not a creepy sex thing, because then he'd be drooling over Estella. Or Ronan. Or Gabe. Anyone other than me. No, I see the glint of warning in his eye. He's still worried about what I said about computers. Worried I might know something. Which makes me sure that there's still something left to find out.

Which is important, because in the kitchen we're plotting a revolution.

Okay, maybe not plotting a revolution. That's going a little far. But we're digging into what we found, or to be more exact, haven't found. Ina, Jasmine, and I huddle in the corner of the kitchen after lunch service, ostensibly menu planning for dinner.

"I've been asking questions about Maisie," Ina says. "Nobody saw her leave."

I ask about the Albertsons. Ina's eyes light up. "I remember them. Nice old couple, always complimented the food," she says. Then the light goes out. "They're not here anymore either."

And yet there are other people living in their houses. That's what Ina was doing that night: swinging by Maisie's trailer to see if she could find anything. She didn't. Only that another person is living there now.

"Did they kill everybody who used to live here and take over?" Jasmine asks, her voice too loud. A few people look toward us. I widen my eyes at her, an admonishment to stay quiet. She lowers her voice to the sound of your average person speaking. "Sorry. But did they?"

"But who are *they*?" Ina says, frowning.

"There's got to be something computer related," I say. "Philip—the guy who welcomed us here—totally freaked out when I said something about computers."

"I haven't seen any computers," Ina says. "Just electricity. I'm not sure if the people who lived here before were really fans of the internet. If these people did somehow install some kind of satellite internet hookup, it would probably all be in one central place."

"A lot of computer fans together would make some noise," I say. "Like . . ." I trail off. The building with the humming inside. Could that be . . . ?

I square my shoulders. "Cancel your plans tonight," I say.

"We didn't have any plans. We never have any plans," says Jasmine, which kind of ruins the whole effect. But it doesn't matter.

We're going in.

49

I don't even bother alerting Estella and the others to our plan. I'll tell them if we come up with anything. Honestly, it'll be kind of nice to have a break from Gabe's hollow staring and Estella's constant nervous chatter and Ronan's attempts to hold everything together.

I know it's their grief. I know it firsthand.

But that doesn't mean I can take it on my shoulders. I already have too much to carry. Both figuratively and literally, since I'm toting my crossbow by my side. If something really is shifty here, I'm not letting anyone catch me without it.

I meet Jasmine and Ina outside the humming building in the black of night. Without the usual chatter of people and general society around us, the humming is especially loud. "It could be bees," Jasmine says. "Like, an enormous hive of bees that'll all sting us when we go in."

"I don't think it's bees," I say, placing a hand against the wall. It's warm.

The door, of course, is locked. I figured that. I just count us lucky that it's not watched over by an armed guard. "Do any of you have a special talent for picking locks?" Jasmine asks doubtfully.

"Kind of," Ina says. She steps forward. I wait for her to pull out the lockpicks.

Instead she pulls out a hammer and smashes the doorknob.

"Ina!" I gasp.

She shrugs. "What?"

We open the door and steal inside, then shut it behind us. My fingers find a light switch on the wall, but turning it on could alert anyone who walks by outside that we're in here. So I settle for my solar flashlight, which I turn accusingly on Ina. "Now they'll definitely know we were in here! And they'll set a guard!"

She shrugs again. "They won't know *we* were in here, just that *somebody* was. And so what if they set a guard? We'll already have what we need."

Hopefully, she's right. It's not like I had any better ideas.

Inside, the room is full of screens, set up on tables around a few chairs in the middle. Wires twist from electrical outlets in the walls. I'm left feeling wistful, almost nostalgic, at the sound of all those computers humming. That used to be the background noise to my entire life. My fingers flex, ready to get to work.

"They're password protected," Jasmine says after clearing a few screen savers. "So much for that."

My fingers flex again, tingling, almost as if they were asleep this whole time and are now waking up. "Step aside, guys. I can pick locks of the digital variety." During those first computer classes in

LA, the ones that consumed me because they were the only thing that didn't make me flash back to the compound, some of the other kids got annoyed—got jealous—that this newcomer was picking things up so fast. They started messing with my devices: resetting passwords, deleting my stuff, and so on. Rather than run to the teacher, I took it as a challenge. And paid them back in turn. It took *them* a lot longer to figure out how to reset their passwords than it took me. Just saying.

As long as these guys' computers aren't protected by anything too complex or encrypted, I have a fighting chance. And I doubt they've gone that far. This is probably just a simple password screen.

It's funny: I thought my skills might have gotten rusty in all these weeks not going near a keyboard, but it's the opposite.

It's like I'm home.

I get tunnel vision when I'm doing stuff like this. The world narrows to just me and the screen. Time slows, or quickens, or both.

For once, my dad's voice in my head is blessedly silent.

Sure enough, the people here did indeed have a satellite internet connection. And beyond their initial passwords (which are laughably insecure), there isn't much hiding going on. So I narrate as I go, the pit in my stomach growing deeper and hollower the more I talk.

It's the computer belonging to Philip—the ringleader. Now I know his last name: Philip Shields. As in, Philip Shields, the "men's rights" fanatic. And this isn't men's rights as in seeking out better treatment for fathers in custody battles or evening out gender ratios in fields where men are underrepresented, like teaching or nursing. No. This is men's rights as in white men should be on top, with women and people of color under their boots. The figurative fathers and older brothers and uncles of the jerks in our AP

Computer Science class who didn't think Estella and I deserved our spots because we're women. Men's rights as in they are entitled to whatever they want and screw everybody else.

Which is what they did. They were communicating online on various 4chan boards and other places before the power went out about what they'd do in an apocalypse scenario, because men like that always liked to fantasize about what they'd do with lots of guns and no laws.

Men other than my dad, of course. Because . . . well, my dad is different. Right?

Anyway. When the power went out, they quickly made a plan to meet here, where one of their members lived. Enough of them heard about it before generators and cell towers started to die. The rest is history. The people who lived here once . . . don't live here anymore. There are photos of the bodies, presumably taken for blackmail purposes in case Philip needed to threaten one of his men into submission. And . . .

"It wasn't a garden," I say. "It was a grave."

My words meet a hush in the room. For a moment all I can hear is the humming of the machines.

Jasmine breaks it. "But then why would they let all of us in here?" she says. "Wouldn't they want to keep everything all for themselves?"

My heart's beating quick and fast like a rabbit as I read on. "Because it's part of their plan," I say. "To lure people here, make us dependent on them. And once they've got their society, that's when they start making changes. Small ones at first. And we'll go with it, because we need them and their electricity to survive. And they'll keep using that . . ." I trail off because I don't want to vocalize what the guys were suggesting. Suffice it to say, you wouldn't want to be a woman or a person of color here in a few months.

A light flashes on overhead. I immediately go to spin in the direction of the door, but before I make it, I hear a man growl, "What are you doing in here?"

50

It's only one man. We outnumber him. But with the light on, and him able to signal his friends, we won't outnumber him for long.

I raise my crossbow in his general direction. He freezes, what looks like a walkie-talkie halting on its way to his mouth. "Don't move," I direct him, centering my crossbow at his throat. And I finally realize that it's Philip. His eyes widen as he recognizes me. "I knew you were too interested in our computers," he says. "You little bitch."

"I'm the bitch?" I say. "Aren't you the one seconds away from a crossbow bolt punching through your windpipe, leading to a slow, bloody, agonizing death?"

He glares at me in response but doesn't say anything. I guess there really isn't a good response to that if you don't want a slow, bloody, agonizing death.

"Do it," Ina whispers behind me. "You know what he is."

Jasmine gasps. "You mean kill him?" She sounds horrified. "No. We're better than that."

Ina snorts. "He's done way worse to others, and he'd do way worse to us if given the chance. And he'll have the chance if we don't get out of here *now*."

Ina's right. I know she's right. She's saying exactly what my dad would say. *You must look out for yourself first, Zara. Do not be soft. Any immediate threats to your life must be taken out.*

I stare Philip down. He's shaking, but I could definitely still hit him. He doesn't beg. I'd expect a coward like him to beg.

I shoot. He screams.

The arrow punches through his walkie-talkie with a loud crack. His hand, too. He screams again, falling to his knees.

We run for the door. Jasmine's the first one out, her black hair whipping behind her. She hesitates for a moment in the doorway. "I volunteered as an EMT back home," she says, glancing over at me. "Maybe I should look at that hand." But I shake my head, and she scurries out.

Ina follows more slowly, stepping on Philip's hand as she goes.

I'm last. Just as I did with the man with the vine tattoos outside the ward, I hesitate over Philip. Because Ina is right. He could follow us. He could have us all strung up to die.

So, one at a time, I shoot him through the knees.

He's crying now, and my stomach lurches as I pull out my bolts, which makes him pass out from the pain. Good. It makes it easier for me to turn off the light and shut him in the computer room. The lock doesn't work, but I doubt he'll be able to get up and open the door anytime soon. He'll have to wait for someone to find him in the morning.

Which leaves us some time. "We have to leave," I say. "Immediately."

Ina gives me a grim nod, but Jasmine's face is still frozen in horror. "We can't just leave everyone here, knowing what's going to happen," she says.

The idea already has me grieving too, but we have no other options. "We can't fight them. There are too many of them, and they have most of the weapons."

"Yeah, but we could make a plan—"

"With what time?" Ina interrupts. "We have to get out of here before morning, or the guy we stupidly didn't kill will rat us out."

Jasmine's eyes are shiny, and her lips are trembling. I go to pat her on the shoulder with sympathy, but I can't help hearing an echo of my dad's voice. *Crying is a waste of water.*

So I don't. I harden my voice instead. "She's right," I say. "We need to get Estella, Gabe, and Ronan, and we need to get out."

"But the girls I shared a tent with, right over . . ." Jasmine trails off as she looks in that direction. "Let me go get them."

I want to shake her and tell her we need to get out *right now*, but that's not being fair. I can't stop her from doing the same thing I'm doing for my own friends. "Hurry," I say. "Meet us near the entrance."

She disappears into the night, and I really hope this isn't the last time I see her. Or that this isn't the last time she sees us.

51

At first Estella flat-out refuses to come. "You're making this all up so we can go see your dad," she says, her chin jutting out stubbornly.

I show her my crossbow bolt. The blood looks black in the darkness, but there's no mistaking that smell of damp and rust, the stains from the parts of a body that are supposed to be safe on the inside. "I'm not making anything up," I say urgently. Ina murmurs confirmation. "Don't you trust me?"

She eyeballs me . . . then nods. She stands slowly, pulling Gabe up after her. "Pack everything," she directs him. "Hurry."

Ronan hesitates, but he follows too. I hope that means he's beginning to trust us more and not that he's afraid of being left behind.

I direct them quietly as we move through the camp, past tents shivering with snores, past guards standing like shadows against the gates, to the entrance. There are guards there, but to stop people from coming in—not leaving. Still, we linger at the entrance, waiting for Jasmine.

"We can't take too long," Ina breathes. "If she doesn't get here soon . . ."

Then we'll have to leave her behind. The thought makes my stomach lurch unpleasantly.

But she's right, my dad says sternly.

So we wait, and wait. But the guards are starting to look at us suspiciously, even when I tell them we're just planning on moving on to the Midwest, where Ina's family is, and the sky is starting to turn from black to a dark gray. We're running out of time.

"Okay," I say finally. "I guess we—"

And then I see her, flying toward us, her feet thudding over the packed dirt. Alone. "Where are your friends?" I ask, even as we're already moving out of the gates. A truck growls past us, stopping at the entrance; a few men hop out and enter the compound.

Jasmine's face is haunted. It looks as if she's aged two years since I saw her last. "They didn't believe me," she says, and her voice breaks. "Told me I must have had a fever dream or something. I tried and tried to convince them, told them about everything these guys were planning, but . . ." She trails off, her eyes pleading. "I couldn't let you leave me behind. I don't need to go to your compound with you, but I want to go in that general direction. Toward my family in New Jersey. We can at least go most of the way together."

"You did the right thing," I tell her. "You can't save everyone."

She shakes her head. "But thinking about them left here, when—"

"If we leave on foot, they'll track us down," Ina interrupts. It takes a minute for me to switch gears, and by the time I do, Ronan is speaking.

"She's right. We need to get out of here fast."

I'm about to ask them what they think we should do, then, when I notice them both staring at the truck.

52

So we're car thieves now. That's a thing.

It ends up being way easier than I think it'll be. Gabe knows the guards from his shift work. He forces a smile on his face and distracts them while the rest of us sidle over toward the truck, which is still idling. He jumps into the front seat, Estella beside him, refusing to go anywhere she can't reach out and touch him. The rest of us leap into the truck bed while the truck's already moving, and the guards start shouting behind us. We push aside crates of supplies and even some water. Nice. There's a compass back here too, heavy and brass, slightly dinged on the case. I pick it up and roll it through my fingers, taking it as a sign.

The gates of Partytown recede behind us. We drive as fast as we can, leaving it in the rearview mirror.

53

I don't stop holding my breath until we're through the Rockies. I don't mean that literally, obviously, since it takes us several hours. But the entire drive through those snow-dusted peaks and rocky roads, there's a tension in my chest like I'm constantly waiting for the men from Partytown to catch up with us and get revenge for shooting Phillip and stealing their truck. For the engine to overheat from the altitude and splutter and die. For two of the tires to burst with bangs like gunshots. For . . . I don't know, an asteroid to hurtle down from the sky and smash our truck into flaming smithereens. Basically for something to go horribly wrong with our one mode of transportation, because without it, we might end up in some Donner Party–like situation.

You know. Eating one another.

When I mention this, Ina says, "I don't think even I could make you taste good."

I'm not sure whom she's talking to, but I laugh heartily. As heartily as I can with the altitude, anyway.

We all want to keep her happy because she works miracles with food. Though we have plenty of supplies in hand, we forage and hunt as much as possible as we move on from Colorado through Nebraska to make those supplies last. She makes our oatmeal sweet and sour with the wax currant berries we pass on the road; she stews up the venison and trout we manage to hunt up with mushrooms or roots or dandelion greens.

We stay mostly in our truck, sticking to side roads to minimize our chances of the Partytown guys catching up with us, venturing out to camp only when we don't see other people around. We do see other people: hiking by the side of the Platte in Nebraska, camped in old ranger cabins, trying to hunt. But nobody ever tries to stop us; they only look at us warily as our group bumps by, weapons in hand. And we never stop for them, no matter how much they look like they need food or water. I learned my lesson on the side of the road in Nevada.

"Please," Estella says to me one day. The two of us are in the cab together, me driving, her sitting on the passenger side. It's a beautiful midsummer day, warm but not too warm, the sun hot and bright, but our road has been shaded enough by trees that the other four are out back in the open air. "Those are kids. They look hungry. Can't we stop and give them something? We haven't eaten half our supplies since we've hunted and foraged so much."

It still feels crazy that she's asking *me*. That the rest of them depend on *me* to tell them when we're stopping for the night and starting for the day, to approve whatever campsite they've picked out. "You're the one who realized right off the bat that something was wrong back there," Gabe said.

"We're almost out of Nebraska," I say. "We have extra gas, thanks to that stockpile we found on the Colorado border, but not enough to get us all the way east without lucking on more. We're going to need our supplies when we're hiking across the Midwest."

"But, Zara." Estella tugs my arm so that I look at her, which is dangerous, considering I'm driving. My heart softens a bit as I realize her eyes are shimmering with pity. "They're *children*. Hungry children. They shouldn't be punished because their parents are bad hunters or don't know what to eat out here."

My heart hardens again as I remember the kids in Nevada. "That's how the world works. It sucks, and it's not fair, but it's them or us." Her eyes start to shine; her lower lip trembles. I soften a little further. "If it makes you feel any better, they're probably all going to die in winter anyway."

It does not make her feel better.

I pat her awkwardly on the back with the hand that's not currently holding the wheel, and remember my attitude toward Avi at the gas station when we were trying to find the Ramirezes. How I wanted him to do something, anything, to help, even if it was small. "Okay, throw them a bag of oatmeal or cornmeal or something," I say. We won't be able to carry all this if we have to get out of the truck anyway.

Or that's what I tell myself.

Estella is glowing when she climbs back into the truck. At least one of us is; I'm tense from having to stop our vehicle. "Thank you," she says. I don't wait for her to buckle up before stomping on the gas, sending us jerking forward. The kids goggle at us in the rearview mirror. "Maybe they'll make it through the winter now."

They won't, but I give her a noncommittal nod.

She sighs, leaning back in her seat. Wind blows through her hair. "These past couple weeks have been kind of a fog."

"I get it," I say.

She turns to me. "It's just, like, I can't believe they're gone. It hasn't sunk in yet."

She's talking about her parents. I can't even bring myself to nod, because I've been waiting for this moment. Dreading it, actually. I suddenly find it hard to swallow.

It's hard enough to survive. I don't know if I can do it while thinking about how my mom is gone forever. If I spend too much brain space on that, I'll just want to crawl under the tarp in the back of the truck and curl up and disappear into the dark.

So I take the coward's way out. "I'm so happy we found you."

She studies me for a moment. Not that I can see her; my gaze is fixed firmly on the road ahead. It's that I can feel her eyes burning into the side of my face.

But she understands. "I'm happy you found me too," she says. "And that Gabe is okay. I can't believe the two of you tracked me halfway across the country." She sniffs. "It really . . ."

"It's not that big a deal," I say quickly, hoping to head off more tears. Her gratitude makes me shift uncomfortably in my seat.

"It is, though," she responds.

She's right, I guess. I glance in the rearview mirror, glimpse the top of Gabe's head. It's funny, how now I'm in the driver's seat and yet I'm still looking at the back of his head just like when we were hiking. Something tender stirs within me. Should I tell Estella about these feelings?

I glance in the rearview mirror again . . . and catch Gabe's eye. He's looking right at me.

I look away. No. No need to tell Estella anything. It's not like Gabe would be interested in me anyway. I'm not beautiful, like his ex-girlfriend, Nina, like Callie Everett of the shiny hair. Callie, who's probably dead now. "So you guys are coming east with me," I say. "You'll meet my dad."

She's quiet for a moment, and I worry I've upset her with the word "dad," until she says, "It'll be interesting, that's for sure. Just from what you've said . . ."

Interesting. Yeah. That's one word for it.

54

We barely notice when we trade rivers, when we blow past the NOW LEAVING NEBRASKA sign and are welcomed into Iowa by another. The landscape is flat plains of corn and grass stretching into the horizon, a shimmering gold ocean. We pull over for a quick lunch—Ina makes some kind of porridge for us out of corn cobs we scavenge in the field—and take a quick inventory of what we have remaining in the truck bed.

"We're good on food and water," Ronan says. "Since we've been finding so much outside."

We have plenty of matches and lighters, bedding and tarp. The only worrying thing is the gas. "We're down to one jug," Jasmine says. "What are the odds we'll find more?"

A gas station won't be good enough—the pumps won't be working. And we've stopped to scavenge at abandoned gas stations for fuel in jugs or bottles and have uncovered nothing since that first lucky find. Which isn't really that surprising—it would've been one of the first things, alongside bottled water, people snapped up when they realized this blackout wasn't ending anytime soon.

Ronan says, "We're in farm country, though. I'd be surprised if the farmers don't have stockpiles. Maybe we could trade for some more."

He's probably right, but it's not as easy as that. Each farm is huge, and it's not like we have maps pointing us toward the houses or barns sprinkled in the middle of each property. It's like seeking out a drop of gas in an ocean of oil, with the fear that we'll use up all our gas gambling we'll find more. And who's to say they'll be willing to trade with us instead of holding us at gunpoint and taking our stuff?

Still, Ronan is looking at me with such shiny optimism, it hurts to think of tarnishing it. "We'll keep an eye out," I say vaguely.

I do, but it's not enough. We're still in Iowa when the truck sputters to a stop. It ticks a bit from residual heat, loud in the sudden silence.

I'm sitting in the back with Jasmine, Estella, and Gabe; Ronan and Ina are in the cab. They get out, Ronan rubbing the back of his head. "Maybe there's just some issue under the hood," he says hopefully.

I shake my head. There's only so much shiny optimism I can take. "Let's divide up whatever we can carry and leave the rest."

Ronan droops, but he obediently starts sorting through our food and water. I exhale, gazing off into the distance. We're not far from the river still. As long as we don't venture too far away, we should be fine. We're more vulnerable on foot, and we'll move much more slowly, but there's a big group of us now. And we all have weapons. I doubt anyone will try to mess with us.

"Zara," Jasmine calls. "Do you think we need all of these potatoes?"

No more gazing into the distance for me. I direct our efforts, making sure everybody's packing efficiently. In the end we have to leave some of our food behind, because I make the executive decision that it's better to do that than risk hurting ourselves by carrying too much.

Ina grumbles but shoulders her pack just like everybody else.

55

Our routine quickly settles into monotony. Not for the first few days—our shoulders aren't accustomed to these heavy packs, and our backs hurt after an hour of walking. Whenever we take off our packs, we feel weightless for a bit, like gravity's lightened. At least we're not climbing through canyons or hiking up mountains like Gabe, Ronan, and I were before, I tell everyone. Ronan is always quick to chime in with support. "Everything here is flat. Try carrying this pack up the Grand Canyon."

Which we did not do, but hey, everyone looks impressed.

At least without the truck we can go off road more. We spend a night in a barn, then another rainy night sheltered in a different barn, and then find somewhere else to sleep a few nights later . . . a barn.

The one we find tonight is almost definitely abandoned: the

stacks of hay are getting mildewy, and one of the windows is broken, allowing a cool night breeze to whistle through. We settle our mats in a circle as usual, close enough to wake one another with a touch, but far enough that Ronan's kicking or Jasmine's sleep-talking won't be too irritating.

And then we sit, because for some reason none of us feel like sleeping. We've grown used to the bone-deep ache in our limbs from all the walking, and the hunger burning in the pits of our stomachs because we're afraid to use up too much of our remaining food.

Estella claps her hands together. "I have an idea."

"Is it a good one?" Gabe asks. He's lying back on his mat, eyes closed, though his entire body is tensed with wakefulness. His long, lean body, grown ropy and tough with all the walking.

Not that I'm looking.

Estella gives him a gentle kick. "All my ideas are good."

"What about the time you decided to stop brushing your teeth for a year to see what would happen?" Gabe asks. "As I recall, the smell of your breath almost flattened me."

She gives him another kick, less gentle this time. "I was *five*. And what about that treasure trove of stiff socks you had under your—"

His eyes still closed, his foot finds her mouth. "Gross!" Estella shrieks, squirming away.

Jasmine sighs dramatically. "You're making me miss my brother, however impossible it sounds."

Gabe and Estella both turn to her, squabble forgotten. "Brother?" Estella asks. Jasmine nods.

Jasmine holds out her fist, and Estella bumps it with her own, saying, "Here's to having someone hold you down and fart on you."

"Or being the one to hold them down and fart on *them*," replies Jasmine.

I shake my head. "Do siblings really do that?"

It's Ronan who answers. "Yes. Do you know how many times I've been farted on? Or beaten up? Or tricked to run headfirst into the wall?"

"How many older brothers do you have?" Estella asks.

"Four."

"That's a lot of older brothers. Older brother solidarity." They fist-bump too.

"Anyway, what was your idea?" Ina asks. She's apparently not sharing how many siblings she has. If any. She strikes me as an only child, used to getting her way. Or an older sister, accustomed to taking no crap.

Estella claps her hands again. "Right! My idea! My *great* idea!" She fixes Gabe with a glare. He only smiles angelically back. "We're going to play truth or dare." Her glare softens. "*Happy* truth or dare. That's the most important rule. No bringing up anything depressing."

Ina raises an eyebrow skeptically, but the rest of them rustle in their seats. "I've never actually played truth or dare," Ronan says brightly.

Me, I'm not so sure. What if someone assigns a dangerous dare, like going out alone into the night? *They wouldn't do that,* I tell myself. None of us are stupid, and we all have personal interest in one another's survival.

But . . . what if someone asks a more dangerous truth?

56

Jasmine's eyes gleam. She won the rounds of rock-paper-scissors to go first. She clasps her hands together as her eyes roam the circle, squinting as she thinks.

They zero in on me. "Fearless leader," she says. "Truth or dare?"

My brain sticks on those two words. *Fearless leader.* Do they really think I'm fearless? Do they really think I'm their leader? "What kinds of dares could we even do here?" I ask. "As your *fearless leader*"—the words feel clumsy in my mouth—"I won't allow anything that might risk our group. Whether that's going outside the barn, where we could get spotted, or trying to climb up into the hayloft and potentially falling."

Jasmine's lips drop into a pout as she looks around. "I guess that doesn't leave us very many options," she says. "Fine, then. Truth or truth?"

What have I gotten myself into? I stifle a sigh. "Truth, I guess."

Her fingers steeple under her chin. I glance to the side to get away from her thoughtful gaze, and my eyes catch on Gabe's. He's looking at me. Again. *Why wouldn't he be?* I ask myself. *It's your turn.*

A smile curls slowly over his lips. I find my throat is suddenly very dry.

"Zara!" Jasmine's saying, snapping me out of . . . whatever state I'm in. "I said, what's your most embarrassing moment?"

"I'm thinking," I say, even though I definitely wasn't. Now I am, though. It's amazing how blank a direct question like that can leave your mind.

I remember quivering with shame at the disappointment in my dad's voice. "You made the wrong cut," he'd told me, standing over the blood and bones and purple-gray meat of the deer I'd butchered. "You punctured the intestines and polluted the meat. We have to throw this away now. This deer gave its life for nothing." I was hor-rifically embarrassed, my cheeks hot and sad, angry at myself as I washed the blood from my hands.

But this is happy truth or truth. "I peed my pants in middle school," I say. I don't mention how it was soon after I got to LA from the compound, how I was intimidated by public school bathrooms and all the girls who gathered in them to gossip and touch up their makeup in the mirrors, how I was so afraid to use them that I held it until I couldn't take it anymore and it all came spilling out. That's not such a happy truth. "In the middle of social studies. I didn't get up, even when class ended, but the other kids smelled it. They knew, and everybody laughed at me."

"Awwww," Estella says. "I wish I'd been there. I would've beaten them all up."

She wouldn't have beaten them up. I'm not sure she would've even talked to me back then, given how odd I was. I was comparatively normal when we met freshman year.

"I peed my pants too when I was a kid," Jasmine volunteers. "On a school trip, when the teacher kept telling us we'd get to a bathroom soon. I jumped in a river and almost drowned, but it was worth it because nobody saw the pee."

Honestly, that sounds like something I would do. So I nod. "Respect."

"Anyway, now it's your turn," Jasmine says. "Truth someone!"

I look around the circle. I already know everything about Estella . . . at least, everything that could reasonably be deemed happy. Ina studiously avoids my eyes as I look at her, and I don't want to force her to say anything she doesn't want to, so I move on by. All I want to ask Gabe is *What do you think of me?* and that's not something I'm going to ask him in front of everyone, or ever.

I stop at Ronan. He stares at me openly, his blue eyes wide and guileless. "Why did you . . . ?" I stop. I was going to ask why he'd left the ward behind, his family and safety and warmth and food, but I had a feeling the answer wouldn't be a happy one. Why would you leave your family and safety and warmth and food, if what's there weren't worse than what's outside?

So I go back. "What's your happiest memory?" There. Happy truth or truth, won.

Ronan smiles. "You were going to ask me why I left the ward, weren't you?"

I hesitate. Then nod. "But this is supposed to be happy, so . . ."

His smile is brighter than our flashlight. "My happiest memory *is* why I left."

Interesting. I prop my chin up on my hand as he goes on.

"It was my first kiss," he says. "We met when I moved from my small town to the ward. I grew up with my passel of cousins and siblings and second cousins, and was homeschooled by my mother. Then I came to the ward, and all of a sudden I was living around a bunch of people my age who weren't related to me. We were assigned on patrol together. Night after night we walked the edges of the ward, making sure everybody else was safe. We were all safe, inside our walls. Nobody even tried to steal food or water or anything else. There was nothing, really, for us to watch for.

"So we watched each other." Ronan smiles dreamily. "Blond hair like mine, blue eyes like mine, but everything else was different in the most wonderful way. The angles of bone, the soft touch of skin . . . we were in the shadow of the church when it happened." He cradles his jaw in a hand, remembering. "One second I was standing there, staring off into the dark of the night, and the next he was kissing me."

The smile flickers on his face as he studies each of ours in turn, eyes narrowed like he's seeking something out. Whatever he's looking for, he doesn't find it, and the smile returns. "Everything around us disappeared. The darkness, the blackout, the suffering of the world. Everything. For a second there was only the two of us wrapped in each other's arms, his stubble prickling against my cheek, his thumb drawing circles on my waist. . . ."

"That sounds *wonderful*." Jasmine's beaming, her hands clasped before her. "I've never been kissed, but it sounds so *romantic*. I wish you'd recorded it so I could watch." Her hands unfold, flutter down to her lap, where they twist together again. "Is that creepy? It's creepy, isn't it?"

"It's creepy," Gabe agrees, his eyes crinkling at the corners.

"*Anyway,*" Ronan says, clearing his throat. "That's my happiest memory. That moment when everything felt absolutely, totally, wonderfully right."

"But you said it's why you left," Ina says. I frown at her, but she doesn't look like she's gloating or anything, just curious.

"Yeah." This time when Ronan's smile flickers, it doesn't come back. "It only lasted a moment before he pulled away and spit, rubbing his mouth like I'd gotten something dirty on it. Told me there was something wrong with us that we liked it and that we'd have to pray for guidance."

"Oh, Ronan." Estella leans in like she's going to give him a hug, but she stops short of touching him. Murmurs of sympathy go around the rest of the circle.

Ronan shrugs, but not nonchalantly. It's like there's something heavy weighing on his shoulders, and he's trying to push it off. "I suspected growing up, but that's when I knew there'd never be a place there for me. Crystal clear. I could be safe, but I'd never be me."

"I'm glad you feel that you can be you with us," I say. Just barely, he inclines his head.

We're quiet for a moment. Ronan takes a long swig of water, the liquid bulging in his throat with every sip. We wait for him to finish, and then to wipe his mouth, and then to say, with authority, "Well, who's going to be next?"

57

We go round and round the circle. Estella describes her dream prom dress; Jasmine tells us all about her family dog, who is fluffy and white and floppy-eared and adorable (and who may have been eaten by now, I do not say); Ronan tells us that he can play the piano blindfolded.

Estella is still laughing at the image when Ronan goes to ask the next question. "Gabe," he says. "Who's your biggest hero?"

Estella's smile immediately falters. I know I'm thinking the same thing as she is: the answer every kid gives to that question in school. *My mom. My dad.* I'd always answer with the former: "My mom is my hero because she's really smart and pretty and she works with the mayor to make Los Angeles a better city." Though maybe really I should always have been answering with the latter. *My dad is my hero because he knows how to survive, and he taught me how to survive too.*

"My biggest hero?" Gabe repeats. He looks around the circle. Looks at me. I look back at him, raising my eyebrows, trying to show how sorry I am. He nods, and I think he's understanding me until he speaks. "I'd have to say that my biggest hero is right here, in this circle." He smiles at me. I'm slow to get it. "It's you, Zara."

I blink furiously. "What?"

None of the others speak. Which is surprising, because you'd think one of them would pipe up that obviously he made a mistake. That he said my name because his brain short-circuited while he was looking at me, and he really meant to say someone's name that sounds similar. I don't know, Lara from *Tomb Raider*.

Gabe shifts awkwardly in his seat. "You're the most badass person I've ever met. Like, who would have ever guessed that the skinny nerd on my headset could use a real crossbow?"

He smiles at me, but all I hear is "skinny nerd." That's what he thought of me?

"None of us would be here if it weren't for you," he continues.

"Or you," I say, waving a hand in the air. I expect the others to chime in and tell him how vital he is, that he's overstating my importance, but again they're silent.

"Not me," he says. "You kept me going. Kept me focused. I didn't know how to use a weapon. How to forage for food. How to *survive*."

I know I should be happy to hear all this. But it really sounds like he's talking about my dad. How grateful he is for the years of training I went through at my dad's hands. Because he's not talking about my brains, or my looks even.

Though I guess those are half my dad too.

I know it's pathetic, but still I ask, "What else?"

"What else?" Gabe repeats.

I want him to tell me that he never really looked before, but now that he's looked, he's realized I'm the most beautiful girl he's ever seen. That my brains wow him, whether they're coding something new and exciting or figuring out the best route from a guarded compound. That his mind buzzes with thoughts of me when we relax onto our sleeping mats at night, that his hand tingles with the desire to reach out and thread his fingers through mine.

"The way you took charge of our group here," Gabe says. "You make sure we're all on track and that we're doing what has to be done, even if it's not easy. You're ruthless!"

He lets out a little laugh, but it feels like cold water running down the back of my neck. *Ruthless. You must be ruthless, Zara, for survival,* my dad whispers. *If you're not ruthless, you're weak. And weak people get themselves killed.*

I push myself up to my feet, standing so quickly that my head spins. "I'm going to pee, and then I'm going to bed." My voice comes out abrupt. Jasmine jumps in surprise. Ronan's eyebrows crease. But I have eyes only for Gabe, whose face rumples in confusion.

"You guys should get ready for bed too," I say, turning so I don't have to see him anymore. "We'll want to get an early start tomorrow."

We're not supposed to go outside alone, but since I'm the one who made that rule, I figure I can break it. I step outside and shut the barn door behind me, relaxing immediately into the cool night air, letting the light of the stars soothe me with their icy brilliance. I just need a second. I take a deep breath, then another, then step around the side of the barn to pee. Not too far, in case there are other people out here, but far enough where nobody will be able to hear my—

The barn door flies open. I stagger back into the barn wall, and I know it's ridiculous, but I can't help but panic that it's Gabe and that he's realized his love for me and that he's going to round on me to confess while I have my pants around my knees. "Wait," I say weakly, but then the person's there, blocking out the light from the stars, and it's not Gabe. It's Estella.

I still stand and yank up my pants, only halfway through my pee. The rest really wants to come out, but it's rude to pee in front of other people. I think. Though social rules kind of get scrambled out here in the wilderness.

Estella rolls her eyes. "You can finish, you know," she says, like she's reading my mind. "It's not like I haven't seen you pee before."

I cross my arms. "What do you want?"

My voice comes out more defensive than I think it will, and she goes rigid at the sound. She says, just as defensively, "None of us are supposed to be out here on our own. I just wanted to make sure you were okay."

"Why wouldn't I be okay?" It's amazing how many stars are visible out here in the middle of nowhere. You don't get this many stars in LA. Light pollution fades them into nothing. Or they did. I suppose that now they're as bright as they are here.

It makes me think of the compound. My dad's probably looking at these same stars. He liked looking at them, liked telling me stories about the constellations. *Better than fairy tales,* I remember he'd say. *This one here is a bear, the—*

"Seriously, Zara?" she says. "You got all prickly and yelled at everyone and ran outside. Obviously you're not okay."

Okay. Maybe I was not exactly subtle.

"Talk to me." Estella grabs my hand and steps next to me, her back up against the barn wall. Then she slides down to sit on the ground, tugging me with her. After a moment of hesitation I follow. I'm not sitting in my own pee. That's a positive. "Was it Gabe? Do I need to beat him up for you?"

I snort, tilting my head back. Somehow it's easier to talk to someone when you're not looking right at them. I imagine I'm speaking to the grand figures of the sky, the heroes of the stories my dad used to tell me. "I'm not some big hero. I'm not special. I just . . . I got trained for years to do all this stuff. That's all."

"And you were hoping that he'd say something else, because you're in love with him," Estella says wisely.

I rest my head on her shoulder. I don't have the energy to argue with her, but I'm not going to come out and say she's right.

"It could be good for the two of you," she says. "We're dealing with so much right now. Go on. I officially give you permission to blow off some steam."

I wait to feel her shoulder jiggling under my cheek with suppressed laughter, but she's as still as stone. Though more comfortable. "I'm going to pretend you didn't just say that."

"Pretend whatever you want." A heavy sigh. "That's what I spend most of my time doing, anyway."

I don't have to ask her to elaborate. She's pretending everything's all right. That she doesn't have to worry about dying from a broken leg or getting kidnapped by people bigger and stronger than she is. That we're out here stargazing by choice and not because the light pollution has been stolen from us.

"I missed you," I say. "I was so worried when I went to your house and found it empty, with no note or anything."

"We left you a note."

"I know. Gabe told me," I said. "Did you leave Twinkle behind too?"

Estella's exhale seems to shiver the stalks of corn around us. "We took him in the cat carrier, but the men let him go after we were all on the bus," she says. "He bolted off into the wilderness. I cried so much. I hope he's okay."

"This is probably a good time to be a cat," I say. "Lots of meat lying around."

Why would you say that, Zara? I berate myself as Estella's shoulders shake, until I realize it's actually laughter this time.

"I hope he's okay. At least he has a fighting chance out there," Estella says. Her laughter fades. Her head falls on mine. "Do you think we'll ever go back?"

I think about the status of LA right now. Things are really all about the water. Cities on the Great Lakes or on other major bodies of fresh water are probably still populated (we'll want to avoid Chicago), though I assume there's probably been looting and terrorizing going on in search of food. It's been a short-enough time, the summer weather warm enough, where they probably haven't had any major die-offs in the those areas, outside of waterborne illnesses. Those will come in the winter, when the cold shatters bones and sets deep into veins, when the lack of food hollows out stomachs for good.

But cities like LA, Phoenix, Austin, Santa Fe? Cities in the desert, where heatstroke kills people suddenly living without AC, where the beating of the sun sucks any drop of water from you as soon as you step outside? They're probably ghost towns now. Either people have fled or they're . . . well, ghosts.

"I don't know," I say. I don't know if I even want to, honestly. LA was home because of my mom. Because of Estella. Now nothing is there for me but the dead.

"Part of me hopes we do, and part of me never wants to step foot there again," Estella says. "It's my home. I've never lived anywhere else." She pauses. I can feel her throat working as she swallows hard. "But I'm afraid. I'm afraid of what it's going to be like there. Part of me wants to just keep it in my memory the way it is, bright and shining and happy, and not have to face reality, you know?"

I do know.

The barn door opens again behind us. The flashlight inside doesn't provide a ton of light, but in the star-filled world out here, any glimpse of unnatural light is immediately apparent. "Zara? Estella?" Jasmine calls. "Are you guys okay?"

Estella lifts her head. I lift mine. I stretch. She stretches.

I sigh. "Yeah, we're coming back in."

"Don't forget to finish peeing," Estella says helpfully. I do, and then we head back inside, where the group is quiet and subdued, not wanting to talk.

I fall asleep beside Estella, marveling at how lucky I am to have a friend like her. Romance is fleeting. It's full of drama. Who needs a boyfriend when you have an Estella? I dream of our past, Estella and me at school pushing our way through crowded hallways, wearing tattered clothes and carrying our homes on our backs, and then I realize that none of our classmates have a face, but somehow they're shouting "Smoke! Smoke!" through their mouthless skin, and they have Ronan's voice, and then my eyes are opening and they sting and Ronan's still shouting.

And the world is on fire.

58

I pop awake, everything already crystal clear, and take a quick inventory of my surroundings.

Ronan is yelling, half his hair matted to the side of his head as he runs around shaking us. The others are blinking awake, sitting up confused. Estella's face is split in a yawn. Jasmine is still on the ground, her pillow over her head.

And above us smoke is billowing.

Flames are rising up one wall, crackling hungrily at the wood. They must have come from outside. The whole field must be on fire. Which isn't surprising, really. With no electric light, matches and lighters and candles are probably being used everywhere, and on a hot, dry night like this it wouldn't take long for flames to—

A piece of the roof falls, landing on the dirt with a shattering crash, throwing up sparks that catch on pieces of hay.

We have to get out of here. Now.

I kick Jasmine in the side as hard as I can. "Hey!" she yelps, lurching upright, but her eyes widen as she takes in what's going on around her.

I grab for my pack, which I was using as a pillow, but many of the others weren't so expeditious. Their packs are piled together over to the side, where the flames are bright.

"We need to get out of here!" I shout, turning around and around, looking for the door.

Our exit is blocked by fire.

When I take my next breath, I feel it scorch my throat. Is it my imagination, or is my head getting dizzy and light? "This way!"

I drop closer to the ground, where the smoke is lighter, and crab-walk to the end of the barn farthest from the fire. Please let there be a window, please let there be a—*there*. Better than a window: a back door. Right. We bolted it shut earlier. I tug the bolt open, hardly wincing as the metal sears my skin. "Get out!" I shout. "Go!"

The captain goes down with the ship. So I stay right where I am and shove Estella out into the night, then Gabe right after her, then . . . where are the others? "Guys! Hey!" I scream in the direction of the camp, but it's just a cloud of smoke now, and it absorbs my words like they're nothing.

A horrible cracking sound. A shower of sparks. My stomach heavy with dread. I have only a second to make my decision.

Another crack. I suck in a deep breath of not-smoke, as deep as I can, and I plunge back into the barn.

The first time I flew on an airplane was when I left the compound and came to LA. I remember sitting in the window seat, my nose pressed up against the dirty plastic, mouth agape as the trees faded into broccoli stalks faded into green dots. *Wow*, I thought, stunned, and then we were inside a cloud, white puffs around us in every direction. I panicked and tugged on my mom's shoulder. "The pilot can't see! We're going to crash!"

That's how I feel right now, except I'm not safe inside a sanitized bubble, I'm right in the heat and the chaos. I stoop low, avoiding the darkest gray of the smoke, but there's nowhere I can go where breathing doesn't hurt. I know I have only a few minutes before I pass out—and that the others might have passed out already.

I flail blindly, the seconds ticking by in my head, and by some miracle I brush up against a T-shirt, then an arm. Standing up. I don't know who it is, but I close my fingers around that arm and *pull*.

They resist. I pull again, as hard as I can, but the figure is rooted like a flagpole, as if they're holding tight to something. They lean in toward me, and Jasmine's face emerges from the fog. "Ina is trapped!" she shouts. "Under a beam! Ronan is trying to—"

I don't waste time listening to her, just plunge forward. I find Ronan sprawled out on the floor, unconscious. I grab his hand and connect it to Jasmine's. "Drag him out before you pass out too!" I try not to think about how passing out from smoke inhalation is bad, how it means something bad for your lungs, and then I crouch down.

I'm already dizzy. I try not to think about what that means either.

Ina's arms are limp. She's passed out too. I run my hands over her body, feeling points where the clothing has burned away. Also bad.

The beam's holding down her left leg. It's hot, but not on fire. Small blessings. I kick it as hard as I can. It doesn't move.

I wipe sweat and grit from my forehead. It takes an extra second for my arm to move. That's bad. Really bad. I should scramble for the door after Ronan and Jasmine. But if I leave, then Ina's going to burn to—

Strong hands seize my shoulders. "Come on!" Estella shouts in my ear, and then Gabe's there too, in front, and we're all pulling Ina together.

We tumble back as she pulls free. I'm weak enough now, my brain fuzzy enough, where I wouldn't have been able to make it on my own. But with the three of us pulling together, with Gabe and Estella's fresher minds and surer hands, we stumble out of the smoke-filled barn and into the night.

We can't stop and rest. My mind quickly goes sharp out in the cool night air, but the fire's roaring in the cornfield. I marvel at it for a moment, the flames against the darkness, stretching out into the horizon.

The smoke blocks out all the stars.

The bare stretch of dirt around the back side of the barn has stopped the fire's progression for now, but it's only a matter of time before it eats through the barn and into the grass and crops on the other side. We have to keep moving.

"Gabe, carry Ina," I say. He stoops and throws her over one shoulder in a fireman's carry. "Estella and Jasmine, do you think the two of you can manage—"

But Ronan's already stirring. I shake him hard. "Come on, wake up!"

He's up, and wincing in pain. We don't have time to figure out where his pain is coming from. I pull him up.

Running through a cornfield—or any field—with a fire coming is probably a death sentence. Fire runs a lot faster than people. Which is why the whole time we're crashing through the field toward the road, I'm looking over my shoulder. Waiting for the flames to overtake us and burn us to ash that'll blow away in the wind. The razor-sharp leaves of the cornstalks cut us as we shove our way through, and the sound of the fire is a muffled roar. The endless rows of waving cornstalks around us make me dizzy . . . dizzier. Are we even running toward the road, or circling back to where we began?

Somehow we do make it to the road. We run onto the pavement, coughing and wheezing, sweat slick on our arms and grit caked in our hair. And we keep running. I take a quick survey as I run. Estella and I are the only ones with packs. Ina's still passed out. Ronan's slow, clutching at one of his arms.

None of this is good.

I honestly don't know how we keep running. We go away from the flames, hoping to find somewhere that isn't on fire, and we find it. Somehow. After what feels like an entire night—after what *is* an entire night; the sky is pinkening into dawn—the smell of smoke is no longer in the air. Well, it is, because it's on us. We reek of smoke and fire and sweat.

A truck rumbles by. We duck into the fields, hiding ourselves from view. When we emerge, the truck is gone. "Maybe they could've helped," Ronan says, his voice raspy, but the rest of us know better. He should know better by now too.

59

"We shouldn't set up here," I say from our little clearing in the cornfield. Around us green stalks rustle, reaching for the sky. Yes, we're sheltered, but we're *too* sheltered. Nobody can see us, but we can't see them coming, either. Even the sound is oddly muffled here in the middle of the corn.

"We need to rest," Estella says firmly, and I can't argue with that. Every part of me aches, even my lungs. I feel like my head is full of sand.

I sit—or rather, I collapse. All I want to do is lie down and close my eyes, but the leader can't show weakness.

Especially when other members of the group are weak. Ronan's breathing is tight and thready, his voice thin and raspy. He's cradling one of his arms, which is pink and oozing with burns; the side of his leg that was closest to the flames is burned too. Jasmine has minor burns and bloody scrapes all over her body from where she was struggling to free Ina.

But it's Ina who has it the worst. She fluttered awake while we were on the move but went in and out of consciousness as she bounced up and down on Gabe's shoulder. The leg that was trapped under the beam hangs limp and makes her cry out when we touch it—"Might be broken," Jasmine confirmed grimly. And Ina's burns are worse than Ronan's or Jasmine's, covering the injured leg and creeping up her torso, red and swollen and blistered, with speckles of white in the worst-hit patches.

I take a deep, shaky breath. She's going to need help. So will Ronan and Jasmine. I don't need Jasmine, our doctor-in-training, to tell me that burns can easily get infected, since they're open wounds and pathways to the soft tissue below. And we don't just have to worry about infection; we have to worry about Ina's leg. She won't be able to walk on that for a long time.

Ina moans. I want to rest a comforting hand on her shoulder, but I'm afraid it will hurt her more. "It's going to be okay," I say. I don't think I sound very convincing. She must not think so either, because she moans again.

"Just leave me." Her voice is so faint at first, I don't think I've heard her correctly. I lean in.

"What?"

"Just leave me!" she says. She looks like she's shouting, but the voice that comes out isn't much more than a puff of air. "Leave me and go!"

I blink at her. "Are you insane?" I'm surprised by the words that jump out of my mouth. Because why should I think she's insane for saying that when it's the best thing for the group? When she would just drag us down?

Why am I not nodding and saying, *Yes, it's unfortunate, but survival is about the individual, and we can't afford to take care of you*?

Estella jumps to my side. "She didn't mean that," she says hastily. "We know you're in a lot of pain and under a lot of stress right now, and—"

"I said to leave me here," Ina says. "I'm not addled. I still have a brain. Just go. Just do it."

"We're not leaving you," Gabe says over my shoulder.

"I'll just slow you down." Ina sounds like a deflating balloon, and then her eyelids flutter shut again.

"Okay, we're probably better off with her out of it," I say. Though I feel bad that she would tell us to leave her. True, she hasn't exactly been the most dynamic companion. She may have helped save the day at the compound, but I still don't know her last name, or where she's from, or where she's going. But I know that she feeds us things that taste good, and she takes her shifts on watch without complaining.

She's one of us.

And we don't leave any of us behind. No matter what it takes.

I'm not sure if this represents a change to my philosophy, or if I just feel a responsibility toward my people. I'm their "fearless leader," after all. What kind of fearless leader would I be if I abandoned members of the group I'm leading?

"We need to rest," Estella says again.

"As the group medic, I agree," says Jasmine. She doesn't wait for me to respond, just plops down on the ground. Sweat pearls over her forehead; the edges of her lips are white. She's in more pain than she wants to admit.

But I stand firm. "We can't stay in the field like this. It's not safe."

"Then where are we supposed to go?"

I haven't thought that far ahead. But I can't let them know that. "We need somewhere covered. Somewhere inside. Somewhere like the barn."

Jasmine mumbles something that sounds like, "The barn's on fire."

I bite my tongue. "We can rest here for a little bit, but then we have to keep moving."

"This is a farm. A big one," Ronan says. I have to lean in to hear his voice. "There should be sheds scattered around the fields for tools and storage where we can rest."

Gabe leaps up. "I'll go look."

"Not alone," I say. I picture the corn swallowing him up. "And take a whistle or something in case you get lost. Move in straight lines."

"I'll go with him," says Estella.

They don't wait for a response, just head off. My whole body clenches at the thought of having them away from me. They should be here. What if they get lost in the endless waves of corn? It's not like one stalk of corn looks different from any other. There are horror movies set in cornfields for that reason, because it's so easy to disappear in them, so easy to vanish forever.

"Did we start the fire?" Ronan's voice is even fainter than before.

Jasmine shakes her head. "We couldn't have," she says firmly. "We didn't light any candles or anything."

"I don't think it started in the barn," I say. "It looks like it started somewhere else and managed to make it to—"

A crash. Gabe reappears, panting, a smile on his face. "There's a shed just over here. On the side of the road."

Perfect. If it's on the road, it'll be easy to find again. Yes, I'm already thinking about finding it again, because I know what we need to do.

Ina's still out, so Gabe and I gently carry her between us, trying not to jar her leg. She must have been in excruciating pain while Gabe was running along with her, I realize. And yet she never said anything.

The shed reminds me a bit of that first shed I stayed in way back when I was trying to get to the Rose Bowl, when I still had a mom. It's cramped and dim, crowded with farm tools, like hoes and rakes. It smells faintly of gasoline and dried grass.

It's probably not a great place for anyone recovering from burns. Or a broken leg. Jasmine grits her teeth. "We need medical supplies," she says. "If any of these burns get infected . . . and Ina's leg . . ."

I rifle quickly through my bag, though I know perfectly well I don't have any medical supplies in there. Gabe had the rest of the ones we took from the stadium. "We don't have anything." I take a deep breath and clutch my mom's plastic dog for luck. "We're going to have to split up. You, Ronan, Ina, and Estella stay here. Stay safe. Don't let anyone in the shed. Gabe and I will go find things to help you."

Gabe nods, but Jasmine shakes her head. "We should all stay together."

"I wish we could," I answer. "But Ina can't even walk. Ronan shouldn't be walking either, or you. You guys shouldn't be stressing your bodies."

Estella purses her lips, chewing on the inside of her cheek. She knows I'm right. She just doesn't want to admit it. I don't blame her.

Splitting up in this new world is scary. Before, she could just text me where she'd be; I could give her a call if plans changed and I had to meet her somewhere else. We could snap each other pictures of our locations, allow each other to track our GPS coordinates. Worse came to worst, we'd go home and get in touch via landline and meet up a little later.

Now? If they're driven out of this shed, how will I ever find them again?

Maybe that's why Estella says, "No. No way."

"You know we can't move—"

"I mean I'm coming with you two." Her eyes flit from me to Gabe, Gabe to me. "I can't take the chance of losing you. Even the slightest chance. I can't. I won't."

"But we need you here," I say patiently. "Ina's pretty much out for the count. Ronan and Jasmine are both injured and off their game."

"Can you be off your game if you never had any game to begin with?" Jasmine asks. I ignore her, even as a smile twitches at my lips. She *has* been pretty terrible at target practice.

"You have to protect them," I continue. "And besides, you don't even know where we're going."

"I don't need to know where." Estella crosses her arms. "All I need to know is that I'm going with you. I swear to God, I'll follow you if I have to. You're all I have left, and I'm not losing you." She glances over at Jasmine. "No offense to you guys. You're great."

"Where *are* you going, by the way?" Jasmine asks. "We're in the middle of nowhere. Anywhere you need to walk will probably take ages. And by the time you get all the way there and back . . ." She trails off, leaving it unspoken. *Infection will have already set in. You'll need a lot more than rubbing alcohol and antibacterial ointment and numbing cream and bandages to save us then.*

"We're not going on foot," I say.

"What are you talking about?"

I let a deep breath out. I didn't even know I had so much air in me. "Let me worry about that. You worry about getting better." It's the kind of platitude that my mom used to say when members of the public used to confront her about things that were stressing them out. It was a way to express sympathy while saying exactly nothing.

"Then, where are you going?" Ronan pushes himself up into a sitting position, wincing in pain.

We've lost Ronan's maps. But I remember enough of them from poring over them every night, our heads bowed side by side. "We've been traveling northeast, roughly along the Boyer River, straying from it when we need to but always keeping its location in hand," I say. We've learned since our time in the desert. "We're not far from the town of Denison. It was a smallish dot on the map, which means it's probably under ten thousand people, but bigger than a few hundred. There's probably a hospital there, or at least some kind of clinic. Even a veterinarian's office would be okay for what we need, I think."

"So you're going to magic yourself there and somehow get some supplies," Jasmine says skeptically. "We don't have anything to trade."

"Maybe they'll be good people and just give us what we need," Ronan says. "That's what my people did back at the ward, with nothing expected in return."

"Maybe," I say grimly. "Maybe not."

60

I try again to leave Estella behind as Gabe and I head out, but she literally won't stop following us. "I don't care what you say," she tells us, her chin jutting out stubbornly in that way I know so well. "I'm coming with. Try and stop me."

"Stell," Gabe says, his voice so gentle it makes me want to curl in on myself. "I just want to keep you safe."

Her eyes go flat. Dead. Now I want to curl around *her*. "Nobody can keep me safe," she says. Then, as if she sees the shock and sadness in our eyes, she forces a smile. "Gabe, you really should've become one of the Eyes. We'd already be out east then."

Gabe cracks a tiny smile in response. "We'd still be in our original car. With our parents. And the power would be back on."

But Gabe's not an Eye, and from the misty look on Estella's face, I can tell she wishes she hadn't joked about it. She comes along, one of Ronan's guns at her side. "Be safe, you guys," I tell Jasmine and Ronan. He has his other gun—thank goodness he slept with them on him—and he's a crack shot. Even if he can't really move. "Stay hidden. We'll be back soon."

Jasmine lifts her chin. "I'd say we'll wait a few days, but I don't think we could go anywhere if we tried." She sounds defiant anyway.

As Gabe, Estella, and I trudge down the road, I tell them what I know. "A truck drove by us this morning, heading this way," I say. "The truck bed was empty. There was one guy in the driver's seat, and he looked pretty old."

"So?" Estella asks.

Gabe finishes for me. "If the truck was going a long distance, like we were going with ours, the truck bed would've been loaded up," he says. "Which means he was probably driving only a short distance. Maybe to pick up water or check on a friend nearby."

"Exactly."

"So the truck is somewhere nearby, hopefully within walking distance," Estella says slowly. "You can't mean . . ."

"We're going to steal the truck," I confirm.

She gasps. "We can't! I know we already stole one truck, but that was from bad people. Not innocent people who haven't done anything to us."

"We have to. We don't have time to search the whole farm for a free tractor or extra vehicle. People driving have probably siphoned any gas left from them anyway," I say grimly. I glance sidelong at Gabe. I know he won't like this plan, but I hope he'll agree we have no other options. He's staring ahead, mouth set into a firm line. "We'll bring it back. I promise."

"Then, we can ask to borrow it," Estella argues. "Then maybe think about taking it if they say—"

"Stell, I don't like it either," Gabe interrupts. "But if we ask and they say no—which they probably will, because we're random strangers and gas is precious these days—they'll be on the alert. Maybe even try to scare us off. So we just need to do it."

I should be happy that he's on my side, but instead an ache spreads through me. Sadness. He's different now than he was before. Different from the guy who was totally shocked and horrified when that couple stole almost all our water while pretending to fix our car, because he could never imagine doing such a thing himself.

And yet, as we keep on walking, hoping the truck will come into view, I find myself sympathizing with those people more and more. Like us, they did what they needed to survive. They sacrificed their morals to save members of their group. Sure, I plan on returning the truck, unlike the way they obviously didn't plan on returning our water, but you know what they say about the best-laid plans. And about the scarcity of gas. Maybe we'll be using up the last they have. I'm not even sorry.

Okay, yes, I am sorry. But not enough to not do what we've planned.

We're walking in the opposite direction of the fire, and it feels good to be leaving the curls of smoke behind. Just as I'm starting to think that we'll be walking beside sweet-smelling fields for the rest of my (surely short) life, a dirt path branches to the side, and I see the fields turn into parched brown grass, and then, sure enough, there's a quaint white home with a truck parked out front.

The relief that sweeps through me is nearly indescribable. It's like that deep breath when I got out of the smoke or that first sweet sip of water back in the ward.

Until now I haven't been absolutely sure I was leading my group to the right place. I haven't even let myself think it. What if I was wrong?

I push those thoughts away. "Stay out of sight," I say. "We need to case the place."

I'd prefer to wait till dark, but we don't have time, not with infection potentially setting in at any moment. "Estella, you stay back here with Ronan's gun," I say.

"But I don't know what to do with—"

"That's fine," I say. "Let me turn the safety off. All you would have to do is point at the sky and pull the trigger. We probably wouldn't need anything more than a warning shot. Just in case."

I glance over at Gabe and nod. He nods back. Together we creep toward the house.

I brush against the truck as I pass by; it's warmer than it should be merely from the heat of the sun, meaning that it was likely recently driven. Whoever drove it should be nearby, then. I peep through the window, hoping that maybe they'll have left the keys in the ignition, but no such luck.

Through the front window of the house, I can hear clanging coming from inside, sounding maybe like pots in the kitchen. The back of my neck prickles uncomfortably in the open air. Anyone could be behind me. Any minute I'll hear the sound of a gun being cocked in my direction. A shotgun, probably. Something that would splatter my brains all over—

"I don't see anything," Gabe whispers.

The truck ticks behind us, as if reminding me someone was just inside. "We don't need to see anything in particular. We need—"

"Can I help y'all?"

The voice comes from behind us, friendly and cautious at the same time. I turn, my hand pulling up my crossbow.

I'm pretty sure it's the same guy I saw driving the truck earlier. He's tall and stocky with a broad, mustachioed face and shaggy black hair. Wearing overalls and dirt-smudged boots, he's exactly what I pictured in a farmer. Even if I didn't think Midwesterners said "y'all."

I take a deep breath. Once the words come out, there's no turning back. "We need your truck."

The man's mustache quivers. His eyes narrow. Thick black brows form a *V* beneath his forehead. "Excuse me?"

I raise my crossbow. Shame rushes hot through me. I push it away by focusing on the key ring dangling from his belt. "I'm really sorry, but we need your truck. It's a matter of life and death." He probably doesn't care about that. No, scratch that—he probably does. I think most human beings would.

It's just that he doesn't care about our life-and-death situation as much as his own life-and-death situation.

"We'll bring it back if we can, I promise," I say hastily. "We're not trying to steal it. We just really, *really* need it for a few hours."

He stares at me, unwavering. Actually, that's not right.

He stares at my crossbow, unwavering.

"We need the keys," Gabe says gently. "We're really sorry."

The man doesn't move. He doesn't look angry. He looks . . . disappointed. Like teachers look when you forget to turn in an important project. Like he expects better of us, even though he doesn't know us or what we're going through.

His eyes dart to the side. His tongue darts out to lick his lips. He might be thinking about yelling out to whoever's in that house making clanking noises in the kitchen. His partner? His child?

It doesn't matter.

I heft my crossbow in what I hope is a threatening manner even as I swallow over a lump in my throat. "Drop your keys," I say. "Or I'll . . ." My voice dies out. I can't say I'll shoot him. I can't shoot an innocent man. Somehow realizing that gives me comfort. "I have great aim."

His face has faded from tan to a sickly yellow. His hands shaking, he unfastens the key ring from his belt and lets it fall to the ground. Gabe takes a step toward him, but I tell him to stop. Gabe stops without even asking why. Maybe he realized what I did: the guy could be luring us close, planning on grabbing Gabe to use as a human shield.

"Kick them over to us," I direct. His first kick is feeble and goes short, but after I give him a death stare, he kicks it hard. The keys skitter close enough for Gabe to bend over and scoop them up.

But I don't move my crossbow. "Start the truck," I direct Gabe. "Make sure there's enough gas."

The man and I stand like posed statues as the truck engine ticks, then vrooms. "Half a tank," Gabe calls to me.

That should be plenty to take us an hour or two away and back. Hopefully. "Estella!" I shout over my shoulder. "In the truck!"

Estella's footsteps crunch against the dry grass. My eyes still trained on the farmer, I hear her thump into the passenger seat, the door close behind her.

"Like I said, we're really sorry, and we'll return it," I tell the guy, backing up toward the truck, my crossbow still raised. "Thank you."

As soon as my butt bumps against warm metal, I lower my

crossbow and leap backward, landing in the truck bed. The man shouts and runs after us, but Gabe revs the engine and reverses fast, fast, fast, and the man has to jump out of the way to avoid getting hit.

I think I hear a voice calling out to him from the house as he grows smaller and smaller behind us.

61

The Iowa roads are not in great shape. We stick to the main one, since we have no idea where we're going on back roads and barely know where we're going this way, and we have to slowly maneuver through an obstacle course: Of cars, though luckily for us, most have already been pushed off to the side of the road. Of a fallen telephone pole, its wires a tangle around it—maybe a failed attempt to see if there was an issue up there. Of the occasional car zooming past us. My heart always hammers when they do, thinking the farmer might have borrowed a car to come after us, but we wouldn't have had to steal his truck if there were cars to be borrowed.

I know we're getting close when we start passing buildings: a few manufacturing plants, some houses, a hotel, and a cinema. If I weren't sitting in the back of the truck, I'd make a crack to Estella about how maybe we should stop and see what's playing.

I catch glimpses of houses in the distance as we turn left onto Route 59, passing more plants and hotels. I wonder if people are staying mostly in their homes, making the trek for water and defending whatever food stores and private spaces they have, or if they decamped for shelters like the Rose Bowl and never looked back. I wonder how many of these hotels and factories have been taken over by desperate people looking for safety.

On the outside it all looks so peaceful.

Gabe slows as we pass a McDonald's and a Pizza Ranch. I glance at him questioningly, and he raises an eyebrow at me. We've been traveling together long enough that I know exactly what he's saying. *Should we stop to see if there's food? We don't have much food left.*

I shake my head. Whatever was left in those restaurants has either gone bad or was looted long ago. Besides, we have to get back to the others; we can go foraging later. The human body can live a surprisingly long time without food.

Gabe nods, turning back to the road, continuing to follow the signs for Crawford County Memorial Hospital.

When we turn into the drive, I survey the land with a critical eye. There isn't really anywhere around here to hide a truck. We'll just have to park somewhere easily visible and guard the keys with our lives.

There are fortunately a surprising number of cars in the parking lot; if someone is looking to hot-wire one, the odds are in our favor that they'll choose someone else's. We park and walk toward the main entrance, our weapons tucked away but in easy reach.

As we walk, the uneasiness from before continues to ripple in my stomach. "So," I say to Gabe, though Estella also looks over. "Am I still your hero?" My voice breaks, but I cover it up with a cough. It works. I think.

"Of course." Gabe's smile is a little crooked. "Maybe even more so. Did you forget how you ran back into a burning building for your squad?"

I take a deep breath, then let it all out. "I just threatened an innocent man and robbed him." Somehow, saying those cold, hard words out loud makes what happened sound even more insane. "That's not exactly something a hero would do."

"You didn't have a choice," Gabe says. "Did you also forget that I was right there next to you?"

That's true. Maybe neither of us is a hero. Then again, what exactly *is* a hero? Is it someone who does the right thing every single time? Who decides what that right thing is? The law? It was illegal to hide Jewish people from the Nazis and to help runaway slaves make it to the North, but those were definitively the right things to do. Not that I'm even remotely comparing my stealing a truck to righteous gentiles or abolitionists, but still.

I stand in front of the automatic doors for an embarrassingly long ten seconds before realizing that, duh, there's no electricity and they're not going to open. Gabe shoulders them open. Inside we're met with a sticky wall of heat. Sweat immediately pops from every crevice in my body; I pull at my collar to get some air into my shirt. None of the big glass windows are open. I guess they're not made to open. Whoever built this place probably assumed it would always be filled with the icy chill of air-conditioning.

There's not much else in the room besides rows of chairs and a long, gleaming desk. All are empty except for one of the chairs at the end, where a figure is slumped over, surrounded by plastic grocery bags. I exchange glances with Gabe and Estella, asking wordlessly, *What do I do?*

The air smells slightly rotten, like when you drive by a dead deer on the side of the road. My stomach stirs uneasily. There's something about that smell that screams, *Get out! Get out, Zara!*

But we can't get out. We have to help our group. Though it occurs to me that there might not even be anything here. Aren't a lot of these medications kept refrigerated? Except I think antibacterial ointment's usually on the shelf at the pharmacy.

Estella's footsteps are loud in the silence as she moves toward the slumped-over figure. She has her hand on her gun, tucked in the back of her pants, though not wrapped around it. More like she's touching it as some sort of good-luck charm. "Hello?" she says. Her words bounce around the high ceiling. *Hello? Hello? Hello?*

The figure turns her face up. It's a woman swathed in blankets, with only her head visible. She's on the older side, maybe in her fifties or sixties, and she blinks blearily at us from behind a pair of round glasses. She opens her mouth with a sticky sort of sound, like pulling your bare skin off leather on a hot day. She croaks, so quietly that I can barely hear her, "So . . . thirsty . . ."

We'll have access to water again once we get back to the river. I go to grab my water bottle, but Estella beats me to it. She turns around and takes a plastic cup from the (dry) water cooler on the edge of the waiting area, pours some of her water into it, and presents it to the woman, who snatches it and drinks greedily, drops splashing down into her lap.

When she lowers the cup, Estella asks, "Do you want some

more?" only to be met with moaning. The woman rocks back and forth, then turns to the side and vomits up a stream of clear water all over the chairs beside her. That done, she settles back into her chair, panting heavily.

"Are you okay?" I ask.

She looks at me like I'm an idiot. Obviously she's not okay. Gabe says, "Is there anything we can do to help?"

The woman closes her eyes. "Not unless you're carrying a refrigerator and a supply of insulin in that pack."

Oh. She's a diabetic. I remember reading books about a diabetic girl when I moved to LA, about how she had to stick herself with needles full of insulin to regulate her body's supply. How without those regular injections, she would die.

The woman rasps, "I ran out of my own supply, then came here just as their backup generator died. But of course I wasn't the only one. They had to ration their insulin, and mine ran out almost a week ago. Some people are still upstairs. Or they died."

"I'm sorry," Gabe and Estella both murmur. I don't say it. It's not like an apology from me will mean anything.

It occurs to me for what shouldn't be the first time how lucky I am to be healthy and able bodied during this whole thing. What if you needed an electric wheelchair to get around? Or refrigerated medications? Or treatments like chemotherapy or dialysis?

That's why the hospital is so empty. Everyone is dead.

"I'm so sorry," I say, and I'm not speaking entirely to her.

"Why are you here?"

What do I have to lose by telling this woman what happened? So I tell her about the wildfire, about our three wounded friends waiting for us at home. No, not at home. That shed is not a home. "We're hoping to find antiseptic ointment, bandages, antibiotics, anything else that might help." Those were the big three Jasmine told us to get. Antiseptic ointment to cleanse the wounds, bandages to keep them covered so other stuff doesn't get in them, and antibiotics in case one of them actually does get infected, which it probably will if we don't apply the antiseptic in time.

"If they don't need to be refrigerated, you might get lucky," the woman rasps. "The only people left here are the dead and the dying."

She struggles to sit up straighter, moving her hand beneath the blanket. In a few seconds it emerges, clutching a worn leather wallet. She thrusts it at me. When I don't take it, she thrusts it at me even more impatiently. "Open it."

I flip it open and find a few twenties, some shiny credit cards, a punch card halfway toward a free coffee, and a driver's license. She points at that with a trembling finger, so I remove it, still not exactly sure what she's getting at.

Her name is Donna Pearson, and she lives nearby outside Denison. She's five three when standing. Donna Pearson points insistently at the license. "Yours," she rasps.

"What?"

"Yours," she says more insistently. Her hand moves around under her blankets again, jingling as it emerges with a key ring. She holds it out to me. It jangles even more as she trembles. "Take my house." She quickly tells us how to get there. It's not far from the hospital, on our way back to the shed where we left the rest of our group, and not far from the river, either. "On one condition."

She's really telling us to use her house? My breath catches in my throat as I realize how lucky we've gotten. Well, probably lucky. A safe, hopefully clean place for the others to recuperate, maybe even with supplies of food or water, near enough to the river?

Donna Pearson points at Estella. Estella steps aside, looking over her shoulder, probably assuming the woman is pointing at something behind her. But Donna's finger travels with Estella, punching at her. "I saw the bulge in the back of your pants when you got me water. A gun, right?" she says. "I'm already dead. All I'm doing now is suffering on the trip there."

Estella pales. She swallows hard. "You want me to *shoot* you?" Her voice climbs a staircase. "Like, with a *gun*?"

"That's why you have it, isn't it?" Donna rasps.

"Yeah, but . . ." Estella trails off, then starts again, her voice even higher. "What if the power comes back on, and you can get more insulin, and then you—"

"I'm a nurse," Donna says flatly. "I have five more days at most, and they're going to be awful, painful days. My brain will start to swell and press against my skull. Please. Help me."

I understand her. I'd rather die quickly, cleanly, than linger painfully in hopes of a miraculous cure. Of course, I'd rather not die at all, but that's not the game we're playing. "I'll do it," I say quietly, nodding first at Donna, then at Estella. "Give it to me."

"Thank you," Donna says, but Estella shakes her head.

"Estella—"

"I can do it," Estella says firmly. "Just give me a minute." She takes a deep breath as she reaches for her gun. Her hands tremble as she removes it, and her lips start moving. I think she's praying, which surprises me somehow. I know Estella always believed in God, but surely that belief faded after all that happened to her?

Apparently not.

While she prays, Gabe talks to Donna. "You're absolutely positive you want to do this?" he asks. She nods. "You're still in your right mind. You want to die." She nods again, her face set and resolute. "Can you say it aloud?"

"Talking hurts," Donna rasps. "Just get it done."

"Do you have any last words?" Gabe asks. "Anything we could write down and pass along?"

"Said everything already," Donna says. "Please. Just do it."

Estella steps up, her whole body shaking now. How can she even hold a gun, shaking like that? I move forward, trying to communicate that I can do it for her, that she doesn't have to do this, that she can stay soft and—

She fires. Donna drops, falling to her side as if with relief. Estella steps back, looking up toward the ceiling, lips moving even faster now. But she's not shaking anymore. She's not crumbling.

Maybe she's not that girl in the bathroom that I need to rescue anymore.

62

I catch up to Estella as we head toward the stairs, Donna Pearson's wallet clutched firmly in my hand. "Stell—"

"I don't want to talk about it," she says, just as firmly as I'm clutching that wallet. "Not right now. Let's do what we need to do and get out."

The hospital in the dark is an eerie place. I pull out my pocket flashlight, but that just makes all the shadows seem more menacing. We hear the occasional shuffling noise but don't see any people.

But the smells. Oh my God. The smells. They crawl inside me, stuffing up my nose and my throat, threatening to choke me. Each of us has to stop and retch every so often to try to clear it out, but there's nothing we can do. Even breathing through our mouths, we can taste it.

I feel like I'll be tasting it for the rest of my life.

We rummage through every closet and nurse's station and dead fridge we come across. Some are empty, some were clearly already looted, with bits of paper and empty plastic containers scattered around them. But as Jasmine told us about the hospital she volunteered at back in New Jersey, antibiotics and antiseptic and bandages are incredibly common items, and we only have to go through two floors before we find enough to help our group, plus some extra just in case.

On our way downstairs and back out into the parking lot, we steer clear of Donna Pearson's body. It might be mental, but the lobby smells thickly of iron and rust. I hold my breath until we push our way through the no-longer-automatic doors into the parking lot.

Where we're confronted with another question. "Did Donna say anything about a car?" Gabe asks, looking around. Abandoned cars gleam in the sunlight.

I shake my head. I don't know. Even looking at the key ring doesn't help. I click the unlock button on her car keys as we wind our way through the rows, but nothing beeps at us. And we don't have time to go through every single row of the parking lot, plus the parking garage. "She might not even have driven here," I say. "Or someone could have stolen her car already."

So we pile back in our truck, me in the driver's seat, Estella on the passenger side to navigate, Gabe in the back to keep a lookout behind us. I glance at Estella as I start the truck. "So, now can we talk about it?"

She sits still, staring straight out the front window. "Talk about what?"

"You just killed someone," I say. She doesn't respond, just looks intently at the blank stretch of road before her. I shift into gear and tap the gas. "That's kind of a big deal."

"It's like she said. She was dead already." Estella's voice shakes a little, but underneath it's firm. "We were doing a good thing for her. I'd hope if I'm ever in the same situation, you'd do the same for me."

That's a big ask of someone. But I'd do anything for her.

I just hope I'll never have to.

"I saw you were whispering to yourself," I say. "Before you did it. Were you . . ."

"Praying?" Estella says. "Yeah. I was." She notices my skeptical eyebrow raise and matches it with one of her own. "Why not?"

"Um, because any god that would let all of this happen"—I wave my arm wildly out the window, probably smacking down a bug or two—"might not bother sending you help?"

"I wasn't asking for help," Estella says. "God helps those who help themselves." She takes a deep breath. "I was asking for strength."

"I don't think you need any of that from God," I say. "I think you've got plenty of that on your own."

63

Donna Pearson's house is nice. It's small and squat, far enough off the road where we probably won't see much foot traffic, but only a ten-minute or so walk to the river. As we pull into the driveway, I hope fervently that we won't see broken windows and kicked-in doors . . . and we don't. When we unlock the front door, all that greets us inside is stale air and dust. There's canned and dry food in the pantry, plenty of it—the woman really liked pasta and tomato sauce—and even some bottled water.

We have less luck in the garage: it's empty of any vehicle. "She must have driven to the hospital, or else somebody stole her car," Gabe says gloomily. "Should we go back and look again?"

I shake my head. "No time," I say.

Estella lets out a cheer, clapping her hands. At first I'm mystified why she'd cheer my words, and then she points at some red plastic canisters stacked in the corner beside a lawn mower. Gasoline. We refill the farmer's tank, with extra left over.

The mood is relatively cheerful as we get back into the truck, having locked the house up carefully behind us, but I know it won't last. Not when I tell them what we're doing next. Or to be exact, what Estella's doing next.

Because now that we have more gas, we can use the truck to transport our wounded friends to Donna Pearson's house to recuperate without endangering them more. Estella nods along as I say that, then stops as I continue on. "We promised the farmer we'd bring his truck back. Gabe and I are going to keep that promise, then hike back to join you guys."

Estella frowns. "I told you, I'm staying with you guys."

I take a deep breath. "It has to be done. I keep my promises, and it should only take us a few days at most. And I need you, Estella, to take care of the others. They're hurt. Keep things going there, and protect them if you need to. I know you can do it. I just saw it."

She's still glowering at me, but at least she's not shaking her head.

"Gabe and I made it through half the country on our own," I say. "I promise we can make it forty miles on the river."

She sighs deeply. I know she's going to agree before she even opens her mouth. "You're the leader. Fine. But . . ." She looks away, and I don't need the frogginess in her voice to tell me she's on the verge of tears. "You guys *can't* die. Or disappear. You can't leave me on my own."

"I promise we won't," I say. "And like I just said, I keep my promises."

64

It's not like I expected them to be gone, but I still exhale a great whoosh of relief when we make it back to the shed and find everybody inside waiting. "We come bearing medical supplies," I announce, breezing through the door like I haven't just been worrying. In case you're wondering, I totally cribbed that whole thing from the president's speech at the beginning of the blackout. Seeing their leader so calm and self-assured made the Ramirezes feel safe and confident. Never let them see you sweat, right?

"That's seriously the sexiest thing I've ever heard," says Jasmine from her seat up against the wall. Pearls of sweat sparkle on her forehead, and she doesn't get up to greet us. Ronan gives us a limp wave from beside her, and Ina doesn't move at all.

It's a good thing we got those antibiotics.

I let Jasmine instruct me, Estella, and Gabe on how to clean and bandage their wounds, which we do, swallowing hard to avoid wanting to throw up. "We found a brace for Ina's leg, too," Gabe says, brandishing it. "But let's wait to put it on until we get to the house. We should go now."

I'm nervous again as we load everyone into the truck, the unconscious Ina lying down in back, with Estella and Gabe there to stabilize her; Ronan and Jasmine pile in next to me, where hopefully the closed windows will protect them from any flying particles that could get in their wounds. "I'm glad to leave the cornfields behind," Jasmine says, shuddering theatrically as she looks out on the waves of green swaying back and forth in the breeze. "They're so creepy."

"You know what's *really* creepy?" Ronan doesn't wait for a response. "New Jersey."

Jasmine mock-frowns at him. "I would elbow you right now, but I don't want to peel any more of our skin off."

"New Jersey's the worst," I agree.

"Better watch it! I *can* elbow you," she warns, but ruins the threatening effect with her smile. "Neither of you are even from the East Coast! You have no idea what a Jersey girl can do in a brawl."

"How about a nice LDS boy?" Ronan says. "Don't forget my four older brothers."

"I could still take you," says Jasmine.

They spend the rest of the drive debating each other's merits in a fight. I don't chime in, keeping my eyes on the road. Besides, I already know I could easily beat either of them. Especially with them all burned up.

Jasmine and Ronan both coo with excitement over Donna Pearson's house. I let them bring Ina in and get her settled as Gabe and I refill the farmer's truck with more gas. "Okay," I say, and take a deep breath. We've also refilled our packs, taking some trail mix and granola bars, which should get us through the next few days of walking. "We'd better go."

"Rest here for a bit first," wheedles Estella. She's slumped into Donna's couch like it's in the middle of swallowing her, and we'd return to find her fully digested. "At least sleep well for a night."

I shake my head. I won't sleep well as long as we have something that isn't ours. As long as someone out there thinks I'm a dirty thief. "If I sleep well here for the night, I won't sleep at all on the road. I can only sleep out there when I'm really tired."

"Do you have everything you need? Crossbow? Pepper spray? Compass?" Jasmine asks, her thick black brows knitted together.

For a moment she sounds so much like my mom that I want to cry. I reach instinctively for the plastic dog and give it a squeeze. Then swallow the tears and go on. "Yes. I have everything we need."

She taps two fingers to her forehead in a salute. "Then Godspeed. Come back to us soon."

I nod. "Godspeed to you, too." I wonder if Jasmine believes in a god, like Estella. We learned on our travels that she's Hindu, part of a religion that believes in thousands upon thousands of gods, but it didn't sound like she's all that devout. Should I say "godsspeed" instead?

I banish the thought just in time to brace myself for a fierce hug from Estella. "Don't die or I'll track you down and kill you again," she says, and sure, it's a joke, but there's a very real fear in her eyes. I squeeze her extra tight, hoping to show her my strength and vitality.

"Rest and heal up," I say to them all. "When Gabe and I get back, we'll stay and recuperate for as long as it takes you guys to mend."

Or until we run out of food. One or the other.

65

The farmer runs out his front door as soon as we pull up in front of his house. This time he's brandishing a shotgun threateningly before him, his mustache turned down over a huge frown.

I know I should feel afraid that he'll shoot. But as I step out of the cab, my hands raised before me, I'm mostly just sad that I've made him feel this way.

"I told you," I tell him. "We brought it back. We even filled up your tank."

Gabe steps out of the passenger side, hands raised as well to show he doesn't have a weapon. He moves a lot more slowly than I do, and he doesn't speak. Estella told me in hushed whispers once about how she'd overheard her parents talking to him about the realities of existing in our world with brown skin. How he had to be extra careful when interacting with the police or anyone else who held a gun, because it took a lot less for people like him to get shot than people like me.

The farmer squints at us, then at his truck. "You did bring it back." He sounds almost like he can't believe it. *I* almost can't believe it when he lowers his shotgun. "Well, I'll be. And you really filled up her tank?"

I nod. Gabe nods. The farmer squints at us a moment longer, and then his face relaxes. "You really needed her?"

"Our friends were hurt," I say. "We had to get to a hospital. And then we had to transport them somewhere safer where they could heal."

"I see," the farmer says. "Well then, I'm glad you stole my truck for a bit. And I'm glad you brought her back, too." I start thinking about asking him to drop us off at Donna Pearson's house, but then his face darkens, the cloud of a thunderstorm passing over it. "Now get out of here before I shoot you."

He doesn't have to say that twice.

We jog out of the man's driveway and back toward the road. The sun is already beating down on us, but we don't want to seek shade in the corn and risk getting lost and maybe devoured, so we stick to the road. We'll come out near the river soon enough.

We're walking in silence, concentrating on the steps ahead, when Gabe speaks. "I failed Estella," he says heavily.

"What are you talking about?" I want to stop and look him square in the face, but I know how eager we both are to get back to the others. No stopping allowed.

He doesn't seem to want to look me in the face anyway. "She had to kill that woman while I just stood there, stunned and silent. She's going to carry that with her for the rest of her life. I should've spoken up, I should've done something, I should've—"

"Are you forgetting that I offered to do it for her?" I ask. His mouth snaps shut. Yes, he forgot. He was too far into his own head. "And she still chose to do it. She's strong, Gabe. Stronger than either of us knew."

His head inclines the barest amount. I continue, "And all of us have already experienced things we'll carry with us forever. Especially her." A beat of quiet. "You're a good big brother, Gabe."

His sigh is mournful. "I guess she doesn't need me anymore."

I elbow him. "Of course she needs you! Don't be so dramatic."

"I just keep thinking about what my parents would say."

I tilt my head up and look at the sky. Maybe I should look directly at the sun. Let it burn out my retinas.

Gabe's voice wavers. "I don't want them to be disappointed in me. I need to be there for her."

"You *are* there for her." I'm so bad at this. At peopling. This is supposed to be *his* job.

What would my mom say? It hurts to picture her in my mind, a dull, steady ache in my chest. *Be kind, Zara. You've all lost so much. He needs you to soothe him and keep telling him he's doing good until he believes it.*

No, he needs to look it head-on until it doesn't make him cry anymore, my dad says. *Crying is for the weak, and the weak die. Are you weak, Zara?*

No, I tell him, and I actually believe it. I'm *not* weak, even if I'm vulnerable sometimes. If there's one thing Gabe taught me, it's that it's okay to not be okay for a little while.

I suck in a breath through my teeth. "I've told you guys about the compound."

"You did."

"I didn't tell you why I left."

"You didn't."

The sun is white and blinding overhead. I blink into it until dark spots dazzle all over my field of vision, and then I look away. The corn is blurry, but it'll clear up soon. I didn't look at the sun long enough to permanently damage my vision. No matter how much I try, there are some things I just can't do.

Like forget.

66

It was a normal fall day. Well, a normal fall day on the compound. Birds tweeting in the trees as the last little ones either learned to fly or died trying. Leaves turning red and gold and brown and fluttering off their branches to decompose under my feet. A chill in the air, even with the sun clear overhead. Animals fattening themselves up for the lean winter months.

We were also fattening ourselves up for the lean winter months. Figuratively. Every day for the past couple of weeks my dad had gone out hunting, gathering enough meat to dry and preserve to last us until spring, while my mom had stayed back at the compound, canning as much produce as she could. I'd split my time between them: one day with a crossbow, the next with glass jars. "It's important for you to learn both, Zara," my dad told me, and I knew he was right. He was always right.

I preferred the hunting, though. Being out in the open woods, padding carefully over leaves and filling my lungs with cool, clean air instead of fruity steam. My attention laser-sharp, my ears pricking for animal footsteps. I'd brought down two deer on my own. One my dad had already started drying; the other I helped him carve for a harvest feast. It wasn't like I enjoyed killing a living creature or skinning it or turning it into meat, but there was a certain satisfaction to it. Knowing that the animal had lived a good life until its clean end, that I was feeding myself and my family without the horrors of factory farming my dad had regaled me about.

So on this normal day I was buzzing with happiness as I trotted after my dad into the woods, carrying my crossbow, the child-sized one he'd specifically carved for my small hands. I still have small hands, but back then, at ten, they were even smaller. "I'm going to bag another deer," I told him authoritatively, practically skipping to keep up with him. His longer legs meant that he walked faster than I did, but he never slowed down to wait for me. I liked that. It meant that he thought of me as an equal, no matter how small I was. "A big one. You'll see."

He stared at me solemnly. "Do you promise?"

"Yeah! I promise!"

He shook his head. "You should never promise something you cannot control."

(He would be very disappointed that we promised Estella we'd get back to her alive.)

(My dad very rarely made promises.)

I tried to explain to him how I *knew* I was going to make a good shot today, just *knew*, and therefore I *could* control my circumstances—yeah, I know, I was a kid—but he hushed me by holding up a finger.

Then kneeled, squinting into the brush on the ground. A hoofprint. The edges crisp and defined, likely fresh. My dad leaned farther to smell it and confirm.

He rose to his feet and pointed to his right. *This way.* I crept alongside him, raising my crossbow so I'd be ready to shoot at a moment's notice. Excitement thrilled through me with every tip-toed step. My dad was going to be so proud of me once I bagged the big one. I'd show him that I kept my promises. And our harvest feast was going to be delicious.

We heard the footsteps as we got closer. *Loud for a deer,* I thought, but that only made me more excited, because surely that meant it was a massive deer that would feed us for a month.

I got into position. My dad said, "Go, Zara, shoot!"

I squinted. I couldn't see much more than a flash of brown in the trees, which made it impossible to aim. Aiming was important if you wanted a clean kill, which I did.

My dad's hand thumped onto my shoulder. "Hurry, Zara, shoot! Before it gets away!"

"But I'm not—"

"Come on!"

My dad was always right. So I fired my crossbow. *Thwip.* A thud. A scream.

Deer don't scream.

67

I stop talking, drawing in a great, shuddery breath. Gabe looks at me with an expression I can't quite read.

"I'm a great shot," I say. Not a brag. A fact. He's seen it. "It was a great shot. She didn't live long."

"She?" Does he sound disgusted? Does he sound angry? I try to hear the emotion in his voice like I'm listening for footsteps in the forest, but it's no use.

"It was a woman out hiking." I'll never forget the shock on her face, the blood in her blond hair, the blood on her brown leather jacket, the blood everywhere. It didn't smell any different from a deer's blood, but it made my stomach lurch, made me seize immediately with great, wracking, paralyzing sobs. "She'd taken a wrong turn on the Appalachian Trail and wandered off deeper into the woods. She thought she was going to be lost forever."

We gathered those facts after from the map clutched in her hands, the texts on her phone that hadn't sent, since there wasn't a signal way out there. The crossbow bolt had gone right into her chest. Right near her heart.

"I totally melted down," I say. "I don't even know how I got back home, how my feet kept me up. I was basically nonverbal. Couldn't stop crying and vomiting. I thought I was going to go to jail, and I thought I deserved it."

This time when I stop, silence hangs in the air, the only sound the rustle of the cornstalks and the crunching of our footsteps. Just as I think that, a tractor whirs in the background. Like the last time I was vulnerable with Gabe, I actually feel slightly better now. As if a little bit of the weight holding me down has been lifted off my shoulders.

I duck my head. "We don't want to be spotted," I say. "We should move toward the river. Get away from the road."

My compass in hand, we navigate our way through the cornfield in the direction of the river. For once I welcome the way the cornfield blots out the outside world, mutes its sound and dulls its light. I don't try to avoid the stalks brushing against me. I welcome the cuts and the scratches. I deserve them.

I manage to endure Gabe's silence only for our walk through the corn. Once we emerge near the river and the light bathes me again, I can't take it anymore. "You think I'm a monster."

"What?" He sounds startled. "No! Of course not!" He actually stops walking, grabs my shoulder, turns me to face him. "I just have no idea what to say. What I could possibly say to that."

Yeah, because you can't speak to a monster.

"You were a little kid," Gabe says. "Living in an environment that sounds really stressful. Maybe even harmful, from what you've told me. You didn't kill her on purpose, and I'm sure her family understood that."

My insides all squirm. I remember fighting my mom as we left the compound. My dad was fighting her too. She was being assailed on all sides. I'd expected her to yell at us, but every time she spoke, her voice was deadly quiet. "I can't do this anymore," she said. I didn't know if she was talking to me or my dad. I still don't. And now I guess I'll never know. "Look at what it's doing to Zara. I'm done. I'm out. *We're* out."

My dad stepped in front of her, blocking the front door. I was dead weight in my mom's arms, feet dragging against the scuffed hardwood floor. My dad had crafted that floor himself, cut down the trees and chopped them up and sanded them and everything. I'd bled on that floor. "You're not going anywhere."

Usually when my dad took that tone with my mom, it would make her shoulders droop and her eyes fall to the floor, and she'd do whatever he said because otherwise he'd get angry. But not this time. This time she raised her chin up and looked him directly in the eye. "You can't stop me."

"You are my wife and you have my child." Sure enough, my dad's voice rose. "You *cannot* leave."

He took a step toward her. I felt all her muscles tense, but I didn't take the opportunity to slip free. I just watched him, my body suddenly tense too.

My mom took a deep breath, squaring her shoulders. "It's taken me a long time to realize it, but I *can* and I *will*," she told him. "I've put in a call to your old friends. You know who I'm talking about."

My dad took another step toward her. From that close I could feel the heat coming off his body in waves. "You wouldn't dare."

"I haven't told them anything yet, but I've scheduled a release of documents," she said. "Online. Something you can't get into. If I am not there to stop it, evidence will be released. They'll finally have a cold, hard reason to bring you in."

A muscle worked in my dad's jaw. "You . . ."

"Yeah. Me." My mom smiled grimly at him. "I didn't realize how much I haven't been me in a long time. So this is me. Me, and my daughter. And we're leaving."

She stepped toward him. And to my surprise, he stepped aside.

"My environment wasn't harmful," I say now, maybe a little too loudly. "It was home." And it's where we're going. Would we really be going there if it were that harmful?

Probably. It's not like we have any other options.

No, that's not true. We could've gone back to the ward and fought on their side. We could've taken our chances in Partytown. We could stay in Donna Pearson's house for a while, longer than it would take for everyone to get better. We have other options, and we keep moving forward anyway. Because I'm the leader, and it's where *I* want to go. Besides, what my dad taught me has saved our lives so many times already. How can the compound be harmful if what I learned there has saved our lives?

My insides squirm again. "You don't have to come, you know," I say. "I won't be offended if you and Estella decide you want to go somewhere else. Or stay here."

"Zara," Gabe says slowly. I can't look him in the eye, so I focus on the parts of his face that have changed during our time traveling together. He was always clean shaven before; now he has black scruff concealing his jaw and upper lip. His hair was always short for sports; now it's long and shaggy. His face was strong and filled out before; now he has hollows in his cheeks that make him look older, less innocent.

I don't even want to think about how much less innocent I must look. I try to avoid looking at my reflection these days.

"Zara," he says again, and then the scruff is brushing my jaw, the hair is silky against my forehead, the hollow of his cheek is right there, touching my own, and before I can blink, his lips are on mine. Soft and hard at the same time, insistent, urgent. They move against mine, and somehow mine are moving back. I have no idea what I'm doing, but my body does, and it's taken over for me.

My body also presses against his, a wave of heat rushing down through me, starting at my lips and smoldering in my throat, my chest, my belly, farther down. I wrap my arms around him, pulling him as close to me as I can, like we're trying to fit into each other.

I'm dizzy with the wanting, so much so that I don't hear the footsteps until they're nearly on us. Gabe and I break apart, panting, just as a pair of men hike by us, nodding at us as they hightail it out of there. We're lucky they weren't planning on robbery, because they would definitely have had the jump on us.

As much as I want to, I can't get distracted. So when Gabe's face ducks toward mine again, I step away. His face falls. I say hastily, "Not out here in the open. We need to pay attention."

He flexes his fingers. "Oh. Okay. No problem." His voice is casual. Too casual. I can hear every bit of the tension he's using to make it sound that way.

I start walking. He follows. "I really liked it," I say so that he doesn't get the wrong idea. "And I want to do it again. Just . . . not out here where any distraction could get us killed."

This time when he speaks, there's a smile in it. "Got it."

I jump as his hand finds mine. As his fingers twine through my fingers. As he squeezes and he smiles and I smile.

Lightness spreads through me. I've been through so much, seen so much, but this? This is a moment of pure joy.

It makes it even better that it comes right after telling him my darkest story. The worst thing I've ever done. Because now he knows all the worst parts of me, and he wants to kiss me anyway. Wants to hold my hand anyway.

"I used to get so excited when you drove me and Estella home, because I'd get to stare at the back of your head without anyone seeing," I say.

His fingers tense in mine. His forehead scrunches.

Oops. Did I accidentally say something really creepy? It is kind of creepy, I guess, to say that I enjoyed staring at the back of his head without him knowing. I jump in with "I didn't mean—" but get interrupted by him laughing.

"That's maybe the cutest thing I've ever heard."

Okay. Creepy, but cute. I can live with that.

Still, maybe I won't tell him about how I stared at his feet poking out of his blanket while he was sleeping. He doesn't have to know everything.

"I never thought you'd be interested," I say. "I always thought you just saw me as your little sister's best friend."

"Well, yeah," he replies. "I did always see you as my little sister's best friend."

Oof.

"But all of that changed with us traveling together," he continues. "Like I said: you're my freaking hero, Zara. You're strong. You're brilliant. You're calm under pressure, and you keep *me* calm under pressure. And all of that? Yeah. It's really hot."

I know we can't afford distraction, but I let him kiss me again. Just once. And then we walk on along the river, hand in hand, side by side.

68

As we near Donna Pearson's house, I find myself wishing the distance would magically extend itself by a few hours, a few days. Not too long—I don't want Estella standing at the window holding her breath for ages.

I just want a few extra nights sleeping curled up against Gabe: lying on our mats with my back tucked against his front, then turning over and cuddling up against him, his arm thrown over me. A few extra days of glancing over at him for an unobtrusive peek, only to find him already glancing at me. Just some more time to run my hand over every muscle in his arms and dip in his neck and memorize them for future reference.

And yes, I know that we can keep doing these things once we're not alone anymore. At least, I hope we will. But it's a totally different dynamic, going from just the two of us to all six of us again. And

Estella? What's Estella going to say? Sure, she gave me her permission to go for it. But there's a big difference between the funny idea of her best friend making out with her brother and the actual cold, hard reality of her best friend making out with her brother.

Though in Donna's house we will have access to a real bed instead of sleeping mats and the hard ground. . . .

I quicken my pace.

69

As I expected, Estella is waiting for us in Donna Pearson's front window. I shake my head at her, since I told her before leaving that she should stay out of sight when inside, but she's already leaping up from her seat in the direction of the front door, and then the front door is flying open and she's bounding outside, a huge grin on her face.

She thuds into me with a hug, spinning me around, before launching herself at Gabe and burying her face in his shoulder. The same place I very recently kissed. My cheeks warm. It's good she can't see me. "Oh my God, you're alive!"

I'm much more alive than I was when I left her. I just smile and hug her from the back.

"Stell, we should tell you something," Gabe says, and as much as I don't want to talk about it all right now, happiness fizzes through me. Because him wanting to talk about it makes it real. It means that it wasn't just a one-time—okay, two-time (okay, eight-time)—deal. "Zara and me—"

"Are really excited to see everybody else," I say hastily, putting a hand on his arm. I want to tell her everything, but not this second, with my body aching and my bladder ready to burst.

Estella's eyes zero in on that casual touch of my skin to his, then raise to meet mine, so wide it almost looks like she's in pain. So I'm pretty sure she knows what Gabe was about to say anyway. "Tell you later," I mouth to her as Gabe nods and heads to the front door.

"You'll tell me soon," Estella says, her voice deadly.

I nod and catch up to Gabe. Honestly, it's not just about my body and my bladder. Gabe and I didn't talk about whether we meant anything. So I'd really like to clear that up with him before hearing him say whatever he's going to say to Estella.

It's still hot and muggy inside, definitely hotter than it was outside. The three others are waiting in Donna's living room, where they've opened the windows, but not much of a breeze filters through. It's a room straight out of the past, with thick carpeting underfoot and big, squashy sofas and armchairs scattered around. Knickknacks are on every open surface, from a collection of glass cat statues to photos of various children and old people who all look vaguely like Donna Pearson's driver's license photo. A massive TV stands sentinel at the center of one wall, black and glossy and empty.

Jasmine waves at me as I enter the room. She's sprawled out belly-down on the carpet, her arm and her leg wrapped in bandages, a half-finished puzzle before her. "You're back! How was your trip?"

Ronan snorts from the couch, where he's reading what looks like a trashy eighties romance novel. "You make it sound like they went to Disney World." He catches me staring at the book and shrugs. "Turns out Donna only seems to like books with half-naked men on the cover. It could be worse."

"And I'm awake." Ina's voice is raspy but sure. She's sitting in the armchair, her splinted and bandaged leg extended before her on the footrest. Bandages swathe her arms and bulge out under her shirt, but her eyes are clear and there's a hint of a wry smile on her face. "Thanks to you."

"Thanks to her," I say, pointing at Jasmine, who I assume was the one to administer the splint and the bandages and the antiseptic and the antibiotics. "She knew exactly what you needed."

"I already thanked her," Ina says. "And Ronan. But you're the one who ran back into a burning building. For me."

"Anyone would've done the—"

"I wouldn't have done the same," Ina says bluntly. She shifts in her seat, her freckled face screwing up with the effort. "Not for you, not for any of you, probably. At least not then, before you did this for me. But you did. I'd be dead if it weren't for you. So thank you. Seriously. With every bit of my cold black heart."

Why does accepting a sincere thank-you always feel so awkward and uncomfortable? It really shouldn't. *You* did *save her life*, I remind myself. And my dad has nothing to chime in about thank-yous. He rarely said them.

And still, my face heats up, and I have to clear my throat before I can speak. "You're welcome. But it's really not a big deal."

She shakes her head. "Whatever you say."

I go and use the bathroom—they've set up a chamber pot–type situation, which they take turns emptying outside when they're sure it's safe—pausing at the back door to examine the security system they've set up: a precarious stack of metal cans and glass jars that'll tip the second someone tries pushing in the door or punching in a window, not just waking us up but forcing the intruder to wade through broken glass and a veritable can obstacle course. It's actually not too bad; I'm oddly proud of them, and I know my dad would be too.

"So."

I look up to find Gabe there in the hallway, arms crossed over his chest. I can't help but smile at the sight of him, only he doesn't smile back.

I might not be the most adept socially, but I know what that's about. "It's not that I don't want to tell Estella," I say quietly, moving closer in hopes that the others won't overhear from the front room. "I just . . . I wanted to know what *you* were going to tell Estella before you told her."

His face softens. "I was going to tell her that there's something happening between us. Is that okay with you?"

It's a little vague for my liking, but I don't want to push, so I nod. It seems ridiculous to be worried about making a relationship "official" right now anyway. I don't know if I even want that. What if the power comes back on and it's like shining a literal light on me? If he realizes that I'm still just his little sister's best friend, not this confident, heroic savior he thinks he sees?

He quiets my doubts with a gentle kiss, one of his hands coming up to cup the side of my face, stroke the line of my jaw with his thumb.

And then there's a gasp. It can't be one of us, on account of how occupied our mouths currently are. We break apart, eyes searching.

And find Estella standing at the end of the hallway, her hands on her hips. Her face looks almost stricken, but when she sees us looking at her, she gives us a wide smile. "I knew something was going on," she says. "This is wonderful. You guys are adorable."

That wide smile of hers doesn't quite light up her eyes. I move toward her, Gabe moves toward her, but she steps back. "Stell," Gabe says as I say, "Estella."

"Seriously," she says with a brittle laugh. "I am seriously happy for you."

Her voice is genuine, or at least I think it is. I can kind of see what's going on in her head, just because I know Estella so well. *My best friend and my brother are in love or whatever. That's great for them, but what about me? What if I become the third wheel now? They're the only ones I have left.*

"You're still number one," I say. "For both of us, I'm pretty sure."

Estella's face relaxes even as she says, "How insecure do you think I am?"

I answer her with a hug. Gabe comes at her from the other side. *How sweet,* I think, until he loops his arm around her head so that his armpit's right in her face. She gags. "Gross!"

"As long as I have pit stains, you'll get to smell them," Gabe says magnanimously. She rolls her eyes, pushing him away.

"If you hold me down and fart on me, I swear I'm leaving."

"How dare you," Gabe says. "I haven't done that for at least a year."

Estella rolls her eyes again, though a smile plays on her lips. "Take him, Zara. Please. He's all yours."

She claps her hands together before I can think of something clever to say back. "Oh! We should do something to celebrate! Like our end-of-the-world party, remember?"

How could I ever forget? But how am I supposed to party when my mom is dead? When the Ramirezes are dead? When we're living in a dead woman's house, and the world is falling apart around us? I look into Estella's eyes, ready to gently decline, but see her staring fiercely back. They're almost glowing with ferocity.

She knows. She feels it too. And she wants to party it out.

I make a split-second decision. "Okay." We're going to be stuck here for a couple of weeks anyway as Ronan, Jasmine, and Ina recover enough to get moving again. "Let's have a party!"

70

We decide rather quickly on our party theme—or rather, Ina decides rather quickly. "We're living in her house," she says grimly. "We should have a celebration of her life, considering we're the only ones who even know she's dead."

And so we dub our party the Donna Pearson Extravaganza.

We gather all the information we can from the photos she has hanging everywhere around the house, and from some other context clues. "She preferred reading books about shirtless men, so obviously Gabe and Ronan shouldn't wear shirts," Jasmine says with a devilish smile. "Maybe they should oil themselves up, too?"

"Try it," Ronan says dryly.

"Maybe I will."

"Donna seems to wear a lot of makeup in her pictures," Estella says loudly over Ronan and Jasmine's bickering. "So I'll do every-one's makeup."

"I don't wear makeup," Ina says.

Estella shrugs. "Fine, then I'll do Zara's, Jasmine's, and my makeup."

Ina is quiet for a minute. "Okay, maybe I'll wear a little makeup."

"I'm opposed to makeup on philosophical grounds, but I'll wear some for Donna Pearson," says Jasmine.

Ronan raises an eyebrow. "Philosophical grounds?"

"Yeah!" Jasmine says, her tone heated. "Men don't get told they 'look tired' or asked if they're 'feeling sick' when their faces are bare, but . . ."

As Jasmine goes on, Ina beckons me over to her chair. I make the trip happily, not wanting to hear what happens when Estella—who views her makeup skills as an art and a way to express herself—jumps into the conversation. "I think I should be able to make a really nice cake if I have someone to help me with the moving around," Ina says. "We're lucky she has an old stove. It looks like we can light it manually, so I should be able to bake."

I'm not sure about the luck regarding having an old stove—who knows how much ancient food is crusted on that thing?—but she doesn't have to ask me again. The argument behind us is getting louder and louder. "Let's go." I move around the back of the chair to shove it into the kitchen, but Ina surprises me by setting her mouth into a thin line and pushing herself gingerly to her feet. With her splinted leg held stiffly, she hobbles in the direction of the kitchen, holding on to the wall for balance.

"You shouldn't be on your feet," I say, trying to take her arm, but she pulls it away.

"It's not broken. I can walk," Ina says, but her good leg is trembling with the effort. Still, she manages to make it into Donna's small, cluttered kitchen before collapsing into a chair, grimacing and massaging her good leg.

"Seriously, you need to rest it," I say. "Or you'll never be well enough to keep going." Looking at her is stressing me out, so I look around instead. Donna Pearson seems to have really had a thing for chickens: the wallpaper is patterned with blue and white chicken silhouettes; the dish towels are covered in chickens rooting for corn; little chicken statues line the counters and the shelves. In the center of the kitchen table sits a big chicken cookie jar, its head held high as if it's about to crow. You'd have to remove the head to get at the cookies inside, which is kind of macabre for a cookie jar.

"I'm using it *because* I have to be well enough to keep going," Ina says. "Get the flour."

I get the flour, taking a moment to admire Donna's pantry, which is stocked full from floor to ceiling. Lukewarm canned soup and dried pasta might not once have been my idea of a delicious meal, but my standards have changed over the past couple of months, and now they make my mouth water. I thump the flour down on the counter, a white cloud puffing around it.

"Get sugar, baking soda, baking powder," she says, her eyes wandering to the open pantry. "It's been long enough without power that any butter and eggs would be bad. Does she have a jar of applesauce? How about vegetable oil?"

"Why applesauce and vegetable oil?"

Ina grimaces. "They are . . . *tolerable* substitutes in baked goods for the things we don't have."

Donna does indeed have applesauce and vegetable oil, along

with the cocoa powder Ina asks for too. My curiosity grows as I clank cans and bottles aside, and I peek as I turn with the items to see Ina watching me openly, a thoughtful expression on her round, freckled face.

I set everything on the Formica counter, which looks just as old as the supposedly ancient oven, then move them all to the kitchen table with Donna's measuring cups and bowls. Ina sets about measuring and sifting, pouring and stirring. Her hands are sure and confident as they move, knowing exactly when to start and stop. "Where'd you learn how to cook?" I ask.

Whenever any of us have asked before, she's just rolled her eyes at us. But she's really calm right now: her shoulders have relaxed from their usual sentry positions below her ears, and there's even the hint of a smile on her thin lips. Still, I'm surprised when she answers me. "I worked in a restaurant. For two years. Started out washing dishes, became a line cook, and did some of the desserts. It was a small restaurant, so we all kind of played double duty." She pours the vegetable oil into the batter slowly, whisking in its gleaming stream. "I would've been running that place someday."

That explains the cooking skills. "But . . . aren't you our age?"

She looks at me sourly as she stirs the batter. It's actually starting to smell like cake. "I'm nineteen. I started at fifteen."

"But . . ."

"I dropped out of high school," Ina says. She keeps her face trained on the bowls in front of her. "Worked part-time until then. Did it as soon as I could. I wasn't any good at school, but I was good with food."

I don't want to pull that sour look or tone out of her again, but I'm dying to know. "What about your parents? They let you do it?"

The bowl judders against the table with the force of her stirring. Somehow I don't think the force is part of the recipe. "My parents haven't been in my life since I was a kid. My foster parents encouraged finding a practical job." She doesn't sound sharp or bitter. In fact, she sounds calmer than I've ever heard her. It's almost like it's a relief getting her story out after holding it back for so long.

"My restaurant was just outside Denver. We were working overtime, trying to feed the hungry with our supply before our generator went out and everything spoiled, but then we decamped en masse for the commune in Colorado before things could get bad. I didn't mind leaving. It wasn't like I had anything to stay for." She motions at me. For a second I think she's asking for a hug, and then I realize she just wants the cake pan. I hand it to her. She sets it down in front of her and starts pouring the batter in from the bowl. "You know, I can't help but wonder how they knew to take us there. My exec chef was the one who told us we should go. That means he was probably in on the whole thing with Philip, right? He was one of *them*."

Her voice is a monotone now. "I trusted my exec chef. I looked up to him. He gave me career advice and encouraged me to keep working, and the whole time . . ." She stops short and sucks in a quick breath. She turns her face away from me, but not quickly enough to stop me from seeing how red her eyes are. "Did you already turn on the oven?"

I leap up. "I'll do that now."

By the time I've fiddled with the pilot light and lit a few matches that fizzle out without hitting the right spot, Ina's face has cleared. "When you do it, set it to three hundred and fifty degrees. And then you can get me the powdered sugar. I'm not sure how good of a frosting I'll be able to make with vegetable oil, but . . ."

She trails off, but I think I know what she was going to say. *But I still have to try. But we all still have to try. Life might be terrible and hard and getting worse, but we still have to try.*

She clears her throat. "But any frosting is better than no frosting, right?" She gives me a tiny smile. "Is it just me, or does that sound weirdly profound?"

"Extremely profound," I say. I watch in silence as she whips the bowl of oil and powdered sugar, trying to make it form into peaks. "So you decided to come with us. . . ."

Ina sets the fork down. "This looks okay. Now go put the cake in the oven."

I slide the cake into the hot oven and cross my fingers. When I return to the kitchen table, I wait for her to tell me why she came with us, but she only stares at the oven like she can will it into cooking. Maybe she forgot what I said. Or maybe she thinks she's shared enough.

It's okay: I already know. She wanted to get away. She wanted to throw her fate into the hands of random strangers because she couldn't stand to be where she was anymore. She's not going to a particular place, like we are. She's getting away from a particular place.

I don't ask her any more questions. She doesn't volunteer any more answers. We just sit there in a dead woman's kitchen, staring at the oven, waiting for the cake to come out chocolatey and moist and whole.

71

We have a cake. We have other party snacks Ina creatively put together from Donna's pantry. Ronan and Gabe are suitably shirtless; they tried to persuade us girls to dress up in Donna's clothes, but we drew a hard line at that. "Gross," Jasmine said. "No way," said Estella.

We did use her makeup, though. Only the unopened things, not so much because we saw the used stuff as dirty or sacred, but because Jasmine informs us all that it could give us eye infections, and if there's one thing we don't need right now, it's an eye infection that, left unchecked by medication, could eat out our eyeball and into our brain. Estella has us sit one by one and looks us over with a critical eye. She already knows my colors, so my appearance in the mirror afterward doesn't come as a huge revelation—I still look like me, just with longer, thicker eyelashes and some pops of color on my lips and eyes. But when Jasmine and Ina see what *they* look like, they both gasp.

Ina because, "I've never seen myself look like this before." She turns her head, examining herself from every angle. Just like with me, Estella didn't seek to change what she looked like: her freckles are still on full display because, as Estella opined while she worked her magic, "freckles are not a flaw, and it's a crime that the beauty industry tries to tell us that." Ina adds, "I like it."

Jasmine because, "My face feels weird." She prods at her cheeks with a finger, causing Estella to reprimand her for smudging her hard work. Because Jasmine's dark brown skin tone is similar to Donna's, she's the only one of us wearing a full face. "It's like I'm wearing a plastic mask."

Estella picks up the facial wipes. "We can take it off. I'll only feel mortally wounded, no big deal." She smiles to show she's kidding.

Jasmine squints into the mirror, ignoring her. "I *look* weird too. It's like I'm my own evil twin."

Gabe even manages to find something better than the Holy Grail: an ancient iPod touch with half a battery's worth of charge. "These songs are pretty new," he says, scrolling through Donna's playlists. "She must actually have been using this until recently. I didn't even know Apple still made these."

"Her taste in music isn't too bad," Jasmine says, looking over his shoulder, blinking furiously. Not because of anything on the screen; she's just been blinking furiously ever since Estella put on eyelash extensions, like she's having trouble holding her eyes open with this new weight. "Some good dance tunes." She holds her fist up in the air. "Thanks, Donna!"

We don't have speakers or anything, but we take out the headphones and turn the volume all the way up. Estella and I lay out the spread of food over Donna's coffee table as Ina directs us, making sure it matches the display in her head. She even has us scatter around some of the fake flowers we found in the bedroom.

The only thing that could make the living room look better is fairy lights, and since those require electricity, we have no such luck. Still, as the room grows dark, its boundaries and lines grow fuzzy, and it gets harder to see the couches, the cat statues, the old-fashioned rug.

We could be anywhere.

"A toast," Estella proclaims. I'm not generally into girls, and still, looking at her takes my breath away. Her eyes, large and dark and smoky. Her lashes making shadows on her cheeks. Her hair in a long side twist, falling over one bare, sparkly shoulder.

I love her so much, it hurts a little.

"We don't know much about you, Donna Pearson," Estella says. "Or should I say, Ms. Pearson. That might be more respectful. We met you on your last, most vulnerable day." She glances over at me. Her lips shine glossy pink even in the dimness. I give her an encouraging nod, not sure what exactly she's told the others about Donna's last day.

I'm not going to ask. That's up to her if she wants to share.

"We were there with you as you died," Estella continues. "When your suffering came to an end. And while we don't know much about you, we do know one thing: you were a good person. Your last act was to give us your home as a refuge as we recovered and grew strong again. Your last act . . ." She pauses for dramatic emphasis. "Was to help us survive."

She raises her glass. I raise mine, too. They're fancy glasses we found covered in dust: elegant wineglasses with dainty crystal stems. Very dainty. Jasmine already broke one, which is why we're making her use a plastic juice glass.

"To Donna Pearson!" Estella cries.

Our glasses clink. Jasmine's clacks. We drink. Gabe, Estella, Jasmine, and Ina all make varying exclamations of disgust. I suppose the warm vodka we found in the cabinet under the sink mixed with canned tomato juice—also warm—isn't all that appetizing.

That's not why I'm not drinking, though. I down my warm filtered water with the rest of the group, as does Ronan. We nod at each other in solidarity. He doesn't drink for religious reasons. I don't drink because I know I have zero tolerance, and getting surprised by attackers in the middle of the night already sounds like a nightmare without me being drunk on top of it. I need to be able to count on myself and my reflexes, because even here in this house, I'm not truly safe.

I can't forget the man with the vine tattoos. He's still out there, assuming the wound I gave him didn't kill him. It shouldn't have . . . or maybe it *should* have. Then I wouldn't be worrying right now.

The chances are extremely slim that he's going to find you, I assure myself. But they're not zero. He managed to find us at the ward. Who says he won't find us here? That he won't track us down?

Maybe I should've stopped and reasoned with him. Told him I didn't have anything to do with the blackout—that I'd only seen it coming because I'd been trained to pay attention to the signs.

Except that gun didn't exactly make him look reasonable.

72

The party music plays. More of the party drinks are poured and choked down.

But the party itself? It's not exactly raging.

An hour after that opening toast, the six of us are sprawled in an awkward circle around the snack table, pudding skins thickening over bowls and creamed-corn nuggets congealing on plates. Estella's the only one moving even a little, swaying back and forth to the frantic beat of Donna's iPod. "Who wants to dance with me?" she says, swaying a little harder. She's moving languidly, like she's drunk, but I can see the sharpness in her eyes. She might want to be drunk, but she's not there yet. "Jasmine, c'mon!"

Jasmine's lying flat on her back on the sofa, staring at the ceiling. "I've never drank this much before," she says dreamily. "I don't know if I like it."

Estella frowns. "Okay, I don't want you throwing up on me," she says. "Ronan! Come on!"

Ronan's sitting in Donna's armchair by the window, nursing his warm water, staring out into the night. He doesn't respond. "Ronan!" Estella shouts, and he jumps, dribbling water onto his lap. "What?"

Estella sighs. "Never mind." She collapses onto another chair. "You both suck."

Ina says, "You all indeed suck. You're wasting my hard work."

"No one's wasting food," says Estella. "We'll eat it tomorrow if it's not finished tonight. Gabe? You're my brother; have pity and dance with me."

Gabe's staring at me. I stare back. He gives a little grin. I give a little grin back.

As if it's a sentient being, Donna's iPod shuffles itself up a slow, moody ballad. Estella says, "You two should at least dance, then."

"I'm not being the only ones dancing," I tell her. Gabe shakes his head too.

Estella slouches into the chair. It looks like it's trying to eat her. "You guys *really* suck." She sighs again. "Okay, then, let's play a party game. Spin the bottle!"

Ina snorts. "Pass. I have zero desire to kiss anyone here."

Nobody else puts up a protest, because really, it was kind of a silly idea. I know that Gabe and I only want to kiss each other, and Ronan doesn't want to kiss any of the girls, and if Estella or Jasmine are interested in each other, they can go kiss each other in a closet and leave the rest of us out of it.

"I wish we had, like, a deck of cards," Estella says. "You guys looked, right?"

"We couldn't find one," Jasmine says gloomily. Ronan stares out the window. Jasmine stares at the ceiling.

"We had some crazy parties at the restaurant," Ina offers. "Lots of alcohol. Clouds of smoke. The partiers would go all night, then wake up in a ditch somewhere the next day." The others are gawking at her, unaccustomed to this amount of sharing. I hope none of them will say anything stupid that'll make her stop. "One time one of the line cooks found himself in Canada. He had to call out sick the next day as he hitchhiked back."

"Now, that is some pretty impressive partying," Estella says. "Let's channel the spirit of that line cook, okay? How about truth or dare?"

The look in her eyes is so hopeful that I can't say no. I nod at her, and her eyes brighten.

"My truth?" Jasmine says. She's slid over on the couch, so that her head hangs off it now, upside down. "My truth is that I think my family might be dead, and I'm making this whole long journey for nothing."

"*Happy* truth or dare," Estella adds hastily. "And it wasn't your turn. Okay, who wants to go—"

"I mean, my dad has a heart condition," Jasmine continues, like she didn't hear Estella. Only her voice is even louder, so probably she did. "How long could a man with a heart condition survive all this? Is my mom supposed to keep him alive? My little brother? What are they going to do?" She pauses. "Maybe I should've left with that first group when they tried to drive home. Maybe they made it back."

"You never know," says Gabe. But his voice is flat. "At least they're not *definitely* dead. Like mine and Estella's parents and Zara's mom."

"You know, New Jersey is the most densely populated state in the country," Jasmine says. "When I was a kid, I didn't know what it meant, only that we were the *most* at something, which I automatically assumed was good. Except it's not so good now, right? It's a ton of people crammed into a small space, all desperately seeking out the same things. If there's only so much water to go around, do you think people are going to step aside and give it to a man with a heart condition and his round wife and a weedy thirteen-year-old with asthma?" She shakes her head no, only the motion seems to make her queasy. She shuts her eyes and swallows hard, wrapping her arms around her stomach. "Do you think they ate my dog?"

"This is the worst game of happy truth or dare ever," Estella says, but her lower lip is trembling. "Ronan! I dare you to put on Donna Pearson's most horrible pantsuit and do the Macarena!"

"That doesn't seem very respectful to our host," Ronan replies. "And I don't think your family is dead, Jasmine. I don't think they could die while you're still out there. They know you're coming."

Jasmine rolls her eyes, but that seems to make her queasy too; she screws eyes shut and gulps. "That's ridiculous. Of course they don't know. It's been ages. It's not like they have some psychic connection to me all the way across the country."

"Guys, let's at least relax and not talk about heavy topics," Estella says desperately. She pops up and claps her hands. "Come on. This is a party! For Donna!"

Jasmine says morosely, "Donna is dead and rotting in a hospital lobby."

The room goes silent. Nobody seems to know how to respond to that.

This isn't good. Estella's eyes are glimmering. Everybody else is frowning. Gabe moves toward his sister, reaching out for a hug, but she jerks away.

"How about singing," I chirp. "Estella, sing us a song! You guys, you wouldn't believe how good her voice is!"

But Estella is done. She slumps onto the couch, shaking Jasmine, so that Jasmine slides off onto the floor like an eel. "Whatever," Estella says. "We'll all die, then. Whatever."

None of the others protest. Even Gabe just slumps forward. They all look like they might actually die right here, right now, of dreariness and disappointment.

I can't let this stand. As the group leader, I have to take care of them.

I just can't believe this falls to me. I would laugh if the situation weren't so urgent. "You guys," I say. "This is awful. We're going to have a tough enough time making it the rest of the way east." No! Don't talk about things being tough! "So let's at least have a fun time right now." Callie's words from the end-of-the-world party come floating out of my mouth. "If we're all going to die, we might as well enjoy tonight."

I step forward, grab Estella's arm, and yank her to her feet. I worry for a moment that I've ripped her arm out of her socket, but she just stumbles into me, smelling of tomato juice and vodka and sweat. "We're going to dance," I say, kicking over Donna's iPod, which is playing some weird electronic dance beat that absolutely does not work in this situation. "And we need music. So sing me some music."

Estella just stares at me in shock as I shimmy from side to side, probably looking like I'm in the process of being electrocuted. But then her mouth falls open, and words start pouring out—one of pop's biggest hits from our elementary school years, about a girl shaking off her haters.

The more she sings, the more into it she gets, her shoulders relaxing, her eyes scrunching closed as she belts out the words. I bounce around with forced enthusiasm that grows less and less forced the more I twirl her around. As the song ends, she segues immediately into another one, and now she's shimmying in a way that looks a whole lot more natural than mine.

A hand lands on my shoulder. Gabe. He pulls me away from Estella to twirl me around, and it's okay, because Ronan's on his feet now, doing a funky kind of bunny hop with Estella. She's struggling to get the words of her song out now that bubbles of laughter are trying to escape with them.

In the corner of my eye I see Jasmine writhing around on the floor, her arms waving in the air. "Floor dancing," Gabe says as he raises my arm. I lift a skeptical eyebrow at him but let him spin me anyway. For a moment I rest with my back against his chest, feeling the warmth of him down to my bones, before spinning back. "The domain of the excessively drunk."

Ina's smiling and bobbing her head. Ronan is grinning and doing the twist. But it's Estella's laughter that sparks joy in me the most.

A bit of music. A bit of laughter. On this night, while everything's going to hell, that has to be enough.

73

Saying goodbye to Donna Pearson's house after a few weeks feels curiously emotional. Or maybe it's not so curious. This house was a gift to us, after all, and it pretty much saved our lives. We couldn't have nursed Ina and Jasmine and Ronan back to health in that dusty shed by the side of the road. Not without protection. Not without access to food. Not having to hike through those occupied cornfields to get water and having to worry about the farmer whose truck we stole coming after us with his shotgun.

And it feels scary, leaving it behind. Because what if this is the best that's out there? What if in a few months, when we're starving in the woods of the frozen Northeast, competing with all the frenzied survivors of the country's most densely populated state, we wish we'd stayed here in Donna's house?

"Nothing is forever," Gabe tells me as we stand in Donna's front yard, looking back one last time. "Eventually we would've run out of food. Or somebody would have come along and broken in. We have to believe we're going toward something better."

Toward my dad. We've crossed more than half of the United States by now, but it's already mid-September. It's going to be getting cold by the time we near him. If he's even still there.

If he's even still alive.

I swallow something bitter rising in my throat. What if this is all for nothing? What if the pot of gold I've promised my group at the end of this long, hard journey turns out to be coal?

Coal is useful, my dad whispers. *You can use it to heat your house. Gold? Gold is useless. I'd much rather have coal than gold.*

He has to be there. On his compound. I would've heard if he died or went somewhere else, right? Somebody would have told me.

Even if he was the only one who lived out there. If nobody visited him, because his ex-wife and only child moved all the way to the other side of the country and never visited.

Once when I was elevenish, not too long after I'd entered the real world, I asked my mom if we could go back and visit sometime. "I bet Dad misses us," I said. "And I bet he needs our help with the canning. He was never that good at canning."

I'll never forget my mom's face. It was almost panicked. I assumed she didn't want to go back on an airline, because she'd spent the entire plane ride to LA crying, which I'd figured had to be because of a fear of flying. She told me that I couldn't miss school, so I said we could go during winter break, and then she said it would be too hard to get to the compound in the snow, and that was it. By the time summer came around, I knew better than to ask again.

I swallow down my guilt. I square my shoulders. "Everybody feeling okay?" I survey my group. Ronan and Jasmine are pretty much fully recovered, only some light scars left to show what they went through. Ina's burns are mostly better, though they're still bandaged, and she's shaky on her leg. We're lucky it wasn't totally broken; I'm not sure if we would've been able to wait the months for that to fully heal. Winter is coming, and it's not going to be kind when it does.

74

It takes three weeks to get out of the Midwest. Every day is largely the same: fields of corn, fields of wheat, fields of what's probably soy, occasionally a wooded area that brings us a much-needed break in the monotony. Not many people. It's amazing how big this country is, how sprawling. "I went to India once with my grandparents," Jasmine tells us one night at camp. We don't find any other houses or sheds to rest our heads in, but we get lucky in that it never rains harder than a drizzle. "They were talking about how India has three times the people packed into one third the space of the US, and yet India's still full of farmland and open spaces."

She's right: the US is *massive*. It's more surprising that we've seen as many people as we have. It's not like there's much hunting or foraging to do out here in the farm fields, though occasionally we pass through a wooded area that bags us a game bird or two. Unlike in the West, where people fled the cities, I bet people out here are clustering in places like Chicago and Milwaukee and Toledo and Cleveland. They're on the Great Lakes, after all. More fresh water than anyone could use or need, at least for the next few years.

It's enough to make me curious how those places are doing, but not enough to make me stop there. We don't have time. It's October now, and the dew is already beginning to frost over in the mornings, a lace of ice placed gently over us as we sleep.

"I can't wait to see forests again," Jasmine sighs one night around a crackling campfire. Though I know it's a risk to leave it lit after eating, we were all shivering, our hands numb. And we haven't seen any people lately, so why not take the chance? "I'm so sick of *flat*."

Ronan sniffs. "The East is still pretty flat. At least compared to the West."

Ina clears her throat from behind us. "Sorry to interrupt what sounds like a scintillating conversation, but, Zara, can you come here for a second?"

Gladly. I hop up, leaving Jasmine and Ronan to argue about what counts as an interesting view. Ina pulls me a few steps farther away, letting the corn envelop us and muffle the sound of our conversation.

"If you're going to kill me, this would be an excellent place to do it," I joke. She doesn't laugh. Okay, is she actually going to kill me?

She reaches out and grabs my arm, bowing her head. "I'm sure you've noticed that we haven't been hunting very much food or scavenging up very much."

She's right. We've been out hunting every time we pass through a wooded area, but there haven't been many animals to be seen. I have a bad feeling as to why. Everybody in the area flooded out to hunt and scavenge up food once their own supplies ran out. And it doesn't take long for a hungry army of desperate people to pick an area clean.

"We're going to have to start drastically reducing rations soon, which is bad with all the walking we've been doing."

Unease stirs within me. That's bad. Really bad.

But I can't let it show. "Well, we have plenty of access to water." Once we leave one river behind, another one pops up, all flowing toward the Great Lakes in the north. Should we take a detour to one of the cities and see if we can find food there? I don't know. I thought those cities would be full of people, and while they might not have to worry about water, they probably are touchy about food. No new shipments of food have been coming in, after all. People are probably fiercely guarding and going after what's left.

So, scratch the idea of a detour. It'll only be dangerous and not likely to bear fruit. Literally or figuratively. "We're almost through Ohio," I tell her, trying to sound reassuring. "Once we're through Ohio and into Pennsylvania, the hunting should get better. A sparser population and more forest. Ronan and I are both excellent shots."

"I hope you're right," she says dubiously.

I hope so too.

75

I am right, kind of. Deer don't quite abound in northwestern Pennsylvania, but we see more animals here than we have where we've been. Ronan takes one down our first night in the state, and we rejoice with a feast. Ina builds a roaring fire as I gut and skin the deer, my hands working slowly and clumsily through its warm insides, sawing away with the dull blade of my Swiss Army Knife. I'm out of practice, but the skills are still there. The skills have always been there.

Gabe stares at me, fascinated, as my bloody hands separate muscle from sinew, guts from bones. There's something hungry in his eyes, and not just for the meat. I raise an eyebrow, my arms wrist-deep in deer. "Do you have a fetish for gore or something?"

He shudders in revulsion. "That's one fetish I definitely don't have," he says, which begs the questions: Which ones *does* he have?

Did I inadvertently hitch myself to someone who can't get off without seeing me sit on balloons or smear cake all over myself?

Before I can ask, he goes on. "There's just something really hot about you getting in there," he says. "There's blood on your cheek." He reaches out and rubs it off. I close my eyes, which is probably not the wisest idea when I'm holding a knife, and enjoy the feel of his thumb warm on my skin. . . .

A throat clears behind me. Estella. My eyes pop open to find her standing there, frowning, her arms crossed. "We're all hungry," she informs me. "You guys can make out after."

"We weren't . . ." I trail off as she stomps away.

Gabe shakes his head. "As much as she says she's cool with this, she really isn't, is she?"

"I think she's having a hard time with everything in general, not just us." She lost most of her family, she got kidnapped and thought she was going to die, and now the two people she has left in the world are getting close to each other. She's worried and sad, and she's taking it out on us. "It's going to be okay." We just have to make it to the compound. Once we're there, the daily stress and pressure of survival will be mostly off our shoulders. It takes a toll, this constant looking behind us, this constant worrying about what we're going to eat or even *if* we're going to eat.

We don't have any spices or herbs, but Ina chars the meat perfectly, so that it's tender and delicious, and we all chow down with relief. We'll have enough meat for tomorrow, too, if it stays good that long—it should, considering how cold it's been getting at night. I wish we had the time and space to dry and smoke some of it, but we don't.

Still, I hate letting meat go to waste. "Eat more," I urge the group.

We eat until our stomachs are full to bursting, until even Gabe groans at the thought of taking one more bite.

"If we get lucky, we'll be able to forage up some nuts, berries, and wild onion," I say. "Delicious with venison."

Ina's brows wrinkle dubiously. "I don't know the foraging out here," she says. "I'd be too worried about accidentally poisoning us with the wrong berry."

I roll my shoulders. "I know how to forage out here." We're on my home turf now. I grew up in these forests, skinning my knees on these rocks and climbing these trees. Not these exact ones, but I know what to look for. What to avoid. "I'll go first with whatever I find. If I die, don't eat them."

"Ha, ha," Estella says dryly.

Sure enough, as we continue on east, we forage up some delicacies: red berries that pop tart on our tongues; wild onions that, charred, make a squirrel stew surprisingly delicious; black walnuts and acorns that don't taste great but give us enough energy to keep moving. We even trade with a group around a campfire that we don't skirt in time, giving them some of our antiseptic in exchange for some chicken and pickles—the most delicious chicken and pickles I've ever eaten.

The night after the chicken and pickles, we're settling in around our own fire. Our pickings are scarce, just some vegetables we found, but we're well-fueled from the night before and the leftover meat this morning, so it's not that big of a deal.

Then Gabe says they all have something important to tell me, and they look at me with solemn eyes.

I tense immediately. It's never a good thing when someone says they have something important to tell you—my mind immediately goes back to Ina telling me we were almost out of food. I shiver at the frost in the air. "What is it?"

Gabe stands up from his rotted log. We discovered that rotted logs are softer and much more comfortable than other logs, so we were lucky to find a whole set of rotten logs tonight. Jasmine springs up beside him. "While you were peeing, we were trading with the guys who made the chicken and pickles!"

I relax a little bit. "Oh, cool. Did you guys trade for some more pickles? They don't have much caloric content, but the salt is good for us."

"We didn't trade for some pickles," Ronan says as he stands too. "We traded for something else."

Before I can ask any more questions, Estella also pops to her feet. "Something for you!"

Ina turns to me from her seat nearby. "I am also part of this, though I'd rather not stand up."

I blink in confusion at the group surrounding me. It's feeling weird, sitting here while they're all standing up, so I stand too. "What are you talking about?"

"We're all here, all alive, because of you," Gabe says. "And we noticed that you have your crossbow, and that's great, but you were sawing away at that deer with a dull knife from Donna's house. . . ."

"So we decided to get you a present to thank you for being generally amazing," Estella says. "Here. For you!"

Gabe takes his hands out from behind his back and presents me with a knife. A gorgeous knife. The handle is heavy and carved out of some kind of metal, and the blade is deadly sharp, coming to an elegant point at the end.

I'm touched, and yet there's my dad's voice in my head saying,

You shouldn't be focusing on using a knife in close combat; you should be focusing on running, so that you can use your crossbow.

I push his words away. Whether this gift is practical or not, it still makes me want to cry with how meaningful it is.

And yet I can't help but try to talk their points down. "I'm not really that amazing," I say. "You're not alive because of me. Jasmine is the one who treated your wounds, and Estella, you practically rescued yourself, and Ronan, you got us alive out of the—"

"But you brought us all together," Gabe says, marking this as one of the few times I won't get annoyed at being interrupted by a guy. "And you led us. Yeah, we each bring our individual skills to the group. But you're the one who makes us work as one."

"And you *are* really that amazing on your own," Estella adds. She holds out a holster, worn leather with a strap that's clearly meant to go around an arm or leg.

I can't help the tears pricking my eyes. I look down as I put the knife on, so that they won't see. "You *guys.*"

They nearly smother me in a hug. It's a good thing I've holstered the knife.

I think that . . . that my dad truly is wrong. We're stronger together. And I can't wait to show him that.

76

We should prepare to see more people, I think, as we continue on. The East is more densely populated than the West, though we've crafted our route to avoid as many population centers as possible. And we don't see many people in the small towns we sometimes stop in overnight; trees and vines are already starting to reclaim buildings. Their residents are either hiding inside or out roaming the wild, or dead.

I don't know exactly when we cross the Pennsylvania–New York border. There's no fancy blue sign like there would be on the roads, just more of the same trees and forests and creeks. We've given up on our map—there's not much use for maps in the middle of the forest—relying instead on our compass to keep us moving in the right direction.

Every night is cold. The six of us huddle together in the shadows of the trees, our breath making clouds in the air. "I think we're almost there," I tell them one night. It's almost more to convince myself than it is to notify them; I can hardly believe that, after so long, I'm going to be back home again.

I brief them all on the traps around the compound, on what my dad looks like, on what they need to say if he surprises them. "And you." I turn to Jasmine. "You're welcome to come to the compound. I know you want to go to New Jersey, but . . ."

"I'll come to the compound for now." Jasmine's face is resolute. "And I'll head down once it's not winter."

I know she thinks her family is dead. I know she doesn't *want* to think that her family is dead. And I know that the longer she doesn't go down there, the longer she doesn't have to know one way or the other.

"It's going to be so weird to see my dad again," I whisper to Gabe at night when everyone is sleeping. We might not officially know that we're in New York, but I *know*. I feel it deep down in my bones. "I hope he's not mad at me."

"Why would he be mad at you?" he whispers back.

"I left him."

Gabe rolls over, slinging one strong arm over me. I nuzzle deeper into his side, inhaling the smell of him. Not for the first time, I wish I could get to know *all* of him. But there's no privacy out here, not to mention birth control, and the only thing that would be worse than dealing with everything we're already dealing with is getting pregnant . . . and still having to deal with it all.

"You were a little kid," he says in what's probably supposed to be a soothing tone. It soothes nothing. If anything, my hackles rise, though I'm not sure what exactly hackles are. "He can't blame a little kid for doing anything."

My stomach roils uneasily. "That's not how he'll see it. I didn't fight back enough against my mom. I—"

I stop because something's rustling in the brush. Maybe that was why my hackles rose in the first place—they sensed before my brain did that something was out there.

I hush Gabe with a finger on his lips. Could it be an animal? Coyotes roam the forest, but they aren't typically threats to big mammals like us. A deer would've been scared away by the sound of us talking. A wolf? Do wolves still exist around here?

The sound of a birdcall. Far from putting me at ease, it makes every muscle in my body tense.

I've heard that birdcall before.

It's him.

The man with the vine tattoos.

77

I leap into action immediately. If they're birdcall-ing to tell each other that they're in place—another one trills in the darkness—then we have only minutes at most, seconds at least, until they attack. "We need to get up," I whisper at Gabe. "Get ready. Get your weapon."

I push myself to my feet, not waiting to see if he's listened to me. I know he has. My crossbow in hand and my new knife strapped to my thigh, I feel a little bit better. I kick each group member to wake them as I circle around our dying fire, shouldering on my pack so that, even if I have to run for it, we won't lose everything again.

A third birdcall. My group is awake now, rubbing their eyes, which widen as they see me standing there with my crossbow at the ready. I jerk my head in the direction of the first birdcall, but they probably have us surrounded.

And they won't hesitate to shoot. Maybe they're aiming even now. I shiver, and not just from the cold.

"What's going on?" Estella whispers. She's standing, fingers scrabbling for her gun, but she's moving slowly, way too slowly.

Maybe I'm wrong. Maybe the calls are just birds seeking a mate, and I've roused them all for nothing.

A crack in the brush behind me, and I whirl, and *there he is*, bathed in the light of the moon. It must be my imagination, but those vines snaking from the collar of his camouflage jacket look even bigger than they did before. Like they're reaching out to strangle me.

"Zara Ross." His voice is a snarl. He takes a step toward me.

I could shoot him if my hands weren't shaking so hard. If there weren't a bunch of other rustles in the woods around me, indicating that his friends are here, surrounding me.

But I have my friends here too. They fan out into a circle with me at the top, their weapons pointed at the woods. Even Ina wields her cast-iron skillet like it was crafted as a weapon and not a cooking tool, hefting it menacingly over her shoulder.

"I've been looking for you a long time." Now the man sounds less snarly, more sure of himself. He's got his gun in his hands, but it's not pointed at me. "We need to talk."

It feels like the next few seconds last for a thousand years. I glance around at my friends, all of them standing in my defense, their faces fierce. They're ready to fight what sounds like, to my estimation, at least four other henchmen. Henchmen who probably know how to use their weapons, assuming they don't laugh themselves silly at the sight of Ina and her frying pan.

Henchmen who *will* use their weapons on my friends. Anything to get to me.

Me. The man's here because of *me*. He has no issue with Gabe, or Estella, or Ronan or Ina or Jasmine. He only wants me.

And if I'm gone, maybe he'll leave my friends alone.

"Hey," I say, and my voice cracks. I can't look at my friends. "Hey, if you want me, you're going to have to catch me first."

The man's eyes widen as I come at him, the whites bright against the blackness. He raises his weapon, but I'm already darting past him into the night.

"I'm going after her!" he shouts behind me. The trees rustle as if in response. I don't wait to hear if his friends respond too.

I'm already gone.

78

Feet thumping. Leaves crunching. Heart pounding. That's how I run away. Or not run away. That's not what I'm doing. I'm leading the men away from my friends, because that's what a leader does. They don't put their people in danger. My dad would be furious. *Survival is about the individual.* And now here I am, taking the individual and sacrificing her on behalf of others.

The man's footsteps are steady and sure behind me. I resist the urge to look over my shoulder to see how much he's gained on me. Years ago I could've evaded him without a second thought, my feet dancing lightly and surely over familiar ground, but now I'm slow and I stumble. We've been hungry the past few days—the area's been overhunted and overforaged by desperate people. I catch my toes on roots and bruise myself on branches. My breaths come in whistles and pants.

And I have no idea where I'm going. At first I try to keep mental track—*I'm running in the same direction we were walking in, that's northeast, so all I have to do to get back is go southwest*—but I'm forced to take too many twists and turns to get around ditches, over rocks, around thickets of brush, and soon I've lost all sense of where I am.

"Zara!" the man shouts. "I just want to talk!"

His lie might send shivers up my spine, but at least it tells me where he is.

Close. Too close.

A male scream goes up behind me, then another. Ronan? Gabe? Either way, they're both cut short.

I stumble and nearly fall. *No.* The whole idea was that I run and draw the men to me, keeping my group safe. But I hear only the one man's footsteps behind me, and with that screaming . . .

I stumble again. I have to get back to my group. What are the men doing to them right now? Attacking them? Hurting them? Killing them? But I have no idea what direction they're in. They're not screaming anymore, so there aren't any sounds to follow.

What if they think I ran away and left them to die?

My eyes blur with tears. *No!* I don't have time for this. I blink them furiously away, but not before my shoulder slams into a tree trunk. My body reels, my arms wheeling to keep me upright.

His hand touches my shoulder. I scream, my leg lashing out.

It's a lucky kick, I swear. It catches him on his kneecap and he stumbles, and in an effort to catch himself, his hand flies off my shoulder and finds purchase on a nearby tree trunk. I dart back off into the night, sweat cool on my forehead.

I don't know how long I run. How long the man chases me through the darkness. Occasionally he lets out a birdcall, but nobody responds. Which is good for me, I guess.

Unless their absence means they're back at camp, torturing my friends. I falter at the idea. Nearly freeze.

Breath scrapes the back of my throat. *You need to keep moving, Zara. You need to lose him.*

Only it seems we're locked in a stalemate. Me running, him always not too far behind. It feels almost like he's pacing me, the way a pack of lions hunt antelope. They follow them, forcing them to run on and on and on until they collapse from exhaustion, and then the predators can do whatever they want.

Because the man doesn't want me dead. I know that already, even before he chooses not to shoot me as I run. Which I should be a little bit grateful for, I suppose. That he doesn't shoot for my leg or foot or some other nonvital part of my body that would nonetheless cripple me. Grateful not to the man, of course. Grateful to the laws of physics that make it nearly impossible to hit a moving target in the dark with any accuracy, especially considering the trees and all the other things in the way. He could easily aim for my leg and put a bullet through my chest, so I'm glad he's not shooting.

If I can't outrun him—and it's pretty clear that I can't—I need to come up with some way to outwit him.

But it's like my brain is frozen. All my energy is focused on putting one foot in front of the other. It's a terrible paradox: I can't think while I'm running, but I can't stop running because he'll grab me and I won't be able to think.

I'm going to have to kill him, aren't I?

I shot that woman on the compound and am still having nightmares about it, and that was an accident.

This man will do worse than kill me if I don't kill him first. And not just to me. To my group.

I grab my crossbow, waiting for the right moment. Too many trees here. Too many stickers there. A clearing—*there.*

I leap to a halt in the clearing and spin, raising my crossbow as I do. I expect him to skid to a stop as well, raise his hands in the air, widen his eyes at my crossbow, so that I can see all the whites. A perfect target.

But he doesn't skid to a stop. He doesn't skid at all. He barrels right into me and tackles me to the ground. All the air flies out of me in a pained "oof" as my back hits the ground hard. My head bounces against the carpet of dead leaves.

For a moment everything goes black. When my vision clears, the man's face is sneering down at me. Most of his face is in shadow, but I can see the vein pulsing on his forehead, the twist of his thick lips.

Terror makes my whole body rigid. I feel myself shaking as if I'm an outside observer, looking on from a distance. From that distance I notice the way his back curves over me, the way his hands clamp down on my shoulders, the way he straddles me so that no matter how much I buck and twist, I can't get free.

I slam back into myself as he speaks. "There. Now we can *talk.*" Only my lower arms and lower legs have some freedom of movement. And my right hand still holds fast to my crossbow. I curl it, trying to angle it toward him. "Zara Ross, if you stay—"

My finger twitches. *Thwip.*

79

The man with the vine tattoos shouts. I can't tell if he's startled or in pain.

Please let it be the latter.

I get my answer when he collapses on me, his full weight pushing me into the ground. His grip on me is gone. I squirm out from under him, gasping and scrabbling for purchase, jumping to my feet as soon as I've rolled him off me.

He doesn't jump to his feet. He lies there, panting and groaning. I kick him in the side, trying to push him onto his back, but he only groans more, pain twisting his face.

My crossbow bolt sticks out of his side, pointing toward his stomach. "That's a gut wound or a lung wound," I tell him. I don't feel happy, not even any sort of vicious glee. I just feel drained. It's like all the stress and panic of my run has dripped away, and there's nothing there to replace it. "You're going to die."

At that he props himself up on one elbow and rolls onto his back. His face is smeared with black dirt; a scrap of dried brown leaf sticks to his forehead, but he doesn't brush it away. "You made a big mistake, Zara Ross," he rasps.

"I didn't let you hurt or kidnap me." A cold wind blows through my hair, but I'm done shivering. "Yeah, big mistake. So sorry about that." A beat of silence. If I have anything I want answered, I'd better ask it now. "Why did you track me all the way across the country?"

He breathes in a shuddering gasp. It doesn't sound like it satisfies very much, because he immediately tries for another one, which sputters on his lips. "Didn't track you . . . after the ward . . . I knew you'd be coming . . . here. . . ."

What? How would he know I was coming here? Unless somehow he knows . . .

He grimaces. Blood dribbles from the corner of his mouth. "Needed leverage . . . against him . . . to fix it . . . make it stop. . . ."

He coughs. More blood froths over his lips. Maybe I should wipe it away, but I'm as still as stone. What is he trying to say? That he knows my dad somehow, that he knows about the compound? And he needed me to use against him? For what? Why?

He gags on the blood now dripping over his lips. I stare at him, unmoved. Maybe I should be moved.

But I'm just cold. Focused. "Why would you need me as leverage?"

He spits, clearing out some of the blood, and manages to get a few words out. "You need to . . ." They're garbled, but I'm pretty sure I'm hearing them right. "Stop him. . . ." And then his head drops to the side. It's a cliché to say that the light goes out of his eyes, but that's exactly what happens: something dulls in them, a spark escaping. I stumble back a few steps, my legs blocky and numb.

I don't like being this close to the body. But it's better not to shy away from the truth of what I did. Like how I think meat eaters should spend a day at a farm or go hunting to understand where their food really comes from, that it's an animal that gave its life so you can sustain yours, not a sanitized chunk of flesh that sprang intact from a plastic-wrapped Styrofoam tray in the grocery store. I'm not antimeat—obviously not. I'm a hunter. I've bowed my head respectfully plenty of times and watched the life drain out of an animal's body. But I think it's sacred, eating the body of another being, and that body should be honored and respected, and what better way to honor and respect something than to know it fully?

I'm babbling on to distract myself from what the man said. Does it count as babbling if it's inside your head? Or is it not just a distraction, because his body is nothing more than meat now? Not that I'm going to eat him. That would be awful.

But . . . stop *whom*? My dad? But how did he know my dad? What the hell is going on?

I draw in a deep, shuddery breath that, horrifyingly enough, reminds me of the ones the man tried to take before the blood bubbled up. That makes me need another one, and another one, until my head is so dizzy and light, I might float away.

80

I'm not sure how long it takes me to calm down. I'm not sure I *have* calmed down, actually. All I know is, an indeterminate amount of time later, I'm cold and alone in the dark woods with the dead body of a person I've killed, and if I don't figure out what to do next, I'll be a dead body in the woods too.

I have my pack and my knife. That's good. I have my crossbow. That's better.

It occurs to me that I should search the man's body. And not just because he might have necessary supplies.

I just don't want to go near him. Still, I lower myself down to the ground and crawl gingerly over the rotting leaves until I'm back at his side, right where I was when I shot him. I pull the crossbow bolt out, my stomach flipping at the awful sucking sound it makes, and try to wipe it clean on the ground. It's been long enough that blood doesn't pour out of the wound, but the metallic smell is all around me. I imagine it coating my hands and spreading black and thick over my arms, sticky and hot.

I lean over and vomit. Not much comes out, and when I'm done heaving, I wipe my mouth on my sleeve and get back to work.

I take the gun and set it a safe distance away so that I don't accidentally hit it while I'm going through his stuff. He doesn't have a big pack like me, meaning that he and his friends were likely traveling by car and this was intended to be a shorter trip on foot. My mind automatically goes to finding the car and whatever supplies he has, but we shouldn't need it. We're almost where we've been trying to go.

Inside his small pack is a half-full water bottle, which I take, and some water purification tablets, which I also take. Some beef jerky and protein bars—take. A detailed map of the area with indecipherable marks all over, stars and jagged lines—maybe marking off where he's been or where he wants to go? I take that, too, because why not? Some other supplies, which I transfer to my own pack.

And a wallet. This I open and flip through with interest. I leave the cash—cash is useless right now, though the man has a whole lot of it. Hundreds of dollars in crisp new bills. Various credit cards.

And his driver's licenses. Yes, licenses, as in multiple. He's got three of them right on top of one another, his unsmiling picture with different names: Jeremy Hall from Connecticut; Joseph Brown from California; James Richmond from Florida. Which is real? Are any of them real? I shuffle through them, my fingers sliding over the smooth laminate, and then realize there's one more card behind them all.

This one's not a driver's license. It's got the same unsmiling picture with yet another name: Jake Latham. The laminate card glitters all over with security holograms as I tilt it back and forth, and there's a design on the edge like a QR code or a barcode. Right next to a design of two black circles, one inside the other, with an eye inside the smaller one.

I've seen this design before. It nags at the inside of my mind. Where?

I can't remember. I'll have to let it come to me. I pocket his wallet and continue my search of the man's body. Of Jake Latham's body. I have no idea if that's his real name, but something about that card makes me think that's the real version of him.

His skin is cold by now and a little bit damp with the coming of the dew, and I don't linger on any of it as I pat him down, seeing if he's got anything else on him. Through his pants I can feel the knot of scar tissue I gave him on his leg. Other than that, I find nothing but some gum and a crumpled receipt in his pocket. I uncrumple it just in case maybe he scribbled some notes on it, but there's nothing there except a record of the onion and cheese omelette he ate for breakfast at some diner in Nevada before the blackout.

The whole process leaves me feeling strangely unsatisfied. I didn't realize until now, but I wanted my search to tell me something. Like who Jake Latham actually was. Why he tracked me across the country. Why I killed him.

But all I have are some fake driver's licenses and a weird ID and the questions whirling around my head, making me dizzy.

81

At some point I drift into a fugue state that's half sleep, half waking dream. It's like my dad is standing there, right in front of me, shaking his head with disapproval. *You let yourself depend too much on others, Zara,* he tells me. *If you'd gone at this alone like I taught you, you would be fine. You'd get up and continue on your way. You wouldn't be paralyzed by this guilt or fear or whatever this is.*

I shake myself out of it as the first rays of sun are beginning to break through the stars. I sit with my back up against a tree, my legs limp before me, and watch the sky turn pink and orange and blue. I'm so cold I can't even feel my fingers, but that's okay. I deserve it.

I ran off and left my group behind. They might be dead now. The thought feels like a kick to my stomach. I was trying to save them, but I might have gotten them killed. Because those men came in pursuit of me, but running away didn't make them all chase me.

Maybe the men shot my group or strangled them or tied them up and left them for dead. I should go back for them, but I'm not sure if I can handle the sight of their bodies. I can barely handle the sight of this body, and I killed him in self-defense. But seeing the bodies of my friends, the people I care for, the people who trusted me . . .

If you'd gone at this alone like I taught you, you would be fine.

I'm not fine. They're probably not fine either. And it's all my fault.

82

I'm so close to the compound, and yet I seem to have lost the will to go on. I sit there by Jake Latham's cold corpse, staring vacantly into the trees. I've avoided alcohol this entire trip, but I can't help but wish I'd scored a flask of vodka off him. I wish for the scorching burn of the alcohol down my throat, for the sweet floating obliviousness it would bring.

Or else it would just make me feel more depressed. Maybe it's best I'm stuck with nothing but water. Which I remind myself periodically to swig, by the way. I don't have a death wish.

It's just that I don't really have a life wish right now either.

I don't know how long it's been when I hear footsteps crunching toward me. By instinct I reach for my crossbow. It's got to be Jake Latham's friends. They've finished with my group, and now they've tracked me here, and when they see I've killed their leader, they'll—

"Zara?"

That's . . . Gabe. That's Gabe's voice.

I push myself up on tottering legs, propping myself against the nearest tree. My feet tingle, the blood flowing through them. Warming them.

I clear my throat. My voice is rusty. "Gabe?"

"Zara?"

There's a crashing sound as branches break, and then there he is. Gabe. His face dirty, his shirt torn. His eyes find me first, then flit to the ground, where Jake Latham is congealing, then come back to me. His lips open in a shout. "Guys! She's over here!"

More crashing sounds follow, and then there they are, faces popping up behind Gabe's shoulders. Estella, her hair a mess and a cut bleeding on her cheek. Ronan, his eyes wary, his rifle in his hands. Jasmine and Ina, Ina limping on her injured leg, Jasmine holding her up.

They're all here. All alive.

My mouth drops open. "How . . ." I trail off because it sounds like a terrible thing to say. *How are you all alive?*

Is this a hallucination? I heard them screaming, after all. I suck in a deep breath, then another, then another, and they start whistling in the back of my throat, and my head starts getting light again. . . .

A hand clamps on to each of my shoulders. Estella. She stares into my eyes, speaking in a low, soothing tone. "Look at my eyes, Zara. Tell me what color my eyes are."

I focus on her eyes. "They're brown."

"But not just brown. Focus really hard. I know you can do it."

I squint. My breaths stop whistling. "They're brown, with black spots, and I can see a red vein in the corner. . . ."

"Right. Good. Now breathe."

I *am* breathing.

"Breathe in for five. Match me. Tap me on the shoulder at every fifth breath."

It's like I'm back in the bathroom the first time I met her, hiding during the lockdown, only she's speaking *my* part.

I breathe in. Breathe out. Tap her on the shoulder every five cycles. My head stops feeling so light.

I feel okay.

Estella moves back with a small smile. "Good."

I don't think I'd feel a hallucination touching me. "But . . . how . . ."

Gabe steps up. "We're not entirely helpless without you, you know."

Clearly not. "But the men . . ."

Estella steps up beside him. "You don't have to worry about them," she says grimly. "We took them down for you."

My mouth drops open. "You did? All four of them?"

"We're not saying it was easy," Ronan says, stepping up too. They're all here. For one another.

For me.

"Or fun," Jasmine says. "I literally thought we were all going to die."

"I just want you to know I knocked one out with my frying pan," Ina says.

My friends. They used their weapons. The way I taught them. They got in formation. They didn't abandon one another, like I did.

"They're all dead?"

Gabe gives me a slight nod. "Yes." A piercing look, like he can read my mind. "It was lucky you ran. I don't know if we could've taken their leader the way you obviously managed to." A nod at Jake Latham's body, which I notice the others are steadfastly refusing to look at. Death isn't so easy to face. Though they're going to have to face what they did. Eventually. I assume that now they're pushing off the feelings so that we can keep pushing on. "You drew the attention away from us, and it threw the other guys off. They didn't seem sure what to do." They must have been hired guns. "A couple tried to chase after you guys but must have lost you and then doubled back. Which helped a lot, because we only had two to face down at a time."

"We're lucky Ronan's such a good shot," says Ina. "All the rest of us had to do was distract them." She shudders. "They shot at us, but it doesn't seem like they were very good at it, and we made sure to zigzag and weave around to make it even harder."

"I got grazed!" Jasmine says, holding up a bloody arm as if it's a trophy. I lean in to see if she's okay, but she grins at me to show me she is.

"And then we tracked you down," Estella continues. "It was hard. But we remembered all those things you told us about hunting, about how you used to track deer through the woods. Ronan led us, since he has the most experience."

"A broken branch here, a footprint in the mud there," says Ronan.

Jasmine waves her hand in the air. "It wasn't actually *that* hard." Her grin goes a little shaky, and I know that it may not have been that hard for them to take the men down, but it *will* be hard for them to deal with it when it hits them.

But we'll be safe at the compound. And I'll be there to help them.

Tears prick my eyes. But I can't cry. Not right now. "You guys . . ." My voice is froggy. I swallow hard, trying to force the tears down, but it's no use. I sniffle, and then they're leaking out, sliding noiselessly over my cheeks and making my lips taste of salt. I cover my eyes with my hand, but it's too late. Everyone's already seen me cry. "I'm sorry. I shouldn't . . ."

Shadows fall over me. Then hands land on my shoulders and rub. "It's okay to cry," Estella says. From my other side, Gabe goes on, "You can't be strong all the time."

I wipe my eyes. The world smears before me. "I have to be strong all the time if I'm going to survive."

"No, you don't," Ronan says. Jasmine says, "That's what your team is for!" Even through the blur, I can see Ina nodding.

And maybe . . . no, not maybe—they're right. They're definitely right. I already learned that it's okay not to be okay all the time, but it's also okay not to be strong all the time. That's why you have a team. Maybe strength isn't only saving yourself. Maybe it's allowing other people to save you sometimes. Trusting in other people to be there for you.

I let them all hug me. Envelop me in their warmth and their strength, and that's when Ina murmurs in my ear. "No way in hell we were going to let them take you, Zara."

And that's when the tears really start flowing.

"Besides, we can't take *all* the credit," Jasmine supplies. "One of those guys almost got me—the one who grazed me—but he fell into some kind of random hole in the ground and died."

My heart nearly stops. "A hole in the ground?" In my mind I see my dad digging, my feet dangling over the edge, his face shining with sweat as he smiled up at me, explaining some fact about the dirt or earthworms or rocks.

"Yeah," she says. "It was all covered in brush like the rest of the forest floor, but he went crashing right through it. It was weirdly deep, too. Do you think it was some kind of animal's den?"

I take a deep breath. "No," I say. "I think we're here."

83

I make sure to lead the way, because if my dad is watching, he needs to see me first. He needs to see me and know not to shoot.

If he even recognizes me. I'm a lot different from the scared ten-year-old whose mom plucked her shaking from the woods.

Am I, though? I pick my way through the trees with my crossbow swinging lightly at my side, the same way I did seven years ago. I squint into the sun, filtering through the trees the same way, and wipe sweat out of my eyes the same way, and to be honest, I'm not much taller than I was back then.

Except now? I'm not alone.

I'm not sure if the woods around me actually look familiar, or if I'm just thinking they do because I know we're close to the compound. Every step swamps me with nostalgia. Is that the tree I climbed to shoot my first deer? Is this the clearing where I found bushes and bushes of fresh raspberries that my mom made into the best pie ever?

It's slow going because we have to keep a careful eye out for traps and snares. Back in the day, my dad made sure to tell me exactly where he'd put them so that I wouldn't accidentally stumble into them. Now I'm stuck looking for signs that they're there so that we don't lose an arm or a leg to a trap wire.

When we start finding more and more, I know we're getting closer.

And then I do legit start recognizing my surroundings. That *is* the rock I used to pretend was a huge mountain and would clamber up with my short legs and act like I'd reached the top of Mount Everest. This *is* the pond crowded with lily pads where I used to wash off after a long day of climbing Mount Everest. I know where I'm going now. I move forward with purpose, my chest swollen with confidence, my squad behind me, backing me up. Gabe grabs my hand. Squeezes it. Estella links her elbow through my other arm. Kind gestures, and I smile at them before neatly disentangling myself. I need my hands and arms free. Just in case.

The foliage grows thicker as we approach the compound. This was on purpose, to hide our buildings from view as much as possible, to discourage any stray hikers from fighting their way through stickers and bushes and convince them to take an easier route the other way.

But we push through, of course. I talk the whole time, nervous prattle intended to reach my dad's ears and tell him that it's me, that he shouldn't shoot, that I've come home again. I don't even know what I'm saying. I don't even know if he'll recognize my voice.

I snap the branches off one final bush. I pry some thorns out of my pants and step free.

Here. At long last I'm finally home.

84

The compound looks smaller than I remember. That's the first thing that pops to mind. As a little kid, I remember it being sprawling, our house huge, the greenhouses dazzling in the sun, the warren of warehouses endless.

As a slightly larger kid, I see that the house is just a long brown building, low to the ground, covered in solar panels. The greenhouse is full of green, but there's only one. The warren of warehouses is made up of only a few small sheds for storage and the chicken coop.

Wait. I backtrack to the roof. Solar panels? Have those always been there?

Yes. I remember my dad telling me about them as a kid. "They're for capturing electricity from the sun," he said. But what did we need the electricity for? The whole point of the compound was that we had to survive without it.

"Zara."

It takes me a minute to realize my dad's voice isn't coming from inside my head, the way it's been for years now. It's coming from the outside. It's coming from right in front of me. I look up, and we lock eyes.

He looks exactly the way I remember. It's like he hasn't aged a year in my absence. His hair is still thick and reddish, if maybe starting a little farther back on his forehead, and his eyes are still a piercing blue. His face is broad and tan and craggy, his lips thin and, right now, turned upward in the slightest hint of a smile.

"Zara," he says, his voice low and deep. It's like it travels up from the ground itself, rooted deep in the earth. "You've come home."

He doesn't spare a glance for any of my friends, just keeps his eyes trained on me. I open my mouth to respond . . . but nothing comes out.

I've traveled all this way and have no idea what to say now that I'm here.

"You took your time," he continues. "I've been waiting."

Just like that, the words break free. "It's chaos out there," I tell him. "We're lucky we made it here at all."

He nods at me. Again he doesn't look at my friends. "We have much to practice. Welcome home, Zara."

He stares at me. I stare at him for a moment, waiting for him to acknowledge the group of people behind me, and when he doesn't, I wave my hand in their direction. "These are my friends. I would never have made it here without them," I say, ignoring how his lip twitches with disapproval. "Gabe and Estella came from LA with me. We met Ronan, Jasmine, and Ina along the way."

A beat of silence. "You wouldn't have made it here alone, hmm?"

The disappointment isn't just in his lips. It's in his voice. "Then we truly do have much to practice." Finally he glances over at my friends, his eyes narrowing with thought. "Please, all of you, join me for lunch inside."

He turns to go, walking toward the house without looking back.

Gabe breathes out. "So that's your dad, huh?"

"It explains so much," Estella murmurs.

I don't want to ask what that means, so I start jogging after him. "Let's go!" I call over my shoulder, trying to force some lightness into my voice. "You can see where I grew up!"

None of them answer. They just follow along.

85

It's so *weird* to be back. It feels at once like I've been gone for a hundred years and like I never left at all, like I just stepped out for a moment and now here I am, back in our kitchen.

An onslaught of memories rush over me the second we step inside: The three of us huddled around the woodstove on a cold New York night, my dad's arm around my mom's shoulders, pulling her close to him. The three of us sitting around the table for a dinner of a goose I'd shot, my parents exclaiming about how this was surely the best goose anyone had ever bagged and cooked up. The three of us taste-testing jam, licking preserves of strawberry and raspberry and blueberry and apple off our fingers until we were sticky with the sugar, ending with split results—my parents preferring the strawberry-rhubarb, me declaring raspberry the winner.

The room still looks the same as it did back then. Just maybe the wooden slab of a table is a little more scarred and pitted, and the big woodstove whose metal chimney pipe stretches from floor to ceiling is cold and dark, the inside filled with charred bits of wood.

As before, there are only three chairs around the table. The one at the head of the table is bigger than the other two, flanked by arms while the other two are armless. That's my dad's. I usher Ina into one of the other two, because of her leg, and the rest of us stand awkwardly around, not wanting to take a seat while the others are left standing.

My dad's at the counter, pulling something from the icebox, putting a pot on the stove. It's an oddly domestic scene, especially odd as I don't think I ever saw him cook. That was my mom's job. But of course he would've had to cook for himself since we left—there was no one here to do it for him.

I swallow the heavy lump of guilt. It sits uncomfortably in my stomach. "Dad," I say, and the word feels like a stone in my mouth. "Do we have any more chairs?"

He doesn't turn. I'm speaking to the back of his russet head. "You may drag some in from the living room."

As we transport some of the living room chairs to the kitchen, where they don't quite reach the height of the table, I keep my eyes carefully averted from the walls. My hand-drawn pictures still hang all over the place. He's never stopped thinking about me, has he? Never stopped missing me.

I abandoned him.

I'm glad he's trying, at least. He might be uncomfortable with my friends, but he's trying.

My friends settle in around the table, but I don't sit quite yet. "Do you need any help? Dad?" Again that stone in my mouth—a word I wasn't sure I'd ever say again.

He continues stirring a pot on the stove. "I can handle it on my own."

So I sit down and trade awkward looks with the group. Gabe is watching my dad, studying him almost, as is Estella. Ronan is looking all around him. Ina's staring at the food on the stove, while Jasmine is jiggling her leg so that it shakes her chair.

Before long my dad is carrying the food over from the stove, spreading it out before us. He doesn't have enough uniform silverware and dishware, so some of us get bowls, and some of us get plates; some of us get spoons, and some of us get forks. It's okay, I tell myself, until my dad sets the last of the mugs down with an apologetic look. "You'll have to drink from your water bottle, Zara," he says. "I don't have enough cups left for tea."

That's fine. "I don't like tea much anyway," I tell him, even though from the smell I can tell it's mint tea, which is tasty and is supposed to be good for the digestion. I pull out my water bottle and take a long drink as he dishes out some kind of meat stew from the pot.

He sits. My friends watch him, picking up their own utensils only once he digs in. I take a big bite and wince. A chunk of bone. I spit it out, then chew the remainder thoughtfully. It's not bad. Not enough onion to cover up the gamey taste of the meat. I guess I've been spoiled by Ina's skill with everything we scavenged up.

My dad doesn't start a conversation, so I jump in. "How have things been here since I . . ." I trail off. He blinks at me, waiting for me to go on. "Since I left," I finish lamely.

He shrugs, chewing slowly on his mouthful of stew. He swallows fully before replying. "Much the same as when you were here, Zara. There are no new trends in the forest."

Silence falls over us again. Jasmine takes an enthusiastic slurp of her tea. "This is really good!" she chirps. "What did you say was in it?"

"I didn't say," my dad answers. From the lack of answer that follows, it's clear he's not going to say either.

I take another long swallow of my water.

Gabe is the one to break the silence this time. "You should be incredibly proud of your daughter," he tells my dad. My dad raises an eyebrow slowly, as if wondering why anyone would be telling him to do anything. "We wouldn't have made it here without her."

"I imagine not," my dad says.

We eat the rest of our meal without speaking. Every scrape of teeth on tines, every gulp of tea, seems excruciatingly loud. Has there ever been a more uncomfortable meal in the history of the world? Probably, but this one's definitely up there in the rankings.

Finally my dad pats around his mouth with a napkin and regards us calmly, taking in the empty bowls and empty cups. "And now we wait."

"Wait for what?" I ask, just as Ronan's cheek hits the table with a thunk.

I have no idea what's going on. Neither do the others. Gabe pushes his chair back, going to stand . . . and stumbles, falling to the ground. Estella cries out, but she's turning to a boneless sack in her chair and sliding after him.

Ina's chin droops neatly toward her chest. Jasmine slumps over.

I leap to my feet, ready to fight—*What? What are you going to fight, Zara?*—but my head doesn't get fuzzy. I crouch at Gabe's side and find, to my great relief, that he's breathing normally. So is Estella.

They're not dead, then. I stand to face my dad, with what feels like horror painted all over my face. "What have you done?"

"They're not dead," my dad says. "Only drugged."

Of course. The tea. He didn't give me any tea.

I reach for my crossbow, still hanging by my side, then hesitate. This is my dad. Not some stranger with bad intentions. He's the only reason I made it here alive. He taught me all that I needed. Whatever he's doing, I'm sure he has a good rationale for it.

Right?

"I would never kill your friends," my dad says. Conversationally, lightly, like we're talking about the weather.

Well, it's good to hear that, at least. I let out a breath.

And then he continues. "You're the one who's going to do that."

Suddenly I forget how to breathe in.

His voice deepens. "You still have so much to learn about survival, Zara. You still have so much to learn about sacrifice," he says, and just like that, it's like I'm hearing his voice through a tunnel; it's like I'm ten years old again, with the blood of an innocent woman on my hands, crying and heaving outside the house as my parents talk in tense, low murmurs.

I wasn't able to take my eyes off the hiker I'd accidentally shot. My dad slung her body over his shoulder and carried her back to the compound, me scurrying along behind him, tears sprinkling the ground like bread crumbs meant to lead me back. At the house she was laid stretched out on the dirt, one arm over her head, one cheek against the ground, her eyes staring sightlessly into the trees. I wanted to close her eyes, but it didn't feel right to touch her. Not when I was the one who'd stolen her ability to see.

I hadn't been in the real world since before I could remember, but somehow I knew about prison. Maybe from stories my parents had told me, or books I'd read in our little library. In any case, what I knew was that prison was a little room locked up with bars, where people were punished for the bad things they'd done. My mom had always assured me that no, I wouldn't go to prison for breaking a window or forgetting to take dinner off the stove before it burned, because prison was only for people who did things that were *really bad*.

I couldn't think of anything more *really bad* than killing someone. I knew my parents had to be talking about taking me to prison, and even though I knew I deserved it, I really didn't want to be locked away in a little room distant from my family. So I was eavesdropping, ready to run and hide in the woods the second one of them mentioned it.

I strained my ears, just barely able to pick up the deep notes of my dad's voice. ". . . will bury the body in the garden and burn all of its belongings," he was saying. "We're out in the middle of nowhere. Nobody will ever find it."

My mom's voice was muffled, not so much by distance but by tears. "We can't do that," she said. "We *can't*. What about her family? What if this happened to Zara?" She sucked in a quick, sharp intake of breath, like the thought was nearly too much to bear. "We can say we found her dead. That we don't know what happened, but her family needs closure."

Dad scoffed. "You don't think they'll investigate? I know that better than anyone what they can do. What they *will* do. They want an excuse to bring me in." He got quiet for a second, and when he spoke again, his voice was decisive. "This is about keeping my family safe. That is my decision, and my decision is final."

"But—"

"Stop arguing with me, woman." I recoiled at the menace in his voice. He'd never spoken that way to me.

But—I realize, thinking back now—I'd heard him talking that way to my mom. Like, a lot.

After their argument that day, he left my mom where she was and came out to me. He looked straight at me, blocking my view of the hiker's body. "Zara," he said. "Gather the woman's belongings so we can destroy them before we bury the body."

As much as I wanted to be rejoicing that I wasn't going to prison after all, I didn't move. My belly was a block of ice. I'd killed an innocent woman. I was a *killer*. I felt like I was going to throw up again from the sheer guilt of it. Like my mom had said: What if someone had shot me and killed me dead, so that I could never eat fresh tomatoes off the vine again or go swimming in the lake or feel sunshine on my face, and tossed my dead body in a hole somewhere, so that my parents would never even know I was dead?

It was the most horrible thing I could think of.

"Dad," I said, pushing on even though my voice didn't really want to come out. "We can't. It's not right."

Something flashed in his eyes as he looked at me. I wasn't sure exactly what it was. I'd never seen him look at me that way before. But the hairs pimpled all along my spine, like I'd sighted a bear coming my way. "Zara," he said. "You did not do a bad thing, killing this woman. You protected our family. She came too close to the compound. If she'd seen us, she could've told anyone out there where we were, and they could have come for us."

As my blood pumped, it brought horror along with it, spreading quick and cold through my neck, my chest, shivering my legs.

He'd encouraged me to shoot before I was totally ready.

He'd *known*.

"If you hadn't done it, I would have." Maybe the most unsettling thing about my dad's speech wasn't the words he was saying; it was the tone he was saying them in. It was casual. Nonchalant. Like he was saying it might rain later today, or that he'd finished the last of the blackberry jam.

Like I hadn't just *killed* someone on his direction.

"But why does it matter so much if someone finds us?" I squeaked. I was trying really hard not to cry. He didn't like to see me cry. "Maybe it would be nice to have company. She looked nice."

My dad leaned over, placing his hands on his knees so that he could stare me down at my level. "We're only safe here at the compound as long as nobody knows we're here. Sometimes safety requires sacrifice." He stood back up, dusting his hands off on his pants, as if saying that had somehow made them dirty. "Her life didn't matter. None of their lives matter. Only we matter."

None of their lives matter. Only we matter. The words ring at the inside of my head like a bell now, making me reel. Right into another memory.

Going down into the root cellar to hide among the potatoes. Trailing my fingers over the big metal door I'd never seen before and never questioned after.

A big metal door. Solar panels on the roof.

And later, "What's this?" I asked, tracing the symbol on the old phone. My dad replied, "A part of my past from a very, very long time ago."

The symbol of two circles, one inside the other, with an eye in the center. The same symbol as the one on Jake Latham's ID card.

You need to stop him.

I look at my dad. My dad looks at me, his face relaxed. Proud. Does he know I've put all the pieces together?

My heart thumps. Nausea churns in my belly. "It was you," I say. His gaze doesn't waver. "You did this. You did *all* of this."

86

It was you. You did this. For a moment I wonder if I should clarify myself to my dad. *It was you who hacked the electrical grids. You who blacked out the entire country. You who killed Mom and the Ramirezes and Donna Pearson and Jake Latham and nine out of every ten people.*

But as I look at him and his eyes don't widen in shock, as I look at him and he doesn't shake his head and frown and ask what the hell I'm talking about, it confirms that I don't have to clarify. He knows exactly what I'm talking about. And he doesn't deny it.

Instead he smiles.

"I told you, modern life makes people soft," he says. "And not only that. It took you from me."

My stomach roils. That's not why my mom took me from here. My mom took me from here to protect me from *him.* Yes, I learned what I needed from him. Without his teachings, I wouldn't be alive right now, and neither would my friends. That doesn't make the way he treated my mom and me okay.

"Sometimes the greater good requires sacrifice," he says. "If humanity was to be saved—the real humanity, the sweat of it, the innovation of it, not the pale imitation that laughs at trash television and spends more time tapping computer keys than learning the world around them—much of it must be sacrificed. It will rise stronger from the ashes left behind." He nods at me. At us. "Do you not feel stronger than you were before?"

I want to tell him no. I want to seize upon all the horror rising within me and throw it back in his face, shriek that he's wrong, that he's delusional, that he killed my mom and I'm only weaker for it. I'm less for it.

And that's true. Her loss means there's a hole inside me that will never be filled again. But as for me? I *am* stronger. I know myself now. I know where I fit in this world now.

But it's not worth it. Nothing could make all of this worth it.

I survey my passed-out friends. This is part of his plan. He's disappointed in how "weak" I am, and this is how he's going to make me strong again. Self-reliant.

But I don't want to be self-reliant anymore—that doesn't make you strong. It makes you alone.

Back to my dad. He's staring at me patiently, like he's waiting for me to agree. I won't. I'll never agree.

Even if he's the one who taught me to survive. Was it worth it? Was it really worth it, if it came along with him yelling at my mom and killing other people and, and, and . . .

I cough. So much is connecting in my head, but there are still points I don't understand. "But how did you . . . ?"

"How did I kill the grids?" my dad asks. It's like he's asking if I'm in the mood for a sandwich right now or if he should save it for later. "What you don't know about me, Zara, is what I *was*, a long time ago."

The scene: thirty years ago, as computers and coding were skyrocketing in importance. Computers and coding had existed for years, been necessary for the moon landing, but now technology was taking off, becoming vital and commonplace all at once. "And I was there in the middle of it," my dad says, his eyes misting over with memory. "Nobody knew we existed. We were in the bowels of the CIA, monitoring threats to our country, overseeing what our people did, how weak and dependent they were becoming."

The Eyes. Like Gabe told me about, or another organization just like it. My dad was one of them. Their logo: two circles with an eye in the middle. Because they were always there. Always watching. Always in the middle of everything important that ever happened.

"Jake Latham," I say. The sound of his name is like a punch in the gut. "You worked together. He *knew* it was you."

That's how he'd known I'd seen the blackout coming: he had listened to my phone call, but not because the mayor's line was bugged. Because *my* line was bugged. Because he was trying to listen to my dad through me. Maybe that was why my dad had never tried to call.

My dad raises an eyebrow. "Ah, you met Jake? How is he?"

"He's dead," I say flatly. He told me the truth, I guess. Maybe he didn't go about it the best way, but he was trying to stop my dad. He must have understood I was the only thing my dad cared about, and when Jake Latham realized what was going on, he tried to grab me to use against my dad as leverage, to threaten my life in exchange for my dad fixing things. He retreated to lurk near where he knew my dad was hiding, in hopes that he could intercept me before I found the compound.

"I learned how easy it would be," my dad continues. "We thwarted attempt after attempt, brought down terrorist group after terrorist group, stopped foreign governments from attacking our people. And over the course of it, I realized . . . why? Why stop it?

"So I ran," he says. "Ran to the wild. I knew I'd need to train myself how to survive without electricity, and to figure out how to do all I would need to do. How I would obtain the proper technology—they were always watching, you know, looking for an excuse to take me down, so it took me a long time to gather everything I would need. Your mom, and you. Perfected my crowning achievement." He smiles. It reaches all the way into his eyes, shines out pure and delighted. "You. A piece of me, continuing on into the future I'd never get to see." Something ugly flickers over his face. "My only one. Your mother wouldn't . . . couldn't . . ." The ugliness clears, is replaced by a placid calm. "How is your mother?"

I can't talk about my mom with him. I'm pretty sure I'd lose it. To the point I'm not even sure what "it" is.

I stand up straight, my crossbow still hanging at my side. Jake Latham told me "You need to stop him" with his dying breath.

Nobody else could get into his bunker. Except me. The "piece" of him continuing on into the future.

I force myself to smile. "Mom is doing great," I say. "She's taking charge in LA. Taking care of people with their emergency supplies. Helping everyone survive." For a moment I relax into the idea, let myself believe it. I'm not sure he does—he must know what LA's state is, how few emergency supplies they actually had—but he regards me patiently anyway, waits for me to go on.

I swallow hard. "I left her to come find you. I knew I had to come home."

It's like the sun is shining out of his face. His grin broadens, stretches from cheek to cheek.

And it's horrifying.

I paste a smile on my face. It feels ghoulish. Gabe would definitely be able to fake a better one than this. *Anyone* would definitely be able to fake a better one than this.

I have no idea what I'm going to do. All I know is that I need to kill some time. For my friends to wake up again, so that they can help me. For me to figure out some kind of plan that will make all of this okay.

I throw my shoulders back. "Could you show me how you did it? How you took out all the electricity?" I ask. I already know where the computers must be: behind the metal door in the root cellar. That's where this all began.

And that's where it's going to end.

87

My dad turns away and heads outside. I follow. With his back to me, I let the smile slide off my face, gripping my crossbow closer to my side. I could end it all with one well-placed shot to the back of the throat. *You need to stop him.* I could stop him.

But this is my dad. The only parent I have left. And he hasn't shown me how he did what he did. If I know more, maybe I'll be able to turn it around.

As if he can read my thoughts, he stops before the root cellar's double doors. "Leave your crossbow up here, Zara," he says. "It's big and bulky, and there are a lot of sensitive objects down there."

He doesn't turn around, but somehow it's like he's staring straight at me. Like his eyes are burning into my forehead. I swallow hard, my throat suddenly dry. "No problem," I tell him, trying to sound breezy. Cold sweat dampens the back of my neck. I slip my crossbow off and set it gently on the ground beside the root cellar doors. "Is it going to be safe here?"

"There's nobody else out here for miles."

"Not even with the blackout? Nobody's shown up hiking through the woods?" I ask doubtfully. We're far from cities like New York and Boston, but not *that* far. Anyone who got out of the city and decided to try to make it in the wilderness could have come in this direction.

My dad pulls the wooden root cellar doors open. Musty air gusts up and out as the doors rattle flat on the ground. "Do you really want to know, Zara?" He doesn't wait for an answer, just embarks on the downward climb. I stand there and watch him disappear, my stomach roiling.

I'd bet my crossbow there isn't just one grave by the garden anymore.

Stop thinking about it. I do my best to push the idea to the back of my mind. I need to focus now. My feet find the top step; the staircase is just as steep as I remember, nearly vertical as I pick my way down it into the darkness underground.

The only light down here comes from the few rays of sun filtering through the open doors, which means most of the root cellar is pitch black. My dad's already disappeared into it; he knows this place as well as he does the woods outside, meaning he doesn't need light to find his way through. I didn't used to either. When I was a kid, I used to be able to scamper down here, not even worrying about falling and breaking my neck, and locate whatever pantry item my mom sent me for by touch and memory only.

I still have a general idea of where I'm heading, but it's slow going; I have to keep my arms out in front of me to stop me from bumping into anything. And it's all for naught when a flashlight flickers on at the other end. "Do you need help, Zara?"

I grit my teeth and slide my feet over the dirt. "No." One of my feet hits what must be a bag of potatoes. My toe stubs with a sharp, sudden pain. I swear silently, shaking out my foot and hitting it on something else.

The flashlight beam finds its way toward me. "Come, Zara. We don't have time to dally."

Following the thin, flickering light feels like I've already lost. Like he's already won. *This isn't about being able to feel your way through a dark basement,* I tell myself, but I don't like starting out at a disadvantage. *Maybe it's even for the better. Let him think that you've lost your edge. That you're nothing without your crossbow.*

My inner voice isn't the most convincing, but it's all I've got.

The flashlight beam takes me to the metal door at the end of the root cellar, the one that so mystified me as a kid. I stop before it. My dad's already standing there, waiting for me to see it before he starts dialing the combination lock, which is high up. I must not have been able to see it as a kid. It's amazing how much results from your perceptions, or lack thereof.

I try to see the combination, but it's too dark and my dad's fingers are too quick. It takes him only a moment before the lock clicks and the door creaks open. He steps back to pull it all the way; it's so heavy that I can see even him strain to move it. And then it's open and—

I'm blind. I blink and blink, trying to see through the sudden influx of bright white light, but the light has taken over. All I can do is stand there, blind and helpless, as little spots of vision start to speckle back.

It's all light. I step into the room—the bunker?—to find a spread of monitors. Some are dark, some blink with lines of code, others are set to a screen saver of a cube bouncing around the screen. Wires tangle in every corner and under every desk; fancy keyboards curve and blink at me. The computers hum quietly to themselves in anticipation.

There are no windows. The walls are metal.

I don't know what to say. "Has this always been here?"

"I built the compound around it." My dad stands so close to me, I can feel the heat radiating from his body. Or maybe it's the heat from all these computers warming the air.

I glance over at him. He gives me a nod, which I take as permission to explore the room.

The amount of information on these screens alone is overwhelming. My eyes scroll through lines of code, which my brain tries frantically to arrange in some sort of order.

"You can feel free to examine them further," my dad says, and I take a seat at one of the terminals, my fingers hovering over the keyboard.

It feels like coming home. The dance of my fingers over the keys. The faint light emanating off the screens that gives people a headache after looking at it too long. The cursor jolting over glowing text.

From what I can see, my dad's been monitoring places in the US that still have power: places like the bunker where they took the president and her family and cabinet officials; isolated communities like Partytown; cities and towns in Alaska and Hawaii, which aren't connected to our grids. Monitoring efforts to send help to our stranded populace—a bunch of other countries have tried to send aid, air-dropping packages of food and water purification tablets and medical supplies, or unpiling them from boats on the coast, but the number of people those are actually reaching are minuscule. I shake my head as horror hollows me out.

"I'm shaking my head at you, too." His voice sounds different than it did before. "You won't *take care* of your friends. I saw that the moment you asked to see the bunker. Do you think I'm stupid, Zara? That I couldn't tell you were lying to me?"

I spin around in my chair to see him standing by the door, his arms folded over his chest, his face frowning with disapproval. "But I don't—"

"If you cannot do it," he says calmly, "then I'll do it for you."

88

Here we are. My dad's underground bunker, where he caused the blackout, and where he just told me he's going to kill all my friends. "You can't do that!" I cry.

"Unfortunately, you can't stop me."

He takes a step toward the door, which I'm sure he'll be able to lock from the outside, and my hand reaches automatically for my crossbow. It isn't there, of course. He gives me a little smirk, and that tells me he made me leave my crossbow outside for just this reason. "You were so pure when you lived here before. Untouched by the outside world. What tainted you, Zara? Was it this?" He sweeps his arm around at all the technology. "Or was it the people?"

The people.

My friends.

"Do you know how many times I almost came after you?" he

asks. "How many times I almost left this place, stole a car, and drove to California to bring you back here where you belonged?" He shakes his head. "But I knew your mom would send the police here. That they'd tear you away from me, and that I'd be hauled off to prison, and that the world wouldn't get what it deserved.

"I was a coward," he continues. "I admit it. And because I was a coward, I let you fall. It's my fault." Quick as a whip, he lunges for me. Before I can stop him, his hand flies out and grabs on to my chin. I try to pull away, but he tugs me toward him, his fingers digging into my jaw. He twists my head from side to side, examining my face. I'm not sure if he's trying to get me to look him in the eye, or if he's trying to see if the outside world has marked me in any way. It has, but not on the skin. My scars aren't on my face where everyone can see them.

Though . . . are my scars even from the outside world? Or are so many of them from my time here on the compound, from the ways my dad tried to teach me to survive?

He was teaching me to survive an apocalypse of his own making.

My dad lets me go with a flick of disgust that sends me stumbling a few steps. "I'll bring you back. Scrub the taint out of you," he tells me. I rub my chin, a shiver crawling down my spine. "You need discipline. The clean, open air. Good, unprocessed food without chemicals. To get out from under your other influences. You'll see, Zara. Everything will be better."

And by *that* he means everything will be better after he kills my friends.

"Don't you worry. It will be painless. They'll bleed out in mere moments." He gives me a small, close-lipped smile that seems as if it's supposed to be reassuring. "I'm not a monster, Zara."

But he *is*. And I'm realizing now that he always has been and always will be. There's no redemption for him because he doesn't think he needs to be redeemed.

He's already turning around. "It's going to be great, Zara," he says over his shoulder. "Everything is going to be great." And he moves toward the door.

But he doesn't know what my friends gave me. Both metaphorically, in my heart, and literally, strapped to my leg.

He always told me to stick to my crossbow.

But he doesn't know me anymore.

It all happens so fast, it's like it's a blur. Me reaching down under my coat for the knife on my thigh. Hefting it in my hands. Flying toward him, the knife raised in front of me, angled at his side.

He never even sees me coming.

89

I'm not careful as I stumble out of the root cellar. I run into every shelf, stub my toe against every can, hit my head on every overhang. By the time I find the steep staircase (by slamming my shin into it with a flash of blinding pain), I'm battered, bruised, and bloody.

Though of course, most of the blood isn't mine.

I'm hollow. Empty. Carved out inside.

I collapse on the ground outside the root cellar, where my friends eventually come to find me. Which means I must have been there for a while, because even though they're weaving a little as they walk, shaky on their feet, they're up and moving.

"Oh my God," Jasmine says, then calls behind her. "You guys! Hurry!"

It's like I put life on fast-forward when I lunged at my dad, and forgot to turn it off. Jasmine the medic looks me over for injuries, while Gabe holds my hand and Estella coos soothing words into my ear. Ronan and Ina keep watch, eyes warily darting from side to side.

"Well, you're not injured on the outside aside from a few scrapes," Jasmine says. "What happened down there?"

I'm not injured because my dad didn't fight back. That's almost the hardest thing to accept. The shock in his eyes as the knife plunged into him. The way he didn't say anything as he fell to the ground, sprawling out onto his back as the blood leaked into a pool beneath him.

I almost wish he'd screamed at me, cursed my name, told me he wished I'd never been born. But there was only silence. I considered ending it quickly, stabbing him in the throat once it was within easy reach, but I couldn't do it. Instead I just ran.

"He's dead," I say, and the words feel oddly sticky. They won't leave; they coat my mouth with their bitter taste. I smack my lips and try again. "He's dead because I killed him." I go on to share the whole thing. I need to make sure they know I'm not a crazed killer. That they're all alive because of the knife they gave me, because of the knife they trusted me with.

Gabe holds me against him as I cry. My shoulders shake, and tears rush from my eyes with abandon. I don't even feel the urge to turn my back or wipe my eyes or hide it in any way. It doesn't mean I'm weak. "We need to bury him," I say. Just like I did for my mom. Burying two parents in the span of months. It's not right. It's not fair. "In the garden."

Ronan nods at Jasmine, Estella, and Ina. Estella gives me a comforting pat on the shoulder as she stands. "We'll go get him."

"Bring flashlights." So that they don't hurt themselves in the root cellar the way I did.

I close my eyes and lean into Gabe. He's warm, and he's strong, and he holds me up. Not forever. But for right now. And it's okay. I can be strong and still need to be held up every once in a while.

My eyes pop open as I hear my friends' footsteps, their worried murmurs. They're moving way too fast to be carrying something heavy and dead up those steep stairs. "What's wrong?"

Estella clears her throat. "Um . . ."

"He's gone," Ronan supplies. "There's nothing there but . . ."

He trails off, allowing Ina to finish flatly, "A pool of blood."

Epilogue

We never found my dad. Let's get that out of the way first.

I could hardly believe it when I followed the others down there. Part of my frenzied, irrational mind thought this was some sort of horrible prank they'd cooked up with him to teach me a lesson. That they'd propped his body up in his chair to leer bloodily at me as I went back into the bunker.

But no. There was nothing there but blood on the ground, a pool of it where he'd lain and smears of it around the floor.

We realized there must have been some emergency exit in the bunker. A hatch. He'd played dead until I left, then made his escape. We followed the trail of blood to the entrance and eventually worked up the nerve to creep through his dark, narrow tunnel. It led out into the woods. We blocked it off, but we've been searching the house for other entrances. Other tunnels. With my dad, nothing stops at just one.

It's been three months since then, and he hasn't reappeared. Maybe he never will, but we carry weapons at all times. We sleep with one eye open. We will not grow complacent.

Aside from the constant waiting for death, everything at the compound is running smoothly. There are a few hiccups, but we've managed to route some electricity into the greenhouse to get a small hydroponic farm up and running, taking what was there already and making it more efficient, more plentiful. I have enough memory of canning and preserving, and we have enough stored supplies, that we're good on food for a while. Fresh water is everywhere. We even have running water, an almost unimaginable luxury.

And we're settled in. Ina is acquainted with the kitchen. Jasmine set up a rudimentary infirmary in case we need one. Ronan hunts. Gabe keeps everyone organized and smooths over conflict. That's really my role as leader, but I'm needed elsewhere for a while. Namely, in the bunker with Estella.

The first thing we did was see if it was possible to fix what my dad had done. "There's got to be a way for us to repair things," Estella said, determined, her hair pulled back from her face in tight french braids, her skin warmed by the faint glow of the screens. "There's *got* to."

There's not.

Repairing our electrical grids depends on replacing the old destroyed transformers and other equipment with new ones, a process that's well underway by our allies and by the remainders of our government.

The second thing we do is figure out how to cut off our access to the grids. Hopefully, that's enough to keep my dad from getting back in for a while, even if he somehow makes it back here and slits all our throats in our—

No. Stop, Zara. Focus. I click the keys. Watch the computers shut down.

So all we can do is wait. Sit here and wait while people die.

I've never felt more helpless.

"No," I say one night at dinner. Everybody blinks at me, confused. Which is not surprising. They weren't all in on my inner monologue.

So I clarify. "We won't just sit here and wait while people die."

Jasmine cocks her head. Ronan stuffs a bite of squirrel stew into his mouth. Ina props her chin on her hand, thoughtful. Which is good. I hope they're all thoughtful. Because I'm about to ask a lot of them.

"It's winter," I say. "People are dying out there." Gabe, at my left hand, gives a nod. He and I have been enjoying the winter, no matter what's going on out there. We have beds, and only so many ways to stay warm. "We have abundance here—there's lots of water, lots of food, lots of space."

Estella's at my right hand. My right-hand woman. She smiles at me. "What you're saying is that we have room."

I take a breath, then let it out. "Exactly."

"But how are we going to notify people?" Her eyes are narrowing, not because she's unhappy, but because she's calculating in her head.

"We're going to connect with people whatever way we can," I say. "We'll range and see if we can find people. Ronan, I'm going to put you in charge of that."

He nods.

"And, Estella, you're going to send out signals online. If there are still people to receive them. See if you can connect with the government or with aid groups. Maybe they can send out leaflets or direct people here."

Estella nods. "It's like we're making a commune like the one in Colorado, but, like, not evil."

"And together," I say, "we'll start to make everything better."

Those are my words, Zara, my dad's voice whispers in my head. I don't shudder. He's always going to be there. A part of me. I'm a part of him, after all, and he did give me some things I needed to survive.

I'm proud of you, Zara. That's my mom. Because she gave me things I needed too. Things I still need.

I think that's what growing up is. Accepting who I was. Who I am. The things I cannot change, and the things I can.

Gabe raises his glass, which is full of blueberry wine my dad had been fermenting in the root cellar. "To our fearless leader!"

"To saving the world!" Estella says.

The others raise their glasses. For a moment I look around at them, at the light shining off their glasses, at the way it makes rainbows in the air. My eyes well with tears of pride, and I let them overflow down my cheeks, not hiding them, not ashamed.

And then I drink.

Acknowledgments

I had a lot of nightmares while researching this story. Until I started reading books like *Lights Out* by Ted Koppel, watching films like National Geographic's *American Blackout*, and getting absorbed in various articles online from places like the *New York Times*, I had no idea how possible this book's premise was, how deadly it would be, and how much of our modern life revolves around the presence of electricity. The statistic Zara cites about 90 percent of the country dying in the event all our electricity shorts out is a true one, taken from the Koppel book. Fortunately, an attack like the one showcased here is still a very remote possibility.

The publishing team behind this book is so excellent I find it hard to believe they wouldn't be the one in ten who could survive anything. Thank you to Pete Harris, without whom this book wouldn't exist; Alli Dyer; and the rest of the team at Temple

Hill Entertainment. Thank you to my agent, Merrilee Heifetz, her assistant, Rebecca Eskildsen, and everybody else at Writers House. And of course my editor, Sarah McCabe—thank you for just "getting" Zara and this book in the best way—and all the others at Margaret K. McElderry Books and Simon & Schuster for supporting this book and making it happen: Justin Chanda, Karen Wojtyla, Anne Zafian, Bridget Madsen, Elizabeth Blake-Lin, Greg Stadnyk, Lauren Hoffman, Caitlin Sweeney, Lisa Quach, Savannah Breckenridge, Anna Jarzab, Yasleen Trinidad, Saleena Nival, Emily Ritter, Annika Voss, Nicole Russo, Cassie Malmo, Erica Stahler, Christina Pecorale and her sales team, and Michelle Leo and her education/library team.

Finally, I couldn't do what I do without the support of my husband, Jeremy Bohrer. I don't know which I need more: you, or electricity.

AMANDA PANITCH

spent most of her childhood telling stories to her four younger siblings, trying both to make them laugh and scare them too much to sleep. Now she lives in New York City, where she writes dark, funny stories for teens, kids, and the pigeons that nest on her apartment balcony.